Singled Out

Singled Out

Trisha Ashley

Thomas Dunne Books
St. Martin's Press ⚑ New York

This one is for Jean Ashley, with love.

THOMAS DUNNE BOOKS.
An imprint of St. Martin's Press.

www.stmartins.com

ISBN 0-312-32712-9
EAN 978-0312-32712-5

First published in Great Britain by Judy Piatkus (Publishers) Ltd.

First U.S. Edition: August 2004

10 9 8 7 6 5 4 3 2 1

Prologue: Resurrection

If Mary Shelley hadn't been able to let her own dark demons out, we wouldn't today have her classic novel Frankenstein. *Now Cass Leigh's demons are on the loose in her debut novel* Twisted Sister, *and darker than most ... Genuinely original, sincerely terrifying ...*
Charlie Rhymer: Skint Old Northern Woman Magazine

It was in spring, when living things were pushing green fingers up through the earth like a resurrection (and dead things were doing much the same in Chapter Sixteen of *Lover, Come Back To Me*), that three catastrophic things happened in quick succession: Max's wife died, my sister Jane came to stay, and the vicar sold me as a slave.

You don't think any of these night-moth harbingers of chaos sound that bad?

Maybe you're right, and perhaps it really *shouldn't* have surprised me that Max's wife, Rosemary, came back to haunt the ghoul who'd waited to step into her shoes for over twenty years.

Then there was my sweet twin sister, the Three Horsewomen of the Apocalypse in one person. While dear Jane's presence is always as welcome to me as a wart, she doesn't usually stay. This time she brought *luggage*.

Even the vicar's annual charity slave auction took a turn for the worse, when Dante Chase, who is far scarier than anything I've ever written into a novel, paid so much for my services I feared (or should that be *hoped*?) that he expected somewhat more than a fortune-reading and a little light dusting.

But I suppose things really first started to unravel long, long before that, when Max left for a sabbatical year at a Californian university, taking Rosemary with him ...

1

Chapter 1: Oh, Hell Again

Twisted Sister, *Cass Leigh's debut novel, takes elements of both traditional Gothic horror and the fairytale, and weaves them into something altogether darker and nastier. While the horror genre is not generally noted for restraint, Cass Leigh drives her narrative along with the brakes of good taste permanently in the 'off' position.*

Fiction Today

By December, Max's luxurious trappings littering my cottage had ceased to be poignant and tear-provoking mementos of our love and more a reminder that *I'd* been discarded for the duration, too: an abandoned Abandoned Woman.

He'd left traces of his presence everywhere like he'd been marking out territory, yet when it came to packing his possessions up they made a pathetically small heap of boxes. (Or rather, Fortnum and Mason hampers, Max having profligate tastes in food and wine.)

When I came down from stashing them away in the attic the answering machine was frantically winking at me. *Three messages. Three messages. Three messages.*

'Play it cool,' I advised it, 'you know you're the best offer I've had all year.'

And no, loneliness has not reduced me to the depths of talking to inanimate objects because I've always done it, particularly with my worn (but still handsome) black leather Italian handbag, Guido.

When I pressed Play Messages, Pa's voice boomed with unchristian fervour: 'You'll burn in hell, girl!' Then he added on a rising note: 'Spawn of Satan! Seed of Beelzebub!'

'And the Season's Greetings to you, too,' I said, deleting him right at the start of what was clearly destined to be one of his longer, brandy-sodden rants.

Pa's phoned me at least once a month with the same message since I became Max's mistress, so Hell hath rather lost its sting over the years.

As you may have guessed, Pa (who converted to the Charismatic Church of God as a young man on a trip to the USA) has had quite a strong influence on my life, some of it good, some bad. Or maybe it was all bad, and I've turned it into good?

I mean, think about the way he frequently locked me in the cupboard under the stairs in order to force the devil out of me! (And had he never tried to take it out of me, I might never have known it was in there in the first place, although his habit of addressing me as 'Seed of Satan' and suchlike from my infancy onwards, should have given me a pointer.)

You know, I never realised he was crackers until I was sent away to boarding school and could compare him with other people's fathers? Mind you, I don't think he was quite so unhinged before the demon drink took hold of him, but even so my childhood experiences seemed to be pretty unique among my peers.

Still, it was great training for a horror writer, because I now know I'm invulnerable to ghosts, spectres, ghouls or any other supernatural manifestation. I often felt their inimical presence in the darkness of the cupboard, and if any of them had been capable of physically harming me they would surely have done so then when I was at their mercy.

... she heard others breathing a different rhythm in the darkness, and hearts pounded to a different beat to her own until sometimes the cupboard walls seemed to wildly pulsate ...

But sometimes now I wonder if such apparitions only exist because I let them escape from some Pandora's box in my brain, so that they owe their existence to me, their creator, La Frankensteina?

Who knows? The denizens of my novels *certainly* owe their existence to me, though on paper my monstrous creations have a more tangible presence in order to better curdle the blood and chill the spines of my readers, who do not believe in ghosts and their like but are afraid of them anyway.

4

Of course with me it is quite the reverse: I believe but I am not afraid – or not afraid of physical harm, anyway, though I do admit to an unnatural fear of birds and have a terrifying recurrent nightmare about cupboards.

Still, I believe I am a walking example that good can come from bad, though if you read some of my book reviews or listened to Pa, you might think that bad was coming from bad.

Emerging from my reverie, I listened to the second message, which was from my sister Jane and just as predictable in content as Pa's. After briefly gloating over her immaculately conceived verse, life, and marriage to her adoring spouse Gerald, she proceeded to plant as many wasp-like stings as she could into my quivering flesh.

Max's leaving me for a year's sabbatical at a Californian university, taking his wife Rosemary with him, has given her fresh ammunition. She can sense vulnerability, and his absence has left me feeling strangely exposed, especially since his communications have slowly dwindled to sporadic and unsatisfactory phone calls.

Jane is erroneously considered by many, including Ma and Pa, to be the nearest thing to an angel in human form, so she needs to say these things to me, because her pedestal would probably corrode and crumble under her if she couldn't drain the poison from her fangs occasionally.

I deleted her pretty swiftly, then listened to the third and last recording.

'Hi, Cass, it's Orla. Guess what, I've got a Perfect Partner tonight! I'm meeting him at a restaurant, but if he's as useless as the last one I'm climbing out of the back window and coming home.

Oh well, hope springs eternal in the female breast.

By-ee!'

I wiped that, too, hoping against hope that Mr Perfect Partner would at least be approaching human this time, for poor Orla was getting desperate.

Could this be me all too soon? Old banger, high mileage, one careful owner from new, reliable and in good running order?

It was an unsettling thought: but then, when had I ever had any other kind?

I dialled the familiar vicarage number and impatiently waited, imagining Charles waking up from a light snooze, working out what the ringing noise was, and then plodding across to answer it.

'Charles, there wouldn't be a lot of virtue in giving Max up if he'd already discarded me first, would there? I mean, I'd still be damned even if I did the sackcloth and ashes for ever thing that Pa's so keen on?' I demanded without preamble.

'Yes, Cass my dear, but God is love, don't forget,' he said, then yawned. 'Good heavens, is that the time? I must have dozed off in my chair.'

'Pa's God isn't love, it's punishment and vengeance and retribution and stuff.'

'Love takes strange forms, and possibly your poor father is not always in his right mind. But I sincerely believe his phone calls to you are a manifestation of his paternal love.'

'You do? What about the locking me in the cupboard to drive the devil out episodes when I was a child, though? Was that a manifestation of his love?'

'In his own misguided way, I believe it was. He perceived your physical resemblance to an ancestor he thought evil, and took the Bible's message that sin was handed down the generations too literally. Didn't you say that he punished your brothers and sisters also?'

'Not Jane – never Jane. She couldn't do any wrong,' I said bitterly. 'But the boys were physically punished if they misbehaved.'

'Well, dear Cass, he was misguided, and the law would intervene on your behalf should such a thing happen these days, for which we must be thankful.'

'But Charles, even my mother doesn't like me!'

'I have told you of the many examples I have come across of families where one child is less regarded than the rest, for no discernible reason: it is *not* your fault.'

'But *am* I innately bad?'

'Of course not: you have many good qualities. But you have sinned, as you yourself realise, in your relationship with a married man. Yet God will understand how needy of love you were, and at any time you can repent and start afresh, the one lamb that was lost and is found again.'

You know, I might not always follow what Charles is on about (or want to do what he suggests), but I always feel better after talking to him.

'You should come into the church sometimes,' he suggested.

6

'I couldn't come to a service – I haven't been in a church since I left home.'

'I didn't mean a service, although you are always welcome. I meant just come in, in order to meditate in the house of God. The door is always open.'

'Not at night, though, surely?'

'Yes, even at night. Of course I lock the vestry, and there's a CCTV camera in the gallery, but I would only look at the film if something was taken, which praise the Lord hasn't happened yet,' he said practically.

'Well I might try that, Charles, if you really think a bolt of lightning won't crisp me on the threshold, even if I am still a married man's mistress.'

'I am sure it won't. Oh dear!' he added, sounding alarmed.

'What?'

'Mrs Grace left a shepherd's pie in the oven for my supper, and I'm afraid I fell asleep and forgot about it! It smells a little singed …'

'Like me, really,' I said, but he'd gone.

After this somehow soothing conversation, instead of going down to the village pub for dinner as I generally do, I heated up my second pizza of the day (garlic chicken), poured a glass of red wine, and settled down to consider the whole Max's Mistress situation, which is not something I've bothered to do for a considerable number of years.

But in his absence I'm slowly starting to wake from Max's thrall (and he has a lot of thrall) like a somewhat aged Sleeping Beauty, and question just where my life is heading. If anywhere?

Who hung the 'Gone To Lunch, Back In Two Decades' sign out?

Look how we've all jogged comfortably along for so many years, Max and his two women in their separate, non-interlocking worlds, once long habit had dulled my initial feelings of guilt; a guilt that now seems to be slowly seeping back in.

Max once assured me that Rosemary tacitly accepted our affair, since she was not interested much in the sexual side of marriage even before her dreadful accident, and at least I *was* sharing him – I mean, I hadn't taken him entirely away from her, as I might have done.

But now that golf (once merely his face-saving excuse for frequent weekends away) has become more of a passion than I am, I'm wondering if perhaps he could get by quite nicely with that and Rosemary?

Am I extraneous? Suddenly surplus to requirements?

Vague daydreams of the 'poor Rosemary hasn't got long to go, and then we can marry and have a family' kind have sustained me over the years, but suddenly here we are a good twenty years down the line, and every cheery sundial is saying: *The Time is Later Than You Think.*

But strangely enough, all this sudden angst seems to be doing wonders for my writing.

Is this another example of good coming out of bad?

Whenever Orla has a big problem she writes down the reasons for and against doing whatever it is she is worrying about, so I settled down to compile a list of the pros and cons of being Max's mistress:

For:

1) Lots of time to write in.
2) Independence.
3) Don't have to wash his dirty underwear.
4) Do not have to look wonderful all the time.
5) Max is tall, handsome, clever, charismatic, and distinguished. (And sexy.)
6) My brothers are all still in contact with me.
7) Have my friends for company when he isn't there.

Against:

1) Guilt, because of his invalid wife, Rosemary.
2) Loneliness.
3) Max not interested in horror writing.
4) He's never there in an emergency.
5) When he is there, he expects me to look great and be in the mood for lurve, like I've got an On and Off switch.
6) I now play second fiddle to his new love, golf.
7) Max resents my sneaking out of bed in the middle of the night to write and visit graveyards.
8) Max adamant about not having children until we can marry, which looks like being never.

9) Having committed to the relationship with Max, have to remain faithful due to inbuilt Puritan streak. (But haven't been terribly tempted by anyone else for years, anyway.)

10) Max spooked by my mind-reading skills, even though I've promised never to do it to him ... again. (And all I read was exasperated affection, lust and guilt, which figured.)

11) Ma hasn't spoken to me since, and Pa only rings me up to curse me.

12) My sister Jane is always phoning me up or dropping in uninvited.

13) Max jealous of my long-standing strong friendships with Orla Murphy and Jason Shaw (and his wife Tanya, until she took off a couple of years ago.)

Conclusion:

Clearly, the game is not worth the candle!

But then, no one else has tempted me seriously in all these years, so even were I to ditch Max I would still have most of the disadvantages. Besides, whenever I get fed up with things as they are I only have to see him again and I'm putty in his hands.

This charisma, Svengali touch, or whatever you want to call it, is not something that works well via occasional transatlantic phone calls.

In the grip of a depression like a dank fog I resorted to desperate measures.

'It is a truth universally acknowledged that a single man of over forty is in possession of a *major* defect,' Orla stated, walking past me into the cottage and flinging her coat and bag on to the nearest chair.

Then she stared glumly at her reflection in the mirror over the fireplace.

'Yes, just as I thought,' she said. 'Hair blonde to the roots, curves in all the rights places, minimal crow's feet, luscious lips, big, baby-blue eyes. What a waste!'

'Do I take it that your Perfect Partner wasn't?'

'Forty-six and still lives with Mummy. I've had every variety of unmarried man now: Divorced, for which read rejected by wife for a very good reason; Mummy's Little Boy, like tonight, and Widowed, Wizened and Smug, like last week's offering.'

'You haven't had Reclusive or Gay yet,' I pointed out helpfully.

'They don't join dating agencies – or at least, not Perfect Partners. What's that you're drinking?'

'Max's bottle of Laphroaig from under the sink.'

'I thought you didn't like whisky?'

'I'd never tried it before, because Pa's drinking spirits put me off the idea. But it's like gold: hot liquid gold.'

'Very poetic. I'll have some. Got any ginger?'

'You can't put ginger in good whisky!'

'You can if your friend's snooty lover isn't there to see you do it.'

She kicked off the stiletto shoes that had raised her to the level of my chin, then curled up on the sofa. 'Phew, that's better! You know, it's simply impossible to believe in the theory of evolution, because if it was true by now women's feet would naturally have pointed toes and thin, four-inch heelbones.'

'Mine wouldn't, I've been wearing those Nanook of the North knee-length suede moccasin boots all winter. And Max *isn't* snooty!'

'Of course he is, and he's getting worse the older he gets. He's turning into a boring old fogy right under your nose. Just think about it,' she added earnestly. 'The sudden passion for golf, imagining he looks good in Rupert Bear trousers, droning on about why expensive wine is the only sort worth drinking, trying to get you to write literary novels instead of the horror you're so brilliant at: I rest my case. Come on, let's be young and reckless and desecrate his whisky!'

'You're an idiot,' I said, pouring her drink. 'And Max isn't like that at all!'

But then I actually *thought* about what I was saying instead of letting my mouth run on automatic pilot and realised she was right: 'OK, yes he is – and selfish, too! Why hadn't I noticed that before?'

I took another swig of whisky, which was helpfully reconnecting parts of my brain that had long since stopped communicating with each other even by semaphore. Laphroaig Gets you Clean Round The Bend.

'Until he took himself off for this sabbatical thing, I'd just been drifting along never really questioning anything, Orla. I mean, I did all the agonising years ago when I fell in love with him and realised he couldn't leave Rosemary, and once I was committed to the relationship I suppose it was just like a long marriage, where the changes are so gradual you don't notice them.'

'Except it *wasn't* a marriage, and it's a bit significant that he took his wife to America with him and not you,' Orla pointed out helpfully. 'You're still only The Mistress even after all these years. Or maybe *because* of all these years? Your novelty's worn off.'

'Thanks.'

'Well, it's no worse than me, is it? Dumped for a younger model, and destined to be divorced, single and desperate for ever. I'm a Trade-in, and you're a slightly tarnished Spinster Of This Parish.'

Since we seemed to have empty glasses I poured us both another generous measure of peaty goodness.

'At least you still have parents who love you, Orla. Mine always treated me like a changeling or a cuckoo in the nest, just because I took after my gypsy great-grandmother, and then they cast me out entirely when they found out about Max.'

'Yes,' she conceded. 'Though Daddy can't always remember who I am these days.'

'*I* was an unwanted throw-back for the first half of my life, and I've been a married man's mistress for the second. That's not going to look good on my tombstone, is it?'

'No, but then, you're not going to pop your clogs yet, are you? You've probably got years left, and you can write your own epitaph before you go.'

'*She dealt horror and death wherever she went?*' I suggested.

'That's more like it. And it's always seemed to me that you had your life arranged to suit you pretty well – perhaps better than you realised.'

'Oh yes, apart from feeling permanently guilty about Rosemary, only seeing Max for occasional weekends had a lot of advantages. He devoted himself to me when he was there, and the rest of the time I could write, and research, and bum about in my old dressing gown looking an absolute dog.' I sighed. 'Of course, the downside was that there was never anyone but me to cope with the blocked drains, or the blown fuses, or even just keep me company when I felt lonely or down.'

'And the infrequent sex,' pointed out Orla, whose list of life's priorities was perhaps not in quite the same order as mine. 'Why you've remained steadfastly faithful to the Unfaithful is one of the great paradoxes of all time. Max was definitely getting the best deal: a wife, a comfortable home and a career, plus someone young and pretty on the side. All he had to do was turn up when he felt like it with his little hamper of goodies and expensive bottles of plonk. No strings, no worries.'

'He loves me!' I protested, then paused. 'Or – he did love me. He really did, Orla. When I finally agreed to this arrangement he actually cried! And he promised he would be faithful to me always.'

'But was he?' she queried cynically.

'As far as I know, and I don't really see how he'd have the time to be anything else, because he's either been working, or under Rosemary's eye, or here. Or playing golf, I suppose, which was originally only a cover story for his weekends away. If Rosemary hadn't been an invalid, I'm sure he'd have left her soon after we met. But he always meant to marry me when she . . . well . . . when she—'

'Died?' Orla suggested helpfully.

'That sounds so crude, but yes,' I agreed guiltily.

'You're so credulous! Just because she's partially paralysed after that skiing accident it doesn't mean she won't live as long as anyone else if she has the proper care – which she does, doesn't she?'

'Yes, of course, the best of everything. And I never wanted her to die just so Max and I could marry . . . or not entirely. I'm guilty enough as it is.'

'Oh, come on! You were a naive student from a strict family, desperate for love; he was a lecturer, your typical suave, hand-some, older man in a position of power. It's only surprising that you resisted so long. Max should have let you go when you got that teaching job and moved here to Westery. You'd probably have found a nice man and have lots of children by now.'

'Who knows? You thought *you* had a happy marriage until Mike suddenly asked for the divorce, didn't you? But I would have liked the chance to have children, and that's the only thing I've ever argued about with Max. He's never wanted them, and I have, and the years pass so quickly. And then suddenly he tells me he's off to America for a year with Rosemary!'

'The bastard,' comforted Orla. 'Have the last of his whisky.'

'He even said it would probably do our relationship good to be apart for a few months!'

'The *absolute* bastard!'

'Yes, and it was when he said he couldn't pass up an opportunity like that, that I suddenly saw him – us – from a different perspective. Things sort of shifted.'

'I should think so, after all the opportunities you've passed up for his sake.'

'That's what I said, and then we argued about the baby thing again, because I wanted to try and get pregnant before he left. I expect he thinks I will be past it when he gets back, and I probably will be too, if I'm not already.'

'I don't know what you want one for anyway,' Orla said. 'But then, my maternal instincts are completely absent. How old are you now?'

'Forty-four.'

'Mmm . . . late, but you could still give it a go. You can get some sort of kit, can't you, to test if you're still fertile?'

'Yes, but Max won't be back for months, and even then I'd still have to persuade him.'

'Not with Max. Someone else.'

'But I don't know anyone else except Jason, and he's such an old friend I couldn't possibly. And even if I could, just look how his son's turned out!' I shuddered. 'Who'd want offspring like Tom?'

'That's a point *and* he's as old as you. Whereas if you got a younger lover you'd probably have a better chance of getting pregnant – if you're really serious about it. Maybe younger lovers are the way to go anyway? I mean, if I'm not going to find good sex and a soulmate combined in one package in my age group, I might at least have the good sex.'

'I *thought* I had a soulmate, but he's really keener on the golf than me these days. I'm just a habit to him.'

'Convenient Cassy, always there when he wants you,' agreed Job's comforter. 'Probably convenient to Rosemary too, because although she knows he's unfaithful, at least it's only with one person.'

'I suppose so. But whenever I wonder if I could bring myself to break with him, I remember all the good times. And when he rings up and says he misses me, I just can't do it! He can be so charming when he wants to be that the things I mean to say go right out of my head, and I can't ring him back and say them later, because I've no way of contacting him.'

'What, none?' Orla said, startled. 'Email?'

'He doesn't trust it.'

'Right. New-fangled invention, I know. He could write?'

'He could – but he doesn't. I tell you, Orla, when I take a clear look at my life, what have I got apart from my writing?'

And an empty glass.

'A clear case of rebellion?' she suggested. 'It's not like you to drink Max's precious whisky, for a start! And now I come to think of it, where are all his things?'

She looked around, her eyes so wide that the spiky lashes spread like a sooty sunburst. 'I mean, we're drinking whisky from the bottle, not a cut-crystal decanter, and these glasses look like Woolworth's finest.'

'They are. I've just packed all his stuff into empty Fortnum and Mason hampers and put them in the attic while I was up there getting the Christmas decorations down.'

'Sounds like a fair exchange. Are you going to put the decorations up now? Can I help?'

'Why not?' I said, waving my glass expansively. 'There's the tree, and I've made gingerbread stars, and I've got two dozen candy canes, and little chocolate umbrellas and—'

'You do go over the top at Christmas, don't you? Must be that strict childhood you had.'

'I love Christmas! Even Christmas on my own,' I enthused.

'You haven't been alone on Christmas Day since Mike left me,' she pointed out. 'You, me, Jason and turkey at my house as usual?'

'And Tom,' I added.

14

'Into every pot of ointment a fly must fall. With any luck he will drink too much and pass out like last year, and Jason will have to take him home early,' she consoled me.

Actually, it turned out that there were three flies in the jar of Seasonal Balm, and the major one was that by Christmas Day Max had failed to send me even a card, let alone a present, and I knew there was little chance that he would be able to slip away and phone over the holiday.

Tom, bluebottle number two, was indeed present at Orla's house for Christmas dinner, the price we have to pay for our friendship with Jason. It is a constant amazement to me that he could father so objectionable a child. (Or *man*, I suppose I should say, since he is now at university.)

After Jason and Tom had finally gone home, replete and bearing foil-wrapped parcels of left-over turkey and pud, Orla revealed the existence of the third fly to me.

'I've thought up a new act for Song Language,' she told me as we cleared the festive board.

Song Language is the name of the singing telegram service she set up after Mike left in order to try and maintain the standard of living to which she was addicted.

She's a Marilyn Monroe look-alike herself and she'd soon talked *me* into a Vampirella costume (which was not much different to my normal look, actually) and a couple of other people into even more improbable garb.

'It's a great idea,' she said now, tossing the turkey carcass arbitrarily into the dustbin, because as she pointed out, who wants to see turkey ever again after Christmas Day?

'You have?' I said cautiously, hoping it didn't involve me.

'Yes. *You're* going to double up as Wonder Woman! Won't that go down a bomb?'

'Me? Wonder Woman? You mean, like that old TV series with Lynda somebody – Carter – terrific figure and a mouth like a ventriloquist's dummy?'

'That's the one. You're tall and dark-haired, and you've got the figure for the costume, *and* the legs for the boots, too.'

'I haven't got the mouth though, or her really light-coloured eyes. Mine are just grey, putrid grey.'

'Putrid?'

'Sorry, I meant pewter. Must have been thinking about something else.'

'As usual. And you don't have to be an exact copy, just near enough to give the impression,' she wheedled. 'I bet it would be even more popular than the vampire thing.'

'Yes – with men. Why does the thought of walking into pubs and parties dressed only in a push-up swimming costume and kinky boots not sound all that attractive to me, I wonder?'

'And tights and a tiara thing,' Orla said persuasively. Seeing I was far from convinced, she added: 'We could send Jason out with you as a minder, if you're afraid things might get a bit out of hand.'

'No thanks, he's bad enough when I'm dressed as a vampire! As Wonder Woman I'd need a minder to protect me from the minder.'

'Think about it. It would mean even more money.'

'I'll think about it, but I can't imagine doing it! It takes me all my courage to do the vampire act, Orla.'

I resisted all her persuasions, but she is unlikely to let her idea go that easily.

While I knew it was unlikely that there would be a message on my answering machine from Max when I got back, I was illogically deeply upset when there was nothing more than the standard message from Pa, who takes no account of such debauched festivals as Christmas.

'You will burn in hell, girl, for your sins lie heavy on your soul! Yet the adulterer is gone from you, and if you truly repent now and serve the Lord, you may yet escape the fiery flames of eternal damnation! Your brother James, too, is a drunken harlot,' he added.

Clearly sweet baby Jane has been telling tales again. I wonder what poor old Jamie has been up to now? And aren't harlots usually women?

'Spawn of Beelzebub,' he finished rather predictably, and I was just thinking: 'Ho-hum, nothing new there, then,' when his message was followed by my name uttered in a small, breathy voice. Familiar – yet strange.

'Repent, Cassandra – it's not too late,' whispered Ma, before quietly replacing the phone, a pale Ghost of Christmas Past.

Why? Why did she send me a message after so long? Did it mean that she did, deep down, care about me?

16

Or perhaps it was just that Pa had told her to do it?

Unsurprisingly, I felt somewhat forlorn and unsettled for quite a time after this. Do not think, though, that I sat moping and alone on Christmas evening without a greeting or gift to my name.

I'd already exchanged presents with Orla and Jason (a book called *Everything You Need to Know About Last-Minute Pregnancy* from Orla, and an antique mourning ring from Jason), and Mrs Bridges next door had given me an adorable hand-knitted toilet-roll cosy in the shape of a white poodle. It was the sort of thing Max absolutely loathed, a factor that just then endeared it to me all the more.

My four brothers (who have steadfastly kept in touch since my ejection from the family nest) had also communicated according to their different natures.

George and Philadelphia sent their annual pre-printed Christmas card, Francis a pair of skiing socks (though I could no more ski than I could fly), Jamie the harlot a box of chocolates with a card sending 'lots of snuggles to Little Huggins' (who was presumably now puzzling over why Jamie should be sending her brotherly greetings with *her* chocolates), and Eddie a battered parcel wrapped in handmade paper full of strange lumps, bumps and stalks, containing one of those stick crosses wrapped in coloured yarn which for some reason are called God's Eyes.

I have never heard that God is at all into psychedelia, especially Pa's God, and I bet Eddie sent one just like it home.

Jane's offering was a coffret of bathtime goodies, though why they call them coffrets I don't know, since it has very *ashy* connotations to me. Maybe it sounds posher than box?

The contents were all rose-scented, which suddenly and painfully reminded me of walking with Max down a path covered in velvet-soft pink petals, long ago. He'd said that he'd strewn roses before me, and what more could I ask?

But there, alas, was the basic difference between us: he'd seen rose petals, and I'd seen dismembered flowers.

As usual, I sent everyone a copy of my last book, *Grave Concerns*, for Christmas.

Happy Yuletide reading.

Chapter 2: Pregnant Pause

Even aficionados of the horror genre will be shocked, stunned and revolted by Cass Leigh's latest offering on the altar of bad taste ....

The Times

Max did eventually send me a Christmas present (in January) of some expensive but noxious perfume. It smelt like it had been extruded from the nether regions of a musk rat, and probably had.

The musk rat was welcome to it, because I *never* wear perfume. Why doesn't he know these things by now?

... from the unstoppered bottle rose a strange, evil, dark miasma that took form and shape and a greasy solidity before her eyes ...

He is still calling me when the fancy takes him, though his conversation is more and more about golf, the excellence of Californian wine, and their new personal fitness trainer Kyra, than about how much he misses me.

Still, with no other man in the offing he remains in pole position.

Meanwhile in a fit of pique I bought my own late Christmas present of a Predictova fertility kit, although it took me a week or two to break open its pristine cellophane wrappings, especially after reading that book Orla gave me for Christmas: *Everything You Need To Know About Last-Minute Pregnancy*.

Actually, I *didn't* need to know most of that.

I am not sure how good an idea Predictova is either, because if I'm not ovulating at all I will be devastated, and if I am, I will be perfectly frantic in case each egg is the last one.

And it's all very well for Orla to tell me to get a young lover, but you can't just pick one up in the supermarket with the weekly shopping. Buy one, get one free? I don't think so.

It's a pity my handbag can't turn into a dark, handsome and comfortably worn lover. I contemplated kissing it, but I think that only works with frogs, besides seeming a little weird.

Orla was quite right about all available men having major defects though, because when I actually came to look around, there were no possible baby-fatherers in the offing except Jason, whose progeny speaks for itself, mostly using the F-word.

We don't know how Jason can carry on being so nice to Tom, unless he's got the drop on him. After all, there *was* only one witness who saw Tanya driving off in the middle of the night after that row she had with Jason (who has a fearsome temper), and it's been two years since then with no word.

Still, he did report her disappearance to the police and they looked into it, so they must have been satisfied.

Wonder where she went?

Have now paid several nocturnal visits to the church, especially on rainy nights. Dim lights burn all night, making it look pleasantly eerie, and I can settle in a little nest of tapestry cushions in my favourite pew next to the Templar's Tomb.

The knight is wearing a pair of those knitted-looking chainmail tights with pointed wrinkly toes, which makes him look rather endearing. His wife lies next to him, looking serene: she was probably glad of the rest, going by the number of named offspring on the sides of the tomb.

I find the atmosphere conducive to thinking about the current novel, and contemplating Max and motherhood, but not, so far, to repentance.

When I told Charles this he said God was always happy to welcome me to his house whatever I thought about. He has such a cosy view of God, so unlike Pa's that I only wish I could share his comforting vision; but even if I should undergo some miraculous conversion, I fear I will never be the type to cover myself with little fish brooches and dance about singing 'Jesus Wants Me For A Sunbeam'.

Yesterday being stormy, I settled down (in the night, by the Knight) to do another of the pros and cons lists, although the first one didn't really help: it showed me what I should and shouldn't do, but then I ignored the information. Like horoscopes, really: you only take any notice of the bits you like the look of.

Having a baby in your forties:

For:	*Against:*
1) I want one.	1) Max doesn't, and he *always* takes precautions.
2) I'm fit and healthy.	
3) I'm financially solvent. (Just.)	2) Even if he agreed, according to that book Orla gave me I probably wouldn't get pregnant now anyway, but if I did, would have a high risk of miscarriage, or something wrong with the baby, or medical risk to myself.
4) I work from home. (Except for the singing telegrams.)	
5) I want one.	
6) I want one.	
7) Max has gone to America for a year, making me question my conscience (and my fidelity.)	3) Max adamant unless we can marry, and Rosemary seems to be going from strength to strength.
8) I don't have time to wait.	
9) I'm no longer one hundred per cent sure I want Max back anyway. Out of sight, out of thrall.	4) If I had a baby by someone else, I'd lose Max and be completely on my own.
10) I want one.	5) Don't know any other possible man except Jason, and his offspring is no advert.

Conclusion:
I still want one.

Biologically it's now (if I'm very lucky) or never. I'm still in working order, but for how much longer?

I ought to give Max an ultimatum, but this is not easy when we do not currently share the same continent, and not only might it be too late when he gets back, but I have always been putty in his hands.

I'm sure he's too stubborn to change his mind, and I can't wish for Rosemary to die (not that she shows any sign of doing so) because it would make me feel even guiltier than I already do.

So if I want to try for a baby I will have to find another father for it and forfeit Max for ever, only after so many years with Max I am unversed in the art of finding another man.

Even Orla is finding it difficult, and she is not only terribly attractive but by no means picky.

At my age I'm sure it would take considerably more than a couple of one-night stands to achieve the desired result even if I fancied that idea, which I don't; but equally I don't want the biological father hanging about interfering with my life.

And speaking of fathers, if I have an illegitimate child Pa will not just ring me to tell me I will burn in hell, but consign me to become eternal spit-roast on Hell's Rotisserie, basted at frequent intervals by Satan and all his little minions.

Clearly the cons outweigh the pros: but hell, logic has *nothing* to do with the issue of my Issue!

At this point the battery in my Maglite went out, which might or might not have been a sign from God? If so, it was unclear just what the message was.

Don't think about it any more?

It now being too dim to write, and the sound of rain having ceased, I went out into the newly washed churchyard.

To celebrate the publication in February of my new novel *Nocturnally Yours*, I treated Orla and Jason to dinner at the village pub.

Not that it is a novelty to go to the King's Arms, since we eat dinner there together most nights like some sad singles club, but one has to mark these twice-yearly occasions in some manner other than the obligatory bouquet of rather pleasantly funereal lilies from my publisher.

Orla and I got there first, giving us an opportunity to air our more personal preoccupations before Jason arrived.

'I've got an American antique collector staying,' she confided. 'He's a bit old, but he's not bad-looking. He's gone out to dinner with local friends, or I'd have offered to cook him a little something.'

This was desperation indeed, for Orla absolutely hates cooking.

One of her phones jangled, and she snatched it up. 'Hello, Song Language? Can I help you?'

'Wrong phone,' I hissed, because the leopard-print one is the B&B.

'No, no, I didn't say strong language,' Orla was saying soothingly. 'You must have misheard me. This is Haunted Well B&B speaking. Can I help you?'

The phone quacked.

'Certainly. From Friday? Yes, Bed and Continental Breakfast. No, only Continental. Yes, do let me know by tomorrow – I only have one vacancy for that weekend. Yes, goodbye.'

She put the phone down on the table next to the pink Barbie Glitter one and sighed. 'Honestly, do they think I've nothing better to do than run around cooking cholesterol in the mornings?'

The Barbie phone rang before I could answer that, as far as I was aware, nothing better *had* offered lately.

'Song Language. Tonight? Tarzanogram? I'm afraid all my operatives are fully booked this evening. Yes, it is late notice. So sorry. Bye.'

'*You* could have gone,' I pointed out.

'Not to a hen party. Same applies to you. And anyway, we're celebrating!'

She raised her glass: 'Here's to *Nocturnally Yours*, *and* to finding someone nocturnally mine!'

'You will,' I assured her. 'There must be interesting unattached men out there somewhere.'

'Well hidden,' she said gloomily. 'How about you? It's nearly six months since Max left, and you must be missing the sex, if nothing else.'

'Well, not really,' I confessed. 'It hasn't been terribly memorable for a while, and sometimes I think Max goes through the motions out of habit now, and only gets excited thinking about a particularly good round of golf.'

'I don't know how you can live like that, *or* like a nun now that he's away.'

'To tell the truth I don't mind most of the time . . . but every so often I get the urge so badly I feel like jumping on the postman. Do you ever feel like that?'

She looked at me, astonished: 'All the time! Why don't you do something about it? Not the postman, because poor old George isn't up to it, and anyway, Agnes wouldn't like it. But you could look for another man.'

'I have looked *at* other men, and I've discovered that I don't find many of them attractive. Hardly any in fact, even when I was younger and lots showed some interest in me. I must be too choosy.'

'Pity they didn't catch you in one of your brief mad-for-sex times then.'

'But until recently I was only mad for sex with Max, and if I'd gone with anyone else I would have felt horrible, and unfaithful, and all the rest of it.'

'You're such a Puritan! Why don't you lighten up a bit? *I* certainly don't feel like that.'

'But you were faithful to Mike while you were married, weren't you?' I said, because it's always seemed to me that she has only gone off the sexual rails since the divorce. She and Jason used to flirt quite a lot before Tanya vanished but it was just harmless fun.

Orla went faintly pink. 'Sort of. Now I don't have to be faithful to anyone.'

'I'm conditioned by my upbringing and it's too late to change now, even if I found a man I fancied, I think,' I pondered doubtfully, for who knows where desperation will lead us? 'And after charting my ovulation cycle I've come to the conclusion that my sex drive switches on only around the time I might get pregnant – assuming my eggs aren't cracked, addled, or blown – so presumably when I stop getting the urge at all it'll mean I've run out for ever.'

'Jump on Jason at the right time then, Cass. You like Jason.'

'Of course I like Jason: he's big, cuddly, attractive – and a *friend*.'

'He's not cuddly when he's in a rage,' she pointed out. 'Though that's when *I* find him sexiest.'

'You have him, then. He always seemed to fancy you more than me, until he saw me dressed as a vampire. Worryingly kinky.'

'Interestingly kinky,' she amended. 'And it's me he only sees as a friend these days. Marilyn Monroe obviously doesn't do it for him . . .'

She sighed and I looked at her sharply, because there had been a certain tension between them just after Tanya disappeared that I'd never quite understood, and although they were the best of friends again now there was no more flirting.

'Wonder where Tanya went?' she said, obviously pursuing a similar train of thought.

'You know, I was just thinking that a few days ago, and how

odd it was that she's never contacted Tom, at least. And although we know Jason argued with her the night she disappeared, before he came down to the pub, he's never said what about. You don't think he did anything to her in one of his rages, do you ?'

'There was that witness who saw her car on the Kedge Hall road out of Westery in the early hours of the morning,' she reminded me.

'They might have seen the car, but maybe it was Jason driving it with the body in the back,' I suggested.

He drove fast along the road, conscious of the limp, bloody thing in the back that had lived and laughed and loved – once too often.

Then he heard a soft scuffling noise, the scratching of long fingernails on fabric, as some travesty of Lara began to drag itself between the rear seats ...

Orla gave me a sharp nudge with her elbow. 'Come on, Cass! If Jason had hurt her, it would have been accidentally in the heat of an argument, and he'd have been ringing the police and ambulance two seconds later!'

'Yes, you're right,' I said. 'And he did report her missing to the police.'

'There you are, then. And he walked me home from the pub that night because Mike was away, and when we passed his house Tanya's car was still there,' she reminded me. 'And he stayed for coffee and a chat, so that by the time he got home not only had she vanished but her car had been seen. She took a load of her things, too.'

'Jason could have done that, though,' I pointed out stubbornly. Not that I wanted poor old Jason to be guilty, it just made for a more interesting story. 'He might have—'

'Shhh!' she warned. 'There he is!' She waved, and Jason, looking very bear-like in a hairy brown jumper, ambled over.

'There might have been an argument and an accident,' she whispered hastily before he reached us, 'but you don't think he'd ever hurt someone on purpose, even in a temper?'

'No, of course not,' I assured her.

'What are you two looking so furtive about?' Jason asked, sitting down in the chair opposite.

'Cass wants a baby,' Orla said quickly. 'Before it's too late.'

'Orla!' I protested, going pink.

24

'Anything I can do to help, you can count on me,' Jason said, eyeing me speculatively from his deep-set brown eyes, and my heart sank.

Thanks to Orla, I was going to find him even harder to handle than before. It was easier when we were all just friends: Mike and Orla, Jason and Tanya, and odd-girl-out me. (Max never mingled on his visits.)

Though come to think of it, there always were undercurrents, like Tanya and Jason's arguing over her flirting with other men, especially Jack Craig, the lodgekeeper at the Hall. And as I said, Jason and Orla had this long-running, seemingly lighthearted flirtation going, that hit a blip after Tanya vanished. Orla's ex, Mike, tried flirting with me soon after I moved to Westery, I *think*, but I didn't seem to pick up the signals very well: perhaps they were on the wrong frequency. Or perhaps I am permanently on the wrong frequency?

I've always been the odd one out: I don't date, I don't flirt, and I don't have a social life.

And maybe now I don't even have a lover any more?

Proudly read my *Times* review out to Max when he next called, only to find he was quite shocked by it.

'My God – how dare they! Darling, are you terribly upset?'

'Upset? Are you mad? I'm absolutely delighted! A *Times* review could boost my sales no end.'

'Yes, a good review, but this is so—'

'Max, it's *The Times*. And they do say that bad publicity is better than no publicity.'

'Not this bad, surely?'

'Oh, it's not much worse than I've had before, and I think it will make lots of people go and look for the book from sheer curiosity, don't you? My agent says they ought to quote it on the next cover.'

'He was joking.'

'No, he wasn't. And my publishers were pleased, too, even though I might become a sort of minority cult, so they'd have to give me bigger advances. Then I could stop doing Crypt-ograms whenever some unexpected bill comes in. The Batmobile is making clunky sounds on corners again, and I think the alternator's getting dodgy.'

'Aren't cult writers usually *literary?*'

'No, of course not, you highbrow snob. And there's nothing wrong with my writing anyway.'

'It's not your style, it's the content, Cassy. If you didn't write about things ordinary people don't even admit to *thinking* about, you'd probably be a respected author by now.'

'What, like Jane? And starve to death? No thanks.'

'Her work is certainly respected and she doesn't seem to have starved.'

'No, but only because she's been supported by Gerald since she left university. Besides, I wouldn't call someone who's had two slim volumes of pared-down poetry published a real writer, even if she has got every literary grant going on the strength of them.'

'Her haiku are generally considered to be brilliant.'

'Yeah, she must have sold *dozens* of copies of "Red Sun, Falling Leaves".'

'Is that a bit of sour grapes?'

'Come on, Max – if there's any jealousy it's the other way round. I've always known my gift lay in curdling the blood and making the hair stand on end, not writing twisty little sushi gobbets.'

'How are you, anyway?' he asked, abruptly abandoning the subject as a lost cause. 'Missing me? Still got that no-hoper from the antique shop sniffing after you?'

'Jason isn't sniffing after me, he's a friend,' I said shortly and quite untruthfully. He isn't quite a no-hoper either, considering he's the only man currently on the horizon who actually fancies me, and who knows where desperation will lead me?

'How is Rosemary?' I enquired politely on that thought: I mean, just pretend I care.

'Fine. California suits her. I haven't seen her this lively and cheerful for years, and Kyra's been working with her to build her upper body strength. It's really lovely here – you'd like it, Cassy.'

... the power of his voice poured over her like warm honey, and she felt herself grow weak with desire ...

'I expect I would,' I agreed. California, sunny California, sounded very enticing, with everything warm, and green and fertile. Even me, perhaps, were I to go there?

'Max,' I said persuasively, 'if I did a couple more Crypt-ograms and ignored the Batmobile repairs, I could afford to fly out for a holiday somewhere near you and we could—'

'No,' he interrupted firmly. 'You know we agreed that it wouldn't be practical to try and see each other while I'm here. Besides, it would hardly be worth it for a couple of weeks, would it?'

'Wouldn't it?' I asked wistfully. 'Don't you miss me, Max?'

'Of course I do, but I'm also working hard, you know, this isn't a holiday for me. Anyway, I'll be back before you know it.'

'Yes, but Max—'

I stopped, realising that whatever I said wouldn't change his mind once he'd made it up, and most of the things I find myself wanting to tell him lately are unsayable anyway, like: Max, I get so lonely without even your weekend visits.

Max, I'm forty-four and my reproductive possibilities are melting faster than the snow in California.

Max, didn't you once assure me that Rosemary's doctors didn't give her more than a very few years to live, and that one day we would marry and have a family?

Max, were you a liar?

I've been treating the Predictova kit with the watchful reverence that you might accord to a ticking time bomb in your bathroom: I mean, are my internal organs pace-egging to extinction, or what? (Not that the damn thing actually *tells* you, it just points out the probabilities.) But outwardly at least my life has resumed its normal (or maybe abnormal) rhythm.

Nature intended me to be nocturnal, so by night I write *Lover, Come Back To Me*, wander for inspiration in the village graveyard and nearby reputedly haunted places (though not the Haunted Well, because Orla and I made that one up), before finally retiring to my virtuous couch in the very early hours of the morning.

There I'm awoken at dawn by Birdsong, the new baby in the adjoining cottage, until I finally rise in late morning to research, visit haunted venues, take naps, do Crypt-ograms (but *not* as Wonder Woman!), go to the pub with Orla and Jason, and start all over again.

The life-cycle of the Sombre-Plumaged Horror Writer.

And my publishers have brought forward the publication date of my next novel to April, due to sudden demand for my books, so at this rate they will soon be publishing them before I've written them.

I am also working at weakening the defenses of Jack Craig, upon whom I have serious designs, though unlike Jason's missing wife Tanya mine are not of a sexual or romantic nature.

No, his sole attraction lies in the fact that he's the caretaker of the local haunted house, reputedly the most haunted manor in the country. But then, aren't they all? It has stood empty since the death of its reclusive owner, and I was desperate to get in there. The heir had apparently taken a quick look round when he inherited before leaving the country for foreign climes: but who knows when the fancy might take him to return, or put the property on the market?

All I want is the key for one night, and a blind eye turning. He knows very well that I won't harm anything, but despite his villainous appearance – and reputation – he is proving remarkably resistant to my bribes.

Jack is a small, wiry, feral-eyed man who has an inexplicable attraction for some women, but personally, I find polecats much more appealing.

Chapter 3: Twisted Sister

Local author Cass Leigh 's newest novel, Nocturnally Yours, *will please all her fans but is not for the faint-hearted – or weak-stomached ...*

Westery and District Voice

March, and Max's phone calls have dwindled further to perfunctory golf bulletins, (may all his niblicks crumble to dust) and though I expect he still possesses a manner that could charm the birds from the trees, he has ceased to waste any of it on me.

Had Prince Charming come along at this point (or even a reasonably attractive frog) I would have been easy meat, especially in view of the fact that my egg count is so far one hit and one miss, and heading for the clincher: watch this space.

As Meatloaf so aptly puts it, life's a lemon and I want my money back.

But despite the zigzag crevasse slowly opening between us, you'd still think Max would have managed to give me the news of Rosemary's accident before I heard about from someone else, wouldn't you?

Well he didn't, and to make it worse the someone else was Jane, maliciously pleased to discover that she was first with the information. While her phone calls have always been of the circling-hornet variety, this one had a scorpion sting in its tail.

That's Jane for you, but you'll have to take my word for it, since if you met her I expect you too would think she was the sweetest, most unselfish, truly beautiful person you'd ever met: an angel come amongst us. Sometimes I suspect her of having studied the Dark Arts to achieve this result.

To understand the relationship between my fair, angelic, success-ful, *and* respectably married twin and myself (and we are so non-identical it is hard to believe we're even related), you need look no further than the opening pages of my very first novel *Twisted Sister*, where only the names have been changed to protect the guilty.

I dedicated this book to Miss Josepha Brand, one of the wealth-ier members of Pa's flock, since she paid for me to go away to boarding school; though whether she did it from some stirring of compassion, or because Pa's preoccupation with casting out my devil was taking up too much of his time, I don't know. Whatever the reason, she gave me an escape ladder that led to university, teaching and writing, even if I finally burnt the rungs behind me by becoming Max's mistress.

Twisted Sister Chapter One.

Once upon a time a baby was born, as fair, sweet and good as a cherub, the longed-for daughter after four sons. And then, un-expectedly following hard on her heels, came a second girl-child, dark and clearly devil-spawned.

A changeling, or at best a throw-back to some disreputable gypsy ancestor that her fire-and-brimstone godly parents would have preferred to pretend never existed

In other times, other places, she would simply have been quietly disposed of, but that not being possible her parents moved their family of golden-haired children, together with the cuckoo in the nest, to a remote part of Scotland

There the father could practise his own rigid version of a faith that was harsh, unforgiving and stark, and as his followers slowly moved into the nearby houses there grew up a sort of community about him. He wanted for nothing, for he was a tall, austerely handsome, charismatic man, and his growing flock featured many widows and divorcees of independent means.

It is a tribute to the physical stamina of both babies that they survived a baptism of total immersion in an icy loch, Julie pale and quiet but Carla angrily screaming her protest.

Afterwards while they slept, Julie's fairy godmother scattered her crib with magic dust, rose petals and witty bon mots before airily rising and winging away, complacent in the knowledge that her protégée would flourish.

Sole attendant at Carla's hastily borrowed cot was the Angel of Death, who flew over heavily, letting fall a crystalline powdering of ground bones and hollow laughter, before landing with the heavy deliberation of a vulture to grip the crib in pale bony hands.

Who invited her? Was she just passing, and, sensing a party of the muted kind so suited to her tastes, gatecrashed?

However it was, finding herself thrust into the role of sole sponsor she hastily bestowed what gifts she could muster on the baby's restless head.

'Ah yes,' she muttered, peering down at the sleeping infant with wall-eyes like milky marbles, 'She looks like a horror writer in the making to me.'

Was the baby that ugly? Surely not, though it is hard to tell from the one faded photo of Carla that lies loose in the album charting Julie's precious babyhood.

But perhaps it was the only gift she had to give, caught on the hop as it were before, flapping ponderously, she became airborne and drifted away on the breeze like a crumpled black rag.

See what I mean? You'd have to read the rest of it to decide just who is the twisted sister.

Suffice it to say that when you've been brought up from the cradle to believe you are inherently bad, evil, and devil-spawned, and even your mother takes a dislike to you for no reason other than it's her side of the family with the gypsy blood, it doesn't give you much incentive to change; so it was fortunate that I discovered an outlet for my darker imaginings in my writing.

First I scared the living daylights out of my schoolmates (which made me, for the first time, strangely popular), and then I began to have the odd (very odd) story published, until finally, not long after I'd moved to Westery and my first teaching post, *Twisted Sister* was accepted.

Now evil pays the bills: not lavishly, but well enough to enable me to give up the teaching long ago, and I've never taken money from Max even on those rare occasions when he's actually offered it, because I'd rather be a Best-kept Secret than a Best-kept Woman.

Meanwhile Jane, on the strength of her poetry books (and she writes poetry like there's a word famine), and the literary merit in which I am so singularly lacking, has been teaching one day a week on a postgraduate creative writing course at the same university as her husband and Max.

This is why she knew about Rosemary's accident so quickly, for her ear isn't just pressed permanently to the ground for gossip, it's sent down invisible suckers, and thus it was that she phoned me, agog for a reaction to something she assumed I knew.

'Isn't it great news about Rosemary?' was her opening gambit. 'Unless they arrest Max, of course. It does sound dodgy that she should fall out of her wheelchair hard enough to hit her head and kill herself when she's paralysed from the waist down, though, doesn't it?'

With astonishment I watched the hand holding the phone suddenly wilt like a dead stalk – most peculiar. Then my knees followed suit, and everything shifted dizzyingly, like it does in one of my recurring nightmares, the long dark corridor ones.

'Any moment now,' I thought with resignation, 'and I'll start somersaulting backwards towards the cupboard door.'

The door I really don't want to open *ever*.

'Cassy? You're very quiet. Are you still there?' demanded Jane's barracuda-toothed voice, piercing my shock and enabling me to lift the receiver to my ear again.

'You did know, didn't you? Or – no, don't tell me Max hasn't even phoned you yet? I'm the first with the news?'

'No. Yes . . . I mean, he must have tried and I was out or . . . or something,' I hedged lamely. 'Jane, are you absolutely sure about this? Rosemary's dead?'

'Yes, two days ago. He came home and found her on the sun deck. Or rather *off* the sun deck.'

'But what about the live-in carer? Max said they'd got one through an agency.'

'Rosemary' d argued with her and sent her packing, that's what I heard. Probably caught her flirting with Max. After all, he may be getting on a bit, but he's still attractive. Bet he looks good with a Californian tan.'

'Max wouldn't flirt,' I said automatically.

'And you really hadn't heard a thing? Well I *was* going to congratulate you, since you can at last be made a respectable woman of and then even Ma and Pa might speak to you again. But if he hasn't told you, then perhaps he's tired of you, or found someone else or something?'

'Thank you for that kind thought,' I said coldly, but she was only saying what I was thinking. Why *hadn't* he phoned me?

'Oh well,' consoled Jane. 'Perhaps it's because they've arrested him. Two major accidents in one lifetime is a bit of a coincidence.'

'Of course it's an accident!' I said hotly. 'Max would never have hurt her! Think how he's stayed married to her all these years, and looked after her. And you can't blame her skiing accident on him!'

'I suppose so, and of course if he *was* going to kill her so he could marry you, he'd have done it when you were young and pretty, wouldn't he? I don't suppose he's bothered now.'

'That wasn't quite what I meant. He didn't love her, but he was fond of her – and her death has probably hit him harder than he'd expected, that's why he hasn't got round to phoning me. It would be sort of disloyal.'

'Not half as disloyal as seducing one of his students, and then keeping her as his mistress for the last twenty or so years,' Jane pointed out helpfully.

'He hasn't kept me!' I protested, though I suppose it was true that he *did* seduce me.

She ignored that. 'He's probably bumped her off because he's picked up some nubile young student out there. Some of them go for the sophisticated father-figure stuff. Gerald's friend over there said that female fitness trainer they've hired is young and quite pretty, too.'

'You'd better not repeat any of your fragrant little theories to anyone else,' I warned, but I knew she wouldn't: Jane only lets her mask slip and her mouth off-leash with me, and to some extent, our brothers. Even her husband still thinks she's Little Miss Angelic.

'Don't be silly. Anyway, now you know, you can phone Max, can't you?'

'I don't have his number. He always calls me: I couldn't afford all those transatlantic calls.'

'You mean he didn't leave you any way of contacting him? Not even in an emergency?'

'He's never been here when I've had any emergencies. I'm used to coping alone.'

'I'll find his home number for you,' Jane offered eagerly. 'Now, who would be best, and why would I want to know . . .? Oh yes, that would work,' she mused. 'Right, I'll get back to you later with the number, but only on condition that you call me and tell me everything he said, mind.'

Like hell I will.

'Thanks, Jane,' I managed to say between gritted teeth, but only because I really needed that number and she was the only one who could get it for me. 'You might have to leave it on the answering machine because I'm doing a singing telegram later.'

'You can't be serious! After that news? Surely you'd rather hang on until you've spoken to Max?'

'I need the money: Crypt-ograms pay well, and they're easy. I may not be as popular as Orla's Marilyn Monroe act, and the jokes do get a bit much sometimes, but they don't take much time. The Batmobile's so old now it's a constant drain on my bank account, and I think it needs an expensive op.'

'You should trade that old banger in for something reliable. And why the hell didn't you milk Max for everything you could get while he was still mad about you? It's probably too late now – but I'll get that number and ring you back anyway. Byee!'

Getting Max's number must have been harder than she anticipated, because she still hadn't rung back by the time I'd arrayed myself in my best vampire outfit, streaked my long dark locks with silver, and rendered my face even more luminescently pallid than nature had already made it with stage make-up.

Jason phoned, though, to ask if I was going to the pub tonight.

'Probably,' I said, warmed by his lovely, treacly dark voice.

Had it not been for his far from lovely teenage son I might just have succumbed to temptation with Jason by now . . . and I might still, if my next egg-xamination is a Null Pointer. I'm obviously running out fast, and this is no time to be choosy.

'I've got to go and do a "greetings from beyond the grave-ogram" first, though.'

His voice perked up: 'Oh goodie! Are you coming to the pub in your vampire stuff? You know that really turns me on!'

'Everything turns you on,' I said dampeningly, though actually it is quite consoling in the face of Max's recent neglect to have Jason lusting after me.

'Everything *you* do turns me on,' he amended. 'Come down later and I'll buy you chicken in a basket.'

'I'll buy my own dinner, thanks. See you later, Jason, I've got to go.'

I felt a little better after that, though. Max might take me for granted, but other men still found me attractive even if I *was* sliding down the slope towards fifty faster than an Olympic bobsleigh team on their last run.

34

And Max was probably just being ultra-cautious. He would never have dreamed that Jane would winkle out the news so fast, or he would have rung me by now.

Finding that actually I had ten minutes to spare before it was time to leave I filled in the time with yet another self-questioning list, though I didn't expect to find anything I didn't already know:

Writing horror versus 'literary' novels.

For:

I) I'm a natural-born horror writer.

2) It's cathartic to let the demons loose from time to time.

3) *I* could have been the monster if I hadn't had this outlet.

4) I make a living from it.

5) You can't eat a literary reputation.

6) I enjoy it.

Against:

1) While we're all peddling our own versions of reality, mine is blacker than most. You don't get literary kudos for horror unless your name's Mary Shelley or Bram Stoker.

2) I'll always be just the Sister of the more famous Jane and her pared-down poetry.

Conclusion: I feel strongly that I have to write these things. Maybe I'll never get on the Booker short list, but with a bit of luck I could be laughing all the way to the bank, even if I'm never quite in the Stephen King league.

My roots are in the graveyard, so let Jane make with the harp in the rarefied atmosphere above.

Draping a nylon cobweb over one black velvet-shrouded shoulder (think early Kate Bush on a bad day) I snarled at my image in the mirror, which is more than most vampires can do, and went out to deliver a Ghastly Greeting.

As Orla is fond of saying, Song Language's motto is 'We serve you right.'

As I stepped out of my front door all girded up to sing for my supper, Mrs Bridges upstairs' window flew open and she leaned out perilously far, her loose grey hair dangling like a dingy unravelled bellrope.

'The fuzzy-wuzzies are coming!' she screeched.

Shouts and rhythmic thumping noises came from the room behind her.

I cupped my hands to my mouth and screamed: 'MRS BRIDGES, TURN *ZULU* OFF!'

'What? Is that you, Cass? Are they after you? The fuz—'

'THE VIDEO – IT'S ONLY THE VIDEO!'

She looked down at me, confused.

Perhaps this wasn't the best time to explain how politically incorrect her terms of reference were, either?

'THE VIDEO, MRS BRIDGES!'

She turned and vanished, and the sound abruptly ceased, only to be replaced a few moments later by her reedy soprano warbling along to *The Sound Of Music*.

'I am sixteen, going on seventeen . . .'

Yeah, right. Sixteen going on seventy-nine.

The room throbbed with a strange beat, and greenish light pulsated as the familiar figure of her neighbour swiftly aged before her eyes, adolescent to elderly woman in seconds, before crumbling to dust with a soft sigh . . .

Not that I want Mrs Bridges to turn to dust, because I am quite fond of the noisy old bat, and she is knitting me a nice, big warm cobweb to wear on those chillier Crypt-ogram occasions.

'Oh, it's only you, Cass!' Chrissie Fowkes said, peeping out of her front door like a timid albino gerbil. 'I thought I heard shouting.'

'You did, but I've stopped now.'

'Oh?' she said doubtfully, then came out a bit further, clutching her tightly and squarely packaged baby. It was making noises like a kettle slowly coming to the boil.

'How's my little Birdie?'

'She never seems to stop screaming, and now she's got this really peculiar rash. Do you want to see it?'

'No, I think I'll pass on that one, thanks.'

'Do you think she's possessed?' she asked fearfully.

'No more than other children,' I reassured her, and then left quickly before she could show me the rash, or Birdsong demonstrate her lung capacity.

If Birdie hasn't put me off the urge to procreate, nothing will.

Chapter 4: Lover, Come Back To Me

I picked up the new horror novel by Cass Leigh, Nocturnally Yours, *out of a spirit of curiosity. Then I couldn't put it down. I couldn't keep any food down for three days either* ...

Expose Magazine:
'On The Shelf' with Lisa-Mona Bevore

As I drove through the twisty dark lanes to deliver the Cryptogram, Clive the rubber vampire bat dangling from the sun visor, my twisty dark mind began to take over, rudely elbowing my real-life problems into the bottom drawer.

This often happens, since I'm a creature of the night. All my best writing is done in the graveyard shift between about midnight and four in the morning, that spooky time when nothing seems quite real. You could punch your fist through the reality around you then, and it would give like cellophane, which I suppose pretty well sums up what I do.

Strangely enough, it's always annoyed the hell out of Max to wake up in the night and find me hammering the keys in the back room, but he forgets that I have to write to eat. (Unless you count his occasional hamper contributions, but I find all those tasty little goodies much too rich for my taste.)

Besides, I am a writer: ergo, I write. And if my most creative time is in the middle of the night, so be it.

The way I slide in and out between the two parallel universes of my life and fiction without conscious volition, the one adding substance to the shadows of the other, unnerved him.

'Where are you, Cassy?' he would often say, which is about as much a conversation stopper as: 'What are you thinking about?'

'Chapter Sixteen of *Lover, Come Back To Me*' is still giving me problems, Clive,' I said, as he bobbed and flapped against the windscreen. 'It just isn't *chilling* enough. Listen to this:

Keturah returned to the grave again and again each night, to fling herself like a penitent across the freshly mounded pall of earth that separated her from her lover, hot tears searing down through the cold clay.

She yearned to feel his presence there with her, for that illusion of comfort was all she could hope for now that the old woman's childish resurrection mumbo-jumbo had failed her, as she had known in her heart it would.

But she had done what she'd promised Sylvanus in his last throes: she'd tried every possible means to call him back to her and all had been fruitless.

Perhaps it was her fault, for not truly believing it could happen? Or deeply dreading that if it did *work, what came back would be some horrible travesty of her lover ...*

'The dead don't come back, Sylvanus,' she whispered, too blinded by tears to see the pale fingers clawing out of the earth towards her, like new shoots to the sun.

She was about to find just how wrong she was.

'But *what*, exactly, is coming back, Clive?'

I wasn't sure, and my publisher's deadline was approaching faster than that grisly set of suppurating fingers.

The only way I'd ever get it finished was to pay a little grave-yard visit later tonight after the pub shut and *scare* myself into the next chapter. If I was very lucky the conditions would be right for that strange, low, smoky mist to hang about at tombstone level like an old horror movie: sometimes it did.

First, though, there was the little matter of the singing telegram to deliver – if the thread of country lane I was currently driving along was really the one I thought it was, that is?

It was, and with relief I turned into a marginally wider road and pulled up outside a brightly lit pub with a full car park.

I hooked Clive's elastic over my arm, checked my greenish pallor in the mirror, and added another layer of crimson lipstick. Then I took a deep breath and issued forth to sing for my supper.

*

38

I shouldn't have bothered.

That is absolutely the last Crypt-ogram I do, because the money could never be enough to compensate me for what I've just gone through!

Even *supply teaching* would be preferable.

I mean, I knew it was a stag night, but no one warned me that the said stags would be huge, burly, drunken rugby players, all of whom wanted me to bite them at the very *least*.

One of them even kept trying to stick his finger in my mouth to test the sharpness of my fangs, until I bit him. (Fangs for the Memory?)

I was lucky to escape with little more than shredded drapery, though I fear my bat would never have been the same again, even had I stopped long enough to retrieve him. (Poor Clive: although I knew his body was hollow, I hadn't realised quite how stretchy it was. Sort of symbolic of the whole thing really – a hollow mockery.)

I beat them to my little black Mini with inches to spare. It was unlocked as usual – you'd have to be desperate to steal it – but as soon as I was in it I slammed down the door locks.

I was just in time: they streamed around the car, baying, then lifted it up bodily only to set it down again sideways in the road facing the hedge.

It took me something like a sixteen-point turn to get free, weaving between huge, drunken bodies while they leered through the windows and banged on the roof But at least that was better than them banging *me*, which seemed to be what they assumed came with the package.

I tell you, it was seriously scary.

'Come back and strip!' they howled, among other more unrepeatable things. 'Call yourself a Strippagram?'

Well no, actually I don't. And Micheline Brown, the unfortunate fiancée of one of these louts, had hired me to sing 'The Monster Mash', nothing more.

She might have warned me: though now I came to think about it, on the phone she'd sounded like the sort of girl who could sort even this lot out, so she had probably assumed I could, too.

I drove off at speed in the wrong direction, and promptly got lost in the small lanes trying to get back to Westery.

It took me ages, and I stopped for a tearful interlude in the first lay-by I came to, though whether the tears were from humiliation, fear, frustration, or the Max situation, I really couldn't say: maybe all of them.

After some time I wiped my face with a wad of tissues, and decided that what I needed was a drink and something solid in the food line, which was fortunate since Something Solid In The Food Line is the only sort of catering the King's Arms does. Not for them the nouvelle cuisine offerings of a teaspoon of cat vomit decorated with a trickle of vivid sauce and two leaves. (And while I am *forever* seeing pubs called the King's Head, or King's Arms, where is the rest of him? Why no King's Leg, or King's Torso, or even King's Knob?)

It wasn't by any means the first time I'd appeared in the pub in full vampire gear, eliciting no more attention than when I'd appeared at more or less fortnightly intervals with a suave, increasingly silver-haired lover.

Mind you, I'd have taken out my fangs had they not by now been well and truly rammed down on to the adhesive gum by having those grubby masculine fingers testing the points for sharpness – and I think I bit down pretty hard, too, which wouldn't have helped. I'd have to work them loose later.

It was quiet in the back room, although the rattle of the slot machine and a low moaning from the juke box gave evidence of the regulars in the bar. Or it could be the moaning of the regulars and the rattling of the juke box, as *something uncoiled itself from a nest of old Elvis 45s and started to slither—*

I shook the image firmly away and looked around.

It being Friday, the vicar was sitting at his usual table, where he holds an impromptu counselling clinic for all comers, while imbibing dry sherry and putting the parish magazine together.

''Evening, Charles,' I said, and he glanced up with a pre-occupied smile.

'Cass, my dear,' he said absently. 'Terrible, terrible stuff!'

I didn't take it personally. Poor Charles is something of a poet, and finds the reams of religious verse that flow in by every post almost too bad to bear. But he stoically reads them, and even prints one or two in every edition.

Seeing he was absorbed I carried on over to the corner where Orla was sitting in Marilyn Monroe mode.

Well, I say sitting, but actually she was slumped in a heap, shoes kicked off, with her gold dress looking a little the worse for wear.

'Hi, Orla,' I said, and she opened mascared eyelashes and looked at me. 'You look like I feel. Bad one?'

'You're not kidding.'

'Where's Jason? He said he'd be here.'

She indicated the limp figure propping up the bar like a wonky gremlin bookend. 'Celebrating selling that hideous screen he's had in the shop for years – to my American guest, too.'

'Did he? No wonder he's celebrating, then. Well, I need to eat, and boy do I need a drink! Do you want anything?'

'Large dark rum and coke. Chicken and chips.'

'OK.'

Jason had looked right out of it, but as I approached he straightened slowly upright and smiled at me, his brown eyes lighting up: 'Cass? Thought you were a figment of my over-heated imagination.'

'Drunken imagination,' I corrected, leaning past him to order food. 'Are you going to get something to eat and come and sit down? Or just carry on drinking until you slide down the bar like last time?'

'You've got your teeth in,' he said sapiently.

'I know. I'd better have curry, it'll be easier to eat.'

'And you've losht . . . *lost* your bat.'

'I'm just grateful that's all I lost,' I said darkly. When I carried the drinks over to Orla he followed me. (It sometimes seems to me that he may be the reincarnation of an Irish wolfhound, except that they are the most equable of dogs and Jason has a quick temper.)

Orla was looking a little more alert. 'How was the stag night?' she asked me.

'I was thinking maybe supply teaching is safer.'

'That bad?'

'Rugby players. I was lucky to escape relatively unscathed, except for the mental scars, and poor Clive is a goner.'

'Clive?' she asked, puzzled.

'My vampire bat.'

'Oh? Well, he's made of rubber, isn't he? He'll probably bounce back.'

'I don't think so, and I don't intend going back to find out. How did yours go?'

41

'Birthday party. They were drunk and persistent – made me sing "Happy Birthday" three times, with lots of pouting, so I'm all pouted out. But please, Cass, don't stop doing the Crypt-ograms. You're one of my most popular acts.'

'What do you mean, "one of"? You've only got four including yourself.'

'Yes, but I'm still building the business. And I promise not to send you on any more stag nights,' she wheedled.

''Cept mine,' slurred Jason, who had been sitting sleepily staring down into his glass looking deceptively cuddly, though actually those sudden bursts of bad temper were probably what had finally driven Tanya away. Who wants to live with a volcano?

'Jason looks like Alice's dormouse,' Orla observed critically.

'More like a Wookie.'

'Are you getting married, Jason?' she asked.

'When Cass says the word.'

'The word is *no,*' I said automatically. 'And not only are you not divorced, Jason, you know you don't really want to marry me.'

'Come on, Cass!' he said, smiling at me. 'Marry me, live with me – whatever you want!'

He really is rather attractive in a large, loose-limbed, craggy way.

'Why waste any more of your life waiting for an old man, when you could be sharing it with me?'

'He's not an old man,' I objected automatically, though Max is certainly no spring chicken. He's a whole decade older than Jason and me, and *our* dewy bloom of youth has long since evaporated.

Somehow this didn't seem the right moment to tell them that my lover was Suddenly Single but hadn't bothered to inform me of the fact, though it might have explained just why I found it balm to my wounded feelings to have Jason looking at me tonight as though I was everything he'd ever wanted for Christmas.

Perhaps I might even have given him just a bit of encouragement . . . unconsciously, of course, for my feelings for him are really more of the sisterly variety.

And after a couple of drinks I certainly began to wonder just why I was being faithful to someone who was, as Orla often pointed out, unfaithful. Who had made promises he hadn't kept, and hidden me in a sort of limbo for half my life (and just about *all* my reproductive life.)

Can there be that many eggs left in the basket at forty-four and counting? How many of the little lions have climbed off and ambled away, yawning? For we are born with all the eggs we'll ever have, and no one's ever gone to work on my Year of the Lion cache. I'll be even older by the time Max comes back and we get married – *if* he comes back and we *do* finally get married – and it might be too late even now.

Too late.

Also to be taken into the reckoning is Max's performance in bed, which has declined over the last few years to the disheartening point where I think the sight of his golf clubs excites him more than I do. This is not likely to help.

I was starting to feel really dismal, not to mention a teeny touch of the bitter and twisted. I may even have been muttering under my breath like a malevolent hag. It was the perfect mood for my graveyard shift, though, so wrapping warmly in my purple velvet cloak I set off.

Tonight, for some reason, Orla and Jason were both twitchy about letting me go off on my own, even though I do this sort of thing all the time and am not at all afraid. I had to be quite firm about needing to be alone.

After all, nothing *living* would harm me in Westery, and the dead can't.

I left the Batmobile outside my cottage in Graveyard Lane, resisting the urge to go in and check for phone messages, which isn't really a *huge* temptation when you live in the central one in a row of three, like the filling in a dubious sandwich.

On one side of me Mrs Bridges has her TV switched on full-volume between the hours of 7am and midnight, sending me subliminal messages through the party wall that I don't want to hear; and on the other side, of course, live the Fowkes with their possessed baby, Birdsong.

They call her Birdie, which might be all right for a tiny tot, but could be a bit sick-making when she's adult, I fear.

Shots from number one and squalling from number three slowly faded behind me as I strode down the lane, warmly wrapped against the chilly breeze in my cape with its quilted mauve satin lining.

I was not at all nervous of the living, for the road to the

43

graveyard is a dead-end and so not much frequented at night, and since Westery is a very small place, what youths there are prefer the dubious nightspots of the nearest large town. I've always felt perfectly safe walking the lanes in the middle of the night, waiting for the chill awareness of the undead to strike, as it always does.

Orla thinks I'm going to fall prey to some mad rapist cruising the lanes looking for a victim, but I don't think they cruise the lanes looking for extremely pissed-off vampires.

Down the high-hedged lane the small and isolated graveyard sits in its very own Foggy Hollow, giving it on the right night that classically spooky effect. But unfortunately tonight was clear and crisp and even, and I didn't even need my little torch once I was out of the lane because the moon was Werewolf full. The metal gate groaned under my hand, and the gravestones all cast dark, hunched shadows.

I paced about the gravelled paths for a while ... *the gravel beneath her feet grated like broken teeth* ... under the inscrutable gaze of angels, and accompanied by the sobbing, guilty shade of Keturah, distraught at having failed her lover, Sylvanus.

She hadn't truly believed black magic could bring him back, nor deep down had she wanted it to, for she'd been mortally afraid of what form her dead lover would take. No wonder, then, that she cast herself on to the freshly dug earth of his grave in a frenzy of guilt and remorse!

And her lover, Sylvanus? How would he be feeling? (Apart from dead.)

If he did manage to come back in some form without her help, wouldn't he be seriously cheesed-off with Keturah for failing him? Especially, perhaps, if he had been called back by another, whose yearning for him was greater than hers?

Come to that, he'd probably be feeling pretty much as I do about Max just now.

Finding I was starting to emphasise with Sylvanus more than Keturah, which wouldn't do in the least at this point, I plunged suddenly off the path and cast myself full-length over the newly sodded grave of Isaiah Kettlewell.

How surprised (but not displeased) he would have been had he been able to appreciate it, the old rogue!

Turf had been jigsawed back over the mound so I couldn't dig my fingers into the soil like Keturah, but actually the image of those other fingers coming up between the sods to close on her as she lay there was much, much better . . .

Then something cold squirmed under *my* cheek and dragging fingers closed on my shoulder.

'Eeee-yaargh!' I screeched, wrenching free with one mighty bound and leaping away in an acrobatic manner I hadn't realised was in me, except in my nightmares.

As I was about to hurdle the nearest gravestone a familiar voice stopped me in my tracks: 'It's only me, Cass,' Jason said apologetically.

He uncurled his long body from a graveside crouch. 'I followed you to make sure you were all right, but I didn't mean to frighten you.'

'Frighten me? I nearly died when you touched me, you imbecile! My heart stopped beating. Three million brain cells ceased to exist. The shock could have—'

I stopped, illumination suddenly dawning. 'Of course! That's what would have happened!'

'What would have?' said Jason, puzzled. 'When?'

'Keturah would probably have passed out from the shock, if not died of fear on the spot. She's such a weak-spined creature.'

'Look, Cass, just who is this Keturah?' demanded Jason. 'And why were you lying on Isaiah's grave? I hadn't realised you were so fond of the old villain!'

'Keturah is the *living* main character of my new novel, *Lover, Come Back To Me*.'

'Appropriate title, with Max going off like that, isn't it?' he quipped unfeelingly, and I glowered at him.

'No, it isn't. And although I quite liked Isaiah, I was just using his grave to get the feel of what it would be like to—'

I didn't finish the sentence, since Jason was looking at me with puzzled affection, like a large, friendly, but not terribly bright dog.

I gave him a pat. 'Never mind, Jason. I think I've got what I needed, and certainly more than I intended, and I'm going home.'

'Can I come?' he asked pathetically.

'No. It's too late, I have a tattered reputation to uphold, and if you were cherishing any hopes, forget them, because I don't intend being unfaithful to Max.'

Not yet, anyway.

'But *I* wouldn't take you for granted like he does, and anyway, why stay faithful to a married man when you could play the field a bit with an unmarried one – sort of? Besides,' he added, 'Tom's home for the weekend and I don't want to go back. Strange music will blast the air until three in the morning, and the lounge will be littered with bodies.'

'I think that sounds pretty much like the next chapter of my book,' I mused, seeing my way forward at last. 'A sort of *Wreck of the Hesperus* effect.'

Their naked bodies slithered and writhed together like snakes in a pit? No, perhaps that's a cliché.

Jason was still thinking along different lines . . . or maybe not. 'You could come back to my place and distract me,' he suggested.

'No thanks,' I said shortly, brushing grass and earth off my cloak and not feeling even remotely tempted. Tom makes rather gross sexual suggestions to me whenever Jason is out of the room, and he's not only young enough to be my son, but has spots the size of puffball mushrooms.

'Well, I'd rather come back with you,' he conceded, removing a worm from my hood and tossing it aside. Then he swept me into a warm embrace which, since I was still wrapped in the cloak, was rather unpleasantly strait-jacketing. 'Cassy, you know I'm mad about you. If Max hadn't taken you away from me when we were students—'

'Jason, Max didn't take me away from you, you were going out with Tanya by the time he came on the scene. And you know we'd already agreed to be just friends.'

'Well, that was then, and this is now. Couldn't you just think seriously about me?'

'I have – I do,' I said truthfully. 'And you know I'm very fond of you, Jason, but that isn't enough, is it?'

'I don't know. Couldn't you try it and see?' he suggested, and kissed me.

'Not until I find out where Tanya's got to,' I thought, but relaxed into the kiss anyway, and very pleasant it was, too, once he'd negotiated his way around the vampire teeth.

But it wasn't *more* than just pleasant, and since Jason was starting to get a bit carried away I wrenched my head back and tried to free myself, before things really got out of hand.

'Jason, stop,' I said. 'No, Jason! I'm sorry, but this just isn't right, and—'

'You don't mean it,' he said thickly, trying to kiss me again. 'Forget Max.'

I was starting to get a bit cross, for although I didn't really think Jason was dangerous (down, Shep!), he was big, focused and had drunk enough to make him stubbornly single-minded. As his mouth closed on mine with passionate determination, I was forced to employ the fangs for the second time that night.

I'd be a full-time vampire before I knew it at this rate.

Jason yelled and let me go so suddenly I staggered back, observing with some interest the way the dark blood welled from his lower lip, and the sudden expression of fury turning his craggy face into a gargoyle's mask.

Scrub what I said about him not being dangerous. Knowing his rages of old I realised it was quite time I removed myself, and so took to my heels through the graveyard and out through the gates into the lane, with Jason in hot pursuit.

Perhaps it was because I was too busy looking over my shoulder to see how close he was, that I wasn't aware of the dark sports car hurtling round the bend until it screeched to a halt bare inches from me, warmly quivering.

The driver, a large, dark and unequivocally masculine shape, was making movements as if to get out and probably yell at me, if not worse, though it certainly wasn't my fault he'd taken a wrong turn down a dead end.

. . . the vampire cruised the dark lanes seeking his next victim, the sleek, fast car making him feel even more powerful than before . . .

Vampires in cars? I hadn't considered the possibilities motor transport would open up to the Undead before . . .

But the driver of *this* one opened his door, and feeling that I was about to turn into whatever the female equivalent of a misogynist is (and contrary to male belief it isn't necessarily a feminist) I bared my fangs in a snarl that he could take either as a propitiating smile or a threat, and began to sidle round the further side of the car towards home.

Do you know, I'd quite forgotten I still had the ghastly greenish complexion and dark crimson lipstick on until the door slammed shut again, the central locking went down with a loud 'clunk!', and the car shot backwards, executed a rapid three-point turn, and roared away.

I took it as a compliment, and it's not the first time this sort of thing has happened either. I am quite tall, dark-haired, and naturally pallid of complexion, with deep-set eyes and a rather lugubrious cast of countenance, and in full escapee-from-the-crypt make-up and dress in a darkened room have been known to scare more nervous telegram recipients into a dead faint.

How people do love to be petrified, don't they? Or maybe they think I'm going to do an Ozzy Osbourne with the Bat? (Ex-bat. Alas, poor Clive! I knew him well . . .)

Once the car had gone, I became aware of blasphemous sounds from the graveyard indicative of Jason's having measured his length over a gravestone, so seizing the opportunity I quickly made myself scarce.

Back home it was midnight at the oasis. Mrs Bridges had gone to bed, and even Birdie was silent in her little nest.

The message light lured me to the phone, but it was just Jane with Max's number. Nothing from Max personally, then or later, though Jason rang the doorbell repeatedly while I wrote through the witching hours with a red-hot pen.

Chapter 5: Mistress Of All She Surveys

'Another chilling little potboiler from mistress of the macabre Cass Leigh, Nocturnally Yours *will delight only her fans.*

Daily Telegraph

At some time during the night, whilst I was pleasantly engaged in causing poor Keturah to pass out with terror as something unspeakable grabs her in the graveyard, only to find when she wakes up that—

No. I'll stop there because I'm not going to tell you what Keturah sees when she wakes up: buy the book and boost my sales.

In any case I am digressing from the point, which is that at some time between Jason's final assault on the doorbell and the first squawk of Birdsong, Jack Craig pushed a key through my letter-box.

Not just any key: *the* key. Large, sturdy, old-fashioned, and the sort of thing that would open Drac's castle or the House on Haunted Hill. Which is pretty close, actually, since it was the key to Kedge Hall that I'd spent so much time trying to borrow.

It came wrapped in a piece of paper that said, thrillingly: 'Tonight!', and included a map of the drive, and the little path under the arch at the side of the house that would take me to the kitchen door, all very Enid Blyton. All it needed was Timmy the dog. Or maybe Jason would do?

The thick plottens.

While delighted that Jack had at last capitulated it *was* odd of him to deliver the key in such a mysterious manner, when he might slip it into my hand down at the pub most nights.

And why tonight? Though of course I will go, because it would be just like him to demand the key back tomorrow, and it's been such amazingly hard work to get the thing at all.

Jack's appearance is clearly against him, for you wouldn't think from looking at him that he had any principles. Indeed, I often wonder how he got the job of caretaker at all, except, I suppose, that Craigs have always occupied the lodge, and he was simply the Last Man Standing.

It's amazing how everything happens at once, isn't it? But having finally worn him down into agreeing, I'll have to seize the moment.

Miss Kedge was a very reclusive old lady who never even bothered answering my letters pleading for a quick look round, and I have no reason to think the new owner, if he ever appears, will be any different. Apart from the haunted bit, Kedge Hall is one of the nicest small manor houses in the country, so you'd think the heir would hotfoot it back if only to put the house on the market, wouldn't you?

Rumour has it that he is – or has been – some kind of foreign correspondent, and is currently abroad somewhere; but other than that no one seems to know anything much about him, or has ever seen him here apart from Jack Craig on that one brief visit months ago.

Dawn was breaking and Birdie was squawking, but instead of going to bed for a couple of hours (with earplugs) like I usually do, I listened to Jane's message again, writing down Max's phone number. And this time I actually registered the end of her message, the scary bit, where she'd added: 'Clear out the spare bedroom, I might just want to come and stay with you soon.'

Stay with me? With *me*? Does she want to get excommunicated from the parental nest too?

Or was it just a Jane thing to put me on edge?

After that I dithered about with Max's number in one hand and the strangely reassuring weight of the Hall key in the other, while I tried to summon up the courage to call him.

When I finally did, it rang for such an awfully long time before it was picked up that I'd started to think Jane had got the wrong number.

Even then, there was silence from the other end, except for the faint seashell whisper of someone breathing.

'Max, is that you? Are you there? It's me, Cass.'

'*Cassy*?' He sounded more stunned than pleased. 'How on earth did you get this number? And do you know what time it is over here?'

'No, of course I don't. I don't know what time it is here, either – what does it matter? Max, Jane told me about Rosemary, and she got your number for me.'

'Jane knows already? My God! Then I suppose everyone knows?'

'Everyone except me! Why didn't you phone, Max? It was so horrible finding out from Jane, not you. And – I'm really sorry about Rosemary,' I added, rather awkwardly. 'I mean, I know you were still fond of her, and—'

'Yes, it's been quite a shock,' he interrupted brusquely. 'I haven't been thinking straight. Sorry, Cassy, I did mean to call, but it's all been so difficult. I knew you'd understand, darling.'

'Yeah, just take me for granted as usual, faithful old Cass,' I thought disloyally, and then felt immediately guilty. Guilt on guilt: I have more layers of the stuff than an onion has skins. (And I *wish* he wouldn't call me Cassy, it's *so* Jane Austen!)

'I'll come over as soon as I can get a plane seat,' I assured him. 'You shouldn't have to be alone at a time like this.'

'No,' he said sharply. 'No, you can't, Cassy! It wouldn't look good at all if you came here.'

'Of course I wouldn't *stay* with you, Max: that would look a bit too "off with the old and on with the new". (Or 'off with the old, and on with the nearly as old'.) 'Why shouldn't a friend come to support you without anyone suspecting there's anything between us? But I must see you and I ought to be with you at a time like this.'

'No,' he repeated with unflattering force. 'You don't understand at all, Cassy! There was a slight difficulty with the police over the accident. They didn't think she was strong enough to get her chair out on to the sun deck like that, and then for it to go over the edge at the highest point, and they've been very awkward about it.'

'But of course it was an accident,' I cried. 'I mean – wasn't it?'

'Of course, and they fully accept that now. Rosemary had great strength in her arms, especially since Kyra's been working with

51

her, and in any case, who would do such a thing on purpose to a helpless invalid? *I* was lecturing all that day, or with colleagues, of course,' he added.

'Yes, of course,' I echoed, thinking the alibi came a bit pat.

'But now it's turned out that the braking mechanism on her chair was faulty, so she probably wheeled up to the low parapet too fast, couldn't stop, and was tipped over.'

'Oh, I see,' I said, relieved. Not that I'd *really* thought Max would have had any hand in it, because he valued his venerable tanned and toned hide too much to do anything illegal.

'So however much I'd like to see you, it's better if you don't come out just now. And there's another thing, Cassy: Rosemary knew all about us.'

'What do you mean? Of course she knew you were having a relationship with someone else, you had an understanding, didn't you? You went off for weekends of "golf", and she never asked any questions?'

'She never asked me anything because she already knew the answers: among her papers are reports on us she'd had done. The police found them, and it made things sticky for a while, until they accepted that it wasn't possible for me to have been there when the accident happened. But it means that you must keep away.'

I felt suddenly like someone had lifted my rock and left my conscience exposed and squirming.

'Max, that's horrible! That she should care enough – be jealous enough to find out about us. And you said when you told her you would never leave her, she more or less said she would turn a blind eye to . . . well to *me*.'

'No, I could never leave her, she knew that,' he said slowly.

'Let me come out and be with you,' I pleaded again, needing to see him face to face.

'No, I've already said. Don't you understand? Besides, I'm flying back with – flying back for the funeral. I'll come down and see you after that, before I return here to finish my year. We'll talk then.'

'But Max, you do still—'

The phone went down with a click.

I don't know what I did for the rest of that morning, except at some stage Pa phoned me again, with his usual message: 'You'll burn in hell, girl,' he assured me with characteristic fervour and no preamble, although he did sound sober this time. I waited for him to put the phone down, but after a small pause he sighed deeply and added: 'And your sister with you!'

Then he put the phone down.

I stared at it like it might suddenly wake up and explain that I'd just had an auditory hallucination, and not to worry, but it stayed mum.

The telephone stirred like a snake under Keturah's hand, the cord rippling and flexing—

What had they found out about Jane? That she only looked like an angel? Well, that took long enough. The evidence has been there before and they've always managed to ignore it, just like all the other poor suckers.

Maybe they've finally discovered what she got up to as a student in Oxford, which was far more than *I* did at my university, before Max began his siege of my heart – and the rest of me.

Whatever it is, I expect Jane will manage to explain it all away to their complete satisfaction, since she seems to weave some hypnotic spell over the gullible so that they believe exactly what she wants them to.

How many years of evolution will it take, before mankind realises that the truth gene does not always go hand in hand with the ones for blonde hair and blue eyes?

But something has clearly cast a blip in her relations with Ma and Pa, and I wonder if this was what caused her to lay claim to the spare room? If so, by now I expect she has realised that staying with me (indeed, even admitting that we ever *see* each other) would not help her cause with the parents.

At eight, the postman brought me a badly wrapped foreign package containing a pair of pink Chinese silk slippers, but no message. They were exquisite but tiny, and I fear it is now too late to have my feet bound.

Not that I don't think I deserve the torture it would cause me, so perhaps I had better try it?

Certainly a punishment is overdue now the comforting bubble surrounding my long-standing affair has well and truly popped, exposing me to the cold blasts of self-doubt and guilt, status quo rocked.

And it's not like I haven't been through all this before, when I

53

was struggling to resist Max. Being quietly pursued by a handsome professor may be flattering, but it is also scary to a young student, especially after I discovered that he was not only married, but his wife had been crippled in a skiing accident a couple of years before.

I am a habitual sinner, but if I hadn't thought Rosemary accepted the situation I would never finally have agreed to it . . . and Max *definitely* let me think it wouldn't be for long, I didn't imagine that.

But I can't blame Max for my sins. What on earth was I thinking of, waiting to step into a dead woman's shoes?

And where *have* the years gone while I was doing that? I'm heading for middle age and I haven't done anything. Well, maybe I have done things, but they were all the wrong things, and most of my life has been spent writing and waiting.

Waiting for Max, waiting for Rosemary to die, waiting for children, waiting for a damned bestseller. (Or even a Damned bestseller.).

Now I feel not so much mistress of the macabre, as macabre mistress.

At lunchtime (ham and pineapple pizza, large glass of Chilean Cabernet Sauvignon), a Jason hangdog and most strangely marked about the lower lip turned up to apologise.

'That's all right,' I assured him. 'At least when I bit you the fangs loosened, so they were quite easy to get out when I got home.'

By then I was so desperately in need of comfort that had he not been in Penitent Mode, the chances are that he could have had from me what he was so keen on having last night, because I would have been anyone's for a good bear hug.

Just as well perhaps that he didn't know that?

Still, we have resumed our friendship as before, the only flaw in our entente being Tom, who apparently wanted to pop round later and tell me how much he'd enjoyed my last book.

Over my blood-spattered mortal remains, he will.

. . . *clutching The Book he stood over her blood-mired corpse, while flies admired themselves in the twin mirrors of her surprised eyes, and . . .*

Jason seems unable to see what Tom is up to, and I seem unable to tell him, but at least I now know to check who's at the door before I open it this afternoon. Tom is larger, stronger and younger than Jason, but without the cuddle factor. Thank goodness he's going back to university tomorrow.

I gave Jason an edited version of Rosemary's death, which depressed him still further, since he assumed it meant that Max and I would be marrying in the near future, even when I pointed out that we could hardly do so immediately after the funeral.

After Jason had gone I accidentally caught sight of myself in the mirror, and really it's a miracle that *anyone* wants me! My face, naturally whiter than white, still had the remains of last night's greenish make-up, my eye-liner was smeared into Alice Cooper streaks, and the crimson lipstick had rubbed off, leaving a ghastly stain. To add the *coup de grâce*, my usually straight, dark red hair now stuck up on one side like a yard brush.

Roll up, roll up, see Max's mistress of the macabre. You saw it here first, folks!

I scrubbed the exterior of the Whited Sepulchre then went to bed for a couple of hours, for after all, I still had a haunted house to visit and a chapter to write that night.

Mental and physical exhaustion meant I fell asleep instantly, only to go straight into The Nightmare like somebody'd dropped me through a trapdoor into hell.

This time the somersaulting was so dizzyingly fast (and why *does* my forward motion always turn into back-flips?), and the cupboard door pulsed so ominously with greenish light, that I thought it would all be over and the door slammed behind me for ever in the time it usually took for the first backwards tumble.

But the pulsing quickly turned to throbbing and then a hard rattling tattoo that jarred me awake: someone was beating hell out of my front door.

I staggered down and threw it wide open, because at that moment I'd have welcomed even Tom for getting me out of that corridor. Could I perhaps survive for ever without sleep? ('For ever' being whatever miserly amount of years I've got left.)

But to my surprise it wasn't Tom, only the small, portly and inoffensive figure of Jane's husband, Gerald. He's the same vintage as Max only looks it, and is nice in an unexciting way. I've always got on fine with him providing I don't malign Sweet Baby Jane, but he's never before crossed my threshold.

'Come in,' I said, staring at him. His blue Pringle jumper was on inside-out and he appeared to be wearing odd socks, one Argyle patterned and the other plain maroon.

'If it's not inconvenient. Sorry to bother you. Were you working?'

Now, that's the nice thing about Gerald, he appreciates that writing is working and not some little pastime you can fit in between shopping and cooking dinner for six. And what is more, he even recognises horror writing as real writing.

'No, that's all right, I was sleeping: but I'm glad you woke me up because I was having my nightmare.'

'Your nightmare?' he echoed, looking round him in some surprise. 'This is all very light and open, isn't it? I expected something more—'

'Dark? Sinister?'

'I was going to say cottagey, actually.'

'Oh. Well, I suppose it is light and bare-ish but I like to keep the dark stuff for the writing. And I *hate* big cupboards.'

'You don't have cupboards?'

'Not with doors. I have cupboard-phobia, you see, hence the nightmares?'

He looked baffled.

'You know, because of Pa locking me in the cupboard under the stairs as a punishment when I was a child? Jane *must* have mentioned it. The devil was supposed to get fed up and come out of me, though if he did I never noticed.'

'I see,' he said, though clearly he hadn't been following what I'd been saying with any great attention. 'I . . . er . . . heard about Max's wife, Rosemary. I'm sorry. Or should I say—'

'Congratulations? Better not to say anything.'

'No – right.'

'Tea, coffee, cocoa, rum, whisky, wine – no, I finished the last bottle of wine with lunch – sherry, crème de menthe, gin?' I offered hospitably.

'Tea, just tea, would be fine,' he said, and followed me into the kitchen while I made it.

'Cass, I came because I wanted to ask you something about Jane.'

56

'What on earth for? You never believe anything I say about her.'

'That was just sister stuff. I knew you didn't really mean it.'

'Didn't I?'

'This is serious, Cass, and I thought you might tell me . . . '

He tailed off and stared helplessly at me, a greying, pleasantly homely man with worried blue eyes. 'Jane's younger than me, and I know I'm not very exciting, but I did think we were happy. Only someone hinted to me that she'd been more than friends with that artist in residence we had last year, and that she was still seeing him.'

We gazed at each other like someone had waved a magic wand and painted us both purple, and neither wanted to tell the other.

'It can't be true, can it?' he pleaded. 'I mean, he left for Cornwall months ago, so when could she have seen him? The only time she's been away is on holiday with me, or all those weekends she's spent here with you. And I *do* understand that you needed her support while Max was away, so don't think I resented that,' he added earnestly.

'Weekends here with me?' I exclaimed, then swallowed hard and said with a weak smile: 'Oh yes – you know how sisters slag each other off all the time, but they're always there for each other in a crisis.'

'Jane's never said a bad word about you,' he assured me.

Big of her. And that's not her way: Jane's skill is to plant the poison dart with such skill and artistry that no one notices she's done it until paralysis sets in and it's too late.

'There you are then,' I said soothingly. 'You can see yourself that she hasn't had time to meet him even if she wanted to. Besides *I* met him once, don't forget, and he was a hairy, rough-looking young man – hardly Jane's type.'

'No, but years younger than me, and Jane's still so youthful and attractive that everyone thinks she's my daughter when we're on holiday,' he added glumly.

Most men seem to be pleased when people say that, but not Gerald. My estimation of him went up.

People always tell *me* I don't look anything like my real age, but they should see me today: round my eyes it isn't so much crow's feet as rookery nook.

I managed to soothe him down, but as Jane should know, once

you let a little tiny doubt lodge into the crevices of your mind it's hard to uproot it totally, and if you're not careful it just grows back again in a slightly different place.

He made me swear not to tell Jane he'd ever doubted her, and took himself off still looking a sad and sorry version of his usual self.

I didn't know what to make of it all. Jane and a non-immaculate, non-famous, years-younger, scruffy painter? I can't see it. But if not, what has she been doing when she said she was here with me?

I tried to phone her before Gerald got home, but there was no reply.

Perhaps she was away perfecting her brushstrokes?

For once I didn't go to the pub for dinner, but instead ate my second pizza of the day (quattro formaggio with sun-dried tomatoes) and spent a quiet hour pasting my review cuttings into a pirate scrapbook with a skull and crossbones on the cover, and renewing my subscription to *Skint Old Northern Woman Magazine*.

Then I went to my study and unleashed the inhabitants of *Lover, Come Back To Me* on to expanses of virgin white paper until it was time to leave for Kedge Hall.

New haunts.

Chapter 6: Tall, Dark and Cadaverous

Cass Leigh's novels form the sludge at the bottom of a very murky pond indeed ...

Guardian

It was a March night so cold that I walked in an ectoplasmic cloud of my own breath and everything, including me, was crispy-crunch-coated with frost. Even the circle of light from my big rubber torch just hung in the air like a yellow reptilian eye.

There was a reasonable moon, but lots of grubby-looking rubber bone-shaped clouds kept writhing about in front of it.

I was wrapped in the ankle-length purple velvet cloak again, not for effect, but simply because of its warm quilted lining. Perhaps it is a trifle over the top for a nocturnal ramble, but definitely in keeping with a night in Spook Hall.

The whole ambience of the night was right for inspiration as I let myself in through the unlocked front gate, pondering subplots involving a vampire full of ancient wisdom, demonic energy, and twisted logic.

... something called to Keturah, compelling her reluctant feet to follow the gravelled drive to where the dark shape of the old house squatted among its dank weeds like a drowned widow ...

He would live, my vampire (if vampires can be said to live?), in a wing of the old house, a dark family secret passed from generation to generation.

I felt strangely excited as I neared the house, though it was not the first time by any means that I'd spent the night hours in a

59

deserted mansion, even if it *was* one I'd been trying to get into for years and rumoured to be the most haunted in Britain. (But then, aren't they all?)

Perhaps even now the shade of Miss Kedge was watching me pick my way up the overgrown drive while rubbing her transparent little hands together with anticipatory glee. There are reputedly so many ghosts up there that the drive might be the only place where there's room for her to stand.

Jack tells all the old ghost stories down at the pub, but most of them I've already read in old books on the subject, especially *Kedge Hall – The Haunted Manor*. You'd expect Jack to be immune to all that superstition too, since his family have been servants there for centuries, but the lodge had been dark as I passed, so he must have been abed rather than doing a midnight round of the property, braving the spirit world. Or just too lazy, now that there was no one to check up on him?

Emerging into the gravelled circle before the low, half-timbered manor house I consulted the map, then followed the path round the side, through an unlocked gate set in a little archway, and into the courtyard beyond.

This bit was new to me, though once years ago I'd seen the front of the house, the single time the rose garden was opened to the public in aid of some charity Miss Kedge favoured. Retirement homes for knitted tea-cosies, or something.

The kitchen door was half-shadowed by encroaching stems of wisteria, and after fumbling for several minutes to insert the key with cold, gloved fingers, I discovered that it was unlocked.

Some caretaker! I could probably just have walked up here any night during the last year, without the wasted time or expense of working on Jack.

Still, I was in. Casting my torch beam around the kitchen I observed with some surprise that the seventeenth-century room had been done out in Ye Olde Worlde style, but with all mod. cons. and every piece of kitchen gadgetry known to woman. Reclusive Miss Kedge might have been, but clearly she liked her comforts and could afford to indulge herself.

The light switches didn't work, so the electricity supply must have been disconnected. I wished I'd brought a bigger torch, especially after I'd opened the doors to a larder and two sculleries (scarily dark-cupboard-like) before finally finding one that opened on to a promising corridor.

The heavy, expectant dark silence awaited me, so I followed my torch beam along the flags until something groaned deep within the stone wall under my groping hand, and I dropped the thing.

It bounced once with a faint tinkling, then went out. So much for unbreakable rubber-cased torches, I thought, berating myself for a clumsy idiot, because all old houses moan and creak with every small change in the temperature, and if walls groan it's usually because there are dodgy water pipes in them.

Then as my eyes adjusted to the darkness, I realised that it wasn't after all total: a faint light outlined the edge of a partly opened door ahead of me.

I groped my way along the (now mercifully silent) wall, and emerged warily into the great dark maw of a hall, where the flickering stub of a candle set on a Sèvres saucer had been left on a dusty refectory table.

'Jack?' I called softly, but answer came there none, unless you count the creaking of the floorboards somewhere above me, which surely must be the maligned caretaker come to make his last evening rounds. Hence the unlocked door, of course: I'd simply arrived before he'd expected me to, but I had wanted to get here before midnight when allegedly all the fun starts.

Who would have thought Jack was this conscientious? What a creature of surprises he was turning out to be!

Still, now my torch was broken the candle was handy, and Jack might even have a supply on him that I could borrow. Picking the saucer up, I climbed the stairs and found myself standing in a long, dark gallery that seemed to run endlessly away from me in both directions, the windows down one side making barely lighter rectangles.

It was *just* like my recurring nightmare, except there was no menacing door awaiting me at one end. (Or if there was, I couldn't see it.)

Then a distant light slowly began to grow, and a giant shadow moved with unnerving stealth across the wall: someone was coming.

'Jack?' I hissed.

Why was I whispering? Did I think the ghosts might wake up if

61

I yelled? And why was Jack's shadow so much more imposing than his small and wiry self?

Maybe because it wasn't Jack. With a soft, heavy padding like a big cat, out of the shadows materialised the tall, gaunt figure of a man.

Unearthly light flowed from cupped hands edged in ruffles to illuminate an austere, hollow-cheeked face framed by two sweeps of dark hair. Add to that a loose white shirt open at the neck, knee-breeches, and a general impression of looming menace, and you get the idea why I nearly did a quick Keturah on to the carpeted floor.

Then he looked up and saw me, and I swear his eyes blazed an unearthly green-blue. He stopped dead and uttered in a low, hoarse voice: 'Emma? My God, Emma, have you come back?'

That horrified, eerie whisper was the last straw. Dropping the saucer I turned to flee, running blindly into the darkness with the sound of his long, loping, strides coming after me.

The gallery must have taken a turn at the end but I didn't, running straight into a door and bruising my outstretched hands. Frantically I wrenched it open, slamming it behind me, heart racing; though don't ask me why I thought a closed door would stop a ghost, or even why I'd run from one of the ghosts I'd come to see.

And it was pointless anyway, for I found myself in a walk-in cupboard and the ghosts were in there with me.

A chill current of air moved my hair as something swooped low over my head – and I went berserk with panic.

It's odd: you think you've subjugated your old demons, and then suddenly you're right in the stuff of your worst nightmares and all the restraints are off. I was probably screaming like a banshee.

When the ghost wrenched open the door I ran right into him. Not *through* him – he was far too solid for that. Solid *and* warm.

So, not a vampire or anything either, then? Clasped to his chest by a sinewy arm I could hear his heart racing even faster than mine.

'What the hell?' he exclaimed.

'The birds – don't let the birds get me,' I pleaded. 'They're in there!'

Still retaining a grip on me, my jailer (or rescuer, I didn't then care which) lifted a small lantern high to illuminate the walk-in cupboard behind me, and observed ironically: 'Open window – no birds to be seen. Most likely it was a bat, but it's gone now whatever it was.'

He had an invigoratingly cold-water-running-over-gravel sort of voice now he wasn't whispering.

Reluctantly removing my face, neatly imprinted with chest hair patterns, from the neck of a shirt opened so far that his swash was almost unbuckled, I took a deep, relieved breath. 'A bat? Of course, how silly of me! And I *like* bats,' I said, pushing myself away shakily, although not very far since he didn't let go of my arm. 'Sorry about that! But I wasn't expecting to see a total stranger – especially dressed like that!'

'Neither was I,' he said thoughtfully, setting his candle lantern down on a little side table and regarding me through narrowed eyes. A trick of the flickering light made them glow aquamarine again, and his expression was so gloweringly unpleasant that the cupboard began to seem almost the better option.

'Who are you, and what are you doing here?' he demanded.

'I'm C-cass Leigh, a local horror writer, and I've got permission,' I stammered, unable for a few long minutes to drag my eyes away from his: and it wasn't just because I was mentally registering all the dark, edgy, don't-mess-with-me vibes he was radiating either, but because I felt an unexpected and scary tug of attraction.

It didn't seem to be mutual, for he frowned down at me and said: 'You look familiar . . . but where from?'

'Perhaps you've seen my picture on a book jacket?' I asked hopefully. That picture was *gorgeous*. It didn't look like me in the least, really. Even my hair looked inoffensively black instead of its real dark dried-blood colour.

'No, I think I saw you near the graveyard last night,' he said slowly. 'In that cloak, too. But weren't you wearing teeth?'

'I still am, all my own.'

'No, pointed ones. You're a part-time vampire?'

'Yes, and I'd just done a Crypt-ogram.'

'Cryptogram?' he exclaimed incredulously. 'Are you trying to tell me you were doing puzzles in the graveyard?'

'No, of course not – it's like a singing telegram. You get dressed up and do birthday parties and stuff.'

He regarded me narrowly. 'So you've been doing one tonight, then?'

63

'No, why – ? Oh, you mean the cloak? It's just so warm, and although it's a bit much for everyday I do love purple velvet. Why wait until I'm old to wear it?'

'Why indeed?' he said dryly.

'So what's *your* excuse for that get-up?' I inquired coldly.

Not that the half-open shirt and close-fitting knee breeches didn't become him: he had a powerful frame even if he did seem to be pared down to sinew, bone and whipcord. You couldn't imagine anything less spectral if you tried.

'I don't need an excuse for being here,' he said loftily. 'But if you must know, I got this outfit through a friend who does historical re-enactment, and I was just trying it on.'

'Oh yes? Something for the dressing-up box?' I said politely. 'You know, my friend Orla Murphy who runs Song Language would employ you like a *flash* if she saw you dressed like that.'

Though come to think of it, I'm not sure what we could market him as. Historical Totty-ogram? The Laughing Cavalier? (Not that I've seen him even smile yet. His is not a face formed for laughter, but would look well standing by a gallows.)

'I wanted to get into the spirit of the place – only when I saw you, there seemed to be more spirit than I'd bargained for.'

'Oh, I see!' Illumination dawned. 'Jack's been selling multiple tickets, and you're a ghost-hunter too?'

'No, I'm not a ghost-hunter, but I might have known you'd be one of the supernatural weirdoes,' he said disgustedly. 'And would that be Jack Craig, he of the missing valuables and empty lodge?'

'What? Which missing valuables?' I asked, confused.

'I've been here since last night going over the inventory, and your Jack Craig seems to have made off with every small portable valuable in the house – and a Roman statue of Diana from the rose garden.'

'Not my Jack Craig,' I corrected as I let this sink in. 'So that's why he wouldn't let me come before, in case I noticed anything suspicious! I suppose he got wind of you arriving and shoved the key through my door on his way to pastures new?'

Another thought struck me: 'And perhaps by "tonight" he meant last night, before you came? Only of course I didn't see the key till much later, and thought he meant tonight. He was probably only trying to do me a good turn.'

'He certainly hasn't done me one! I don't suppose you know where I can find him?'

'No, sorry. Are you from the solicitors? You don't look like one!'

He looked at me rather strangely: 'You mean, you really don't know who I am?'

'No. Should I?' I said, though now I came to think of it he *did* look sort of familiar until it occurred to me that he had the same sort of bony face as mine, with deep-set eyes and straight brows, only his was more gaunt. I'd have looked haggard, but he looked haunted and interesting in a hungry sort of way.

'Are you Irish?' I demanded. 'Only Orla always says I look Irish, and you're a bit like me – though I haven't got your nose, thank God,' I added devoutly.

'What?' he said, looking strangely disconcerted. 'Of course I'm not Irish!'

'Neither am I.'

'Fascinating! Spare me a list of all the other places you don't come from! And what's the matter with my nose, anyway?'

'It's a bit beaky,' I said with a slight shudder, though the fine, hawk-like curve of it didn't actually look out of place on his face.

'Beaky! It is not — ' he stopped. 'I don't know why I'm stand-ing here in the middle of the night arguing about noses with you! And it may interest you to know that I'm not a solicitor but Dante Chase, the new owner of Kedge Hall, and you're trespassing.'

I peered more closely at him. 'You're Dante Chase? Aren't you too young?'

'Too young for what?'

'To be old Miss Kedge's cousin.'

'I'm not her cousin, but I am the next male relative in line. I won't draw up a genealogy for you just now, if you don't mind. It's been a long day, and it seems destined to be even longer.'

'What are you doing up at this time of night, then?'

'I know it's past my bedtime,' he said unpleasantly, 'but I'm allowed to stay up on special occasions.'

'Well, don't wait up for me, 'I said brightly. 'I can find my own way out.'

'I was also giving these famous family ghosts a chance to show themselves until you interrupted me. I especially wanted to see poor blind Betsy run mad and stark-naked down this very gallery at midnight.'

I checked my watch. 'You're out of luck then. And anyway, ghosts don't run about naked – at the most they're drifting shadows.'

'Or mere figments of the imagination? I know that, but you seemed pretty convinced a few minutes ago.'

'Well so did you, when you first saw me. Who's Emma?'

He frowned. 'Did I say that?'

'Yes.'

His straight lips compressed into an even thinner line, like you might have to prise them apart with a crowbar to get any more out of him, but I persisted: 'So who is she?'

'Was. Emma was my wife, but she's dead. For one minute when I saw you I thought . . . not that you're anything like her, really.'

'I'm so sorry.' I put my hand on his arm. 'It must have been a shock—'I broke off and froze as a low hoarse muttering echoed down from above, followed by a heavy dragging noise. I couldn't think of any rational explanation for *those* sounds, and my mind went blank with surprise.

My hand was still resting on Dante's sinewy warm arm where the ruffles had fallen back, and the contact between us combined with that blank moment somehow allowed the door to his mind to open to me, releasing a dark-edged whirlpool of thoughts and feelings.

Mind-reading is not a gift I choose to exercise very much, but this time it came of its own volition and I recoiled, snatching my hand away and backing from him with horror: 'Such guilt, pain and remorse – have you killed someone? Was it Emma?'

He stared back through narrowed, furious, suspicious eyes. 'That's all I need, a bloody mind-reader!' he snapped, and reached out a hand for me.

The sounds from above, which had been rising to a sort of crescendo, suddenly ceased. Dante lunged, I jumped back – and then there was nothing under my feet and I was tumbling and bumping down the stairs, to fetch up against the wall at the first turn.

The Catherine wheel in my head suddenly went out.

Chapter 7: Things Go Bump

Cass Leigh writes of the unspeakable horrors of the night with such familiarity and understanding, that you would think she was on intimate terms with them ...

Independent

I woke up with a thumping headache and a fiery trail of brandy burning its way down my throat.

You could say I coughed my way back to life, which is certainly not in the Haunted House Gothic Heroine style at all, but when I tried to pull away a strong arm held me fast and tipped another fiery dose down for good measure.

'You're awake,' said a relieved voice that was at once strange and familiar, and I opened watering eyes to find myself lying on a four poster bed with the gallows face of Dante Chase looming over me, a half-filled glass in one hand.

'Half-empty – or half-full?' I muttered.

'How many fingers am I holding up?' he demanded.

'You'll be missing a couple if you try and force any more of that vile stuff down me!' I told him, struggling to sit up.

He frowned. 'I suppose I shouldn't have given you alcohol if you've got concussion,' he conceded.

'I haven't got concussion,' I said coldly, fingering the back of my head. 'Only a little bump. No thanks to you, though! I must have fainted from terror when you attacked me.'

'I didn't attack you,' he snapped. 'I was trying to stop you falling down the stairs!'

'A likely story.'

'You've been unconscious for about fifteen minutes – long enough to carry you up here. I was starting to get worried.'

He didn't look worried, just tense, wary and irritated, and suddenly I recalled my involuntary lucky-dip into his subconscious. Was I in Bluebeard's chamber?

The room was lit by a candelabra, the lantern, and a crackling open fire, and was strewn with what must be Dante's belongings.

'Where's Guido?' I demanded suddenly. After all, if I needed to make a speedy getaway there were all sorts of handy things in my bag I could use . . . practically a complete escape kit.

He stared at me. 'Guido? There was someone with you?'

'No – he's my handbag.'

'Of course he is,' he said smoothly. 'And he's sitting right over there on the chair. Perhaps he could keep you company while I go for a doctor? You did bang your head on the wall, after all, and head injuries can be tricky.'

'I haven't got a head injury, just a bit of a bump – and you were holding up four fingers,' I added as final proof 'Terror made me faint. But really, I'm fine now.'

I began inching away from him across the bed. 'I'll just be on my way. Goodness, it's late, isn't it? You must be *dying* to go to bed, and here am I keeping you up . . . I wonder where my cloak is? Oh yes,' I babbled, seeing it draped over the back of a chair. 'Perhaps I could just borrow this little lantern to find my way out, and I'll be—'

A large hand closed like a manacle over my wrist. My pulse went *berserk*.

'You did read my mind before you fell, didn't you?' he demanded. 'I didn't believe it was possible – but I saw your face change.'

'No, of course I didn't,' I assured him, smiling nervously. 'I can't read minds, or crystal balls or anything else!'

He didn't let go, but continued to look at me.

I searched for an explanation that would satisfy him: 'I just . . . well, sometimes if I touch someone and I let my mind go sort of blank but receptive I get a kind of impression of what's stirring in their subconscious,' I admitted cautiously. 'But I don't know what they're *thinking*, really.'

'And you did that to me?'

'I didn't *do* it to you, I just happened to be touching you when that grisly noise started. And believe me, I've forgotten all about it already!' I assured him brightly. 'That noise—'

68

'There'll be some simple, rational explanation,' he said shortly. 'Which is more than can be said for you . . . although you really *didn't* seem to recognise me when we met. But then, you've probably seen me on the TV or read about me in the papers and forgotten about it, except in your subconscious.'

'I only watch horror films and videos on my TV, and I don't read newspapers,' I told him. 'What were you in the news for?'

I sincerely hoped it wasn't wife-murder.

'I was a foreign correspondent for a newspaper,' he said tersely. 'Got caught up by FARC guerillas in Colombia about eighteen months ago and held hostage with another man – a photographer. I made it back out, he didn't.'

'Oh, I see.'

'No, you don't,' he said tightly. 'He – Paul – wasn't just another man, he was my oldest friend.'

His deep-set eyes weren't looking at me, but at something hellish only he could see.

'I'm so sorry,' I said inadequately.

'And you were right about my wife, Emma: she was pregnant when I left for the trip, and dead when I got back.'

'Then it wasn't your fault she died, was it?' I said, relieved.

'According to her mother it was,' he said bitterly. 'Because I might have got her to hospital in time to save her if I'd been there. Emma thought if she got pregnant I'd give up the foreign trips and work closer to home instead, but she was wrong: so you see, I'm not a lucky person to have around.'

I eyed the distant door longingly.

'Don't worry, you're safe enough with me,' he said sardonic-ally. 'Only people close to me seem to meet a sudden end.'

He appeared to have forgotten he was still gripping my wrist, and my fingers were now turning an interesting shade of blue.

'You know why seeing you gave me such a shock? I'll tell you: Emma was so convinced there was life after death that she even made me swear when we married that if she died first I'd call her back – and she'd come. I knew it was all rubbish, but I promised anyway, and for a minute there I actually thought I'd got it all wrong.'

I eyed him narrowly, which he didn't notice because all his thoughts were turned broodingly back into some dark place. He must really have loved his Emma.

His guilt had been strong enough to send me running: but then, everyone whose loved one dies feels guilty to some extent, or blames themselves, and coming straight after the hostage thing where he'd lost his friend, his wife's death must have knocked him for six.

He wasn't a murderer anyway, even if he looked infinitely capable of being one. (And had he really been a psychopath I don't suppose he'd have been bothered about my having concussion.)

I sat up and got interested rather than witless with panic. 'So you've tried to call Emma back, like she asked you?'

'Oh yes! I gave my word, so I tried every charlatan I could find, including her mother, who calls herself a psychic and medium.' He laughed shortly. 'But there were no messages from beyond the grave, of course – except patently bogus ones. The dead don't come back.'

'That's what Keturah thought too, but she was wrong. Mind you, she wasn't just trying to contact her lover, but raise his physical presence!'

He ignored that, still locked away in some dark memory of his own, to the extent that he didn't even seem to notice when I pried his fingers off my wrist one by one until I was free.

'They said it was because I didn't believe, that she couldn't return and contact us. Her mother said that I'd failed her again,' he added bleakly.

'Yes, you did,' I agreed, 'and it's so amazingly like Keturah and Sylvanus that it's uncanny!'

'Who?' he said, suddenly focusing on me again, which was a bit unnerving, especially since he was still sitting on the edge of the bed within pouncing distance.

'Characters in my next book. Keturah tries to raise her dead lover through magic spells, but she's afraid that what comes back won't be quite Sylvanus – and she's right too, as it turns out. It isn't.'

'I don't think I'd like your books,' he said shortly.

'Probably not. Well, it's been an eventful night, but I really ought to be going. I meant to spend the whole night here, because my next chapter's a take on the Haunted House Gothic and I always write better when I scare myself into it,' I said regretfully, because now he didn't appear to want to kill me, it seemed a pity to leave.

70

'Haven't you been frightened enough for one night?' he said, sounding surprised. 'You nearly ripped that cupboard door down, and that was just a bat.'

'But I didn't know that, I thought it was a bird. I have a fear of cupboards and birds.'

'How very Daphne du Maurier. What's the matter with birds?'

'Cruel eyes.'

'They haven't got enough brain to be cruel. And I don't see why you should panic about being shut up with a bird, but right as rain with a bat.'

'Yes, but bats are lovely. They have sweet little faces with crinkly noses. I had a rubber vampire one called Clive, but something nasty happened to it at a stag night.'

The bed was wide and short, like it was designed for the Seven Dwarfs. I cautiously swung my legs to the floor and got up a little unsteadily, but I think that was the brandy. 'Perhaps you wouldn't mind if I had a quick look round the house before I go?' I asked hopefully. 'Only it seems a pity to waste the opportunity, because I don't suppose you'd let me come back another night. And I'd be very quiet and just let myself out afterwards. I wouldn't disturb you.'

'Actually, I intend finishing the inventory of what's missing,' Dante said. 'While looking out for the rest of these so-called ghosts. Do you want to spend the night with me?'

'Excuse me?'

'That didn't come out quite how I meant it to,' he said sardonically.

'I'm glad to hear it. In that case, I'd certainly like to stay until morning, though I'm pretty sure that if there are any ghosts they won't appear tonight.'

They'd probably be too scared to.

He shrugged. 'They won't appear any night, since I'm neither gullible nor susceptible to suggestion. But no one can say I didn't give them the opportunity to show themselves before I open the house up again.'

'You're going to live here?' I asked, surprised.

'In the lonely west wing, mostly. My sister's going to run part of the main house as a sort of guesthouse, doing weekend ghost-hunting breaks. I said I'd suss it out. See what sort of special effects we could use.'

'Special effects?'

'Well, you can't book ghosts to appear, can you? Although,' he added, looking at me in a measuring way that I didn't quite like, 'I could book you as Something From the Crypt. That should scare the punters.'

'No thank you, I only do the Crypt-ograms when I'm strapped for cash.' I shivered suddenly. 'I think I'll put my cloak back on, it's cold even with that fire.'

'Sorry – I told Craig to leave the electricity and gas on, but they've all been cut off. They're supposed to be reconnecting everything tomorrow, although maybe the phone will be a bit longer. The police are coming back then too, for the definitive list of what's missing.'

He looked down at the sheets of paper. 'I was about to do the ground floor and cellars until you disturbed me.'

'I think you were pretty disturbed already,' I told him icily. I mean, who was the one with the bumped head and the crushed wrist?

'Then perhaps you'd better help me finish it, as compensation for breaking and entering?' he suggested.

'I only entered,' I said with dignity. 'You left the door open. But I'll help if it gets me a look at the rest of the place before it goes all hotely.'

'I'm keeping the ambience, it's just the lights I'd like back – and the heating. We could have candle-type sconces on the walls, for that spooky look,' he said distastefully.

'If you're so revolted by anything to do with the supernatural, I can't imagine why you're letting your sister run ghost-hunting weekends!' I said tartly.

He shrugged and looked at me like it was none of my business. (Which it wasn't – just call me nosy.)

'She needs something to occupy her, and it won't do any harm – I'll see to that,' he said firmly. Subject closed.

So I spent the night with Dante Chase, although I expected to see nothing more scary than him, because any self-respecting wraith would have given up and gone away by now.

(And from Dante's fancy dress I suspect that they will soon have some competition, since I think he intends to appear on guesthouse weekends as First Ghost: the Most Haunted Manor in Britain, featuring Britain's Most Haunted Man.)

I was dying to ask about his relationship with Emma, and what she died of, because he's practically guilt-edged. I don't even need to look into his mind to feel it, and it's so like the Keturah/Sylvanus situation that it would be really useful stuff to know . . . but better not.

Checking the inventory took ages, Miss Kedge having been devoted to expensive knick-knacks, but I do not think she was devoted to brandy, so the bottle (or was that perhaps *bottles*?) Dante produced must have been lying forgotten in the cellars.

He carried it round with us, though a cuddly St Bernard he is not, and I got so cold after a while that I had another little nip . . . though I'm positive it was Dante who finished it.

Almost positive.

And I might hate the taste, but it certainly warmed us up on our Quest for the Questionable.

'I doubt you'll ever track most of this down,' I said finally. 'Fifty small items of Tunbridge Ware? A collection of porcelain cockatoos?'

'It's all under the insurance so I don't care it they don't find any of it, except the family miniatures. I'd really like those back,' he said, removing the list from my grasp and ticking off yet another missing memento.

When we'd finished the survey (and a lot of brandy) and given up on the ghosts, it was nearly morning, so we retired back to Dante's bedroom, the only warm place in the house, to wait for old rosy-fingered Dawn.

I woke up stiff, tired and headachy, curled up in a four-poster bed next to a stranger.

The unfamiliar room was fuzzy with grey early-morning light, and it took me a few heart-thumping minutes to remember where I was, and even then I couldn't for the life of me recall how – or why – I was back in Dante's bedroom.

It must have seemed like a good idea at the time.

Under the old eiderdown that covered us his naked arm lay warmly and heavily across me, but his face was half-turned away and masked by long, dishevelled dark hair.

As I stared at him, some confused memories began to bubble disturbingly to the surface.

At least, I *think* they were memories.

Hadn't I been woken at some point from the pounding terror of my cupboard nightmare, and taken into a warm, comforting embrace? And surely I knew – remembered – how the muscles of his broad back moved under my hands . . . *and* how his lips felt on mine.

Or maybe it was the feel of mine on his? For I began to have an awful feeling it was me doing most of the kissing, and desperately wanting him, even urging him, to—

Oh God: it was all coming back to me!

Shivering (but not from cold, for the world's most efficient hottie was right in there with me), I took a quick horrified peek under the eiderdown . . . and then a second, more admiring one.

I must have been *possessed* – and I don't think brandy agrees with me, so clearly I do not take after Pa in that respect either, which is something, I suppose.

Dante was still breathing deeply, so with infinite caution I slid out from under his arm and off the bed, nearly falling when my foot landed on an empty bottle.

He moved restlessly and murmured something, then turned over and settled back to that regular breathing. Reassured, I tiptoed round the bed, collecting clothes as I went, and took a good look at him.

He seemed a lot younger than I'd thought with the grim lines smoothed out by sleep, and a lot of dark stubble softening his square chin. Nothing would make that hawk nose anything other than aggressive, though, and I'm not convinced a mouth so hard and straight could ever break into a grin, although it *could* feel soft and . . .

No. Let's not go down that road. He looked relaxed, anyway.

It's wonderful what physical exercise can do for a man.

Some deeply primal instinct was urging me to go downstairs and make him a huge cooked breakfast, but I was ruthless with it. It wasn't my fault he looked like he needed feeding up.

One hank of springy raven hair still lay across his cheek, and on a sudden impulse I leaned over and gently pushed it away, before drawing back quickly, afraid he would wake up.

My mind slid safely away into the alternative reality of Keturah:

. . . *Keturah took the pillow, meaning to extinguish his life and so never have to face the full enormity of what she had done.*

Then she put it down again, slowly: he might move and act like a man, but he was not mortal. He could not love ... or die.

He could only possess.

Keturah, you're in big trouble. What the hell got into you? Or maybe that should be: what *from* hell got into you?

It certainly wasn't Sylvanus.

With a new plot twist uncoiling in my mind, I left the kitchen key on the bedside table, picked up Guido, and went out into weak early sunshine, where I didn't burn, crumble into dust, or turn into a pillar of stone, all distinct possibilities and no more than I deserved.

Crumpled, creaking, unwashed, unloved, unfaithful and unchaste, I hurried towards the haven of home as the first birds and little Birdie croaked into action.

It felt like a decade since I'd set out.

Cassandra Leigh, I know what you did last night.

What I don't know is *why*.

A writer can take research too far.

Chapter 8: Raising The Spirits

The latest offering from strangely popular horror writer Cass Leigh, Nocturnally Yours, *has no claims to literary merit whatsoever ...*

Observer

It felt strange to be arriving home in the grey light of dawn rather than the dark hours of the morning as I usually did after my little expeditions; but then, I don't usually carry my research to such extremes.

My head still ached, along with all the other portions of my anatomy that had come into contact with the staircase, and I seemed to be developing a Dante-sized bracelet of bruises on one wrist.

That man doesn't know his own strength.

Although I felt absolutely shattered, once I'd had a shower and changed I settled down to write up the events of the night while they were still fresh in my mind.

Those I remember clearly, anyway – and the rest had *better* be forgotten, although perhaps I really hadn't behaved too badly with Dante Chase after all, considering I'd had a nasty bump on the head and quantities of brandy forced down my throat?

Who am I kidding?

But I'm sure he drank much, much more, so hopefully he won't remember a thing about it. And if he does, he probably won't think anything of it . . . unlike me. I just can't believe I did that! And compared to my only other lover, Max, he—

No. Behave yourself, Cass. You weren't responsible for what happened, so just put it right out of your mind. With any luck your

76

path and Dante's will hardly ever cross, which will make it easier: he didn't like you, so he's hardly going to come looking for you, is he?

Right, lecture to myself over and uncomfortable memories consigned to box labelled 'Pretend It Never Happened', leaving the other strange aspects of the night for consideration.

For instance, it was interesting to discover that no matter how I rationalise the supernatural, nor how often I have cheerfully walked in haunted or spooky places, the first sight of Dante Chase frightened me into illogical flight.

Mind you, if it hadn't been for the bird in the cupboard, the second and third sight of him might have had much the same effect. A scary and arrogant man with a temper on a hair-trigger, that about summed up the impression he made, though perhaps I should make allowances for the eagle nose. And the guilt.

He's thin for his height and frame and too fine-drawn, though he still has muscles in all the right places. His knee-breeches and ruffles had suited him very well, but he would have looked even more at home emerging out of the Celtic twilight, wearing a homespun cape and wielding a drawn sword, with snake-headed torques of gold clasped around his muscular bare forearms . . .

Stop it, Cass.

That unnerving way his eyes had seemed to flash green-blue in their deep sockets was clearly just a trick of the lantern-light, and I bet they are that shallow light blue really, like Jane's. It's interesting though, because you somehow expect dark eyes to go with black hair, and it doesn't always follow. I can use that:

'Keturah!' whispered Sylvanus, but where the soft hazel eyes of her lover should have been, burning-cold orbs of aquamarine shone instead.

What a coincidence that Emma should have made him promise to try and bring her back, just like Sylvanus and Keturah! Though in Dante's case, clearly, he was just meant to contact her beyond the grave, not actually try and raise her from it.

It's also fascinating on a personal level to meet someone even more consumed with guilt than me, though I don't understand why he is so guilty about his wife's death, when he wasn't there. What did she die of? An accident, illness, or one of those rare but horrific pregnancy complications that I've read about in that book

77

Orla gave me? And even being the hostage that survived seems to be making him feel guilty too!

He has already taught me one valuable lesson (more than one really, but the rest are locked in the Pretend It Never Happened box), for until last night I hadn't realised it was possible to take an instant dislike to a man but still find him scarily attractive.

I'm going to infuse all that frightening sexiness into the Vampire of the Manor character, an updated Dracula in a biting saga about blood relatives.

Come to that, my vampire can bite Keturah too, because for some mysterious reason she's gone wimpy on me and I'm getting quite tired of her.

At least then she'd actually have some power to battle with whatever evil thing came back in the shape of Sylvanus . . . unless my vampire could choose to take over the form of what was once Sylvanus? Or maybe one of his female vampires was the one who fancied Sylvanus so much that she called him back when Keturah had failed him?

A vampire love-triangle – or pentagram. Mmm. Must think about it a bit more.

And I'm going to call *my* Dracula Vladimir.

By ten it was quite impossible to stop my head slumping forward over the keyboard, so not wanting the alphabet permanently embossed on my cheek I went to bed.

Despite the neighbouring Surround Sound I fell instantly into a deep and mercifully dreamless sleep, and might have slept on and on for ever had a delivery driver not practically beaten my door in, determined not to have to turn his van round in my thread of a lane twice in one day.

While normally paler than pale in complexion, after the night I'd had I must have looked like the living dead, because he silently and nervously thrust the pad for me to sign, shoved a parcel into my arms, and left at high speed on smoking tires.

My heart sank when I saw it was the proofs of my next novel, *Shock To The Spirits*, because whenever I'm getting really into the new novel, the last epic keeps turning up in some ghastly resurrection shuffle; first for a bit of rewriting, then copy-editing, then for proof-checking like now.

It just won't give up and go away.

Still, this should be the last of it, and then hopefully it will march its denizens of the undead into bookshops all across the country with no further help from me.

After another long, hot shower I felt almost human myself, and settled down to do the proofreading so as to get rid of the damned thing fast and return to *Lover, Come Back To Me*. I just couldn't wait to get to grips with my new character, Vladimir: all bite and no bark.

I read through the proofs of *Shock To The Spirits* twice, then repacked it and sent it on its way just before the post office shut.

Westery post office is also Emlyn's garage, hardware, and twenty-four-hour shop, having expanded to cater for all things as the village businesses vanished one by one, to be replaced by entirely useless antique shops such as Jason's.

Emlyn has a prime position right by the village green and Haunted Well, which is in the garden of Orla's big Victorian house. Today, instead of tourists, clusters of daffodils were standing brazenly about on the green, but it's early in the season yet.

Westery is one of those villages on the Welsh border that is not so much a destination as a stopping-off place en route to somewhere more interesting. There is a nice old church, the pub, five antique shops, one second-hand bookshop, and Orla's Haunted Well B&B, and that is about it.

Emlyn's Dutch wife, Clara, was serving behind the till of the supermarket section, and we had a nice chat while I bought a pizza (chorizo with black olives), which I heated and ate as soon as I got home.

Then I settled down to some hard work on *Lover, Come Back To Me*, which went very well once I realised that Vlad's crucial mistake was biting Keturah just as the sun began to rise, because the whole vampire-transformation thing wasn't nearly completed when he had to make a bolt for home in his flashy black sports car.

Keturah is now not quite human and not quite vampire, and a whole lot more interesting.

Go, girl.

Orla rang, very late and not quite sober, to say that she'd just had a drink with a gorgeous man, and all he wanted to talk about was me.

'I don't know any gorgeous men,' I said vaguely, what mental faculties I possessed still focused on the alternative universe inhabited by Vlad, Keturah and Sylvanus. 'Apart from Max, and he's in America.'

'Not Max, idiot! *His* patina may be authentic, but his veneer's crackled.'

'You've been hanging around Jason too much, Orla. Or drinking. Or both.'

'Both. But I'm sober enough to recognise a good thing when it walks into the pub and strikes up a conversation with me. This man is years younger than Max – younger than either of us, come to that – and he said he bumped into you last night, and he understood you were some kind of writer. Tall, slim, longish floppy dark hair, and sort of greeny-blue eyes.'

'Oh *him*' I said shortly, with a sudden weird feeling in the pit of my stomach, compounded of panic, guilt and embarrassment. 'He's not gorgeous, he's got a huge beak of a nose!'

'Aquiline, and just the right size. And I love those hollow cheekbones, and the way his lips are so straight they make a sort of arrow shape when he smiles.'

'He can *smile*?'

'Are we talking about the same man?' Orla demanded. 'He says he's the new owner of Kedge Hall, but his name's not Kedge, it's Gabriel something.'

'Dante Chase?' I suggested dubiously.

'That's it.'

'But that's nothing like Gabriel!'

'Yes it is – I knew it was something to do with Rossetti.'

'He's nothing to do with Rossetti.'

'You know, the Dante Gabriel bit – don't be obtuse. He looked familiar, too, and after he'd gone I remembered where from: he was in the news about eighteen months ago, because he was a hostage somewhere or other. South America, I think, but I'm going to look him up on the internet.'

'So, did you give him the Orla Third Degree interrogation?'

'No, because he wasn't there long, and he made most of the conversational running, bringing the subject back to you all the time. He wanted to know if you were married or anything, so I told him you were in a committed long term relationship.'

'You did?'

80

'Of course. He's *my* type, not yours: tall, dark, clever, tricky, and younger than me. And although he asked me a lot about you, he seemed most interested in the Crypt-ograms and the mind reading and prediction stuff, and your knowledge of the local spooks, than anything more personal about you.'

'I don't suppose he told you why?'

'Well, no, but I suppose it's natural he should be interested.'

'He's going to let his sister run part of the Hall as a sort of guesthouse doing Ghastly Weekends for Ghost-hunters.'

'But he can't do that, the rat! *I'm* the local B&B!' Orla exclaimed indignantly. 'And he can't need the money: Miss Kedge was loaded.'

'A man can never be too thin or too rich?' I suggested.

'Huh!' she said inelegantly.

'But it sounds more like an occasional weekend thing rather than a regular business like yours, so it shouldn't affect you, Orla. I don't think he really wants to do it either, it's more his sister talked him into it.'

'You seem to know an awful lot after "just bumping into each other,"' she said sarcastically.

'I spent the night with him,' I confessed.

'What!'

'In a non-carnal way,' I assured her hastily, lying through my teeth. It was *almost* true, after all, and if I said it enough times even I might believe it.

I told her the Jack and the Enormous Door Key tale and about the abortive ghost hunt, but left out the brandy, the bed, and the black guilty heart bit. (Dante's, not mine.) I need another hands-on session with concentration before I pass judgment on that one, and now he knows I can do it he's unlikely to give me another chance even if our paths cross, which I sincerely hope they don't.

I wonder if I should try reading Jason's mind, as a sort of guilt-comparison? And a couple of random men too, perhaps? Orla knows quite a few random men.

She listened avidly to my story, then asked me if I didn't fancy Dante Chase?

'No, you get him, you can have him,' I said generously. 'He's not my type, as you said.'

'Actually, he *is* your type in that you both look a bit the same.'

81

'You know, that was *my* first impression too – apart from the nose,' I added hastily. 'And the thin lips, and the square chin, and – no, forget it, we're not alike at all.'

'You both have lovely bones, deep-set eyes, hollow cheeks and straight dark eyebrows,' Orla pointed out. 'You're beautiful, he's sexy.'

'I'm *not* beautiful, and he's not sexy,' I said stubbornly.

'Oh, come on! And he's got one of those lovely, gravelly, slightly gin-and-cigarettes voices, while yours is melodious but mournful even when you tell jokes.'

'Thanks.'

'It's all right: part of your charm is that you're not like everyone else.'

'It certainly never charmed my parents.'

'No, but it isn't your fault you take after some tall, dark, wicked forebear while all your brothers are medium-sized blue-eyed blondes, is it?'

'You'd think so,' I said. 'My sister Jane's a little Goldilocks too, so it's just me with the unhealthy white pallor and dried ox-blood hair.'

'Darkest auburn.'

'Whatever. Anyway, you're the beautiful one. Mike must have been out of his mind to leave you.'

'For a younger version of me? You know, I've just had one of my brilliant ideas!' she added.

My heart sank

'We're such a terrific contrast to each other that we should put a lonely hearts ad in a magazine *together*. That way, one man out of every two we pull might be halfway decent.'

'No thanks, I'm not doing anything hasty until I've seen Max after the funeral.'

Anything *else* hasty, that is.

'Funeral? Which funeral?' she said, baffled. 'Who's died?'

'Oh Orla! Haven't I told you? I've had so much to think about that . . . ' I stopped. 'But I'm *sure* I told Jason, so why didn't he pass it on?'

'I haven't seen Jason, he's off at some country house auction. *What* funeral?' she repeated patiently.

'Rosemary's. She had an accident a few days ago and died. Max is coming back for the funeral next week.'

'My God! Does this mean you can get married at last? Do you still *want* to marry him?'

Trust Orla to ask the million dollar question!

'I don't know any more, and I don't know how he feels after all these months apart. He didn't even phone me to tell me the news, Orla! I found out from my sister Jane first.'

'That is pretty bad,' she conceded, 'though I suppose he had a lot to do?'

'I expect so, but he wouldn't let me go out there to help. He's supposed to be coming to visit me after the funeral, and then we will see. I'm just so confused about everything right now,' I confessed. 'And by then too, I'll have performed the last fertility rite.'

'You won't do anything rash, will you?' she asked anxiously.

'Too late!' I thought; but according to the charts, the wrong man had been combined with the wrong time of month, fortunately.

'Seeing Max after so long you might get carried away,' she suggested.

'Max is the one who is always careful about taking precautions: he's got condomania. He's never got so carried away that he forgot,' I said bitterly.

'Right. Anyway, even if there *are* only one or two eggs rolling around in the bottom of the basket, you still don't want to do it at your age. It's too risky. Get a lover and a dog.'

'I've got a lover – I think. But I'll consider the dog. It might *have* to be a dog.'

'Much less trouble. By the way,' she added with seeming casualness, 'have you decided about the Wonder Woman thing yet?'

'Give it up,' I advised her wearily. 'There is no way I'm going anywhere in that outfit.'

'I could do with some new ones. My Tarzan's getting a bit long in the tooth for a leopardskin.'

'He could be a Geriatric Tarzanogram. Wrap some fake vine leaves round his zimmer frame, and it would go down a treat with elderly ladies.'

I was joking but she was quite taken with it. 'That's a great idea! And I could advertise for a new young Tarzan, couldn't I? Do you want to sit in on the interviews?'

'If I ever get off this phone and finish the book,' I said. 'Goodnight, Orla!'

But by then I was definitely jaded, and so went to bed instead.

Chapter 9: Somersaulting Backwards

Movin' on up: the page that tells you what's new in fashion, fiction and much much more!

Booked out. worthy literary prizewinners that want to make you think seriously when you *want to chill out!*

Booked in: Woman-power horror from author Cass Leigh. Don't we all sometimes want to do just what the heroine did to her unfaithful lover in Nocturnally Yours? *It's just a pity she had to die before she took her revenge!'*

Surprise! Magazine

I stood in thick, tangible, muffling darkness, but far away at the end of the corridor a half-open door spilled a beckoning buttery pool of light on to the stone flags.

Half-open: or half-shut?

But sanctuary whichever it was, and my only hope of escape, though even as I started to run towards it I knew what would happen: every step forward instead sent me tumbling backwards like an acrobat into the waiting darkness.

Neat, slow and triangular, the somersaults always finished with an agile twist landing me face to face with the other door. The dark door. The door I really *didn't* want to open.

This time was no different, and I stood helpless as my shaking hand was drawn inexorably to the handle, the bones lit from inside the skin like an X-ray.

Some dark, rancid fluid began to gather and ooze from the

keyhole, dripping with echoing loudness on to the stone flags before reaching a viscous tentacle towards my bare feet . . .

'Cassandra!' shrilled a voice. 'Cassandra!'

The octopus tentacle of filth jerked galvanically then started to retract – and suddenly I was free, cartwheeling away, round and dizzyingly round, until I finally fell into a gasping heap and opened my eyes to the safe, warm, golden light.

A light bearing a striking resemblance to my bedside light: a happy glass sun with a smiley face.

Another face hovered over me, equally fair but far from sunny, and so incongruous that I knew I must still be asleep.

'Jane?' I muttered. 'Were you in the cupboard? Scary!'

But sort of a relief too, because Jane's a monster I can deal with. Turning over, I let my heavy eyelids close, the worst past, the demons all let out.

A skeletal hand banded with gold shook my shoulder.

'Ouch!' I screwed my eyes tighter shut. 'Go away, Jane. You can't frighten me, now I know it's only you in the cupboard.'

'Will you wake up, Cassandra?' Jane snapped, and with a click the room was illuminated by the bright ceiling light.

'*Jane*?'

My sister hovered over me, her fair Madonna face distorted by a weasel snarl of exasperation unfamiliar to her many admirers, including probably her husband. I recognised it, though.

'What on earth are you doing here?' I sat up, feeling disorientated. 'And how did you get in?'

'If you *will* leave the spare key in such an obvious hiding place,' she said scathingly. 'I did ring, but obviously you were asleep. You seemed to be having a bad dream.'

'I was somersaulting backwards.'

'Still? I thought you'd have grown out of all that by now. Lots of children get put in cupboards for being naughty and they don't grow up warped. Get over it.'

'I thought *you* were the awful thing in the cupboard.'

'Thanks.'

'Maybe you really are, and this is still part of the bad dream?' I suggested hopefully, closing and opening my eyes. But no, unfortunately she was still there, Fair, but set for Squally Weather. 'What *are* you doing here?'

'There wasn't anywhere else,' she said simply, and with a sink-ing feeling I noticed a suitcase big enough to hold three bodies parked by the door.

. . . slowly she bent and undid the heavy metal clasps securing the huge trunk, the dust of centuries thick and soft under her fingertips.

Yet something living and desperate bumped and whimpered against the lid, with the imperative, irresistible cries of a small child.

Needless to say, my sleep was even more disturbed after that, and I got up late and bleary-eyed.

There was no sign of Jane other than a beige cashmere coat tossed on to a chair, and a pale pink pashmina, neatly folded, on the window seat. I threw them both behind the sofa (out of sight, out of mind) and hoped that they, and Jane with them, would magically vanish all on their own.

I had lots of post. This little row of houses is out on a limb – literally a dead end, the occupants of the graveyard not receiving much in the way of snail mail – so the postman frequently doesn't bother to deliver our letters for two or three days. Then we get a bundle, wadded together with elastic bands.

I opened the one with the foreign stamp first. It looked more exciting than the gas bill, but it wasn't really, since it was just from my brother Jamie.

Dear Sis
Hope you liked the little present I sent you from out East.

We are still here on manoeuvres. Boz and Foxy and me went on shore yesterday and got absolutely slewed, and Boz fell in the harbour, which believe me is not the healthiest water around here to fall in! Hope his hepatitis shots are up to date. (Ha! ha!)

Had a message from Pa the other day. I knew he'd come round eventually after I got the chaplain to tell him I wasn't a harlot! He's saying Jane's going to burn in hell now, so the poor old thing's definitely losing his marbles. We all know you're the one lined up for the eternal fire. Pa said your feller's wife finally shuffled off too, but even marriage to the adulterer wouldn't keep you from the fiery pit. Still, maybe when you're a respectable married woman they'll come round a bit.

    Boz just came into a bit of money, and he says we could leave the navy early and set up a chicken farm, because at least there's no Mad Chicken disease, so everyone will buy poultry. Foxy says geese would be better – I don't know why. Still, might give it a go before too long!

    See you next leave,

xxx Jamie.

I do not fancy the chances of a poultry farm run by the likes of Boz, Foxy and Jamie, because intellectually the chickens will run rings around them.

Still, at least Jamie's letter explained that battered parcel I had with the pink silk Chinese slippers. Trust my brother Jamie to get the size wrong *and* I hate pink.

Fortunately, Alice's Alternative Clothes Emporium in town, where I purchase most of my rather alternative clothing, had some very similar green ones in stock in my size, and took mine in part exchange.

I don't suppose Jamie will notice the change of colour when he pays one of his flying visits on his way up to make a duty call on Ma and Pa.

You wouldn't think from his letter that he was an officer in the navy, although he's never going to get to the top of the naval tree like George, who not only has a brain but is also deadly serious. He's something in the Admiralty now, married to the runt of a titled family, while Jamie is eternally mentally fifteen.

I suppose it did help that George was sort of semi-adopted by a rich relative when he was eight, because he had all the right connections when he needed them.

I have four brothers. George is the oldest, then Jamie, Francis and Edward. The sea and the church are in the family blood, which probably accounts for George and Jamie's interest in the navy. Eddie, too, ran away to sea at sixteen, and was next heard of via a postcard from Jamaica, which explains his long-standing ganja habit, although he is a New Age traveller now.

None of them have embraced religion, probably due to seeing Pa take it to extremes. He might have gone a long way if it hadn't been for the brandy and going off at a tangent, since he is exceedingly charismatic when sober. Come to that, he's pretty compelling even when not sober, in a hell and damnation sort of way.

Pa went to the USA as a young man, thinking he was some sort of reverse Billy Graham; but instead he converted to the Charismatic Church of God sect and brought that back here, eventually setting up his little community in Scotland. Several American members of the sect joined him there, all, strangely enough, wealthy widows.

I don't know where he picked the brandy habit up, or how he squares that with his God, since he is very strongly against all alcohol in his preaching. In the family, if referred to at all, it was as 'Pa's medicine', so clearly it conveniently transmutes in his mind into something other than spirits.

Francis and I are both sports, I suppose: he climbs things, and has a little shop up in the Highlands that stocks the sort of serious stuff climbers need, and indeed is usually full of craggy, weathered, serious climbers, some wearing plaster casts. He is generally in mild favour with Pa, since they rarely see him and so have not sussed that his climbing and business partner, Robbie, is female.

Eddie and Francis are my favourite brothers, even if they did think up most of the pranks that got us into trouble when we were children, mostly because Jane always snitched on us.

Eddie is Ma's favourite too, and probably the only thing Ma's ever stood up to Pa about in all their marriage. She believes he was called to his wandering way of life because he is touched by God.

Frankly, between you and me, Eddie is just touched. He's as cracked as Pa in his own way, like a pleasantly glazed old piece of pot.

When Pa made it clear that my relationship with Max would mean eviction from the family circle (as well as eternal damnation) I thought: 'Big deal, I never felt I was in it anyway,' though I suppose the hope of one day winning their respect, if not love, never quite died.

But the boys all keep in contact like nothing ever happened, and pop in to see me if they can, except George: his idea of keeping in touch with anyone, including family, not useful to his career or social life, is to send an annual pre-printed Christmas card.

There was a postcard of the Cairngorms hidden underneath Jamie's letter. It read:

Dear Sis,

Am on Channel 5 programme Friday at 6.45: 'Impossible Climbs',

Love, Francis

Friday was today.

I'd just set a video to record it in case I forgot later, when Jane wandered in yawning, with her golden hair falling becomingly over her silk-clad shoulders. Mine felt like a bird's nest, and though the balding violet chenille robe I was wearing was a much-mended favourite, it could hardly be described as flattering.

Still, I learned the lesson when very young that there is no point in competing with Jane, because the race is fixed: angelic blue-eyed blondes win every time.

Just call me Maggie Tulliver. Now *there* was a girl with a dark side!

'Post? Anything for me?' she asked, pouring a cup of coffee and reaching for my pile of letters.

'How on earth would anyone know you were here?' I pointed out, snatching them back, but not before she'd got hold of Jamie's epistle.

'How come you got a present, when he hardly ever writes even a postcard to me?' she complained indignantly.

'Because he doesn't like you, Jane. None of the boys like you, you're a snitch. When we were little you told on us all the time just to make yourself look good and you've never stopped. How else would Ma and Pa know already about Max's wife? You're a little sneak and *I* don't like you either.'

'George's wife likes me,' she pointed out complacently. 'Philadelphia often invites me to stay.'

'Phily's a genetic mutation, that's why she ended up marrying George. He was the only one desperate enough to propose to her.'

'She does look a bit inbred. Just as well they never had any children, or they might have had to keep them in London Z— 'she broke off suddenly, staring down at Jamie' s letter.

'Oh God! Did you see what Pa said about *me*? That bastard Gerald must have told him about—' She stopped dead, frowning.

'About what? Fallen off your pedestal, have you? Is this why you've deigned to grace my spare bedroom with your presence?'

'Call that hell-hole with a campbed a spare room?' she said scathingly.

'Please yourself, I didn't invite you. *And* it didn't seem to bother you on all those weekends you so kindly spent keeping me company while Max was away,' I said pointedly.

'What?' Her jaw dropped and she went all Snow White with just a touch of Dopey. 'How on earth did you know about that?'

'Gerald came to see me.'

'Gerald? And you told him I hadn't been staying with you? No wonder he's—'

'No, of course I didn't,' I interrupted coldly. 'Just because you're a little sneak it doesn't mean everyone else is! Anyway, I thought he'd probably got the wrong end of the stick. Now, spill the beans!'

'I'm in love,' she said dramatically.

'Yeah, with yourself. I already knew that.'

'No, with a man.'

'Strange, I thought that's what Gerald was?'

'Yes, and I'm very fond of Gerald,' she said earnestly. 'But I married too young. I didn't realise what love was until I met Clint Atwood when he was Painter in Residence at the university last year. He wants me to leave Gerald and go and live with him in Cornwall. He's years younger than I am and so impulsive.'

I stared at her, wondering if I was dreaming that my sister was having a relationship with someone called *Clint*.

'That's who Gerald suspected – and I told him he was mad!' It seemed very untidy and unstructured for Jane. Her perfect image wouldn't be just tarnished but blown to pieces; and did she realise just how much satisfaction her friends would gain from rocking her pedestal?

'So Gerald's suspicions have been confirmed?'

'He searched my desk!' she exclaimed, aggrievedly. 'And when he found Clint's letters he went ballistic. And he simply wouldn't believe me when I explained that poor Clint had fallen hard for me without the least encouragement, and how I was just trying to let him down lightly. It was a little difficult, because Clint does get a bit carried away in his letters . . . but Gerald was absolutely horrible, and said the most wounding things to me.'

'So you and Clint *were* having it off, then?'

'Really, Cassandra!'

'You were, weren't you? All those weekends you were supposed to be here with me. And there was I thinking you were the nearest thing to a married virgin possible!'

Jane looked huffy. 'I just wanted for once to have a little fun. It's all right for you, being a mistress with no ties, you can do what you want.'

'Jane, I've been Max's mistress for over twenty years and I felt just as tied as if I were married to him!'

'Well, you don't suppose he's ever felt the same way, do you?' she said waspishly. 'He made a pass at *me* once.'

'Oh, shut up, Jane! You think everyone fancies you, and I know for a fact that Max likes curvy, tallish, dark-haired women, not skinny blonde runts. You're just trying to distract me from your Clint. *Clint* indeed! Really, Jane.'

'Your bit on the side's called Jason, isn't he? I don't think you've got any call to be snide about my lover's name!'

'Jason isn't my boyfriend, just a friend,' I snapped. 'And at least Jason is a good old name, even if it has been over-used recently, whereas Clint—'

'I quite like it. And anyway, there's something about him that makes me forget all that kind of thing *or* that he's years younger than me, when I'm with him. My God, is he young! And strong! He can keep it up all—'

'Spare me,' I interrupted hastily. 'I get the picture – you've fallen in love with good sex.' And clearly she's found what Orla's been looking for.

'I never meant anything serious,' she explained, 'and I thought when he finished his year at the university I'd never see him again, only it didn't turn out that way, and now he wants me to go and live with him at Yurt in Cornwall.'

'Jane, Yurt isn't a place.'

'Yes it is – it's in his letter.'

I decided not to disillusion her. 'So, are you going to go?'

'I wasn't, of course – I've got my job and my writing to consider. But if Gerald's going to tell everybody . . . I mean, he must have told the parents, mustn't he? He was being so un-reasonable that I got the doctor to sign me off with stress and came here to sort things out. I thought perhaps I might go down and visit Clint and just see if it would work out, and you can tell everyone I'm resting, and not seeing visitors.'

'Oh thanks. What will you do if Clint *doesn't* work out?'

'Come back and smooth things over. No one's going to believe Gerald anyway, because even the parents will think he's unhinged once I've explained things to them face to face.'

I'd like to see her explain Clint to them if she abandons Gerald in his favour, but somehow I don't think his cottage in Cornwall is quite what she is expecting.

'Explaining face to face might be difficult from Cornwall,' I pointed out.

'Yes, but they won't *know* I've been to Cornwall, they'll think I'm here with you, stunned and traumatised by Gerald's wildly unfair accusations. That's what I wrote to them. I said I felt like an outcast, so I was going to live with one until Gerald came to his senses. Though of course, if Clint and I do decide to make a go of it, it isn't going to matter, because I'll make a new life down there with him.'

'Jane, being disowned by Ma and Pa might hit you harder than you expect: I found it hard, and I was the least favourite child!'

She wasn't listening: 'Wonder what his cottage in Yurt is like?'

'Jane—'

'Driven by my husband's obsessive jealousy into the arms of Another,' she murmured soulfully. 'Looking for a refuge . . .'

'That might work for anyone except the parents,' I said critically. 'Though it's so Mills and Boon only you could sell it to your friends and acquaintances.'

'I don't know why you think I'm acting a part all the time!' she snapped.

'I grew up with you. And don't think I'm going to tell lies about you being here when you're off on a have-it-away day to Cornwall.'

I began to open the rest of my mail, and from one big manila envelope pulled a bundle of papers and loose photographs.

The top one was of Max: tall, curly-haired and becomingly greying, with his arm around me as we stood looking out at a vista. My hair was whipping out around my face as usual, but apart from the Gypsy Queen impression we looked like an old married couple.

I remembered that day clearly, because later we had one of our arguments about trying for a baby before it was too late and *that* was a few years ago.

The ticking on the biological clock goes manic after forty.

There were lots of other photos, all taken without my knowledge . . . and a letter from Rosemary, to be forwarded with the package by her solicitor after her death.

Rosemary for remembrance: she'd come back to haunt me.

She wrote with a pen dipped into such pure vitriol that when I'd finished reading it my hands were shaking. Somehow, I'd always thought of her as a bloodless creature like Jane; though now even Jane had disconcertingly proved to have something other than milk in her veins.

I'd believed Max when he told me Rosemary had never cared much for the physical side of marriage even before the accident, didn't even mind if he had a mistress, as long as he didn't ever leave her. But this letter was written by a woman eaten with a deep and passionate jealousy, who had obsessively charted every detail of our liaison.

No wonder she never asked Max questions: her detective spies kept her fully informed. I think she knew more about my relationship with Max than I did.

She wrote to me to say that she knew Max was incapable of being faithful, but that he would never leave her, so sooner with me than a string of other women.

She said quite a lot of other things about Max, bitter, horrible things that I hoped weren't true, tortured outpourings of hatred and jealousy.

I read it through twice, feeling horribly guilty and quite besmirched. Having compartmentalised and rationalised what I was doing over the years, I now felt like a complete tart again.

A haunted, heartless tart, for this was a message from beyond the grave in no uncertain terms.

Had Max also had a copy of this whole package? If so, no wonder he was worried about my going over there and getting the police thinking again!

'What is it?' Jane said eagerly, snatching the letter out of my numb fingers and reading it avidly. I'd have grabbed it back if my limbs had been functioning.

'Rosemary – Max's wife? Oh God, did she know all about you? And she never said? And . . . oh, that's interesting. That explains a lot.'

'What does?'

'Didn't you read that bit over the page, where she says: "Don't think you can step into my shoes: you'll always be just a mistress at best. I'm the one with all the money, and I've left it to Max on condition that he never marries you." You know, I wondered how they could afford that palatial house, and the cars and all the rest of it, as well as all the help for Rosemary,' Jane said. 'I know he gets a good salary, but he has expensive tastes. So that's why he never left her.'

'He was fond of her,' I protested weakly, since the thought had from time to time occurred to me, too. 'And he couldn't just abandon her when she was an invalid. With her injuries, we never imagined . . . I mean, Max said she would—'

'Die? But you can go on for ever with a broken back as long as you can afford the right health care,' Jane said blithely. 'I could have told you that.'

'I found it out myself later, thanks. She says . . . she says when she found out she couldn't have children, she made him swear that he wouldn't have them with anyone else until after she was gone! But he didn't tell *me* that. He always said he'd rather have my undivided attention, and also that I'd never cope alone with a baby, so he'd rather wait until we could marry.'

'Well, he would, wouldn't he? You'd never be able to marry, so that took care of that.'

'I feel so dreadfully sorry for Rosemary. But Max can't have known how she felt, Jane, and surely the money alone wouldn't have kept him tied to her?'

'Clearly, when she found out he'd fallen for you she wasn't happy about it,' Jane said. 'But she wanted to keep him, and he wanted to keep her money and you. Though if it wasn't you, it would probably have been a string of other gullible students, so she should have been grateful.'

'He's not like that,' I said sharply. 'He isn't calculating and mercenary.'

'Then after a decent interval he will marry you anyway, and to hell with the money – but I wouldn't hold your breath if I was you.'

'Of course Max will marry me,' I said, although doubts were seeping in even while I said the words. Things had not been as they seemed . . . and even how they seemed had been difficult enough to square with my uneasy conscience.

And Max *does* like the material things in life.

Suddenly I was starting to see a Max I didn't know emerging – a manipulative, selfish stranger.

Had he really thought Rosemary accepted the situation? Or had he coerced her into it at the start, like she said, with threats of leaving her? Had he been sometimes unfaithful to both of us, or was that just spite talking?

Which was the real Max? And did I still want to marry him? Did I still, come to that, want to have any sort of relationship with him?

I wouldn't know until I saw him again, and then either the world would swing back to its familiar orbit, and he would tell me that he loved me and at last we could be together for ever . . . or it wouldn't, and he wouldn't.

And maybe either way *I* wouldn't?

Later, while Jane was off soaking her carcass in coffret-scented water, I phoned Orla and told her all about Rosemary's message from Beyond.

She registered all the right, reassuring emotions, which is what friends are for, after all: a true friend lines up firmly on your side, whether you are right or wrong.

Then, lowering my voice, I told her about Jane and Clint.

'Lucky cow! What's she got that I haven't?' she demanded enviously.

'A husband, for one thing,' I pointed out. 'And she expects me to cover for her while she decides which one to choose!'

'If she'd handled it better she might have had her cake and eaten it. What's her husband like? Is he tasty?'

'Gerald? Small, chubby, and pleasant.'

'Not quite what I'm looking for then, even on the used market,' she said, summarily dismissing him. 'By the way, I looked Dante Chase up on the internet, and I've printed out some articles for you about the hostage thing. It was Colombia – they seem to kidnap each other at random there, all the time. He was freed in a military raid, but another hostage was accidentally shot.'

'That was a friend of his, so it hit him pretty hard when he was killed,' I told her, trying to pretend I wasn't absolutely dying to see the printouts.

I knew I hadn't really fooled her, though.

Chapter 10: Spawn

'Good morning! This is Edge Radio, bringing you news and views from both sides of the Welsh border. For those of you who have just joined us, today's studio guest is writer of horror novels, Cass Leigh.'

'Good morning'

'Nice to meet you – can I call you Cass?'

'Please do.'

'I have to admit that I'm a big fan of yours.'

'You don't have to admit it, you can keep it secret if you want to.'

'Ha, ha! Now, the critics haven't always been kind about your work, have they?'

'No, but that isn't unusual.'

'Aren't they a little more damning than the usual reviews, though?'

'Any publicity is good publicity. But it's my faithful readers' opinions that matter: if they're buying the books, I must be doing something right.'

'Yes. Your work isn't for the faint-hearted, is it?'

'I don't pull my punches, certainly.'

'Could you tell us something about your next book?'

'Yes, it's called Shock To The Spirits *and it's coming out in April. It's a story about murder, and revenge going even beyond the grave.'*

'Well, I'm sure we all look forward to that one. And are you working on another book at the moment?'

'No, I'm sitting in a stuffy studio answering a lot of inane questions. But when I get home I will be working on my next novel, Lover, Come Back To Me.*'*

'*And what is that about?*'

'*Resurrected love.*'

'*Er . . . yes. Now, a little birdie told me something just before I came on air that I find very hard to credit: that you were actually the twin sister of the celebrated poet, Jane Leigh!*'

'*Did it?*'

'*I take it my information is wrong then? We had the pleasure of Miss Leigh's company on the programme last year, and you certainly don't look anything like her!*'

'*No.*'

'*You mean, no it isn't true that you're her twin sister?*'

'*Yes, it's true, but no, I don't look anything like her.*'

'*Oh . . . then perhaps we could explore the relationship between two such different writers originating from the same family?*'

'*Perhaps we couldn't.*'

'*Right. Right . . . er, now listeners, I think it's time for a record request. Mrs Popplewell of Shrewsbury would like to dedicate an Elvis track to her dear husband, Bruce. So here is the King himself with "You Ain't Nothin' But A Hound Dog" . . .*'

My agent phoned to tell me that *Nocturnally Yours* has slithered, crept, wormed, and ectoplasmically materialized its way into the top one hundred fiction chart, which is sort of like Top of the Pops for books.

Clearly, this is what happens when reviewers can't resist looking at some of the non-literary dross that lands on their desks, and then they just *have* to go into print to say how awful the experience of reading it was, so thousands of other people decide they want to share that experience too.

Isn't that weird?

If *Shock To The Spirits* does well when it comes out in April (publication day having been brought forward due to all the publicity), hopefully my agent will be able to negotiate me a much better deal for *Lover, Come Back To Me*. Then maybe I can take my nose off the treadmill occasionally, and not do humiliating things like Crypt-ograms any more.

I told Jane the news simply because she was there, a captive audience, but she was very sour grapes. Her only attempt at novel writing, bloodless as a vampire victim, has so far failed to find a publisher. Mind you, now she's had a taste of passion she could try again.

97

By only lunchtime I was heartily sick of Jane.

This was partly because Jane gets me like that, and partly because I am not used to sharing my house with anyone. (Not counting the visitations of Max, and I'm even out of the habit of those, now.)

Makes me wonder if the status can ever be quo'd again?

'There's nothing in the fridge or freezer except pizza, white bread, fruit and peanut butter,' Jane whined.

'That's my staple diet. Toast and peanut butter for breakfast, pizza for lunch, fruit any time.'

'That sounds very unhealthy. And boring.'

'It can't be too unhealthy, because I feel fine. Glossy hair, shiny nose.'

'Pale as death. No colour in your cheeks.'

'You know very well that I've always been pale.'

'It doesn't *look* healthy. Why don't you use some blusher?' she suggested.

'Because I dare to be different, and at least I've *got* cheekbones. It must be such a puzzle for you to decide where yours are when you're doing your make-up.'

'All my bones are going to stand out a mile if I don't get some real food soon,' she said pathetically.

'They already do: you look like you've been constructed from coathangers. But if you want to go out and forage, feel free. Otherwise you'll have to wait for tonight: I eat my dinner at the pub most evenings.'

'I wonder how Max could stand it!'

'He brought his own food and drink, and he liked the King's Arms. It was one of the few public places we went to together.'

It occurred to me that we were talking about him as if he was dead.

... the way his hair curled on the back of his neck, his stance, the way he moved ... Yes, it was Sylvanus, his own dear self! thought Keturah, *her heart leaping. Then he turned, those familiar hazel eyes a dead two-way mirror for the unspeakable evil that rode within him like a golem charioteer ...*

'You could at least keep some supplies in for visitors. I don't like pizza, or peanut butter,' Jane complained.

'Tough titties, blossom: I didn't invite you,' I told her, but it's all water off a duck's back to Jane.

98

She pouted like a little girl, and while pouting makes Orla resemble Marilyn Monroe, Jane just looked like a very skinny fish.

'If you're interested, Max rang while you were asleep,' she said casually now, smiling angelically as is her wont while doing the cat and mouse stuff.

'What?' I stared at her. 'Why on earth didn't you wake me? What did he say?'

'Not much when he realised it was me and not you, except that the funeral is on Thursday. Oh, and he's flying back to California on Saturday, so obviously he's not planning on spending much time with *you*, is he?'

'Saturday?' I repeated like a parrot. Maybe it was just as well I hadn't spoken to him, because I'm still trying to suppress conflicting urges to confess my descent into Dante's inferno the other night, and to demand to know the truth about his relationship with Rosemary, and I'm not one hundred per cent certain I've got my mouth under control yet on either count.

'Yes. He said he'd try and get over for a couple of hours on Friday if he could.'

'Big of him,' I said sourly. 'Though maybe knowing you're staying here put him off?'

'No it didn't, because I told him I was leaving tomorrow.'

'And are you?' I asked hopefully.

'Yes, I've booked the train, and Clint's meeting me. You can drive me to the station in the morning, can't you?'

'Gladly!'

'Well you needn't sound so pleased about it. You're lucky anyone comes to stay, when you've got no food in the house and only a manky outside toilet!'

'The toilet's right outside the back door, Jane, so I really don't see your problem. I mean, it's not like I hand you a spade and a roll of loo paper when you arrive, is it? And I have got an indoor bath and washbasin.'

'You must be mad and I can't imagine why Max never made you install an inside toilet in all these years!'

'He couldn't *make* me do anything to my own house, and anyway, it doesn't bother me. Although the Plague of Frogs the year before last *was* a bit of a nuisance,' I conceded. 'I don't know *what* I did to deserve that.'

99

Jane shuddered melodramatically. 'Oh, don't! I can't even bear to think about it.'

I'd forgotten that one of her rare visits to me had fortuitously coincided with the frogs. It was one of her shortest visits ever, and clearly she'd never forgotten the experience.

'There were frogs on the seat, frogs in the pan, frogs on the floor . . . ugh!' she said

'They were cute little green ones, though,' I pointed out. 'I managed to get them all out eventually, three whole bucket-fulls, and took them up to the pond in the woods. The garden was still covered in them even so, and I had to block up the gap at the bottom of the outhouse door until they'd all gone. Where they appeared from in the first place is one of life's great mysteries. Didn't you see I'd given my cottage a name sign on the door?'

'No, what?'

'Frog's Bottom.'

'You are joking aren't you, Cass?'

'No, I really have. Go and look if you don't believe me.'

. . . their soft jewelled green bodies gave under her feet as she drew closer to her goal, each shuddering, crunching step a small, precious life extinguished . . .

'Cass? You've gone into a trance again. I *said*, the vicar also phoned, to remind you about the slave auction. Is he mad? What on earth did he mean?'

'It's a charity thing. Every year some of us put ourselves up for auction and people bid for our services for a day of their choice.'

'Sounds weird. What *kind* of services?'

'Just any skills you might have, like gardening, cleaning, baby-sitting, that sort of stuff.'

'What on earth could *you* offer!'

'Light cleaning, dog-walking, chauffeuring, and shopping, though old Miss Gresham bid for me last year, under the mistaken impression that I could read fortunes, and invited all her cronies round to have their bumps read.'

'You *can* read fortunes – and minds.'

'You know I can't read fortunes in the "crystal ball, cross my palm with Euros" way like a party entertainer. It's just that if I take someone's hand and concentrate hard, sometimes I get a flash of premonition. But of course, that's only because life is a sort of Mobius strip, and what goes around comes around. The

Newsflash from the Future is also a Newsflash from the Past
. . . sort of.'

'You are *seriously* weird. Did they know you could read their
minds too? And doesn't that work the same way, so you don't
know which you will get?'

'No, it's a different door in my head to the Newsflash door, and
it just gives me a sort of random sample of what emotions are
bubbling under the surface, not really what they are *thinking*
about.'

'Pity! You could make a fortune in blackmail if you could read
minds!'

'Only if you were morally depraved,' I said coldly.

My Romany gift – if gift it was – was quite enough. I suddenly
remembered reading Dante Chase's exceedingly chill undercurrents and shivered: touching him that time had been like
dipping your hand into dark, cold water, not knowing what was
swimming around in there with you. Well, that time it had; but
touching him later had been equally amazing in its way, but quite,
quite different . . .

I shook the forbidden image away and said briskly: 'I don't do
it much, because I don't want to know how people feel
. . . mostly.'

'You should try Max if he deigns to visit on Friday,' she
suggested. 'Could you tell if he's been faithful to you, or is going
to marry you or dump you?'

I didn't answer, because I'd already decided I was going to,
even though I'd once promised Max I wouldn't do it again.

But then, he'd promised me a lot of things too, and now I
needed to know how he really felt. This was the best way.

Mind you, it was just as well this mind-meld thing wasn't a
two-way street, or I'd be in big, big trouble.

Chapter 11: Gone, But Not Forgotten

As usual, the choice selection of slaves-for-a day at the vicar's annual charity auction includes our own resident author, Cass Leigh, Marilyn Monroe look-alike Orla Murphy and Clara Williams, whose talk at the WI on recycling knitted garments was voted the most popular of the year ...

Westery and District Voice

I almost forgot that I had a Crypt-ogram to do early that evening.

Orla's talked me into carrying on (but not as Wonder Woman), though I am adamant I won't do stag nights any more, and if it weren't for keeping the Batmobile on the road I would have given up after the fiasco with poor old Clive.

This one was a children's party in the next village, so I tried not to look too alarming: no greenish pallor, just my natural ashen complexion, and my hair flowing its own dried-blood red over my shoulders.

When I sang the Monster Mash only one little girl cried, and they were all amazingly quiet. One of the mothers offered me a job as her permanent nanny on the way out, but I expect she was joking.

Jane was waiting for me in the car, since we were going to the King's Arms for dinner straight afterwards. She'd seemed strangely reluctant to be seen driving about the lanes with a vampire, and on the way here had swathed her head in her pashmina like a pastel-tinted babushka. Now she insisted I took my teeth out before carrying on.

Fussy.

I twisted my hair up and secured it with a big diamante comb that I keep in the glove compartment for the purpose. 'There, perfectly normal,' I told her, wiping a layer of crimson from my lips with a tissue.

'Don't you want to go home and change?' she suggested. 'It won't take long, and that crinkle velvet dress you're wearing not only makes you look like a superannuated hippie, but it clings so much you look twice as big as you are!'

'Jane, I'm not fat, just naturally curvy, and if I like my clothes I don't care what anyone else thinks.'

'Max?'

I considered it. 'He used to like the way I dressed, it's only in later years when he started to go stuffy that he complained. But we never actually go out much when he visits except to the pub, so there's nothing to dress up for. Besides, I choose clothes I like and feel comfortable in, not dress to please him.'

'And I suppose you told him so?'

'I certainly did.'

'I don't think you have ever had the least idea how to get and keep a man,' she said acidly.

'Well I must have done something right or it wouldn't have lasted this long.'

'If you'd played your cards right when he first fell for you, he'd have left Rosemary and married you.'

'Yes, I think he would: but how could I have insisted that he left her, when she was an invalid? And I tried not to fall in love with Max – that's why I got the job and moved here without telling him. But he found me eventually.'

'You always were putty in his hands,' she said scathingly.

'That's the problem – there's just something about Max.' I frowned. 'There *was* something about Max. I mean, no matter how logically I thought things out and realised I ought to end our affair, as soon as I saw him again I just couldn't do it. It's still a bit like that when he phones, if he puts himself out to be charming, but he doesn't always bother any more.'

'Why should he? He's got you anyway.'

'Not necessarily,' I said with dignity.

As we walked into the bar I said: 'Orla and Jason are probably already here, so I'll introduce you, and then—'

I stopped dead, because standing at the end of the bar was a tall man with his back turned to me, and an awfully familiar, broad-shouldered back it was too. A mane of too-long, glossy dark hair fell over his shoulders, hair that would feel like springy silk to the touch . . .

My mouth went dry, and waves of hot and cold swept over me like a speeded-up version of the four seasons.

'It never happened, Cass: all you have to do is shut that door on the whole thing and convince yourself it never happened. You were drunk, so maybe you only imagined it anyway.'

Yeah, right. Easy. Thank you, voice of my conscience.

If Jane hadn't been right behind me I'd have bolted.

'What's up?' she said in her rather piercing voice. 'Why have you stopped?'

Casting a nervous glance at the bar I muttered: 'Nothing – come on, Orla and Jason are over there in the corner.'

'Is *that* Jason? He's not bad is he, you dark horse!'

The feeling seemed to be annoyingly mutual, because Jason stood up as we got there and eyed Jane approvingly. I felt like hitting him with the ashtray, because if he has a sudden yearning for a blonde he might at least have the good taste to choose Orla; and going by her sour expression Orla thought so too, though she quickly hid her feelings: 'Hi, Cass! Gig go OK?'

'Yes, fine: I much prefer children to stag parties, because at least they are only *little* monsters. Oh, and speaking of monsters, this is my sister Jane. Jane, Orla and Jason. I know you've heard me mention them.'

'This is your *twin* sister?' exclaimed Orla predictably. 'I can't believe it! You're such absolute opposites.'

'Yes, in *every* way,' Jane said, smiling sweetly at Jason.

He smirked fatuously back until Orla and I kicked him under the table from opposite sides, but although it wiped off the smirk it didn't stop him leaning over and saying, like no one had ever noticed before: 'You look so unlike each other it's hard to believe you are sisters, let alone twins.'

'Ho-hum, boring conversation,' I said to Orla. 'I see Marilyn Monroe is making an appearance tonight: where are you going?'

'Oh, I just love the dress!' Jane said. 'But doesn't bleaching your hair like that ruin it?'

'It's natural,' Orla said coldly.

'Of course it is,' I agreed hastily. 'Where *are* you going? Or have you been?'

'It's a private party later, which sounds respectable, and it's not far away so I don't have to leave for another hour.' She nodded and lowered her voice: 'Did you see who is at the bar? I've just introduced him to Jason.'

'Does Cass know who he is?' Jason demanded, overhearing. 'How come? He's only been here a couple of days, and he seems to have spent most of those sorting his house out and setting the police on to Jack Craig!'

'I bumped into him the other night when I was out ghost-hunting,' I said vaguely. 'He introduced himself.'

'Who?' demanded Jane, and twisted to look over her shoulder.

Dante's face was half-turned towards us, giving me a glimpse of an arrogantly aquiline nose and angular cheekbone. His hair looked like the most attention it had had in months was having fingers run through it (including mine), and it didn't so much need cutting as shearing.

'What's *he* doing here?' I hissed at Orla, and she widened her eyes innocently at me.

'Why not? This is his local now too, you know. Sh . . . he's coming back.'

'Coming *back*—' I began, half-rising to my feet in a panic. Then I sat down again, because if the man was actually going to live here I was going to have to get used to meeting him.

There's supposed to be a time and a place for everything. The one for meeting large, morose strangers you have irrationally done intimate things with is probably *not* while under the suddenly suspicious eyes of your sister, close friend and would-be lover.

It was too late for escape anyway. Dante put a pint down in front of Jason (male bonding rite) then took the chair opposite me and next to Jane, which I now noticed too late had a bulky scuffed leather jacket draped over it.

All his clothes hang on him a bit, like they belong to someone bigger, and I could see that even Orla, the most unmaternal of women, was looking at him as if she wanted to take him home and feed him up. And then maybe *eat* him up.

I sort of half-met his eyes and smiled, like you do when you vaguely recognise someone but can't quite remember who, what or when. Inside, though, I was doing the hot and cold thing again during which some evil gremlin in my head ran an edited Highlights of the Night tape at fast speed.

'Hello, Cass,' he said as easily as though we'd known each other for ever, and if there were any gremlins in *his* head they were in the back room asleep. 'I was beginning to think you were a figment of my imagination. Would you like a drink?'

'Yeah, but only if they stock Instant Cup'a' Poison: Just Add Hot Water And Stir,' I thought, trying hard not to succumb to the urge to look at him.

Some hope.

'No, it's OK, thanks, I'll get one in a minute when I order some food,' I mumbled, stealing a glance at him only to discover that he was looking so unconcerned and even, truth to tell, *uninterested*, that I began to seriously doubt that anything intimate had ever taken place between us.

Was it a dream after all? Or something that was, to him, so unimportant that it was instantly forgettable?

Quite unaccountably, considering I was hell-bent on pretending the whole sorry thing never happened, I began to feel piqued and stopped switching on and off like a thermostat.

Instead I set Jane on to him so I could watch him unnoticed while she worked her mojo on him. 'This is my sister, Jane. Jane, this is Dante Chase, who's just inherited Kedge Hall, the lovely old manor house outside the village.'

The total stranger I slept with the other night.

'Hi,' she said alertly, bestowing on him her full panoply of winsome, white-toothed charm. 'You look so familiar: now where *do* I know you from?'

'No idea,' he said curtly, and turning abruptly met my eyes. His were the greeny-blue of a Caribbean sea – or a glacier's depths – and showed a momentary glint of some emotion.

I couldn't for the life of me decide what it was.

Can glaciers burn?

'Jane's Cass's twin sister: isn't it amazing how different they are?' Orla asked, changing the subject, because Dante was clearly not about to regale us with jolly tales of his hostage days.

He shrugged, seemingly uninterested. 'It often happens that way with non-identical twins.'

'Dante has been telling me his plans for the Hall,' Orla told us, persevering.

106

'You mean, about setting up in competition with your B&B?' I said helpfully.

'It's not a B&B,' Dante said shortly. 'My sister, Rosetta, just aims to run themed ghost-hunting weekends, so there's no competition. There seem to be more alleged ghosts per mile round here than anywhere in the country, most of them haunting my house,' he added distastefully.

'It's noted for it,' I agreed. 'And Hanged Man Lane runs right past it.'

'There's the Haunted Well too, but it's not really haunted, we made that one up,' Orla confessed. 'It's in my garden, and passers-by love to throw money down it. It's great!'

'You made it up?' he frowned. 'But I bought a booklet about it from that general shop this morning. Emlyn's, is it? All about the history of the well, going back centuries!'

'Oh, Cass wrote that.'

'I thought it seemed a bit over-imaginative.'

'So, aren't you afraid of all the ghosts, up there in your lonely old house?' asked Jane sweetly, having another go. She'd been looking a bit miffed at his lack of interest, but perhaps the fact that he'd been equally brusque to me, too, had encouraged her. 'Or – sorry, is there a Mrs Chase?'

'No,' he said shortly, scowling at me like *I'd* asked the nosy questions. 'I'm a widower. And I don't believe in that sort of supernatural rubbish, so I might have to take a leaf out of Cass's book, and create an apparition or two to please my sister's visitors.'

'It wasn't an apparition, just a haunted well,' I said. 'And *our* motives were pure.'

'Yes, my husband had just left me, and I was desperate for money!' Orla agreed. 'Since then, of course, I've started doing B&B's, and the singing telegrams, so I'm managing fine; but the Haunted Well is a permanent fixture.'

'You mean, you just made a well in your garden and people come and throw money down it?' demanded Jane, round-eyed.

'Oh, there was an old well there, but it was covered over,' Jason said. We got some stones from an old garden wall and made it look a bit more interesting, then erected an information board, and off it went.'

'Why didn't you put it in *your* garden?' Jane asked me. 'You never have enough money either.'

'I get the proceeds from the little booklet,' I said. 'And I didn't have a well to start with.'

'If you need the money, I told Orla just before you got here that I'd like to hire you for a couple of appearances over Easter weekend, when Rosetta intends to open for business . . . night-time ones,' Dante told me, looking deadly serious.

Mind you, with that face it must be hard to look any other way. I'd rate his chances of being voted Mr Congeniality at nil.

'What, Crypt-ograms?' I asked doubtfully.

'No. No singing, no vampire teeth, just flitting around looking scary in the rose garden at night – and maybe the Long Gallery,' he added, raising one eyebrow at me.

'No way,' I said hotly, rising to the bait. 'I don't do flitting, and if you have any idea that I'm going to run along the gallery at midnight, stark naked like poor blind Betsy . . .'

I watched, fascinated, as his eyes filled with amusement, and one corner of his long mouth twitched upwards. 'Kind of you to offer – and *I* certainly wouldn't have any objections.'

'You could make a couple of appearances,' Orla said helpfully. 'At the usual rate, of course . . . plus extra for unsociable hours.'

'Orla! There's no way I'm streaking down the corridors at midnight!'

'No, I didn't mean that, just that you could—'

'No!'

'Oh well,' she said resignedly, recognising that tone.

'You know I'm only doing the Crypt-ograms until you find some other acts instead.'

'Yes, and Cass knows I'm always willing to look after her when she's doing them,' Jason said jealously, exchanging a measuring look with Dante. 'She only has to ask.'

'Thank you, Jason,' I said. 'I can look after myself.'

Jane, I could tell, was piqued by the lack of masculine attention, although she remained smiling serenely, our own little Buddha of Suburbia.

Dante seemed singularly impervious even when she did the sort of fluttery eyelash stuff at him that I'm not only incapable of, but would get me certified if I tried.

'So you and your sister are going to run the weekend breaks thing together?' she asked.

'No. I'll be there if Rosetta needs me, but running it will be her concern. I'll be living and working in the west wing, mostly.'

'What do you do?' she persisted.

'I've been travelling round the States for a year, making notes for a book I've been commissioned to write: sort of an auto-biography. I used to be a foreign correspondent for a newspaper,' he added tersely.

'Oh?' clearly Jane had even less idea than me about the hostage-taking episode, but from Jason's face it had all suddenly clicked.

'Have you read any of Cass's books?' Jane asked.

'No, I've managed to resist their dubious charms so far.'

I scowled at him and he raised one black brow: 'I've just ordered your backlist off the internet in case an acute need for a prolonged period of bad taste comes over me. It only surprises me that you write that sort of stuff yet you're too scared to come back to the Hall and brave the ghosts. I thought you told me you didn't believe in that sort of thing?'

'No, I said I knew they couldn't *hurt* me. And I'm not afraid, even though I know there *are* things out there, either echoes of the past, or maybe the dark things from our own minds.'

'Oh, don't!' Jane shuddered theatrically. 'I know none of them exist, but it still frightens me.'

'That's how most people feel, or say they feel, Jane,' I pointed out. 'It's why horror sells so well.'

'When you thought *I* was a ghost you took to your heels fast enough,' Dante said to me.

'You thought *I* was one, too!' I snapped, glaring at him. 'And *you're* supposed to be the sceptic, not me!'

'When was this?' Jane said curiously, looking from one of us to the other.

Jason, glowering suspiciously, said: 'Yes, when did all this nocturnal activity take place? You didn't say you knew each other *that* well.'

'We don't! I told you we only met the other night, ghost-hunting,' I said defensively, then blushed hotly. Considering how pale-skinned I am I might as well have raised a red flag.

'I wish you wouldn't wander about in the middle of the night like that,' Jason grumbled, looking from me to Dante narrowly. 'Who knows what might happen to you?'

Who, indeed?

'You make a habit of it?' inquired Dante.

'Oh, everyone knows Cass walks about the graveyard and Hanged Man's Lane at night for inspiration. She will do it,' Orla said, and gave me a sideways look that meant: 'I know you're holding out on me with some vital information, friend of mine.'

'Cass won't be doing that this Friday though, because her mind will be on other things!' Jane said sweetly, and smiled generally round at everyone. 'Max – do you all know Max, Cassy's lover? – well, he's coming to see her.'

Jason looked gloomy. 'I suppose he's returning for good before long?'

'When his sabbatical year ends in July,' I agreed uncomfortably. 'He's just coming over to see me for a couple of hours tomorrow, after the funeral.'

'The funeral?' asked Dante, frowning at me darkly like Thor about to toss the hammer.

'His wife died recently, in America. He's bringing her back.'

'Right,' he said, then rose abruptly to his feet leaving half his drink untouched. 'I'll have to go, I'm meeting my sister at the station. But I'll try to bring her in to meet you all soon, if you're here?'

'*Some* of us will be here,' Orla assured him, with her special smile 'We meet here most evenings . . . unless something better offers?'

Good old Orla, always willing to give it a go.

'And if you want any advice about the B&B business—'

'Thanks,' he said, and with a brief arrow-head smile, strode off.

Orla sighed after him. 'He's so gorgeous, but he only seems interested in Cass's possibilities.'

'Her *haunting* possibilities,' Jane amended. 'I'm sure he's not interested in her personally. Maybe he's gay.'

I don't think so, Jane.

'He's not,' Orla said definitely. 'Are you mad?'

'Just a thought. So what's he running a guesthouse for? Does he need the money?'

'No, but I think his sister's been in hotel management and she thought the idea up. Luckily the Hall is pretty well ready to take visitors now, because Miss Kedge had it all modernised over the years, so it's in good order.'

'Yes, though hiring big outside firms to do the work didn't endear her to the local tradesmen,' I agreed. 'It was all pretty well kept up until she died, too. There can't be much to put right.'

Except the odd broken window-catch in a walk-in cupboard . . .

'Why won't you do his ghost act for him?' Orla asked me. 'I would, and it will be easy money compared to the Crypt-ograms.'

'You look too healthy to be a ghost. And I'm not going to mock the spirits in person, only in my books,' I said firmly.

'I think Cass's quite right,' agreed Jason who'd gone into a gloomy trance over his beer mug. 'She should avoid the Hall entirely. I didn't like the way Dante spoke to her, as though he only had to offer money and she'd come running.'

Actually, the way he'd spoken to me absolutely *slayed* me.

'And he came out of that hostage situation half-starved and half-mad,' Jason said. 'I've remembered all about it now. He looks unbalanced to me, Cass: you'd better avoid him, especially when you're on your own.'

'Which hostage situation?' Jane wailed plaintively.

Later that night, refreshed by a jolly good blood-letting, I decided to try my hand at a haiku before retiring to my blameless bed:

Spring flushes out new life.
How green the frogs that gaily leap
into the white bowl.

And that was my *best* shot.

Writing them is much more difficult than I expected, and I now realise that every three-line poem is not automatically a haiku.

I'm not going to give Jane any credit, though. She just naturally has a brain that takes a perceived view and turns it on its head in seventeen concise syllables.

She does much the same with gossip.

Doesn't syllable sound like something delicious made with sugar and cream?

. . . Keturah smiled like a fanged angel. 'But I am not the innocent, trusting creature you left behind you, Sylvanus,' she said softly. 'Look again!'

My personal fanged angel woke me up at some gruesome hour of the morning from a brief and inadequate slumber in order to drive her to the train, but she wasn't smiling, especially when she discovered that she had to pour mug after mug of strong coffee down me before I could even hoist my eyelids more than halfway.

As the sky grew slowly lighter beyond the kitchen window she got impatient. 'Come on, Cassy!' she said at last, twitching the curtains aside to peer out. 'I'm going to miss the—'

She stopped and gasped: 'Cass, there's a disgusting old van parked right next to your car at the bottom of the garden, all painted up with big daisies like one of those New Age Traveller things! Before you know it, the whole lane will be jammed with them – hordes of noisy children, dogs, loud music, rubbish, crap behind every hedge . . .'

Yawning, I got up and looked blearily over her shoulder. 'Don't panic, it's only Eddie.'

'Eddie?' she said blankly.

'Your youngest brother, remember?'

'You mean my brother actually lives in that – that *heap*?'

'Yes, didn't you know?'

'No, I thought he was living in some sort of commune. I haven't seen him for ages, because last time he stayed Gerald found him stark naked at dawn in the garden, playing his flute, and he won't have him any more. The neighbours all complained.'

'He still does that, winter or summer. He must be must tougher than he looks – or perhaps the demon weed makes you impervious.'

'Perhaps he's grown out of doing it now,' she said hopefully.

'What, the nude flute playing, or the weed?'

'Both.'

The van looked deserted as we made our way down the path towards the car, but at the rumbling of Jane's suitcase wheels Eddie stuck his head of flaxen dreadlocks and naked shoulders out of the window and said cheerily: 'Hi, Cass! Hi Sister Immaculata! Long time, no see. Did you get your Christmas present?'

'If you mean a bundle of twigs with knitting wool wrapped round it, then yes,' she said icily. 'Excuse us: I've got a train to catch.'

She edged past and wedged her suitcase into the car with some difficulty.

'Eddie, I'm just taking Jane to catch a train to Cornwall, but I won't be long. You know where the key is – help yourself to anything you want. See you later.'

I drove off, the corner of Jane's suitcase sharply nudging my back through the seat, and Jane's disparaging commentary about Eddie and his mode of life buzzing around me.

At least Mrs Bridges enjoys a naked Eddie in my garden. She says he's a lovely boy, and if he wants to mend her washer taps next time in the rude nude, she's no objections.

Were it not for Mr Fowkes, I expect Chrissie would say the same.

While Jane and the Giant Suitcase pursued the road less well travelled to a destination that might not be quite what she was imagining, her car remained parked on the verge at the front of the cottage, solid metal proof that she is in residence, should anyone care to come and do a visual check.

She has dispatched two long missives to Gerald and the parents giving the Gospel according to St Jane, so I expect they will swallow it down like they usually do, and Gerald at least will be beating a penitent path to my door before we know where we are.

If she is still away exploring Clint's possibilities I am instructed to say that Jane is deeply hurt, stressed and incommunicado, but am just as likely to impart the information that she is deeply warped, selfish and a plausible liar.

I told Eddie all about it when I got back from the station, but he just smiled vaguely and then wandered off down the garden to his van in a cloud of wonderweed.

Eddie is well-meaning but not terribly bright (traits he shares with Jamie), so you never know whether he has taken in what you are saying. His eyes don't register anything: the lights are on but there's nobody home. He beams a lot though, having a happy and un-complicated nature, and he is strangely practical and good with his hands.

I wonder if he is inhabiting a parallel universe, and so only appears to us on those brief occasions when there is a kink in the vortex of time?

He did wander back in later, to watch the video I'd recorded about rock climbing. Not that I'm interested in that sort of thing, but it was pretty gripping watching my brother Francis swing under a mountain ledge like an insecurely attached spider.

We already knew he'd survived the experience, because he's currently up in his little Scottish climbing shop regaling his customers with the tale.

Eddie laughed whenever it looked like Francis might lose his grip as though he was watching a cartoon, which was disconcerting; but he does love us all, even Jane, in his way.

And he'd found time to change the leaky washer on the bath tap and mend a wonky kitchen chair while I was out.

Later, I discovered some folded papers in the side pocket of my bag: the printouts of articles about Dante.

Orla must have pushed them in there at the pub, then forgotten to tell me.

FIVE MISSING AFTER COLOMBIAN HOSTAGE RAID. Five men, including British journalist Dante Chase (on right in photograph), American TV cameraman Paul Vance (left), and three German agricultural advisers, were kidnapped yesterday while travelling to Bogota in the same vehicle.

It is feared left-wing guerrilla group FARC are responsible ...

The photo of Dante showed a younger, less gaunt version of the man I'd met, leaning against a car in the middle of what looked like a desert. The one taken on his release showed a hollow-eyed, thin man with a haunted expression and hair even longer and shaggier than it was now – plus rather Che Guevara facial hair.

BRITON FREED IN COLOMBIAN HOSTAGE RAID SHOOT-OUT. Hundreds of soldiers yesterday took part in a raid on a former FARC safe haven, after the lack of progress towards peace talks ...

There were several articles, but most repeated the same facts: Dante and Paul had accepted a lift from the German agricultural advisors, who were there to encourage the growing of crops other than those for the lucrative cocaine and heroin trade. The left-wing guerrilla group, FARC, who derived a considerable income from drug production, promptly kidnapped them, and the other two men with them.

From what I read, someone gets kidnapped and held to ransom

by FARC practically every day there. Dante and Paul were just unlucky – in the wrong place at the wrong time – and Paul was doubly unlucky because he was killed, along with three soldiers and one of the Germans, in the raid.

WIFE OF BRITISH HOSTAGE IN COLOMBIA DIES AFTER TV APPEAL FOR HIS RELEASE.

A fuzzy picture of a pretty, dark-haired woman: Dante's wife Emma. So far as I could tell she didn't look a bit like me, which was somehow a relief. After that, the last hostage story was a short piece in a Sunday paper written by Dante himself, giving a brief description of the conditions they were held in, and a glowing tribute to the two hostages who had been killed. The paper disclosed that he had received an advance to write his auto-biography, and it would be serialised before publication.

I thought that was it, but there was one more sheet with two small news items about Dante: in the first, police and an ambu-lance had apparently been called by neighbours after a fracas at his London flat. A Mrs Dufferin, the mother of his dead wife, was later released from hospital after being treated for a suspected heart attack.

In the second Dante appeared to have been involved in a fight with his sister's boyfriend, who seemed to have got the worst of it, although no charges were made.

That was it, the tantalising bones of Dante's past, already picked over in public and now on the internet, for anyone to see.

I studied the before and after pictures for a while, but they didn't tell me anything I didn't already know.

Chapter 12: Rover's Return

I have recently learned, to my complete surprise, that the sister of the accomplished poet Jane Leigh is none other than Cass Leigh, author of such extreme examples of the horror genre as Grave Concerns *and the very disturbing* Twisted Sister.

No greater contrast could exist between the exquisitely honed haiku of the former and the dark, warped fiction of the latter ...

Wordplay Magazine

No word from Max saying whether he was definitely going to come and see me, let alone what time and for how long. As usual he just took it for granted that I would hang about the house all day waiting for him.

Clearly nature intended him to be a delivery man, not a university lecturer.

Under the circumstances it hardly seemed worth getting his stuff out of the attic, which would have felt like dressing a stage set where the main actor might or might not turn up and there was, unfortunately, no understudy.

Not that I didn't understand that he'd had the funeral and its attendant rites to contend with, but I needed to see him too. And you'd think, after so long apart, that he'd be pretty desperate to see me.

I'm sure all this worry and stress is subconsciously affecting my book, because it seems to be developing strangely: Sylvanus is turning into a blonde, blue-eyed monster, while Vladimir, the supposed villain of the piece, is evil but darkly attractive, with a clever if warped logic and moral code.

Keturah is fighting the bad in both of them at the moment, but since her near-vampire experience she seems to find a little evil quite sexy, so she has to fight herself too. She's not sure what effect biting either of them would have, if any . . . and I might just let her go for broke and find out.

It's all getting quite complicated, but I'm sure she'll sort something out in the end, now she's got over being such a wimp. I can't think what got into her, apart from Vlad, and that was just a Lite Bite.

It will be interesting to see which way she jumps.

Jason popped in during his lunch hour to confess that he'd been flirting with Jane the night before in the hope of making me jealous. He didn't confess that he'd also quite fancied her too, but then, the poor old thing doesn't realise he's as transparent as a jellyfish.

He'd been mulling things over among his bits of antique tat, and what he really wanted was for me to swear I would end the Max affair on Friday and take up with him instead, but I managed to smooth him down a trifle and send him off in a happier frame of mind without actually promising anything at all.

Later I phoned Orla up for a chat, during the course of which I managed to ask her casually if she'd ever really, really fancied a man while realising that he was not only infinitely alien in all ways to her, but dangerously scary somehow with it.

'All the time,' she said promptly. 'Hell's Angels, mostly.'

'Hell's Angels? Orla!'

'Middle-aged ones, with pony-tails and all that black leather . . . and maybe sunglasses. You know?'

'Well yes, but—'

'And Lemmy, out of Motorhead. Part of me wouldn't mind meeting him down a dark alley!'

'You can't be serious?' I said incredulously.

'Yes I can, and you did ask! Dante's got a touch of the dark, intense, scary side about him too, don't you think? I don't know what it is, but he's got it, while Jason, who has *terrific* rages, hasn't. Were you thinking of Dante?'

'No, of course not! I wasn't thinking of anyone in particular, just struggling with the villain-vampire in my book, Vladimir.'

'Yeah, right,' she said.

'Perhaps I *was* thinking about him a bit,' I admitted.

'Objectively – some aspects of his character have interesting possibilities.'

'They certainly do,' she enthused. 'I'd like to research them for you.'

'I think I'll invent some, thanks, but go ahead and research on your own account.'

'I wish!'

There was no sign of Dante at the pub that evening, which I was extremely glad about, because I do not want him glowering disapprovingly at me on a nightly basis. (I *think* it was disapproval.) He seems very moody, and most of the moods are shades of deepest gloom, but I expect a lot of it is due to his awful experiences.

Jason was back in a sulk, after all my hard work too, but whether that was because he felt his nose had been put out of joint by Dante's arrival on the scene, or because he was still jealous of Max's (putative) visit, I don't know.

It was a hot night for the Barbie phone: Orla booked two Marilyn Monroes and a Gorillagram.

On the Friday I arose mid-morning after a hard night's work and, feeling surprisingly nervous, attired myself in Festive Springtime Black to await the return of the rover.

And waited . . . and waited . . . and waited.

I'd eaten a mushroom and black olive pizza, two apples, and a small bunch of green grapes before Max's BMW sports car finally pulled up outside the cottage – or as near to it as he could get, seeing Jane's car was taking up the whole verge in front, and my car and Eddie's van were occupying the parking space at the end of the garden.

I wasn't sure where Eddie'd got to, unless Mrs Bridges was measuring him again for the rainbow Rasta hat and matching jumper she was knitting for him, but he had briefly met Max once and they could not be said to have clicked, so I expect he will keep out of the way.

Eddie doesn't bother me much when he is here, apart from having long hot soaks in my bath, singing Bob Marley songs in a pseudo-Jamaican accent, and depleting my food stores.

When I finally heard the car I opened the front door and watched Max walk up the path towards me, thinking how déjà vu it felt. Strangely familiar . . . familiarly strange.

118

I haven't actually stood back and looked objectively at him for years, but suddenly I saw him as a stranger might.

He is above medium height and slender, although he may go stringy in a year or two like Clint Eastwood, and his dark curly hair is now more grey than black. The loose, silky-looking grey suit he was wearing might have been Armani, and was certainly rather formal for the occasion, though he wore an open-necked shirt with it.

A Californian tan made his hazel eyes look a bit startled, but probably not as startled as mine when I spotted the revolting little manicured beard he had grown since I'd last seen him. It looked like it had been razor-cut out of black plastic and stuck on.

I haven't had such a shock since I followed the advice in one of those alternative women's health books, the ones that urged you to get familiar with your private parts using mirrors, and discovered something so sea-urchin it would have looked more appropriate attached to a coral reef.

He probably assumed I was numbed with emotion at the sight of him, for while I was still staring at his facial adornment in horrified amazement he swept me into a comprehensive and expensively scented embrace.

The feel of the beard touching my face, the unfamiliar after-shave, and the snaky slither of his suit against me all seemed very peculiar and not quite right: like one of those dreams where everything is suddenly just a bit off, and you can't quite put your finger on what it is . . . but – oh my God, yes! Aunt Susie's turned into a triple-headed Martian!

Somehow I seem to have got out of the habit of Max. It was embarrassingly like being over-enthusiastically kissed by a stranger, and an unattractive one at that, since I loathe beards.

And it wasn't only embarrassing: it was downright disconcerting when I realised I was finding his embrace no more exciting than Jason's.

Less, in fact.

And certainly much, *much* less exciting than being crushed against Dante Chase's hairy, half-naked and admirably broad torso when he yanked me out of that cupboard . . . although that, of course was more the excitement of fear. Sort of.

Max did not seem to be sharing my feelings, or even noticing my lack of response.

'I'd forgotten how beautiful you are!' he muttered, kicking the front door shut behind us, and shifting his grip purposefully. 'Let's go to bed, Cassy – we can talk later.'

I fended him off by using both elbows (and I have sharp elbows). 'Later, Max? I understood you could only stay a couple of hours. Didn't you tell Jane you were flying back to America tomorrow?'

He looked surprised and hurt. 'Yes, I'll have to get home tonight because there's still so much to arrange. But I thought you'd understand – and there's still time for me to show you just how I've missed you.'

Unfortunately for him I seemed to be having a complete understanding breakdown, even when he smiled in the way that would once have turned me to putty in his hands. But either it had lost its magic, or guilt over Rosemary's haunting legacy was freezing my heart.

That ridiculous beard didn't help either: it gave him the old-goatish look of a satyr.

Still fending him off, I tried to explain how I was feeling: 'Max, I haven't seen you for months, so everything seems very strange, somehow, and – and wrong. Especially when you've come pretty well straight from Rosemary's funeral!'

'Wrong? Isn't it a bit late in the day to start feeling guilty?' He let me go abruptly, looking irritated. 'This isn't much of a welcome! It was very difficult for me to get away at all, you know, when there was so much to do before I fly back. Now I'm starting to wish I hadn't bothered!'

'You don't understand, Max: Rosemary left me a letter saying how she'd always really felt about our affair, and the relationship between you, and it's deeply upset me. I need you to read it, and tell me whether or not any of it is true.'

'I don't need to read it, she left me a copy, too,' he said impatiently. 'But I didn't expect you to take any notice of her spiteful ramblings. I confess, I simply didn't realise how bitter she felt about things: I always thought she accepted the situation.'

'But she wasn't just bitter, she was obsessed! And *you* told me she didn't really mind, that you'd come to an agreement together!'

Max sighed long-sufferingly, and sat down on the sofa. 'Must we talk about it? Yes, I did think Rosemary and I understood each other very well, but she must have been mad to have had us followed and photographed like that.'

120

'Yes, so madly in love with you she was jealous. It made me feel *besmirched* when I understood that she wasn't complaisant about our affair at all – *and* when she said you'd continued to have a physical relationship! Was that true, Max?'

His hazel eyes met mine with hurt innocence: 'Of course not, darling! How can you even ask? These are all just lies, meant to divide us – and they seem to be succeeding.'

'All lies?'

'I should have told you to burn the letter unopened,' he said, sighing. 'Put it out of your head, and you'll see: when I come back in the summer we can forget the past and think about our future together.'

'And what? Get married?' I demanded. 'I know about the will, too.'

He shifted uncomfortably and this time didn't meet my eyes. 'If you really want to, of course we will: but we're quite happy the way we are, aren't we? You're used to your independence, and you'd probably prefer having separate households – though of course I'd like you to move nearer, so we can see much more of each other.'

I looked at him searchingly, but he still wasn't quite meeting my gaze. 'Max, this is my home, and I'd never sell it even if we *were* getting married. But we're not, are we? You'd rather have Rosemary's money than marry me.'

'Of course I'd marry you if we weren't so happy with our current arrangement! But why lose the money when there's no need? Be sensible, Cassy!'

'Well, thanks for making your priorities plain to me, Max!' I snapped, and the last faint urge to confess about my lapse with Dante evaporated into the air and was gone for ever. In fact, I was starting to feel more inclined to boast about it.

He patted the sofa and smiled in the way that had beguiled and brainwashed me only too often in the past, so sure that he could still manipulate me into seeing things from his own unique viewpoint.

Welcome to Planet Max: please orbit as instructed.

'You look lovely when you're angry,' he said tritely. 'It's strange how I'd forgotten just how beautiful you are. Why don't you come over here next to me, instead of pacing up and down?'

That certain light was in his eyes again. Seeing me after a long

121

absence seems to rate my excitement factor higher than golf unless he's simply been on the Viagra? You can buy it in every sweet shop over there, I expect.

I did sit down, though keeping a distance between us. 'Max, do you still love me?' I asked curiously.

'Of course I do, darling.'

'Then how could you swan off to America for a year without a second thought, with only a few measly phone calls to remind me of your existence?'

'Because it was too good a chance to miss, and I've been very busy. But soon we will be together again for good, and then I'll make it up to you.'

'Or together as much as we ever were, if you've no intention of marrying me?'

'Of course I'll marry you if you really want it, Cassy! But do you? Think about it. It would be stupid to—'

'—whistle Rosemary's fortune down the wind for love? Like I whistled my morals and principles down the wind when I became your mistress?'

'People live together all the time these days, it's not unusual.'

'No, it isn't. But what about children? You said we should wait until we got married, but you never wanted any, did you? Or was Rosemary telling the truth about striking a bargain with you on that one, too?'

He shifted uneasily. 'Was it wrong of me to want you all to myself?'

'But what about me? I'd still like to try for a baby before it's too late – if it isn't already, because I've been doing a test that shows you if you're still fertile, and I've had one hit and two misses, so it's not looking good.'

He smiled like I'd said something amusing: 'I wouldn't worry about that too much, there's plenty of time to think about it when I get back in the summer.'

'Max, I'm forty-four. I'm running out of time.'

His hazel eyes widened in surprise. 'Forty-four? Are you really? I suppose you *must* be, but you look so much younger than your age I forget. Everyone in California thinks *I'm* much younger than I am, too,' he added complacently.

They must all be liars. He does still look head-turningly good (apart from the beard), but he doesn't look younger than he is.

'Look Cassy, let's talk about all this when I get back. Can't we just enjoy being together now? You know how much I've missed you, and we can sort all this out,' he said in his very best warm-honey voice.

He moved up closer and took my hand – and I purposely let my mind go blank, and opened the door to his.

It was a maelstrom of mixed emotions, hard to read, but the surface one seemed to consist of lust. There were black edges of guilt, desire, worry, and a sort of shamefaced shiftiness too.

I couldn't feel any love, or even the exasperated affection I read on the only previous occasion I'd done this, and while the guilt wasn't as strong as Dante's, it was still more than enough to raise a question mark or two in my mind . . .

Maybe I really should take that random reading of several men to see if they all feel guilty?

Max wrenched his hand away and I came back down to earth. 'Bloody hell, Cassy, you promised never to do that to me!' he yelled furiously.

'You promised *me* a lot of things, Max, most of them, I now see, out of your power to deliver. Besides, I needed to know what you were feeling.' I stared at him with knitted brows. 'What part *did* you play in Rosemary's death?'

'How can you ask me that?' he exclaimed angrily.

'I read your guilt.'

'Guilt over the situation, of course, since it was because of me that she was out there in California at all. I swear to you that I had no hand in harming her! It was a tragic accident.'

'I suppose it *could* be just that . . . ' I mused.

'I was miles away, and I have witnesses to prove it!'

'So you keep saying. You're guilty about something, though, I saw that clearly enough. But what I couldn't see in your mind was any love for me.'

'If I didn't love you I wouldn't be here having this stupid and pointless conversation, would I? And I'd have *shown* you how much I love you if you hadn't been in this awkward mood! What on earth's the matter with you?'

'Max, sex can be an act of love, but it can also be just sex. I don't feel loved by you, I feel rejected, used – anything but loved!'

'I don't know what's got into you, but I can see I've wasted my time coming over here today,' he snapped. 'Are you trying to tell me you don't want to see me any more? You want to end it all, now, when the way is clear for us to spend the rest of our lives together?'

'I—' I faltered on the edge of the big step, searching for the words that would admit that I'd damned my soul to hell, cut myself off from my parents, and condemned another woman to suffer the torments of jealousy, all for the love of a vain, self-centred, lying, cheating man, who wasn't, and never had been, worth the steep price ticket.

What a Sleeping Beauty, dreaming of marrying him for years, only to wake up and find I don't really want to after all! But the habit of loving him – or the man I thought he was – made it hard to say the words that would end it all.

Max couldn't believe it either. 'We've been together a hell of a long time.'

'Yes, and I always meant it to be for ever,' I said sadly. 'But you've been away so long, and now Rosemary's death has changed everything and made me see things differently, and I don't know *what* I want.'

'Is there someone else?' he said with predictable suspicion.

Dante's face flashed across my mind like a meteorite. 'No, there isn't,' I said firmly, and looked at him, feeling all at once sad and lonely: 'I just think we've grown apart.'

'Are you telling me you don't love me?' He looked incredulous, as though such a thing were impossible.

'I don't know any more,' I said, because part of me did still love the man he once was – or the one I thought he was, anyway. 'And all you're offering me now is that we carry on as before when you come back, really, isn't it?'

'But we can spend time together freely, and I did say we'd discuss having a baby then, too,' he reminded me.

'Yes, when it might be too late. The clock's ticking and I feel it's probably now or never.'

'Why not now, then?' he said coolly, and to my complete astonishment tried to take me in his arms again.

He can't have been listening to a word I was saying, but that Viagra-fired light was in his eyes again, which might account for it: it had to be that, he hadn't been this frisky for years.

'Not with that revolting beard,' I said, fending him off with

124

revulsion, because suddenly I found the thought of sex with Max quite repugnant, like Rosemary would be in there with us.

'What's the matter with my beard?' he demanded.

'Everything. You know I've always hated beards, and that's such a silly clipped one. Why don't you shave it off?'

'Certainly not!' he said huffily. 'It's plain to me you're just using it as an excuse. I don't know what's the matter with you, but if I'd known you were in this sort of mood I wouldn't have bothered coming.'

'Well, I certainly don't intend sleeping with you just to make it worth your while.'

'I can't think what's got into you, but I can't see any point in carrying on this discussion. I don't suppose you've got any decent food in the house either?'

'No,' I said shortly.

He sighed long-sufferingly. 'I'm not driving all the way home without eating something, so it had better be the pub, I suppose.'

We walked to the King's Arms in silence, two old, old lovers with nothing left to say, and I felt quite cold, empty and somehow bereft. There was a space inside me where I thought our eternal love was burning, but the fire had definitely gone out and the embers were cooling.

I'm sure he loved me once, in his way, but then when he had overcome my resistance he started to take me more and more for granted, which probably happens in a lot of marriages too.

Max clearly still finds me desirable, especially after his absence, but not only would I have to contend with the horrid beard and the ghost in the bed, I find I don't particularly want sex without love when sober and in my right mind, whereas it doesn't seem to bother him in the least.

It is a pity Orla doesn't find him attractive, because then he could just transfer his casual attentions to her, thus fulfilling a useful purpose.

She was sitting in the pub lounge with Jason and waved as we went in, but Jason scowled from under his bushy eyebrows like a grumpy and possibly dangerous brown bear.

Max led the way to a table away from them, and without asking went to order food and drink. He did acknowledge the other two in passing, but that's all he ever does. He always said he wanted to

125

be alone with me, to make the most of our time together, but perhaps he just couldn't be bothered?

It was early yet, so there were few customers in the lounge, and only the jingle of the fruit machine in the bar.

Charles came in with his bundle of parish papers, beamed generally round, and settled himself in his usual seat. I don't think he noticed Max, possibly because his distance glasses were pushed up on top of his head. I gave him a wave to test if he could see me, but the only effect was on Jason, who brightened slightly and waved back.

'Your boyfriend's looking jealous,' Max said, setting a glass of white wine in front of me. Clearly he'd forgotten I hate white wine. He seemed to have managed to forget almost everything I liked and disliked in only a few months' absence. 'You shouldn't encourage him like that. He might think we want him to come and join us.'

'I was waving at the vicar; and you know very well that Jason isn't my boyfriend, so he has nothing to be jealous about.'

'No, I suppose you aren't very tempted by a man whose wife suddenly vanished without trace,' he agreed. 'You never know.'

'What do you mean by that?' I stared at him, astonished.

'Isn't that what you told me? She left her son behind and most of her things, and she's not been heard of since? Very odd.'

'Not odd at all,' I said, leaping to Jason's defence. 'She and Jason were always rowing, and if you'd ever seen her son you'd understand how she could leave him behind, because anyone would. It wasn't like she left a sweet little toddler, he was a big spotty adolescent. Besides, Jason might have a quick temper, but he wouldn't have harmed her!'

'You were quick enough to suspect *me* of harming Rosemary!'

'Not of killing her – it's just that there was that guilt, so I feel sure you know something you aren't telling me about.'

And I wasn't about to tell Max that Orla and I had discussed whether Jason might have accidentally done something to Tanya in a fit of rage, because he was so uniformly nice to his awful son that the foul youth must be holding *some* dark secret over his father's head.

'I think you should seriously consider what you want from life, Cassy,' Max said sententiously. 'Perhaps you will have come to your senses by the time I get back.'

Not unless he shaves that beard off, I won't, and probably not ever where he is concerned if coming to my senses means believing all his lies again

Part of me wished my spell had not been broken by Rosemary's chill breath of suspicion, but it had, and there was no going back.

He sat there looking huffy and pompous, and I looked away, fighting for control, as tears began to well.

At that moment the Demon Prince walked through the door like dark thoughts had conjured him up. His eyes met and held mine, shining the cold greeny-blue of something on a collision course with the *Titanic*.

'What are you staring at?' demanded Max, affronted. 'Didn't you hear what I said?'

I wrenched my gaze away with an effort and half-turned towards Max. 'Nothing. I—'

'Good evening, Cass,' said Dante's slightly gravelly voice behind me, and he rested his large hand intimately on the nape of my neck for a moment, like he was about to measure it for a collar.

Startled, I twisted round indignantly (although I must admit my timbers shivered prow to stern and back again), but before I could say anything he added politely: 'Is this your father?' And taking Max's limp hand he shook it enthusiastically.

Tall and gaunt Dante might be, and dressed in baggy sweater, jeans and the leather jacket that was so scuffed it was practically suede, but Max looked like a desiccated old man in his Sunday suit in comparison.

And whatever Dante's rating on the Richter scale, aftershocks were still rippling up and down my spine.

'I'm Dante Chase, and very pleased to meet you, sir,' he continued, not giving Max a chance to say a word. 'You have a lovely daughter. Did she tell you about that amazing night we spent together? I can tell you now, it was something *I'll* never forget! But I'll leave you two alone, because I'm sure you must have lots to talk about. Catch up with you later, Cass!'

He walked away, leaving Max looking as if he'd been stuffed with cactus and me speechless between anger and a hysterical desire to laugh.

'Who the hell is that? What did he mean?' demanded Max, fixing me with an accusing stare.

'Nothing,' I said weakly. 'He's inherited Kedge Hall, and I – er . . .'

'Spent the night with him? Hence your lack of interest in me? I see!'

'I met him while I was out ghost-hunting, that's all,' I said hastily, but probably looking as guilty as hell, mainly, I suppose, because I *was* as guilty as hell.

'You seem on very friendly terms. Intimate, even,' he said nastily.

'Not really. In fact, I don't even like him. He came over simply to try and annoy me, because he wants to hire me to haunt the Hall and I won't.'

My eyes met Dante's again where he now sat next to Orla, and he raised his glass and grinned like a shark.

'Haunt the Hall?' Max said incredulously, dividing a jealous gaze between me and Dante as if he was quick enough he might find us communicating with mirrors.

'You know, like the Crypt-ograms, only without the singing? Or the teeth. To frighten his guests.'

'Darling Cassy,' Max said softly, moving his chair up close to mine and taking my hand in his dry, warm clasp. 'All this business with poor, unbalanced Rosemary has preyed on your mind, hasn't it? And perhaps I was a bit insensitive not realising that, but it has all been so difficult. But you know how much I've missed you since I've been away, Cassy, don't you? I feel sure that when this has blown over a bit you could come and spend a week or two in California with me, and we can sort things out.'

His soft, mesmerising voice and earnest hazel eyes gazing into mine were exerting their usual effect . . . *almost*. If his persuasive lips hadn't been surrounded by topiary hairclippings it might just have worked – or maybe not.

Perhaps it was the quick glance over his shoulder of dog-in-the-manger possessiveness to check how Dante and Jason were taking our closeness, that ruined the beginnings of the familiar spell.

'Look, if we left now we would still have time to go back to the cottage and spend some quality time tog—'

'*No!*'

It came out flatter and way louder than I intended and he recoiled.

'Sorry, but I need space to think, Max. Time to work things out.'

His lips went all tight and he pushed his chair back, so I could once more see Dante's sardonic face watching us. It was strangely unnerving.

We walked back to the cottage soon after that and Max, angry and ruffled, got into his car and drove away: unsatisfied, unsated, and unloved.

I walked on up to the graveyard, which suited my current mood admirably, plotting to thwart and punish both Sylvanus and Vlad no end in the next chapter as a sort of general revenge on all mankind.

If they weren't already dead I'd have killed them.

Chapter 13: Dead Again

Cass Leigh keeps them coming thick and fast, with another new release in April, Shock to the Spirits. *The covers are quite tasteful compared to the content, and this one certainly gives no inkling of the horrors lurking inside. You either love them or loathe them.*

Bookseller

Even after a considerable period of reflection in the peaceful solitude of the graveyard I was still just one seething pit of dark writhing emotions, so instead of going home to work I returned to the pub.

It was still quite early after all, the hours of the night being infinitely more elastic than those of the day.

I put my head round the door of the lounge carefully, but there was no sign of either Dante, Jason, or even Charles; only Orla, earnestly perusing the lonely hearts page of *Private Eye*. She looked up, her predatory mauve claws marking a particularly luscious advert.

'Have they gone?'

'What, Jason and Dante? Yes, they formed a sort of uneasy alliance after you came in with Max – nice suit, by the way. Armani? – and Jason confessed that he'd bought some miniatures from Jack Craig a couple of weeks ago which he now realised might be from Kedge Hall.'

'I thought he was looking shifty about something.'

'They've gone off to look at them, and Dante says he will buy them back at whatever price Jason paid for them if they are his, which is very fair of him, isn't it?'

'Very.'

'So, how is Max? Things looked a bit sticky between you two even before Dante stopped by and spoke to you – and if you don't tell me what he said to make Max look so furious I will *die* of curiosity!'

So I told her, and when she giggled I saw the funny side too, although it didn't mean I wasn't still angry with Dante.

'Max's face!' I said. 'But just wait until I get my hands on Dante Chase, insinuating we'd spent the night together. What was he playing at?'

'Simple jealousy, I'd say, Cass – and probably with cause! And don't tell me you two didn't get up to *something* that night at the Hall, because it was absolutely obvious from the moment I saw you together.'

'Oh hell, was it?' I said ruefully.

'It was to *me*. And then when you were asking me the other day about being attracted to men you didn't like, I was quite sure.'

'Oh.'

'Did you, you lucky dog?'

'Yes, though I just don't understand how it happened, except that we'd been drinking this brandy he'd found in the cellar – and I'm certainly never touching the stuff again! – and I must have dozed off on his bed.'

'On his *bed*? What were you doing in his bedroom?'

'I'm not sure, but I have a vague feeling I might have left my bag up there earlier in the evening and gone up to fetch it before I left for home. Then I woke up in the early hours under a duvet with Dante, with some blurry memories of having had one of my ghostly dreams in the night; and I have a horrible suspicion that what started out with Dante comforting me turned into me practically jumping on him.'

'Who wouldn't?' she said generously.

'Yes, but we took an instant dislike to each other!'

'But it didn't stop you fancying the pants – literally as it turned out! – off him, did it?' she pointed out. 'And you don't remember him trying to fight you off, do you?'

'Well, no. No, I don't remember any signs of resistance at all. And he was fathoms deep in sleep looking terribly relaxed and peaceful when I sneaked out.'

'Cass, if you didn't even leave him a note saying "thanks, you were great – let's do it again some time" he's probably extremely piqued. I'm sure he only came in here that first night to try and find you.'

'But he didn't come and find me,' I pointed out.

'No, but that was probably because I told him about Max. And then when you two did meet again you both seemed to be pretending that you hardly knew each other, and you were digging your heels in about an absolutely easy, well-paid haunting.'

'I was trying to put the whole sorry episode out of my mind. Not only was there Max to consider, but Dante isn't my type, and he's absolutely eaten by the trauma of seeing his friend killed, and then the guilt about his wife.'

'He's got a wife? I thought he was a widower?'

'He is. I meant he was guilty about his wife because she was pregnant and died while he was a hostage.'

'Oh well, if she's *dead*,' Orla said expansively, 'what does she matter?'

'Dead wives seem to be more trouble than living ones – look at Rosemary,' I pointed out bitterly, and then, abandoning the troublesome – and troubling – Dante, told her more or less everything that had passed between Max and me earlier.

'He did look like an old goat in that beard – it's definitely a mistake,' she agreed. 'And if you're convinced that Rosemary was telling the truth in her letter, then he's been lying to you all down the line. You're going to have to cut loose, Cass – you simply don't love him any more, do you?'

'But there *were* moments when he almost had me believing him again, and I could have – I mean, if it weren't for that beard—'

'He's too mercenary even to marry you after all these years together. And face it, Cass, if he agreed that you could try for a baby and you still turned him down flat, you not only don't fancy him any more, you positively dislike him!'

I sighed. 'Yes, you're right, but things are never that simple, are they? The worst bit was when he first arrived and wanted me to jump straight into bed with him! I felt all shy and embarrassed at the idea, because he was just like a stranger, and a stranger I didn't even fancy, at that. And he couldn't understand how awful I felt about poor Rosemary either, or even *want* to try and understand it. And then, of course, he didn't know what I'd done with Dante, either.'

'Yes *he* was a stranger, but apparently a stranger you fancied,' she said. 'Hard to explain to Max, that.'

'Hard to explain to *me*, never mind Max.'

'Ye-es,' Orla looked pensively down at her immaculate finger-nails. 'With Dante, Cass, you did take precautions, didn't you?'

'I thought of that – too late! – and I shouldn't think so. But I'm not an adolescent, likely to get pregnant from a one-night stand. Anyway, according to the Predictova thing I probably didn't ovulate this month, so that's that.'

'He's young, though – around thirty-five, six, do you think? Good stud material! If you really want to try for a baby, he's your man.'

'He's not my man, he's a drunken aberration, and now he knows about Max he probably thinks I sleep around whenever my lover's away, so I'm just a tart. I'm going to put that night right out of my head, and I'm not going to do his haunting, either.'

'Of course he won't think you're a tart!' she said indignantly. 'And that night you spent together, what I'd really like to know—'

'No, you wouldn't,' I said firmly. 'And even if you would, I'm not going to tell you. Even if I remembered.'

'Spoilsport! And it's sod's law that you get the only available decent man, when you've already got a lover. Or *had* a lover, perhaps I should say. Isn't it odd how everyone we know seems to have lost their spouse?'

I thought about it, and had to agree: 'Yes, Max, Dante and Jason have all lost their wives in one way or another.'

'And I lost a husband, don't forget,' Orla said. 'There's Mike.'

'At least you know where Mike *is*. He ran off with that busty blonde exec with the big briefcase.'

'True,' she conceded. 'And once I knew they were living in Swindon I realised that God had punished them as much as they deserved.'

'Yes, so that only makes two dead wives . . . ' I ticked them off on my fingers. 'One disappeared wife, and one divorced husband. Shall I now officially dump my lover of over twenty years stand-ing (though very little of it was standing, as I recall), and join the Suddenly Single club?'

'You've been single as near as damn it for years anyway, Cass, and at least now there's the possibility of getting something going with Dante.'

'There is no possibility of getting *anything* going with Dante: too young, too big, too dark, too intense, too haunted, too trauma-tised and too scary!'

'That's at least five things you've got in common to start with,' she suggested helpfully. 'You are carrying a load of guilt, rejection and childhood trauma. And what do you mean, he's too scary? This from *you*!'

'He's different scary to my usual scary,' I tried to explain. 'Maybe you're right about us having things in common, but that's surely all the more reason not to go near each other? I may have piqued him a bit, as you say, but really he's only interested in getting me to flit about the grounds of the Hall at night doing ghost impersonations for the edification of his visitors.'

'His sister's visitors,' Orla corrected. 'I wonder what she's like? Clara's met her in the shop, and she says she looks a bit like Dante, and is very nice. She told her she'd already advertised the first ghost party weekend, and she's taken on two cleaners to get the place straight, and hired a garden clearing service to come and sort out the grounds.'

'That's quick work! And there isn't going to be much profit after paying for all that,' I pointed out. 'And if Dante's so well off, which he must be, I don't see why he should be letting his sister do this at all.'

Orla looked surprised: 'Oh, haven't I brought you up to date on all the nice long chats I've been having with Dante? I only wish he looked at me the way he looks at you, so brooding and sombre and—'

'Like he wants to murder me?'

'Actually I was going to say, like he wants to eat you.'

I had a sudden vision of Vlad, in immaculate dinner jacket, approaching Keturah with his knife and fork held threateningly before him and a hungry look in his eyes, but instantly discarded it because of its risibility potential.

'Are you listening?' demanded Orla. 'I was saying that Dante explained – or rather, I winkled out of him—'

'You're good at winkling,' I conceded.

'Thank you. I winkled out of him that he'd been brought to the Hall once when he was a little boy, and never forgotten it, so when he inherited he wanted to live here. He's been commissioned to write a book about his experiences as a hostage, which he thinks will be good for him, but he took almost a year out to tour the USA, finishing up in Alaska where the widow of that other hostage who was killed lives.'

134

'How did you get all that out of him?' I demanded, astonished. 'With an oyster knife?'

'No, but it was slow work. And apparently his sister has just come out of a long, violent relationship – with a chef! Now *that's* scary, all those big choppers. She was in the hotel management business. She refuses to live off him, or accept an allowance, so when she suggested the ghostly weekends he didn't like to refuse. She's called Rosetta, isn't that pretty?'

'What happened to Gabriel? Or Gabrielle?' I interrupted.

'Don't be sarky. Dante says she's got the weekend worked out already, pretty well. She's only offering B&B, but her visitors can come here and eat in the restaurant like mine do. Dante's writing a ghost guide to the Hall to give to them. He's very thorough for a sceptic.'

'And you're very sanguine about this rival guesthouse.'

'I don't think it will really make any difference to me after all, since theirs isn't a regular thing. My guests are usually on their way somewhere else, not ghost-hunting, though they do love the Haunted Well. The compulsion people feel to throw money into water must hark back to some ancient god-propitiating rite, inbred in some of us, mustn't it? Me, I'm more concerned with taking the money out again. It's a nice little earner.'

. . . the coin bounced, and the depths of the pond shifted and gleamed like the golden scales of a great, stirring monster. . . .

'Speaking of great, stirring monsters, when's Kedge Hall going to open for business?'

She looked puzzled: 'Were we speaking of great, stirring monsters?'

'I was . . . maybe. In my head: sorry.'

'Right. They're opening at Easter, would you believe it? They've ordered a whole heap of Haunted Walks Through Westery, too, so their guests can take themselves off in search of extra ghosts.'

'It still seems strange behaviour for a man who seems to have an absolute antipathy for the supernatural.'

'Oh, he thinks it's a load of nonsense, but he's prepared to go along with it if it helps his sister.'

'Did he say so?'

'Yes, and also that he didn't mind ghost-hunters, but he wouldn't permit seances, planchettes or any other dangerous nonsense in his house.'

'That's because his mother-in-law's some kind of medium, and when his wife died she made him try and contact her from beyond the grave, though it didn't work. But why has he banned them if he doesn't believe in them?'

'He thinks they're harmful to weak-minded people.'

'Of whom he isn't one?'

'Apparently not.'

She looked down at her neglected copy of *Private Eye*, and read out an advert: ' "*Strictly* for fun: guy seeks doll, North West/Wales/ would travel." What do you think?'

'Oh come on, Orla! He's looking for a cross between Miss Whiplash and Barbie.' I reconsidered. 'On second thoughts, maybe you're just what he's looking for.'

'No, honestly, Cass: tell me if you think he sounds interesting.'

'He sounds like one of those red-faced sex-maniac types with long-suffering wives: is that interesting?'

'Well, I like the sound of everything except the red face.'

'I think it's probably nature's way of announcing their proclivities, like baboon's bums.'

'You have such a romantic way of putting things.'

'If you're looking for romance, I doubt if you will find it through that sort of advert anyway.'

'And if you're looking for romance, why won't you go and haunt Kedge Hall? I can't see why not – I bet he would pay double the Crypt-ogram fee, and it would be quite easy, wouldn't it? And who knows where it might lead?'

'I'm not looking for romance, and anyway, I don't want to spend any time near Dante Chase.'

'You don't trust him?'

'No, I'm not sure I trust *me*, especially if my hormones kick in again. And despite that book you gave me putting me off pregnancy a bit, at least part of me still wants to try for a baby. I might be tempted to ply him with brandy and jump on him again.'

'What about Jason?'

'Usual objections.'

'Mmm. Remember the night Tanya vanished, when he came to the pub alone after they'd argued, although he wouldn't tell us what about?'

'Probably Jack Craig, since they'd had a fairly blatant "me Mellors, you Lady Chatterley" thing going on for ages.'

'Very likely. But do you also remember that Mike was away that night?'

I looked at her. 'Yes: you said Jason walked you home and stayed for a cup of coffee, and when he got back home Tanya'd gone.'

'Yes,' she said pensively. 'But actually he stayed for something a bit hotter than coffee!'

'I *knew* there was something! Who's the dark horse now?' I exclaimed.

'I couldn't really say anything: Jason felt guilty when he went home next morning early and Tanya'd gone, and he felt guilty about Mike, too, because they were friends, and I felt guilty – so, you see?'

'You've both been pretending it never happened ever since? You're a fine one to talk about me!'

'Yes, but actually I still fancy Jason, only I was just a lapse on his part due to the temper he was in and he regrets it, so I know we will only ever be friends now. And he's got the hots for you these days anyway.'

I stared at her. 'And you keep trying to push him off on to me?'

'Only as a potential baby generator. I know you don't really fancy him otherwise, but I'm sure he wouldn't mind.'

'Probably not!'

'And I wouldn't mind even if Jason and I were together. But we're not, and never likely to be.'

I really couldn't see why not, if he could be cured of his crush on me, because it was always Orla he used to flirt with. Another thought struck me: 'Orla, if Tanya's car was still there when Jason walked you home, and he stayed with you, doesn't that mean he couldn't have done anything to her?'

'Not entirely, because he left while it was still dark. But he did tell the police where he'd been when he reported her missing, so they must have been satisfied, especially after that sighting of her car. When Jason saw she'd gone he went up to Kedge Hall to see if she was there, but there was no sign of her, so he assumed she'd gone right away.'

'That's what he says anyway, Orla, though it does look even more likely now that she just left on her own, doesn't it? If they'd had another row when he got back from your house and he'd done something regrettable in a rage, I don't think he'd have had time to dispose of her and her car and get back before it was light enough for people to see him, do you?'

'No, you're right! So apart from Tom being so awful, there's really no reason why you shouldn't try for a baby with him!'

'Yes, but Tom *is* awful, so I couldn't possibly. And that book said all the risks seem to rise horrifically at my age, even if you achieve pregnancy – which I'm not likely to do without a lover, am I? Or even possibly with a lover.'

'But Max actually offered?'

'He just wanted to get his leg over,' I said crudely. 'I'm not going to get pregnant that easily at my age, am I? And promising to discuss it when he finally gets back from America – that's months away. No, he doesn't want a baby and he doesn't want to marry me when he thinks he can have his cake and eat it as it is.'

'Well, if you're *determined* on trying, there are private AI clinics?'

I shuddered. 'No, I couldn't! Too clinical, and anyway I want to choose the father of my child. If I really did decide to give it a go. I think the temptation factor is weakening.'

'AI by a friend?'

'Back to Jason again, and the usual objections apply.'

'You don't really fancy him, and there's Tom, right.'

'Right. Besides, he'd want more than to donate his sperm, wouldn't he? I don't think I want a long-term relationship with anyone any more. I've done all that. If I have a baby, it will be just for me.'

'Well, Jason is a very good father, even though Tom's so awful.'

'Max insinuated that it was because Tom had the drop on him over his mother's disappearance.'

'Did he? Astute of him, when it took us ages to think that one up! But I'm sure Jason hasn't done anything, and Tanya went away of her own accord.'

'Yes, and even if he had he wouldn't have meant to do it, so he's perfectly harmless,' I agreed.

'But to get back to the point, Cass, the only other way is to go for the Lonely Hearts columns – don't tell them where you live or your real name, and dump them when they've served their purpose.'

'Oh no, thanks. I mean, apart from the Yuk factor, how would I know if they had any revolting STDs? Or even an IQ?'

'You're so fastidious . . . but you have a point,' she admitted. 'So what about Dante?'

'Oh, I don't think so – he'd have felt so guilty afterwards that I'm sure he'd have had to tell me if he'd put me at risk,' I said hopefully.

'You're probably right, *and* you could seduce him again, I bet. The way he stares at you . . .'

'Glares. I think it's his natural expression.'

'You're a fine one to talk! You both look and sound like a tragedy queen – Lady Macbeth to the life – but it seems to work on the men OK.'

'Dante's too young, and I don't really think he's interested in me like that despite the other night. In fact, he seems to disapprove of me, my works and everything I do. And I don't know how to go about seducing anyone anyway. I'm out of the habit of going out with other men . . . I mean, I always meant to be faithful to Max, but he lied to me all the way along the line.'

'That was always perfectly obvious, but it was pointless saying anything when you were so under his thumb.'

I shuddered. 'I nearly was again – there's something almost hypnotic about Max when he really starts to work on me. You know, if it hadn't been for that stupid beard I might just have weakened!'

'No, I think you're beyond that, and that beard is pretty stupid. Besides, maybe you didn't notice, but when Dante was standing next to Max, the contrast really struck you, because he is so big, and dark and *virile*, and Max looked thin, and dry and older and well-preserved, I suppose, and sophisticated.'

'I did notice,' I admitted. 'But I'm no spring chicken either! If I felt shy with Max after only a few months apart, think what I'd be like trying to get off with a total stranger! And how could I bare this forty-four-year-old body to a new lover?'

'What about the other night? And you have a wonderful figure!'

'The other night I was drunk and – well, let's not go into that. And we both have wonderful figures, as in big busty ones, but it's not fashionable to be shaped like a woman, is it? Only anorexic boyish types need apply.'

'I think you'd better abandon any hopes of pregnancy by anything other than divine intervention then, since clearly you'll

139

never come near enough to another man again to make it happen. How about a nice dog?'

'What?'

'You absolutely drooled over the Saluki hounds when we were watching Crufts on my TV. Why don't you have one of those instead?'

'It's hardly the same thing, Orla!'

'Much less trouble though! It's not life-threatening, figure-threatening, wallet-threatening, doesn't involve having random sex with strangers or turning friends into lovers . . .'

Maybe she had something. But the urge to procreate is a powerful one, and it wasn't prepared to lie down and die quite yet.

'How's your other offspring, your latest book, coming along?' she asked.

'Oh, the characters are all off doing their own thing, now I've made Keturah's dead lover come back as something not quite human. And then there's this ancient family vampire that lives in the local hall that she finds quite attractive.'

'You're not going to do anything particularly revolting to him at the end, are you?' she asked suspiciously. 'I always get to kind of identify with someone half bad and half good in your novels, and then you do something awful to them!'

'Of course I am! Don't I always? But it won't be *me* but my heroine Keturah. She might eat him during the sex act, like a spider, since she is half-vampire, half—'

'Oh God!' exclaimed Orla. 'Ugh! Don't tell me any more. How can you sleep at night?'

'I don't, I'm too busy writing.' I sighed. 'After this, I think I'll write a literary novel under an assumed name, and call it *Dante's Compendium* or *Dante's Goldfish* or something.'

'You are joking, aren't you?' she said suspiciously.

I woke Charles yet again with my phone calls. I really must learn to check the time before I call people.

He never seems to mind, but he is not a young man and needs his beauty sleep. Another thing to feel guilty about.

I brought him up to date on Rosemary's letter, and how I'd made her suffer all these years, and how guilty I felt, and about Max now seeming a worthless thing to have swapped for my self-respect.

140

'And Charles, I had an absolutely horrible thought: did I choose Max simply because he was older and very charismatic, like Pa? (Only sane.) Or like Pa was, before he took to drink.'

'You were simply desperate for love, Cass my dear: leave the psychoanalysis to specialists. As to the rest: yes, it is a heavy weight to bear on your conscience, but if you are truly sorry, God will forgive you.'

'Actually, I feel more worried about me ever forgiving me at the moment. And it was a bit shattering to discover that the minute the path is apparently clear for Max and I to be together, Rosemary is always going to be blocking the way.'

'Does Max accept that the affair is finished?'

'I'm not sure that I quite accept it yet, Charles: I mean, I didn't know how I would feel about him until I saw him again, and then we just argued, and then he tried to be nice and get round me, and then he went huffy again and left . . . so it all seems a bit like it's inconclusively petered out rather than ended.'

'So you haven't actually told him?'

'I think he got the idea, but no, I haven't actually come right out with it in so many words. I might have, except he was so much more like the old Max I loved towards the end of the visit – apart from the vile beard.'

'The beard?'

'Surely you noticed, at the pub on Friday? It was disgusting – sort of shaved at the sides. There's no telling what might have happened if he hadn't turned up with facial hair, but I'm glad now that he did, because it made me take a good hard objective look at him and decide to end it all. I must. I *must* finish it.'

'You will feel much better when you do, Cass: but in your own time. God has infinite patience, and infinite love.'

'It's just as well, Charles,' I said, before replacing the receiver.

Chapter 14: Mad Max

. . . and we knew Dante was no good.

Samuel Butler: Note Books

Found myself idly thumbing through the *Dictionary of Quotations*, where there were lots of good Dante ones but, I was extremely aggrieved to find, no Cassandra ones.

Maybe there's a male and female version of the Dictionary and I've got the wrong one? I mean, it's not like she didn't have an interesting life: *someone* must have mentioned her.

Mind you, she is a striking example of what can happen to a woman when she reneges on a promise. Keturah should bear it in mind, although in her case it isn't a lot of petulant gods who are about to become the thingummy in the machine.

Tried to discuss this with Jason when he popped in at lunchtime to share a pizza, for he is not unintelligent, although he has stopped thinking deeply about anything much since he settled here.

All he said was that I was cute when I talked mythological, and then *I* said I hoped he choked on his black olive.

Such childish depths are, I'm afraid, our usual comfortable mode of conversation when he is not fancying himself in love with me.

Later I popped into the Haunted Well B&B, where Orla was fully occupied with a party of Australian family-tree researchers. The house seemed to be covered in people poring over vast photocopies, and Orla was quite distracted.

She said the only Cassandra she'd ever come across before me was Mama Cass, who was a striking example to us all.

I agreed, but afterwards wondered quite what sort of example?

An almost incoherent phone call from Max, who had been 'taken in for questioning' by the American police the moment he stepped off the plane in sunny California.

'Incompetence!' he spluttered. 'They already know I'm innocent of anything to do with Rosemary's death, and whatever Kyra says she did had nothing to do with me!'

'Kyra, as in your personal trainer?' I asked, my heart sinking. 'What *did* she do?'

'Only confessed that she was responsible for Rosemary's death! They had an argument which ended with Kyra giving the wheelchair an almighty shove and walking off. Afterwards, she realised Rosemary hadn't been able to stop it and gone over the edge, but she was too frightened to say anything even though it was an accident.'

'So why is she saying anything now?'

'Goodness knows!'

'And why did the police want to question you again, if you weren't there at the time?' I pondered aloud.

'Some busybody – that home-help we had to fire for incompetence, probably – told them that Kyra was getting a bit . . . well, frankly, she had a crush on me,' he hedged. 'Rosemary told me the day before she died that she'd had enough of Kyra trying to flirt with me under her nose and she would have to go, so that's probably what the argument was about.'

'You were having an affair with her, weren't you?' I asked bluntly, a lot of long-suppressed suspicions bobbing up to the surface, all thanks to Rosemary.

'How can you even suggest that, Cassy, when you know how I feel about you?' he said, sounding deeply wounded. 'Of course I wasn't, and in the end the police just let me go home, because clearly I had absolutely nothing to do with it. Only now the university has asked me not go in until further notice, and I feel I'm being unfairly punished and harassed for poor Rosemary's tragic death, which was little more than an accident anyway, as it turns out.'

I think Rosemary might have described it a little differently – and there was definitely some subplot there that he wasn't telling me about.

143

'So what will happen to Kyra?'

He didn't sound too concerned: 'There were no witnesses, but with any luck it will be brought in as an unfortunate accident. It certainly wasn't premeditated – she had no reason to want her dead, as she told the police – and everyone knows Rosemary was a quarrelsome woman.'

'Was she? I don't think you've ever mentioned that.' It was strange how I was getting to know Rosemary after her death.

'There's no one else I can talk to about the whole sorry affair except you, Cassy – you understand me like no one else does.'

I think he meant that I was blind to all his faults, but hasn't realised Rosemary has ripped the blinkers off, leaving me squirming in the light of day.

'And I'm sorry if I was unreasonable when I came to see you, and that we argued, but I really wasn't myself after the funeral and everything. I'll make it up to you when I get back darling: marriage, babies – anything you want.'

I muttered something non-committal, not wanting to be the straw that broke the camel's back, but longing to tell him that the magic had not only worn off our relationship but the base metal was beginning to tarnish.

Charles is so right: when the right time comes and I can tell Max that I never want to see him again it is going to feel such a release. Guilt has been dragging me like an anchor, and soon I will be able to serenely sail away into the seas of desiccated spinsterhood.

Portsmouth, 19th March.
Dear Sis,

Docked. See you soon on way to my duty-visit to Ma and Pa. Pa says Jane's staying with you, and I'm to take her home with me. No bloody fear! Rather be tied to an alligator than cooped up in a car with Jane for hours.

Boz and Foxy and me are going poultry-farm hunting after that, but don't tell Ma and Pa yet.

Love, Jamie.

Ps. is that yummy blonde friend of yours still single? Give her my best!

Belgravia, 19th March.

Dear Jane,

tried to phone you the other day, but Gerald informs me you are staying with Cassandra and completely incommunicado. I'm surprised you should want to stay with Cassandra in her hideously uncomfortable little hovel when you could stay with us, which is why I was calling: Phily's had a spot of her old trouble, and the court case comes up next week.

Unfortunately I have to be away for several days then, so could you possibly come and keep an eye on Phily and support her, and all that? Her doctor will be giving evidence of course, so there will be no problem. It is ridiculous to put her through this when she cannot help herself, as I know you understand.

Let me know as soon as you can if you will be able to come,

George.

'Do you know what Phily's "old trouble" is, Eddie?' I asked, frowning over Jane's letter. I've started opening all her mail, since she's been gone days now and no word on yurts. No word at all, in fact.

Eddie shook his blond dreadlocks and carried on eating peanut butter with a spoon straight from the jar.

'Well, whatever it is, she will have to cope on her own, because I don't know the address of Jason's yurt in Cornwall. If yurts have addresses?'

'The peanut butter's gone,' he said, smiling vaguely at me as he put the jar down.

Hello, Planet Eddie. Are you receiving me?

'There are four more jars on the shelf behind you.'

'I know Clint Atwood,' he suddenly announced, to my astonishment. 'Crap painter, weird bloke. Nice yurt.'

I stared at him, astounded. 'You never said. And what do you mean, weird?'

I mean, if Eddie thinks he is weird, then there is something seriously off-centre about Jane's lover.

Eddie just shrugged. 'Dunno.'

'Do you know the address of this yurt?'

'No, but I could find it.'

145

'Well, that's a fat lot of good. Eddie, Jamie is calling in some-time on his way home. He thinks Jane is here – everyone thinks Jane is here, not cavorting in Cornwall with her lover.'

'Well, it'll be good to see old Jamie again,' Eddie said amiably, filling the kettle and plugging it in. 'Have you seen my bong?'

'No, and you know I won't let you smoke that stuff in the cottage – it smells vile.'

'I know, but I've put it down somewhere.'

He wandered round the kitchen, lifting things up as though the pipe might be playing a game of hide and seek with him. I had a sudden strange vision of Eddie as the next TV chef: 'Naked Stoned Old Hippie in the Kitchen', perhaps? Buy his new cook-book now: *Fifty Fun Ways With Weed*. Not so much a recipe book, more a way of life.

'Jamie's going to leave the navy and run a poultry farm some-where with those two daft friends of his, Boz and Foxy.'

'Even chickens have souls,' he said absently, turning over the contents of the bread bin.

'I daresay they have, especially compared to Jane,' I agreed, trying to remember where the conversation had started out and failing.

I finished the last of my late breakfast and just sat there feeling exhausted but sated, for last night I worked non-stop like someone cut open a major writing artery.

Lover, Come Back is not far off completion, and so is Keturah – she's pregnant with something, though until it arrives she won't know quite what, or who – or even how. And considering what she did to Sylvanus and Vladimir, I now feel quite benign towards them both and the world in general. Sated, even.

There's nothing like a bit of blood-letting.

'I've nearly finished my book,' I said, more for the glow of saying it than expecting an answer, but Eddie beamed his light-house smile at me and said warmly: 'Clever Cass!'

The doorbell rang, and since Eddie seemed quite happy to stand there and beam indefinitely without even noticing it, I heaved myself up and went to answer it.

A young woman stood on the doorstep, and one glance told me that this must be Dante's sister Rosetta even before she told me, for the resemblance was striking.

In her, Dante's springy, raven's wing hair had been downgraded to shaggy dark brown curls, and her eyes were an everyday blue-grey, but she certainly had the nose. It was not pretty on her, but combined with the rest to give her a pleasantly rangy, Afghan hound sort of appeal, like Cher before the nose-job.

'I'm Dante's sister, Rosetta, and I hope you don't mind me calling?' she asked anxiously. 'Only Dante says you're the local ghost expert, and you were terribly kind to him when he first got here, so he thought you wouldn't mind answering a couple of questions.'

My mouth fell open. What did he mean, *kind*?

'I thought perhaps you might have some books on local hauntings that I haven't found yet – you know, to add a bit of spice to the ghost-hunting?'

'Come in,' I said, finally remembering my manners. 'Your brother said I was *kind* to him?'

'Yes, and I was quite surprised, because he's always been reserved, and now he's so withdrawn and – oh!'

I wasn't surprised at her losing the thread of the plot, because she'd suddenly come face to face with Eddie; and though thankfully he was wearing the clean but tattered remnants of a pair of jeans, he did look like a half-naked Saxon wandered in from the wrong century, though they probably didn't put multicoloured beads on the end of their braids.

'This is my brother Eddie,' I said, but I might as well have been speaking to myself for they were staring into each other's eyes like a pair of telepaths. Maybe they *are* a pair of telepaths, and that's why communication with Eddie has never been entirely straightforward?

Neither of them seemed able to look away. I haven't seen Eddie so serious since the time we were little, and he managed to open the cupboard door with a bit of bent wire to let me out, and Pa caught us.

Then Eddie's pearly smile returned four-fold. He held out his hand, Rosetta took it, and he led her outside without a word.

'Eddie?' I called. 'Rosetta?' But without a backward look they climbed into Eddie's van and vanished from my view.

Well!

I sat down again at the table with another cup of coffee, waiting for them to reappear, but when I looked out later the *van* had gone too.

147

Ruffled by Dante's references to my kindness, I found it hard to fall into my early afternoon doze, and then when I did drop off I was instantly awoken by Max phoning again.

He'd simmered down about the police questioning: seemed to have put it right out of his head, strangely enough, and instead asked me all sorts of inane questions about the slave auction, which he has never shown any interest in before.

Perhaps he was feeling lonely and just making conversation, because he also asked about my new book and the Cryptograms, which is unusual: normally he just talks about himself.

He was at his most charming, too, his voice low and caressing. But somehow it doesn't seem to be working any more, and I don't think the fact that I was still exhausted but exhilarated after my mammoth blood-letting-by-proxy stint and so not in a receptive frame of mind, had any effect on the matter.

After that I tried to settle back down again, but before I could insert the earplugs against the surrounding Birdsong and TV babble, Dante called to ask if I'd seen his sister.

'She left hours ago to visit you.'

'She was here,' I told him. 'Briefly. But then she went off somewhere with Eddie.'

'Eddie? Who the hell's Eddie?' he snapped.

'My brother. One of them: I've got four.'

'He lives with you? Why haven't I seen him around, then?'

'He lives in a van, he's just visiting me. And you probably have seen him around: he looks sort of like a blonde Rastafarian.'

'I've seen him,' he said after a short but menacing silence. 'But I don't know why my sister would go off with him. And where have they gone?'

'No idea. He's old enough to stay out without telling me, and so is your sister.'

'My sister's emotionally fragile. She's just come out of a violent relationship, and the one thing she doesn't need is to get involved with some New-Age weirdo.'

'Eddie's entirely harmless, peaceful and non-violent,' I told him. 'He's vegetarian, he doesn't drink, and he likes to commune with the wild creatures in the woods, playing his flute.' I didn't mention the weed.

'Could he possibly be communing with my sister in the woods?' he enquired rather nastily.

148

It was by no means an impossibility.

'Yours are the nearest woods, so why don't you go and look?' I suggested.

'No need,' he said in a different voice. 'There's an old van with big psychedelic daisies painted all over it coming up the drive. Your brother's, I take it?'

'Sounds like it,' I admitted.

'Yes: he's getting out, and so is Rosetta. They're coming in – and they're holding hands.'

'I think it's legal in public,' I told him. 'I *thought* they seemed to hit it off.'

Dante put the phone down on me. I only hope he doesn't do anything hasty to Eddie, though it's very difficult since Eddie doesn't tend to notice people being annoyed or irritated by him and it's hard to hit anyone radiating indiscriminate peace and love at you.

It sounds to me as though Rosetta deserves a good time, and I only hope Eddie is it.

Eddie's van still hadn't returned by the time I went down to the pub, so perhaps he is staying up at the Hall? And what does Dante think about that?

The vicar and Jason had evidently been having a boys-together session going by the empty glasses in front of them, but Charles was just getting up to go when I got there.

After reminding me once more about the impending slave auction and trying a last, unavailing attempt to get Jason to put himself up for bidding too, he went off to his t'ai chi class. He says when he has mastered the art, he will run classes on the vicarage lawn until the whole village stops and does them every morning like the Chinese peasants.

I cannot see it myself but I'm willing to give it a go, and so is Mrs Bridges.

Before he left, I asked if he would let me hold his hand for a minute.

'Any time, my dear!' he agreed enthusiastically. 'Any particular reason? Not that I'm complaining, mind.'

'You're a sort of control – something to judge other men against,' I told him, and he looked baffled but pleased.

His mind was the equivalent of a sunny cloudless day, what guilt there was being the very faintest tinge of the 'perhaps two helpings of apple pie and custard shows ungodly greed?' kind.

After he'd gone, beaming, Jason held his hand out to me, too. 'Go on – you've been dying to do your mind-reading bit on me, ever since Tanya vanished.'

'You know I don't read minds,' I protested weakly, because he was quite right: I had. 'Only emotions. Do you mind if I take a quick peek into your subconscious?'

'Not really. Not if I can hold your hand and leer at you while you do it. I don't see why the vicar should have all the fun.'

Jason's subconscious was like the bits from several jigsaws jumbled in a bag, one of them a big chunk of guilt. In the ratings chart it was somewhere between Max and Dante.

There was also lust again, but rather warmer in tint, Jason being of an affectionate disposition.

'What's the verdict? Did she go, or was she murdered?'

'She went. You're guilty about it, but you didn't do anything to her.'

'No: except argue, and threaten to throw her out over her affair with Jack Craig, and then not go back that night until too late to ask where she was going.'

'I know, Orla told me.'

'She did?' He shifted uncomfortably. 'What, you mean—?'

'Yes, everything: but I already guessed something had happened between you and Orla, so it wasn't a huge surprise. And we thought your argument that night with Tanya was probably because she'd taken up with Jack Craig again.'

'Yes, it was the last straw: she'd promised me she wouldn't have anything more to do with him, we'd try and start again, for Tom's sake. And then she told me . . . threw back at me . . . ' He looked at me, his brown eyes full of hurt: 'I've never told anyone this, Cassy, because then everyone would think I'd done away with her, but she said Tom wasn't my son.'

'Not yours?' I exclaimed. 'Do you think it's true?'

'Yes, I'm sure it is. I've tried to love the poor brat, God knows, but it's been an uphill struggle. And now he thinks I've done away with his mother. I think he found that easier to believe than that she could abandon him.'

'Poor Tom! So that's why you're always so kind, you're trying to make it up to him?'

'Yes – and he's not entirely bad, you know, Cass. He's just going through a funny age.'

Yeah, one that's lasted for nineteen years.

'So where do you think Tanya went?' I asked curiously. 'And why hasn't she been in touch?'

'That's what worries me the longer time goes on, and she's never sent for her things, or used her credit cards or anything. When I found her gone it was nearly morning, and I thought she might be up at the lodge with Jack Craig, but when I knocked him up he said he hadn't seen her. I hit him anyway,' he added with satisfaction.

'Here's Orla,' I said. 'Can I tell her everything?'

'Yes: I've just told Charles, too. No more secrets.'

Little did he know . . .

When we'd told Orla she made one of her mental quantum leaps and exclaimed impetuously: 'Cass, now you're sure Jason's not a murderer, and Tom's not his son, what's to stop you asking him to father your baby?'

'Nothing, I suppose,' I said startled. 'but I think I'm going right off the idea of m—'

But Jason's face had lit up like he'd just been handed a rather extraordinary present. 'Any time,' he interrupted enthusiastically. 'Have you ditched your old man at last, Cass? Couldn't deliver the goods, I bet. What you need is a good—'

'No, I don't!' I interrupted hastily, and certainly not with Jason, whom I now find I love like a brother, and so do not wish to sleep with in the least. Besides, I'm beginning to think that he and Orla were made for each other if only he could be brought to see it.

'Hi, Eddie!' exclaimed Orla, waving at some new arrivals. 'We don't often see you in here. Are you joining us? And your friend?'

Turning round, I was pleased to see that Eddie'd put on a T-shirt and sandals. With the rents in his jeans you couldn't say he looked respectable, but clean and reasonably decent providing he sat down carefully.

'Hello, Rosetta,' I said, 'Your brother was looking for you earlier. This is Dante's sister,' I added for Orla and Jason's benefit, and introduced them.

Rosetta smiled shyly. 'I've seen Dante. I went to get the key of the lodge for Eddie, so he can use it if he wants to.'

'Yes, I've moved my van up to Kedge Hall,' Eddie explained. 'Parked up behind the lodge. Rosetta wants me to help her do a few things round the house and garden.'

They smiled at each other, hands entwined. It was quite sweet, really. I've never seen Eddie in love before.

'Does Dante know?' I asked.

'Yes, I told him,' Rosetta said innocently. 'He'd asked me to look for a handyman/gardener for the lodge, but I'm sure he didn't expect me to find one so quickly!'

'No, it must have been quite a surprise,' I agreed.

'Are you going to join us?' Jason asked, who'd been sitting there grinning from ear to ear like the Cheshire Cat. 'We're celebrating: I'm going to father Cass's children.'

Even Eddie looked a trifle startled.

'No! I mean, just *maybe*, but if so only by artificial—' I protested, but Jason wasn't listening.

'I'm ready when she is,' he declared, trying to put his arm around me.

'Thank you, Jason, but Orla jumped the gun a bit. I only meant—'

'I know what you meant,' he said, giving me a squeeze that took my breath away and so rendered me speechless and seething in silence.

'I didn't realise! I mean, I must have misunderstood when Dante said that Cass had . . . ' began Rosetta, looking doubtfully from me, wheezing and trying to fend Jason off, to Orla who was smothering laughter, and Eddie looking puzzled.

'It's a joke,' I gasped. 'Look Jason, get off me! I didn't say I would—'

His phone belted out a loud Bond theme, drowning me out. 'Damn, it's my late night customer!' he said, releasing me so he could answer it.

I moved out of his reach, re-inflating my lungs.

'Yes, yes!' he said ungraciously into his phone. 'I'll be there in five minutes.' He snapped it shut and looked irritated: 'I'll have to go and open the shop up, he's a big spender and he's got to leave early tomorrow.'

'I know,' Orla said. 'He's going to stay overnight with me. I'd better go home soon so I can let him in, I suppose, but he'll be ages in your shop: he always is.'

Jason got up, kissed the top of my head and said with a big grin: 'Tomorrow?'

About to disabuse his mind of any hopes he might have, it suddenly occurred to me that although I didn't want quite the personal service he had in mind, there was no reason why I shouldn't still utilise him if I did decide that I wanted to go ahead with late motherhood. Once he'd got over the disappointment, of course. I didn't need to totally close the door on the idea just yet . . .

'I'll *talk* to you tomorrow, anyway,' I agreed cautiously.

Rosetta and Eddie drifted off to a corner where they sat in an entwined heap, like puppies. They seemed to be sharing one orange juice and a packet of crisps.

Orla got the giggles as soon as we were alone.

'Cass, your face! I'm sorry I came out with it like that, without thinking, but you really don't have to sleep with Jason if you don't want to, you know!'

'I know, and there's no reason why he shouldn't father my baby, now we know he isn't Tom's father. Poor Tom!'

'Of course Jason might well only agree to help if you let him in on the act,' Orla pointed out. 'I don't somehow think the idea of donating is going to go down well – and I think he will want to be involved with the pregnancy and the baby.'

'If there is one, because I've been uncertain about the whole idea lately. And you are right – if it worked and I got pregnant it wouldn't be fair to Jason, because he would want more than I could give him.' I sighed. 'No, it isn't going to work, is it? I'll have to tell him tomorrow that I've changed my mind and I'm not going to try and get pregnant at all.'

'Aren't you? Is that your last word on the subject?'

'Oh, I don't know. No. I mean, who with?'

'I think we both *know* who with,' Orla said significantly.

'No, we don't,' I snapped. 'It'll have to be the Saluki hound after all.'

'Much better idea,' she approved.

Chapter 15: Rescue Me

... the one ewe lamb must be saved from the foul beast. Righteousness will prevail. The Spawn of Satan shall not draw her in, though I walk in the fiery pit to save her ...

This rant was awaiting me on the answering machine when I got home last night, and I fear Pa has finally gone right over the edge.

While it is clear that Jane is the ewe lamb, am I the foul beast or the Spawn of Satan, or both? And far from being a fiery pit my cottage is on the dank side, if anything.

He can't possibly intend coming here, can he?

Perhaps he means to get Jane up there and lock *her* in the cupboard? I'd quite like that.

After that I couldn't settle down to work because my mind was going round in circles, wondering what to do about Jason. I mean, he's the only man willing (apart from a reluctant and faraway Max) to offer to father my offspring, it's just that I can't stomach the relationship angle that he clearly expects to go with it.

Maybe I could persuade him just to do the donor thing? But even then he'd still haunt me at every turn, wanting to get involved with the child-rearing.

Now the awful spectre of Tom has been removed from the equation, Jason might make quite nice babies, though . . .

But then there's Orla to consider: I think she really cares about him, but she's not going to get anywhere while he has this misguided crush on my slightly kinky Vampirella persona; and even though she says she wouldn't mind Jason fathering my child, I'm quite sure it would do something fundamentally bad to our friendship.

I don't have so many close friends I can afford to lose any.

Why do I feel this need to have children – a child – at all? What do I want one *for*? The answer, plainly, is nothing: the urge to procreate goes much, much deeper than that. But other women deal with it: they get cats, dogs, or look after other people's children.

It was all very confusing, so after a while I pulled on my boots and cloak and walked up to the graveyard, striking it lucky: it was one of those rare nights with the full Hammer Horror mist-rising-from-the-tombs effect.

I took it as a good omen right up to the minute when I stepped back to admire a particularly spooky vista, tripped over a half-hidden tombstone, and fell backwards into an all-too-familiar embrace.

. . . arms closed about her, caged her in a strong embrace. She felt enveloped in inky blackness as though a dark cloud had forever blotted out the sun and she would never know its warmth again, only the raging fires of eternity . . .

I didn't even have to see him: one touch and I knew who it was.

'You just can't keep out of my arms, can you?' Dante said unfairly, setting me back on my feet and turning me round to face him. The darkly shadowed hollow cheekbones and deep-set eyes were *sensational* by moonlight, but his mouth, unfortunately, looked like it had been firmly folded by an anally retentive origami expert.

'What are *you* doing here?' I demanded angrily, for I rather look on the graveyard at night as my own special place, for refuge, inspiration or comfort.

'I'd heard about the special effects, and came to see for myself.' He looked around, still retaining a seemingly casual hold on me. 'Pity we can't lay it on when we want it, isn't it?'

'No, I like the surprise. How did *you* know it would be like this tonight?'

'The vicar told me. He told me about lots of other interesting things, too, like this slave auction coming up next week,' he added casually, if anything can sound casual when delivered in that curiously sexy, running-water-over-gravel voice.

'Oh, *that's* not very interesting,' I assured him. 'Not worth your while bothering to come, even.'

'Oh, I don't know: I think it has distinct possibilities.' He

155

looked me over, burqa'd head to heels in purple velvet, and amended that: 'Hidden possibilities. Tell me, Cass, how does your lover feel about you selling yourself to the highest bidder, when any man could buy your services for a day?'

He managed to make an innocent charity event sound absolutely indecent.

'You must know from the vicar that it's a *perfectly* respectable affair,' I said coldly. 'And leave my lover out of this! What did you mean, pretending you thought Max was my father the other night?'

He shrugged, but at least he let me go and put his hands in his jacket pockets instead, which was a relief. I took a cautious step back.

'It was an impulse of the moment: you looked miserable, he was looking pompous. You hadn't told him about our little fling, by any chance? Or is sleeping with strange men something you do so often when he's not around it's hardly worth mentioning?'

For a moment I couldn't seem to breathe: but then something terribly Southern Belle swept over me like a savanna fire and I dealt him the most resounding slap on the cheek with the flat of my hand. You could practically hear the theme tune to *Gone With The Wind* building up to a crescendo in the background.

Oh Miz Scarlett, what *have* you gone and done?

The slap echoed like the crack of doom around the graveyard, but fortunately none of the residents took it as a wake-up call.

I stared up at him, horrified and suddenly afraid, because according to all the films I've ever seen he should either chastise me in a humiliating and totally unforgivable manner or drag me into his arms and kiss me senseless. Or one followed by the other.

Dante can't have seen the same films, because he just stood there looking naturally grim and said levelly: 'So I'll take that as a resounding no, then, shall I?'

'You can take it any way you like!' I snapped, although I noticed some innate survival instinct had caused me to put more space between us.

He shrugged. 'You can't blame me for wondering. Rosetta tells me you're so desperate to get pregnant you're even thinking about using your friend Jason to father it, so I thought perhaps your lover was past it and you might be distributing your favours generously in the hopes one of us might do the trick for you?'

'No he isn't – I'm not – I didn't!' I cried hotly and incoherently. 'That was all a mistake, and I'm certainly not going to sleep with Jason even if – and Max isn't—'

I stopped, and glared at him: 'Why am I even trying to explain things to you? It's got absolutely nothing to do with you!'

'It is if that was why you wanted *me*? Don't think I'm complaining, only if you are using me for your own ends I'd like to know about it.'

He was angry: coldly and furiously angry, I could see that now. I took another step or two back and nearly fell over a gravestone.

'No, I wasn't! I didn't want you, it was just the drink and the nightmare—'

'If it didn't work, perhaps you'd like me to try again? Only you might like to remember my track record: a wife left to cope with pregnancy on her own, dead by the time I got back.'

'I wouldn't touch you again if you were the last—' I began, then broke off as what he'd just said sank in and I realised at last that he was far, far angrier with himself than with me. I stared at what I could see of his hawk profile, now half-turned away.

'But it wasn't *your* fault that you got kidnapped, was it?' I said. 'And you weren't there when she died, so that isn't your fault either.'

'She hated being left alone when I was off on assignments, and she hated being pregnant: she only did it because she thought it would keep me at home.'

'But it didn't, did it?' I said. 'That was your job, surely she knew that?'

'I suppose I expected my life to go on pretty much the same after I was married as before, but I might have found work nearer home once there was a baby on the way, if I hadn't found out she'd had an affair last time I was away. I told her I needed time to think about things and left her alone and pregnant in London.'

'Then you got taken hostage and couldn't get back,' I prompted, since he seemed to have come to a brooding halt.

'Emma was complaining of headaches when I left, and it turns out she had an aneurysm, a weak blood vessel in her brain that ruptured. They couldn't save her, but if I'd been home and made her see a doctor perhaps something might have been done. Her mother was there, and all she did was take her to some faith healer!'

157

'But you couldn't have guessed what would happen when you left, and perhaps she couldn't have been saved anyway?'

'Who knows?' he sighed. 'After Paul was killed I thought things couldn't get any worse, and then I was told Emma and the baby had died months before.'

'Well, I still don't see why you need to feel guilty about any of it, and it's really nothing to do with me, after all: I mean, it's not like you've just confessed to galloping syphilis, is it?'

'No,' he said gravely. 'I don't have anything like that.'

'And I don't know why you're telling me anyway, because I wouldn't have touched you with a barge pole the other night if you hadn't made me hideously drunk with that brandy, let alone want you to father my child! Getting pregnant was the last thing on my mind.'

'Was it? How about your subconscious? What's the scenario in there, Cass? Is the biological clock ticking, your lover won't or can't father a child, and no one else is in the offing except poor old Jason?'

Summed it up in a nutshell, the bastard.

'I love Jason like a brother,' I said with dignity. 'I might desperately want a baby, but logically I don't need one, it's just Nature trying to con me into reproduction. I'm going to fight the urge and get a nice dog instead.'

He laughed at me, and I so nearly hit him again that I had to step right away out of arm's reach.

'Haven't you got a faithful old dog already? One called Max?'

'I've given him up,' I said, like he was a bad habit. (Which, come to think of it, he was.) 'His wife has started to come between us.'

'I thought his wife was dead?'

'She is, and now she's an insuperable obstacle.'

'You are the weirdest woman I've ever met,' he stated, gazing at me with knit brows. 'Poor Jason's trying to bite off more than he can chew.'

'I wish you wouldn't keep calling him "poor Jason" in that pitying way! He's one of my oldest friends and I'm very fond of him. He just has this little mental kink about me in my vampire get-up which has temporarily clouded his judgment.'

'I'm not surprised,' he said enigmatically, and I stared at him doubtfully before deciding I didn't want an explanation.

'So, what *was* all that about with me the other night?"

'Comfort, I think, and brandy. Brandy seems to be a family weakness. But you're quite safe, because I'm not going to do it again.'

'No?'

'No. Though at least one good thing came out of that night: I knew Kedge Hall would provide the inspiration I needed to add an extra dimension to my new book, and it did!'

'I just read one of your books, and I don't believe anything good comes into it. How did Kedge Hall inspire you?' he demanded suspiciously.

'Oh – just as a bit of mock-Gothic background,' I said with sudden vagueness, thinking that perhaps he wouldn't like to know that I'd described the house pretty closely, besides inventing a permanent vampire family patriarch of dubious tastes and habits.

Could he sue me for that, when the book comes out?

Unfortunately he seemed to be thinking along similar lines. 'If you are using my house as a background don't you think you owe me something?' he said, surprising me. 'If you still refuse to help us out with the haunting, perhaps you'd like to come up to the Hall and give me some advice, writer to writer, instead?'

'Advice?'

'I've got the notes for the book, I've got an advance to write it, now I have to deliver the goods and I don't know how to put it together. I'm a novice, you're a professional. You used me the other night for whatever reasons of your own, and now you're using my home: so is an afternoon of your time too much to ask in return?'

Got you there, Cass.

'I didn't use . . . ' I began to protest, and then I thought: maybe I did?

'Just a couple of hours to help you with your book?' I asked suspiciously.

'That's all. I don't know any other authors or I wouldn't ask you. Just how to set it out, that sort of thing. I don't really need a Ghost Writer, just a ghost writer.'

'Was that a joke?' I peered at him, but the moon was a little obscured and it was hard to tell. Mind you, with that face it would be hard to tell anyway.

'I suppose I could,' I conceded reluctantly, since I have this hideous, innate sense of fair play, which is unfortunate since life doesn't.

'And maybe while you're at the Hall you can tell that mad brother of yours to keep his clothes on, keep out of my woods, and keep away from my sister!' he said acerbically.

'I think it's love,' I said idiotically. 'It's such a pleasure to see two people so happy!'

'Love? He's not even inhabiting the same space-time continuum half the bloody time! How can she have a relationship with someone like that?'

'Why don't you ask her, not me?' I snapped, and walked away, leaving him there, although the effect of my sudden departure was rather ruined by my having to stop and disentangle my cloak from an encroaching briar.

As I was passing under Mrs Bridge's window something netlike dropped silently over my head. It was a very Gladiator moment until I heard her giggle like a girl and whisper conspiratorially 'Heaven's cobwebs!' before slamming down the sash.

You know, it's very comforting to have someone even stranger than me living next door. She's worth her weight in three-ply.

I poured a glass of red wine and sat down at my desk to work, but instead ended up turning over all the things Dante had said, especially the ones about using him as some kind of stud, and the more I thought the madder I got.

Eventually I phoned Jason (waking him up), and told him bluntly that I would have his baby, although declining his sleepy but enthusiastic offer to start right away.

Then I spent a sleepless couple of hours before phoning him again at dawn when sanity had returned, together with the hellish sound of Birdsong's screaming, to tell him I couldn't possibly after all.

I think the inside of my telephone has melted.

I can't blame him for being mad, but I was quite glad not to have to face him in one of his rages because he can be quite awesome, although he usually simmers down pretty quickly.

After that I'd have tried to catch a couple of hours sleep if the great She-beast herself didn't phone me up at last, sounding fraught and breathless, which is unusual for Jane.

'Cass? Is that you? You've got to help me!'

160

'I thought I already was, Jane: Pa and Gerald have both been on the phone wanting you, and neither were pleased that you wouldn't come and speak to them. Pa's flipped and sent you a biblical rant, and Gerald's written you an absolutely pathetic letter.'

'You read it?' she demanded, sounding more like her old self.

'Gerald sent all your mail on and I read the lot,' I said. 'You read all mine when you were here, after all: fair's fair.'

'Well, never mind that now!' she said. 'Listen, Cass, you've got to help me get out of here! It's dreadful: Clint lives in a big *tent*.'

'I'm told yurts are very comfortable, Jane. And weren't you after a bit of the old back-to-nature?'

'Not this natural! There's a whole field of these yurts, and they live there like a lot of gypsies. And there's nowhere to recharge my phone, and no proper toilet, and everything's muddy. Now my Jimmy Choo's have got dung on them – and Clint's turned so jealous he won't let me out of his sight!' She paused, breathless.

It sounded to me like the excremental Choo's were the last straw.

'So he's there now?' I asked.

'No, of course not! I'm at the pub – and I had to borrow the landlord's own phone, because Clint's hidden my bag with all my money and my credit cards, and I don't know how to get away!'

She sounded desperate, but I expect the landlord was eating out of her hand.

'So where is Clint at the moment?'

'He's gone to Penzance to sell some paintings. His friend Baz's supposed to be keeping me company until he gets back, but he's taken something,' she said primly, 'and he didn't even blink when I got up and left.'

'Get on the train and come here then, while the going's good.'

'Without money? And my suitcase, my clothes, and—'

'Gerald – and possibly Pa, if the spirit moves him – are liable to come to Westery in person at any minute, and insist you talk to them,' I told her, which had the effect of a dash of icy water to the face.

'Oh God, what if they come before I get back? And what if Clint comes back and finds me here? I'll never get away, and—'

'You can go to London. One of your letters was from George. He's got to go abroad next week, and he wants you to keep Phily out of trouble until her case comes up. What, by the way, is Phily's old trouble?'

161

'Shoplifting, only she can't help it. It's kleptomania.'

'Of course, the nobility do *not* shoplift.'

'George wanted me to go down?'

I could practically hear her weasely little brain whirring.

'Yes – and if I do that, he will have to promise to say I've been there all week. And London's closer than you are, especially if I catch the Express. But what do I do for money?'

'Put the landlord on,' I said resignedly, and when she did I gave him my bank card details and he advanced enough to my pathetic sister to get her to London, including a taxi to the station.

'I want it back the minute you get your stuff,' I warned. 'Leave a message with the landlord for Clint, telling him to forward your belongings to London, or you'll set the police on his doped-up friends.'

'Thank you, Cass,' she said, the unaccustomed words coming with creaking reluctance. But she said them.

'Get moving before he comes back,' I advised her. 'I'll tell George to expect you.'

. . . *at last he slept, coffined in marble, and she took the key from its hiding place and turned it slowly and carefully in the huge lock.*

It grated slightly, and behind her in the darkness he stirred and began to wake as she frantically turned the handle and pulled open the heavy door.

She felt rather than heard him spring out and reach for her, but by then the first rays of sunshine barred the way between them.

She was free – until darkness fell once more.

Chapter 16: The Definitive Delilah

Popular Horror Writer Satan's Mouthpiece! says Bishop ...
Daily Mail

I walked up to the Hall in the afternoon, though I'm not sure what drove me. Rampant curiosity? Over-active conscience? Or maybe the prospect of another invigorating little exchange of opinions, for there is no denying that my encounters with Dante do wonders for the adrenalin.

And had he really been offering his services at one point last night, or had I totally misread what he was saying?

Not that it matters now my mind is made up . . . almost. On my way home I would stop by Emlyn's and buy a copy of *Best Dog* magazine and enough pizzas to mean I don't have to go to the pub and face an angry Jason for at least a couple of days.

Call me a coward.

Coward.

A white van marked 'Gardeners To Go' was parked halfway up the drive and a team of men were certainly going hard at weeding the drive and tidying the nearer aspects of the grounds, which seemed to have run riot in the months since Miss Kedge died.

Gardening can't be terribly exciting because they all stopped and watched me walk past, so I gave them a cheery wave and called hello, then crunched on up the gravel to the front door.

No tradesman's entrance for me this time.

Eddie answered the doorbell, holding a large screwdriver. His

163

flaxen dreadlocks were held back by a red spotted scarf and he wore bib and brace overalls over, apparently, nothing.

He didn't seem at all surprised to see me, just smiled as I walked past him and then went back to whatever it was he was fixing.

The Hall looked much more welcoming by daylight. Rosetta and two vaguely familiar local women were polishing the furniture with something that smelled beeswaxy, and she looked glad to stop for a minute and talk.

'Hi, Rosetta, I've come to see Dante. About his book,' I added airily, in case she suspected this might be the start of something big.

'He's expecting you – he's in his study in the west wing. I'll show you, shall I?'

With a lingering look over her shoulder at Eddie, who was halfway up a ladder tinkering with something, she led the way through a side door, along a passage that went up and down and up again and round and . . . well, you get the idea. It started to feel like one of those Escher pictures of endless staircases.

'It's easier to get into from upstairs,' Rosetta said. 'Just one passage and a door. Dante's been looking at the house plans, and he says there was an easier way in from downstairs, too, but it's been blocked off for some reason.'

'Yes, I know.'

. . . there was only one door to the west wing, locked and barred, the keys held by the heir alone, generation after generation. But the door kept people out, not in, for the creature that dwelt there knew no bars to his freedom other than that which came with every dawn . . .

Rosetta gave me a strange look, but didn't question my omniscience, which was just as well since this was just another example of my two overlapping realities.

We finished up in a big bright room with newly whitewashed walls above dark panelling, and a diamond-paned window looking out over what was once the park.

It was set out like a cross between a study and a sitting room, with an individual stamp that told me that Dante had made it like this, plundering the house for furniture to suit his needs.

There was a big old trestle table along one wall heaped with papers, photographs, and a rather elderly looking laptop computer.

At the window end of the room were some ancient and comfortable-looking leather armchairs, one occupied by a far from ancient but comfortable-looking Dante.

He got up when we came in and said: 'Ah, there you are,' as though he was expecting me and I was running late, though I'm sure I didn't *promise* to turn up today – or, indeed, any other day.

Looking serious (as is his wont), he helped me out of my long black, rather military velvet coat with its frogging and silver buttons, then glanced down at my moccasin boots.

The corner of his mouth twitched, which I am slowly coming to realise is a sign of secret amusement rather than a nervous tic, though I do not see what is funny about my boots. I mean, wearing four-inch stiletto heels like Orla is funny-peculiar, not my practical footwear.

Colour-wise we were pretty well matched, since he was wearing a black shirt (open at the neck, but swash most definitely buckled) and ancient-looking black leather trousers, well moulded around his finer assets. (He has fine assets.)

How come he didn't squeak when he got off the leather chair?

While he gravely folded my coat over a chairback and I had interesting thoughts about Leather Food, Rosetta said reproachfully: 'Oh Dante, you haven't eaten any of those lovely sandwiches I made for you!'

'I was waiting for Cass – we'll share them,' he said guiltily.

Clearly the urge to fatten Dante up is endemic in the female of the species. I was just surprised she hadn't also felt the urge to sneak in while he slept and do a definitive Delilah to that shaggy mane with the kitchen scissors, because I certainly wanted to.

Rosetta cast us a dubious look before leaving that plainly said: 'Now, don't argue, children!'

But I for one had no intention of arguing, especially after I stopped thinking about various kinds of hides and really started to take in what Dante had begun to tell me about his book.

It was evident that he really *did* need my advice, but wasn't going to find it easy to talk about what had happened to him.

'I know all about the hostage thing and how your wife died,' I told him helpfully. 'Orla got it all off the internet – all the newspaper articles and stuff.'

'Right,' he said, rather bitterly. 'Well, that's the part that my publishers are particularly interested in, obviously, but I want the book to be more than just another hostage story. I want it to be a celebration of Paul – my friend's – life, too. And I've got all this stuff I've written down, and I don't know where to go from here.'

He ran his hands though his black hair, which didn't do much for it since it sprang back into dishevelled waves as soon as it was released. 'I don't want to go over it all again – reliving it – but I think that somehow I'll feel better when I've done it.'

Clearly writing it was a painful pilgrimage into a past that he would like to forget but could not; and he might achieve some kind of catharsis through setting it all down. And the more he talked about his experiences, the more I felt that he was telling me something he hadn't been able to share with anyone else, opening himself up to me in a way that made him appealingly vulnerable.

'I did write an article about it soon after I was released, but I wasn't really very fit, mentally or physically. And coming home and dealing with the loss of Emma, and having to go through those seances and stuff her mother insisted on – well, it was pretty well the last straw.'

'I should think it was!' I agreed.

'And then I really needed to go and see Paul's widow, who'd gone back to her family in Alaska, although I'd already passed on all the messages Paul had sent in case I made it and he didn't . . . But I felt guilty somehow that I'd survived and he hadn't, and I just spent months travelling around the States, making notes for the book, and putting the trip off.'

'You were travelling in America for nearly a year, weren't you?'

'Yes, thinking about things, sleeping in anonymous motel rooms, slowly going north towards Alaska. Somehow I was afraid to face Paul's widow, Kathy. But then finally I drove up through Canada to Prince Rupert, and took a seaplane to Ketchican, where she lives.'

'And found her?' I prompted, since he seemed to have gone silent on me.

'Yes, I found her, and she was pleased about the book. She was also desperate to talk about Paul, and I'd made her wait for nearly a year before I went there, thinking she'd blame me for surviving. How selfish is that?'

'I don't think you came out of the hostage thing entirely sane and sensible, Dante,' I pointed out. 'There's no point in flagellating yourself for not being Superman.'

I was turning over the photographs on the table, some of a slight, fair man, his pretty wife and two small daughters.

'Paul?'

'Yes, Paul and his family,' Dante said. 'There are more there of him as a boy, and some of his better known photographs . . . all sorts of stuff Kathy's loaned me.'

'And is all this the rough draft of the book?' I asked, pointing to the heap of American Five Star notebooks on the trestle table.

'Yes, but I just started to put everything I remembered down as it came back to mind, so it's all out of sequence, and sometimes something I saw while I was travelling would spark off a recollection . . . I put the date and where I was every time I started writing, so at the moment it's more a series of travel diaries with memories, than a biography.'

He looked at the table and shrugged despairingly: 'See what I mean about not knowing where to start? How do I even begin to get the story out in chronological order?'

'Can I look at one or two of the notebooks to get an idea of how it's written?' I asked cautiously. 'Perhaps just the first?'

'I suppose so,' he agreed in his usual gracious way. 'I'll make coffee – I've got a coffee-maker and stuff set up through there,' he nodded to a door. 'How do you like it?'

'Hot, strong, no milk,' I said, perching on the edge of the table and starting to read the jagged black script that told of a journey to hell . . . and, hopefully, back.

Eventually I looked up and noticed that he'd returned, and was sitting in one of the armchairs with the coffee before him and a patient expression. My leg had gone dead when I got down off the table, so I must have been reading for quite some time.

Putting the notebook carefully back in its place on the table I hobbled over and fetched the plate of sandwiches Rosetta had made.

'Eat!' I said, putting them down in front of him, and feeling a need to feed one kind of hunger at least.

'Don't *you* start trying to mother me too!' he snapped.

'I'm not. I'm hungry, but I'm not going to tell Rosetta I wolfed all the sandwiches down while you sat there starving,' I said, and picked one up. They were good. So was the coffee, although it could have been hotter.

After a couple of minutes Dante picked a sandwich up too, though he seems to eat like he's lost the habit.

'So,' he said, after some silent chewing, 'can I turn all that into a book? Or should I start again?'

'You don't need to turn it into a book,' I told him. 'It already is one. Each notebook is dated, and headed with the place you wrote it from, and these will be your chapters. It's sort of a framework, and you can rove back and forwards in time and memories within that structure. I think it'll work, because it's different. The journal-cum-memoir of a trip across America, slowly heading for Alaska. In fact,' I added enthusiastically, 'I think you ought to call it *Travelling To Alaska*!'

'You do? I thought you were going to say it was useless, and I'd have to get someone to write it for me!'

'No, all you need to do is type it up in the date order of the journals, finishing with Alaska. Then it will just need tidying and checking through. You can type, can't you?'

'Of course – and pretty fast, too.' He sat back. 'But do you really think the publishers will go for it? Won't they think it's a bit rambling and out of sequence?'

'From the bits I've read it seems to be fairly straightforwardly told, only relating to places you were at on your journey, and with occasional flashback memories to happier times. I think they'll love it because it's just that bit different. You have a way with words.'

'I should hope so – I *was* a foreign corespondent, don't forget.'

'OK, then double space, indent your paragraphs, and get on with it,' I said helpfully.

We'd finished the sandwiches, I noticed, and I only hoped I hadn't eaten most of them myself.

Dante's sombre expression seemed to have lightened a bit, so perhaps hunger makes him bad-tempered? Low blood sugar or something. Why doesn't he eat more? Does he have to carry on starving, just because he made it out and Paul didn't?

'You're going to feel so much better when you've written the book,' I assured him. 'I certainly did when I started exorcising *my* demons through my novels, and you're doing the same, only in a different genre.'

His aquamarine eyes lifted to my face and he asked abruptly, 'So what's *your* demon?'

'Me? Oh, I *am* the demon – Satan's Spawn, according to my father,' I said lightly. 'My parents, my four brothers and even Jane are all blond, medium-sized and blue-eyed like a lot of Dutch dolls. I take after a gypsy great-grandmother, hence the mind-reading stuff though I've never worked out quite why that should make me inherently evil.'

'It doesn't,' he said. 'Are you serious?'

I didn't see why he should think he had a total monopoly on suffering just because he'd taken it to extremes, so I told him about my strange childhood, and being Seed of the Devil, and my time-out with the ghosts in the cupboard. 'Which is why I have the recurring nightmare about trying to get away from a cupboard, I suppose,' I added.

He looked slightly stunned. 'It's not surprising . . . I had no idea! But you're free now, aren't you? You've got away from them?'

'I don't see Ma and Pa any more, not since I took up with Max, which was the final, unforgivable offence. Jane's done worse, but they never found out about that. And the boys, too – but somehow their sins are forgivable and mine aren't. But Pa often phones me to remind me I'll burn in hell, and stuff like that. Which I probably will, because Max's poor wife was an invalid and our affair put her through torments of jealousy, although I didn't really under-stand that until recently, when I got a letter she left to be sent on to me after she died. I let myself believe it was all OK, because I wanted it to be: so you see, I'm guilty about that, too. Ma never speaks to me, but she never liked me as much as any of the others anyway. I couldn't understand it, but Charles says sometimes that just happens in families, and it isn't my fault.'

'Your parents sound delightful!'

'Well, Ma just mostly ignored me, and even Pa wasn't too bad until he started drinking more and more on the quiet. He let his brother adopt one of the boys – George – in return for a lot of money, and he started a sort of self-sufficient commune-cum-church up in Scotland. He's a Charismatic Preacher,' I added.

'And I thought my mother-in-law was bad enough, hounding and blaming me for Emma's death!'

'Does she still do that? But that's so unfair!'

He shrugged. 'Life's unfair – and death's even more so.'

'Yes . . . do you have nightmares, too, Dante?' I asked him. 'Mine get worse and worse. I was nearly in the cupboard the other night when you woke me up and—'

Then I remembered the consequences and did the fluctuating hot and cold thing again. I don't think my thermostat is up to dealing with Dante in near proximity.

'Out of the frying pan into the fire?' he said with that quirk of the lips. 'I'm sorry – you were vulnerable, and I didn't realise it.'

Sudden tears came to my eyes. 'It doesn't matter: it was just the brandy really – I'm not used to it. We can forget it, can't we?'

'No, I don't think we can do that, but we could start again? Get to know each other? Especially if you can remove your idiotic brother from my house and my sister's life!' he added acidly, sounding suddenly much more like himself.

'He isn't idiotic, and he's probably being a lot of help. If you mean to take in the first visitors at Easter, you hardly have more than a few days left.'

'No, and we've already got four bookings . . . maybe five. I've left it to Rosetta. It's her affair, and she doesn't seem to need my help now she's got your brother.'

'He's very practical really. And you needn't worry about him, because he never stays in one place long before he gets restless.'

'So Rosetta's going to have a broken heart as well?'

'You can't have it both ways,' I pointed out. 'Do you want him to go or stay? Not that it matters, because he'll do exactly what he wants.'

'I've noticed.'

'Did Jason have your miniatures?' I asked inconsequentially.

'Yes, I'm going to put them up in here.' He looked thoughtfully at me. 'And now that I've bared my soul in writing to you, are you at all likely to reciprocate and let me read the manuscript of your next epic, the one featuring the family pile?'

'That fair play thing again,' I said resignedly. 'It's nearly finished . . . I suppose I could run you off a copy before I send it in.'

'Is it like your others?'

'I don't know – tell me when you've read it.' Preferably when I'm out of the country.

The door opened and Eddie wandered in. 'Hi, Cass. It's dark in here, isn't it?'

Funny I hadn't noticed that while we were talking, but it was now pretty gloomy.

'I'm going down to the cottage to get that screwdriver I left behind. Rosetta said you might want a lift home?'

'There is a sign on the door to the west wing, saying "Private, Keep Out",' Dante observed.

'Yes, I put it there,' Eddie said, beaming at Dante like he was his dearest friend. 'Coming, Cass?'

'OK,' I agreed, because I was feeling a bit limp. 'If you don't mind stopping off at Emlyn's on the way? And I'll let you have a copy of the manuscript when it's finished, Dante.'

'I can hardly wait.'

I checked his face for sarcasm, but it was back to inscrutable Prince Of Darkness mode again.

But then, he had just rather bared his soul to me (and mine to him, to some extent) and so we'd probably never want to see each other again, as is the usual case with full and frank confessions.

He immediately proved me wrong.

'If I go down to the pub tonight, will you be there?' he asked.

'No.'

'Oh?' he frowned. 'I thought you went there most nights? What about Jason – will he be there?'

'I have no idea,' I said grandly. 'And I will be at home, working. I am not a creature of totally predictable habits.'

'Jason says you're blowing hot and cold and driving him completely mad,' Eddie intoned helpfully, as though the phrase was a mantra he'd been practising.

'When? When did he say that?' I demanded.

'This morning?' Eddie said vaguely. 'I've been busy – think it was this morning.'

'Just leave it at cold,' Dante suggested.

'I told you,' I said with as much dignity as possible under the circumstances. 'I'm getting a dog.'

'Much safer,' he agreed, and a sudden shadow seemed to cross his face.

'Lurchers are good,' Eddie suggested, leading the way out. The tattoo of Bob Marley on his shoulder blade peeped out at me over the straps of his overalls as he walked.

'No woman, no cry,' I admonished myself, severely.

Chapter 17: A Slave To Love

Dante – known . . . as an eccentric man in the nature of an Old File, who used to put leaves round his head, and sit upon a stool for some unaccountable purpose . . .

Charles Dickens. Little Dorrit

By 'File', read 'cunning man' in Dickens-speak: Dante the Devious. He's laid himself open to me by showing me his notebooks, and I've told him things about Pa that it took me years to get round to telling Orla (and *never* told Max.) Why? How did that come about?

And how can we be so intimate with each other's nightmares, yet still seem to be circling in some ritual fight? And do I have time to puzzle over these and other mysteries when I've got another world, other characters, waiting for me?

Went incommunicado for three days, not answering the door, the phone, or checking the answering machine, while I galloped up the home straight with *Lover, Come Back To Me.*

It was much easier to face the characters in my novel than deal with the complications that seem to be piling up in my life like spillikins: pull one out of the heap and they all fall down.

Some time around midnight on day three I wrote the very last line, then climbed wearily into bed to the accompaniment of Birdsong's raucous cries and fell into a deep and mercifully dreamless sleep.

What seemed like only five minutes later I was jarred awake by the sound of bellowing, and since it went on and on like a lost Minotaur I eventually staggered downstairs to the front door.

'Ahoy there, Sis!' Jamie foghorned through the letterbox. 'Rise and shine! Yo, dude, the sun's hot and the surf's high!'

When I opened the door he toppled forward on to a nice soft mountain of mail, probably because his rather fleshy lips were jammed in the letterbox: a stocky man with rumpled sandy hair, guileless baby-blue eyes like Jane's, and a pink and healthy complexion.

Just as well you can't see his liver.

He hauled himself to his feet as I closed the door, looking at my Chinese slippers in a slightly puzzled way as he did so. 'Could have sworn those were pink, Sis.'

'No, you must have changed your mind, Jamie,' I said kindly. 'Perhaps you remembered that green was my favourite colour?'

'Must have done!' He gave me a bear hug and a smacking kiss on the cheek: Jamie is affectionate but quite exhausting, due to all that terrible heartiness.

'Jane's not here, is she?' he asked anxiously now, swivelling his blue eyes about like a nervous horse. 'Only if she is, I'm off. I can tell the parents I didn't have time to call in.'

'Relax, Jane's not here. She's in London – I think.'

'Oh? Suppose she's with old George and Phily? Good, good – they can't expect me to take her up to Scotland with me if she's not here!'

I left him in the kitchen with a pile of toast and a pot of tea while I went to shower, dress, and get into my right mind: such as it was. I was beyond exhausted, and into dream-like trance, but it was a happy and satisfied weariness.

Meanwhile, Jamie had been amusing himself by listening to my accumulation of phone messages, but had now got to Pa's latest rant. Judging by the tail end I caught it seemed to be even more demented than the last.

After that, Jamie said he was in two minds whether to continue his journey home. 'What exactly has Jane done, Cass? And why is it your fault?'

'Everything's my fault,' I reminded him, rewinding the tape and listening to a couple of loving messages from Max, who was perversely bombarding me with them now that it was too late.

He didn't once mention Kyra the Confessor or even golf.

I deleted him, and then Jane's voice said breathily: 'I'm here at last. I felt a total dog arriving all muddy and in such a mess, but Phily's been an angel and loaned me all her things.'

173

'Let's hope she paid for them, then,' I muttered, and Jamie looked baffled.

'Are you there, Cass my dear? Saturday, 10am on the dot at the King's Arms,' said a new voice. 'All slaves to be there an hour earlier.'

'Crank?' asked Jamie.

'Charles – the vicar. Don't ask.'

Jamie looked like he'd caught me out in something very dubious indeed (maybe a kinky nuns' and vicars' party?) that maybe his little sister shouldn't really be doing, but obediently said nothing.

There was one call where the tape ran for a few minutes and then Jason, sounding furious, said: 'If you won't answer your door, at least answer the bloody phone!' and slammed his receiver down.

This was followed by a couple of plaintive messages from Orla asking if I was all right.

'Though if you're not all right – I mean, if we were wrong about Jason and you're lying in a bloody puddle in the kitchen, you're not going to get up and tell me so, are you?'

The last message, if you could describe it as one, was just my name, spoken questioningly in an instantly familiar voice. Shivers ran up and down my spine, but don't ask me to try and define whether they were pleasurable or not because I listened to him speak my name five times and I still couldn't decide.

'That one *must* have been a crank,' Jamie said. 'You've forgotten to wipe it. I'll do it for you, shall I?'

'No! No – I'll leave it for now, just in case I recognise it.'

'OK. You get a lot of messages, don't you?'

'Only because I've been working so hard for three days trying to finish this book, so I've just let everything accumulate. But it's done now. Let's see what the post has brought.'

The top envelope was inscribed with the word Urgent! in big straggly capitals.

Dear Sis,

Just to warn you – have been shanghaied by Ma and Pa to drive them down to Westery in search of the ewe lamb that was lost, or something. Pa's off his head, and these days I don't think it's just the booze. They seem to mean Jane by the ewe lamb, but she's more like mutton dressed as, if you ask me.

Booked us all into some B&B in the village – Haunted Well? – for a couple of nights. Do you know it?

They don't want to see you, only Jane, Pa says. Thought I'd better tell you. Hide the vampire teeth and the upside-down crosses. I'll slip out when I can and come and see you.

Love, Francis.

I was still looking at this aghast (and I don't mean by the weak black magic humour and terrible handwriting), when Jamie, who'd been riffling through the pile, said:

'Here's a hand-delivered note from that dishy blonde friend of yours, Orla.'

'Couldn't get you on the phone,' he read. 'Have got three Easter B&B bookings by people all called Leigh. Any relation? Are you all right in there? Love, Orla.'

'Wonder who these Leighs are?' he pondered, his brow furrowed.

'Ma, Pa and Francis – this letter's from Francis telling me they're coming to rescue Jane from my evil influence: but she's not here.'

'Better tell them, then,' he advised, which is easier said than done when you haven't phoned them for over twenty years.

He cravenly refused to do it for me, but there was no reply anyway, and Robbie answered when I rang Francis's shop, and said he'd gone away for a few days.

'They must have set out already,' I said despairingly. 'Jamie, you'll have to stay here too, so you can tell them what's happening. They don't want to see me.'

'No fear, not after listening to Pa on that tape! I'm off back down to Portsmouth again. I'll have to fake an illness, or something.'

'Coward,' I said bitterly, but he just grinned and took himself off. Perhaps it's his survival instinct that has kept him out of serious trouble so far, because it certainly isn't due to intelligence.

When he'd gone I drove furtively round to Orla's and informed her just who she was about to entertain in her guesthouse, but cowardly declined to meet her and Jason at the pub that night, even when she said Jason had now simmered down to mild volcanic bubbling.

175

'I can't – I've finished the book, but there are a few bits of tidying-up on it to do. I'll see you at the auction tomorrow.'

'You certainly will! Dante and Jason are shaping up to have a bidding war over you, and the vicar just told me his housekeeper's going to be bidding for your services on behalf of someone who's abroad. I wonder who *that* could be?'

My heart sank. 'Oh no, he wouldn't – would he? He *was* asking all sorts of questions about it though, and – oh, shit!'

'Max, of course,' she agreed.

'Honestly, talk about too much, too late!' I fumed. 'And what do you mean, Jason and Dante are going to have a bidding war over me?'

'Dante's been haunting the pub the last couple of days looking even more morose, as has Jason – waiting for you to turn up, I think – and whatever they say to each other seems to have some sort of unspoken subplot.'

'Subplot?' I stared at her.

'Yes. What could that be, I wonder?' she asked innocently. 'Maybe something like: whoever buys you can father your offspring?'

'Don't be silly,' I said primly. 'I hope neither of them will waste their money when they've read the list of things I'm offering, because sex is definitely not on it.'

'Oh, I think they're both expecting considerably more than a little light dusting,' she said dryly. 'Especially since Dante's under the impression that you've ended your affair with Max.'

'I was going to – I just haven't quite got round to it yet. And I'm sure you're wrong about Jason and Dante,' I added doubtfully. 'Are they friendly?'

'Not very. Jason is angry and hurt, and Dante has gone quiet, thoughtful, and even more withdrawn. But then, he's clearly worried about your brother and Rosetta too, isn't he? They seem to be everywhere together, like Siamese twins.'

'I think Rosetta's old enough to look out for herself,' I said. 'And anyway, I think they're really in love with each other, so it doesn't matter what Dante says about it.'

'It's rather sweet of him to care though, isn't it? Anyway, I've given her lots of advice about her guests, because we're both almost fully booked for Easter visitors. I've got your family coming, and Rosetta's got three members of some ghost-hunting

176

society *and* a medium with her husband, although she says Dante made her write to the medium and tell her that she couldn't hold seances on his premises. She's called Madame Something.'

'It sounds busy, though my parents probably won't stay more than one night when they realise Jane's really not here.' I ferreted about inside my bag and then handed her a note: 'Will you give this to them when they arrive? It explains where she is.'

'What are you doing for Easter? I haven't got any vampire bookings for you for about a week, and then there are two.' She pushed a bit of paper with the dates of my next appearances on across to me. 'I've got one Marilyn Monroe on Saturday.'

'I'm going to do nothing over Easter, except avoid Ma, Pa, Dante and Jason, and wait for everyone to go away or go back to normal. But I've had an idea for a new costume for you, one that I think would make Jason forget I even exist.'

She looked at me expectantly.

'Barbarella!'

'What *me*? I'd explode out of that outfit!' she exclaimed.

'All the better. I think he might just go for it. Most of his tastes are stuck in a time warp, anyway.'

Orla looked thoughtful. 'Well, it would certainly be striking! I might give it a go. Nothing ventured . . . I'll get on to that big fancy dress suppliers in London, I bet they can come up with the goods.'

'Sock it to him!' I urged.

'I'll do my damnedest, and even if it doesn't work on Jason it should be pretty popular as a singing telegram. Only, what would she sing?'

'I'll think about it, and let you know.'

'Tomorrow!' she said firmly. 'You'll have to come out then for the auction. No trying to fake illnesses from pure cowardice.'

I groaned. 'But if I was really ill, Orla, you could phone the vicar for me?'

'No.'

'Call yourself a friend?'

'Even a friend can enjoy watching you squirm tomorrow!' she said unfeelingly. 'May the best – or worst – man win!'

I drove back by the same circuitous route, thus avoiding passing Jason's shop. Later I rang Charles myself and tried my excuse, but he thought I was joking. 'Teasing again, Cass my dear? And you with a huge reserve price on you!'

I felt like the prizewinning heifer at the show.

'I suppose you mean this telephone bidder? I think I can guess who that is!'

'I'm sure you can, and the amount he will go up to is quite stupendous, my dear! I might just try and run it up a bit . . .'

'That's cheating,' I said. 'It *is* Max, isn't it?'

'Confidential, but let's say I was surprised after what you'd told me. But then, if you are at all uneasy about whoever buys your services, I will chaperone you, my dear.'

'Thank you, Charles, but I'm sure I can look after myself. . . except that I really am *not* feeling very well at all: I don't think I'm going to be up to it tomorrow.'

'Always the joker!' he said with cheery imperviousness, and rang off.

Still, at least if Max wins the bidding for my services I won't be called upon to provide them for some months, by which time I will either have told him definitely that it's all over, or left the country. Or both.

Leaving the country before Dante reads my manuscript is something I was thinking of doing anyway, because I really don't think he's going to like having an evil vampire ancestor in his beloved house, so I can economically kill two vultures with one stone.

Then I had an even better idea, one fulfilling my promise literally to the letter: when Eddie popped in briefly later I gave him a ghost-pale copy of the manuscript to take to Dante. He's sure to give up trying to strain his eyes before the end of the first chapter!

Saturday found me at the pub being issued with a numbered sticker, along with all the other slaves-for-the-day.

After my past experiences, this time I'd dressed down for the occasion. Contrary to popular belief I do have more practical garments than ankle-length crinkle velvet or crimped silk, and today I was wearing plain black jeans and a polo neck.

Admittedly, the said polo neck was made of stretch black velvet and clung a little, but at least it did not display a *centimeter* of cleavage.

'You look terribly sexy in that outfit,' Orla said, grinning. 'What on earth are you offering to do this year? Cat burgling?'

178

'You're joking, aren't you?' I asked anxiously. 'I was trying not to look even remotely sexy, because of all that trouble I had that time with old Mr Browne.'

'Cass, you'd look sexy in a sack, in a hollow-eyed, Morticia Addams kind of way. Oh look – there's Dante and Rosetta. And isn't that Eddie?'

'I'm afraid so. He and Rosetta do seem to be inseparable, don't they? You can't see where one ends and the other begins, and Dante doesn't look too pleased.'

This was an understatement: he'd have put the Grimm into anyone's fairytale.

'No, but I don't know why,' Orla said. 'Eddie's so sweet! I know he's a bit off-beat, but—'

'Not so much off-beat as off his head, but in an entirely harmless way.'

'You don't look too worried about who's going to give the winning bid for you,' Orla said curiously.

'Because I'm sure Max is the mysterious absentee bidder, with a wallet impelled into action by sheer dog-in-the-manger jealousy. Charles says he will chaperone me if I want him to.'

'Bit late for that, isn't it?' she said, then nudged me like a schoolgirl as Dante sauntered over, tall, dark and doomy.

She went all pink when he smiled at her, but he didn't smile at me: just eyed me dispassionately from top to toe, like I was a link in the food chain that might just put him on as a snack until something tastier came along.

The *weakest* link.

I squinted down to check I hadn't somehow lost my clothing without realising it, but I still seemed to be covered pretty well from chin to toes. He was definitely in a rage about something, though, unless it was just natural reaction to having bared some of his soul to me, but I hadn't *forced* him to, after all.

'What will you do for me if I buy you?' he asked coolly, but there was a disconcerting glint at the back of his eyes that caused me to blurt unthinkingly:

'Probably not what you think, Dante Chase!'

'You have no idea what I'm thinking – and let's keep it that way. But you have certain talents that interest me, and if I can't have you one way, I'll have you another,' he said and strode off.

179

'What the hell does he mean by that?' I demanded. 'Orla, stop giggling – it isn't funny!'

'Oh yes it is – your face! But don't worry, I'm sure he just means that he's going to enlist you as First Ghoul for the grand opening weekend of Spooky Hall B&B.'

'He can't ask me to do that when I haven't put it on my list. I didn't even put Crypt-ograms on it, in case he tried to get me to do it when I'd already refused.'

'So you did expect him to bid for your services then?'

'No! Yes – oh, I don't know. I was just being cautious. And thank goodness Jason doesn't seem to be here. I knew you were wrong about them bidding against each other.'

'I put the Marilyn Monroe thing on *my* list.'

'You'll probably get old Mr Browne this year then,' I told her maliciously.

'I sincerely hope not! I was hoping for something a bit friskier.'

'They don't come much friskier than Mr Browne,' I assured her. 'I thought I was hired to give his antique shop a jolly good clean and turn out, but if he chased me round that inlaid pedestal table once, he chased me ten times. I was quite exhausted.'

'Who got you last year?'

'Miss Gresham – don't you remember? First she made me give a talk on writing to the WI, then she invited her particular cronies over and tried to make me read their fortunes, and she just didn't understand when I said I couldn't do it to order.'

'I got her the year before last, and she made me wash all of her little Pekes, and Sung bit me!'

I nudged her. 'Shush – the vicar's about to start.'

The line of slaves shuffled their feet, and laughingly formed into numerical order. I was between Emlyn's wife Clara, and Orla, a thorn between two roses.

Come in, number six, your time is up.

Pushing the twin portholes of his glasses up on to the bridge of his insignificant nose, the vicar beamed at the assembled throng like a friendly turtle.

'Welcome to the ninth Westery Annual Slave Auction, everyone. Glad to see a good turn-out for such an excellent cause, and for those newcomers among you who might think a slave auction an unchristian event, let me just explain: the very idea of real slavery is, of course, absolutely abhorrent to me and to all of you,

180

and I'm sure we all stand firm on that. But today, these good people have volunteered their services for a day, and the money they fetch will go to a very good cause: the fund to send a little local girl, Kylie Morgan, to America for life-saving surgery.

'Now, I have a fine assortment of slaves here, willing to do your bidding. The usual rules, ladies and gentlemen: one whole day, regular rest and food breaks, and don't ask them to do anything dangerous or – ahem! – naughty. But do utilise the talents that they have so generously offered. Thank you.'

His audience of the drunk, the sober, the curious, the convivial and the calculating settled into their seats and waited for lot one.

Dante didn't bid for any of the first lots, just sat there darkly brooding with his arms crossed over his manly bosom, while a parade of slaves passed before his eyes.

Eddie and Rosetta seemed to have vanished, but to my dismay Jason suddenly appeared at the back of the room: he must have closed his shop up especially.

Clara drew the short straw and went to Miss Gresham this year, but she is extremely practical so I expect she can cope even if asked to wash the horrid little Pekes. Or perhaps Miss Gresham wants something knitted? Clara's an ace machine knitter.

Then it was my turn, and I thought maybe I might derive some pleasure (if Dante actually did bid for me), in seeing him outdone from afar, even though it was going to make giving Max the final heave-ho just a little bit more difficult than it already was.

'Next we have Miss Cass Leigh,' the Rev. said enticingly. 'Rumoured, like her namesake Cassandra, daughter of Priam and Hecuba, to have the gift of prophecy. Her talents might be a little on the dark side, but she will hardly be burnt as a witch these days!'

There was dutiful laughter: he says much the same thing every year. Glancing across at Dante I was disconcerted to find that although his head was still slightly bent, his bright eyes were fixed speculatively on me.

It was a bit unnerving, actually, but made me think what a great character he would make for a cartoon strip, *strip* being the operative word. Or in one of my books, as the ghost of some ancient warrior perhaps? With his floppy, unkempt black hair, glistening muscled torso, and maybe leather wristbands or an armlet . . .

Wolfric paused, looking about in a puzzled way. 'This is not my world,' he said. 'I was called from my eternal rest by a power stronger than death . . . '

'Twenty pounds? Who will start the bidding at – oh, thank you, Mr Browne. Now, do I hear thirty – forty – fifty . . . '

The bidding paused, not surprisingly, at this point. Then the vicar's housekeeper, her cheeks red with excitement, said, as one making the clinching bid: 'Sixty pounds!'

'Thank you, Mrs Grace! Sixty pounds . . . ' began the vicar happily. 'Six—'

'Seventy!' said Jason's voice from the back of the room. Every head turned to stare.

'A hundred,' said Dante laconically.

All eyes swivelled back, and the Vicar nearly fell off his perch. 'A hundred!'

He swallowed, beamed, and continued: 'A generous offer of one hundred pounds for Miss Cassandra Leigh, from Mr Dante Chase of Kedge Hall. Would . . . er . . . anyone like to raise that?' he asked hopefully.

Mr Browne shook his head, looking disappointed, as did Mrs Grace.

Clearly Max had underestimated the value of my assets – and so had I. Could somebody have doctored my list of skills?

'One hundred and ten,' Jason's voice said firmly, and Dante immediately capped it, catching me staring at him again and holding me in the tractor beam of his gaze.

Oh, beam me up, Scotty!

Had I somehow tacitly agreed with either Dante or Jason to do over a hundred pounds worth of something? And if so, what? When? Where? *Why?*

I mean, I may be sex on legs personified for Mr Browne or even Jason, but Dante can have no need to pay for anything I might give him . . . except the most expensive singing telegram in the world?

Perhaps he just doesn't like to be beaten?

I came back to earth with a start to find a small bidding war had erupted, though Jason retained enough good sense (or lacked sufficient chivalry) to waste his money and dropped out when Dante offered two hundred pounds.

Just as well, because Dante seemed quite prepared to go on for ever.

This was Survival of the Richest.

'Sold to Mr Chase!' the vicar said, crashing his hammer down excitedly.

'And I'll double that, if I can have Miss Leigh's services for two days instead of one,' Dante called clearly.

The room couldn't have gone more silent if he'd announced that he was about to ravish me on the pool table in the bar.

...the castors squeaked beneath their entwined bodies, the green felt a field of ...

No, scrub that one: I'm definitely not writing that sort of novel.

'Two days?' The vicar, taken aback, looked doubtfully at me. 'Er . . . the arrangement is always one day only, Mr Chase. Though of course it's up to Miss Leigh, and it is a good cause? But no, I can't ask anyone to give up more than one day!'

Everyone looked expectantly at me, including the speaking dark eyes of Kylie Morgan from her photograph on the wall.

A life-saving operation: what could I do?

'All right,' I muttered unwillingly and, I fear, ungraciously.

'Done!' the vicar said delightedly.

I certainly felt as if I had been.

'You lucky dog!' Orla whispered.

'Yes,' Clara agreed enthusiastically from my other side. 'I wonder what he wants? From me, he could have any—'

'Shh!' I said desperately. 'It's the last lot – you, Orla!'

Mr Browne, rallying, bought Orla for thirty pounds, and then as the usual finale the vicar sold himself.

And as always his housekeeper bought him for ten pounds. She uses the day to force him into town for all the new items of clothing and household goods he has avoided shopping for in the last year.

'Here do be coming your young master, wench!' Orla said.

'Ho, ho,' I said hollowly. 'Consider your copies of *Poldark* confiscated.'

Dante stopped in front of me unsmiling, and I stared inimically right back. His eyes looked like cold chips of good turquoise, so perhaps he was regretting his deal already.

'I'm not doing anything that isn't on my list!' I told him bluntly.

'I need your skills,' he said ambiguously. 'Easter weekend – the Saturday and Sunday.'

'What about them?'

'Keep them for me. That's when I want you.'

'But I—'

'I understand the arrangement is the whole day?'

'Well yes, but—'

'It just says "whole day" on the sheet. That's midnight to midnight in my book – or in this case, midnight Friday to midnight Sunday. You'd better come up to the Hall on the Friday evening and stay.'

'You can't *possibly* expect—'

'In the lonely west wing with me – and *Vladimir*,' he said meaningfully. 'Remember him? Rosetta's filled the guest rooms, so you have no choice.'

Oh-oh! Now I think about it he does have the hollow, dark-circled eyes of a man who's spent the whole night poring over a pallid manuscript.

'Now look here, Dante!' I began angrily, beginning to think he was going to spend a fun weekend paying me back for endowing his ancestors with bloodsucking propensities (among other things), but was interrupted by the local reporter.

She congratulated Dante on his generosity, and he made full use of the opportunity to talk about the Ghastly Breaks, and said how he hoped I would help him and his sister on their opening week-end, and also looked forward to receiving some handy hints, author to author, on the book he was writing.

I smiled weakly and said I hoped he would think I was worth it, and he said satisfaction was guaranteed, which made him a clear winner in that round.

It was abundantly evident that the reporter thought he was a clear winner in *any* round, so I gave up sparring with him – for now.

He'd made my bed and I was just going to have to lie on it with as good a grace as possible, even if it was in the remote west wing of the most haunted house in Britain, with the most haunted man.

Our photos were taken, though my expression might have been a trifle frozen, since Dante whispered the words: 'Nice outfit, by the way!' into my ear at the crucial moment, his long hair brushing my face.

Immediately after that he left, though there wasn't a lot of bounce went in me by then.

Jason had turned on his heel and gone when he bowed out of the bidding, but Rosetta and Eddie had reappeared and were staring at me, hand in hand. Then Eddie beamed, and I beamed back automatically as one does, and then Rosetta beamed, and it only needed someone to whip out a guitar and start playing 'Oh, Happy Day!' to put the finishing touch to a glorious occasion.

Maybe my face was reflecting some of this, for Orla said: 'Hey, you don't have to do this alone, you know! If you fancy a ménage à trois, Clara and I are both up for it,' and they giggled.

You know, I think the pair of them deserve to be sold down the river?

Chapter 18: Don't You Love Me, Baby?

Tonight's subject on the 'Factions of Fiction' programme is the horror genre: where has it been? Where is it going? Should it get there?

Later Cass Leigh, extreme modern exponent of the art of terror, will be giving us her views, which she says can be summed up as: 'If you don't like it, don't read it. If you don't read it, don't review it.'

First, though, we have an author from the gentler end of the horror spectrum, Melanie Mandrible.

Melanie, you feel that there is an increasing call from readers for the more spiritual, traditional fairy-story horror novel, don't you?

'Yes, because that's the only kind of book she can write, dimwit!' I said, turning the radio off in disgust.

There was no point in listening further, since I could predict practically every word of what Milky Melanie would say, and of course I knew what I said, having recorded it ages ago.

I was feeling at a bit of a loose end, with an aching void inside waiting to be filled afresh once inspiration struck for the next novel. While this feeling only usually lasts a week or two while I am tidying up the final version of the last book and sending it off to my agent, it is *hell* while it does.

I really didn't know what to do with myself.

Of course, what I should have been doing was sorting out the other tricky aspects of my life, like calling Max and telling him it really was all over between us, dumping the Predictova kit, calling some dog-breeders, and possibly leaving the country for a month or so as an interim measure.

I did sort *one* thing out, though: last night I went back to the pub for dinner, having no excuse any more to skulk at home, and made my peace with Jason. He'd stopped being mad with me, and was mad with jealousy over Dante's outbidding him instead, so I told him that Dante'd read the manuscript of my next novel in which I'd portrayed one of his ancestors as an evil monster, and he probably merely intended to put me through the torments of hell over Easter weekend as retribution.

'Yes, but how?' he demanded, frowning horribly, as only Jason can.

'I expect he'll try and make me do some haunting, and perhaps help Rosetta with the guests?' I said doubtfully. 'He mentioned his book, too, so maybe I'll end up typing his notes up or something, as well. Whatever, I expect he will get his money's worth.'

'That's what's worrying me,' Jason said darkly. 'So I'm going to book myself into Kedge Hall for Easter and protect you!'

'I don't think Rosetta has any rooms left, Jason,' I said, startled. 'But thanks for the offer. You are sweet when I've been so horrible to you!'

'Well, we're still friends, aren't we?' he said, leaning over and kissing my cheek.

I smiled slightly mistily at him, since I'd really been an absolute cow. 'Of course we are! And don't worry about me – I can take care of myself.'

And with a bit of luck, Orla might take care of Jason if the Barbarella costume arrives in time! From the sound of it it is pretty sure to grab his attention, and even if it doesn't it's certain to be a popular singing telegram outfit anyway.

When she turned up later she was definitely not pleased to hear Jason still insisting on asking Rosetta if she could squeeze him in at the Hall somewhere, but he wouldn't be moved even when I told him he would be wasting his time and money: I intended doing whatever Dante wanted, and leaving the minute my bondage ended.

Somehow, that didn't seem to reassure him.

Since Max hadn't phoned me after the auction, I was rather hoping he'd called the vicar instead, and so got the bad news from someone else.

Unfortunately not, for on the Sunday he rang me and said gaily: 'Hello, slave!'

'Er . . . Max,' I began, slightly nervously.

'I bet that was a surprise? And good news – I'll be home even sooner than you expected to claim your services, because I'm not finishing out the whole sabbatical year now! So, what's the damage? How much am I paying for the pleasure of a day in your company?'

'I fetched four hundred pounds,' I said shortly, and there was a small silence.

'But my limit was sixty pounds!' Max said disbelievingly. 'You're joking, aren't you? The vicar said no one ever fetched more than twenty pounds, except for one year when you went to some old antique dealer for thirty.'

'Mr Browne. He got Orla this year, and prices have gone up a bit.'

'So come on, darling, joking aside, what's the damage? I know you're special to *me* but—'

'It really *was* four hundred pounds, Max. Bidding was pretty brisk.'

'So who was it?' he demanded. 'Jason?'

'No, Dante Chase. He wants me to help his sister over Easter when she has her first Ghastly Weekend for Ghost-hunters,' I said weakly, not mentioning the possible byline: 'and also be subjected to the torment of the damned for forty-eight hours.'

'Come off it,' he snapped. 'No man would pay that much money unless he's got an ulterior motive, and he made it pretty clear at the pub that he was jealous of me.'

Actually I think it was the other way round, for if Max hadn't become jealous of Dante that night I don't think he would have dreamed up the idea of bidding for me at the auction at all.

'In any case I absolutely forbid it, even if it is only for one day,' he said flatly.

'*Two* days, actually. Dante offered to double the original bid if I would do an extra day, and since it's for a good cause I couldn't very well refuse, could I?'

'Two?' bellowed Max. 'No way is my girlfriend spending two days with another man!'

Max was getting up my nose but it was entirely my own fault: I really should have ended the whole thing before now in a civilised

188

and final manner instead of all this dithering and indecision. And after being his mistress for more than twenty years I find the word 'girlfriend' singularly inappropriate, since I am neither a girl nor feeling particularly friendly.

'Two days and two nights,' I pointed out, fanning the flames a little. 'But you needn't think this is some kind of Indecent Proposal. Dante's a bit piqued because I turned him down flat when he wanted to hire me to do ghost impersonations for his visitors in case it wasn't haunted enough for them.'

I didn't mention that Dante's recently expressed wish to get to know me better had been instantly changed by the power of my fiction into the desire to punish me.

'It's all harmless, Max,' I said, even though I am by no means convinced about that myself. 'And the house will be full of his sister's guests *and* Eddie, who seems to have become resident gardener/handyman, so it's not like I'm spending the weekend alone with another man, is it?'

Not that I feel it's really his business any more what I do.

'You're not spending the weekend with him, alone or not,' he ordained, like *he* was my lord and master instead of Dante.

From feeling that if only I had a good excuse I'd try and wriggle out of my bondage, I now contrarily refused to even consider the idea. 'Now just wait a minute, Max! That's up to me to decide.'

'If you had any real feelings for me you would have turned him down flat at the auction!'

'If you had any real feelings for me you wouldn't have gone to America for a year with Rosemary and left me behind!'

'You hardly seemed pleased to see me when I did come and visit you!'

'Only because all you seemed to be interested in was sex!'

'So what do you think Dante Chase is interested in? Or is that why you've agreed?' he said nastily. 'Or perhaps you always have played the field when I'm away, and all that innocence was a put-on affair?'

'You know very well I haven't!' I said hotly, for apart from my recent brief encounter with Dante there hasn't been much of a field to play, even had infidelity seriously entered my head.

'Then if you really love me you'll tell the vicar you're turning down his offer, and you'd rather accept my bid.'

'You know I can't do that – it's an open auction!'

'I'll make the money up to the vicar,' he said shortly.

'That's not the point. It's done, I'm going to do it, and that's that,' I snapped. 'And while we are on the subject of loving you, there's something I've got to tell—'

He put the phone down on me.

On the Monday I packed up my manuscript (clear dark copy, printed with a new cartridge) and posted it off with a wonderfully purged feeling: colonic irrigation for the soul.

When I got back home Gerald was sitting on the bench outside looking miserably at Jane's car like it had eaten her.

. . . the windows slowly darkened and grew opaque as the car shuddered hungrily . . .

'It spat the bones out, Gerald, but I put them in the boot,' I said, fishing out my door keys.

He turned a drawn and wan face towards me and I could see he hadn't taken in what I'd said, which on reflection is probably a good thing.

'Hello, Cass. I was waiting for you.'

'I thought you'd turn up eventually, Gerald, but it's like I told you on the phone: Jane isn't here.'

'I know she doesn't want to see me, and I don't mean to try and force my way in or anything,' he said pathetically, looking about as violent as a stuffed koala.

'You don't have to force your way in,' I said opening the door invitingly. 'You're quite welcome to. And Jane really isn't here – she's in London, because George has had to go abroad and Phily's being prosecuted for a spot of her old trouble.'

'You mean she's been in London all this time helping poor Phily?' he said, his face clearing as if by magic.

Fortunately he was not expecting an answer to this question.

'Oh that's *so* like Jane, not to want to tell people when she's helping someone in distress!'

'Yes, isn't it?' I said, possibly a little sarcastically.

'And people have been implying the most horrible things,' he said indignantly, 'like she wasn't really staying with you, but was off with this Clint whatever he was called.'

190

'Really? Well, you only have to ask yourself, George: would Jane throw up her happy and comfortable life with you to go and live in a tent in Cornwall? I mean, how likely is that?'

'A tent?' His slightly protuberant eyes widened like a surprised baby's.

'Yes, Clint Atwood lives in a tent in a commune. Now, can you see Jane teetering about a wet boggy field in her stilettos and beige cashmere? Come on!'

I certainly wish *I'd* seen it, though. It would have cancelled out a whole load of debts.

George glowed happily as if he'd had a transfusion of something. Whatever it was, I wished I could have one too, because I've never managed glowing: a pallid pearly glimmer is about the best I can do.

'What a weight off my mind,' he said. Then his face clouded again a little: 'But will she ever forgive me for the horrible things I accused her of – the things I did? She sent me a wonderful letter explaining everything, and I felt totally unworthy of her!'

I'd like to have seen that letter: clearly there's hope for her novel-writing skills yet.

'I'm sure she will, Gerald, she's dying to see you,' I said reassuringly. 'Aren't you on holiday? Why don't you go down for the weekend? George and Phily have got lots of room and I'm sure they won't mind.'

'Do you think I should? Does she really want to see me?'

'Of course she does!' I said firmly, because by now I'm pretty sure Jane is regretting her moment of muddy madness and is longing to sink back into her usual groove.

'Then I will! But first, perhaps I ought to try and explain to your parents? I mean in the heat of the moment—'

'You said more than you should?' I said. 'I know, Gerald, Pa's been burning the wires with messages of eternal damnation ever since, for Jane as well as me, which is a novelty. But you can't get in touch with them, because they're making Francis drive them here to see Jane and there's no way to head them off. They must be staying with some of the godly en route, and Pa doesn't let Francis drive at more than thirty miles an hour even in an emergency, so they probably won't arrive before Friday when they're booked into a local B&B.'

'I'll have to try and talk to them later, then. But at least their journey won't be wasted even if Jane isn't here, because once they see you again they are bound to want to become reconciled, aren't they?'

'I wouldn't hold your breath.'

'You may be surprised, now you've completely finished with Max.'

'But I haven't quite done that, yet, Gerald.'

His eyes widened in surprise. 'Haven't you? I thought you would have after it came out about his affair with that personal trainer, the one who's admitted pushing Rosemary's chair over the edge.'

'Kyra?' I exclaimed. 'So he really was having an affair with her? I suspected as much after he told me about her shoving Rosemary's wheelchair during an argument, and he denied it! But he said the police were satisfied the accident was nothing to do with him?'

'Yes, though he will probably have to go back for the court case since this Kyra said the argument with Rosemary was because she'd found out about their affair. Sorry, Cass – I thought you knew all this,' he aplogised.

'Never mind – I'm glad you told me. Gerald, do you think Max knew what Kyra had done all along?'

'Apparently she's sworn he didn't.'

'Has she? But then, she might be as firmly under the Max influence as I once was,' I said, and Gerald looked baffled. 'How do you know all this?'

'I've an old friend on the campus out there, and he's been emailing me,' Gerald explained. 'According to the latest story going round, Rosemary found out about the affair and told Kyra to get out, and Kyra said she was pregnant by Max and he was going to leave Rosemary.'

'Pregnant?' I felt a cold clutch at the pit of my stomach. 'She's pregnant by Max?'

'I'm sorry,' he said, looking concerned. 'I probably shouldn't have told you *that*, either!'

'Yes, you should – go on,' I urged him.

'She miscarried, which is when she confessed to pushing Rosemary over the edge. Apparently Rosemary laughed at the thought of Max leaving her, and Kyra snapped.'

Over the edge in more ways than one . . . which is where I felt I was heading, too. Strangely, what was hurting most was that Max, who'd always been so fanatically careful that I shouldn't get pregnant, had been so carried away with another woman that he was careless.

'The university has asked him to cut his year short,' Gerald said. 'You could see him back before long if the police give him permission to go. Probably have to return for the trial, though.'

'I expect he will,' I agreed numbly. 'And he's still guilty of Rosemary's death to some extent, isn't he? Because if he hadn't had an affair with Kyra she wouldn't have had that argument.'

And no wonder I'd read guilt in his mind, because not only had he been unfaithful both to Rosemary and me, he must have had a suspicion Kyra'd done something, too. Yet he'd clearly considered his fling with Kyra as just that, and expected to return to me as if it hadn't happened!

'Are you all right, Cass?' Gerald asked anxiously. 'I know it must have come as a big shock, but I thought it was better to tell you everything. I just wish Jane was still here with you.'

I shuddered. '*I'm* not. But I am glad you told me. Could you – there's a bottle of Laphroaig under the kitchen sink?'

'Laphroaig?'

'Yes, I seem to have developed a taste for it. Could you pour me a glass, do you think?'

He did, and we sat and silently sipped good whisky with bad thoughts, until after a while Gerald downed the last of his very moderate tot and drove off, not without some reluctance and an offer to spend the night, which was kind but ill-considered.

Jane would not have approved in the least, and Mrs Bridges would have counted him in and be waiting to count him out.

I certainly felt as if *I'd* been counted out.

Floored.

Phoned the number for Max that Jane got for me, but there was only an answering machine. I told it to tell Max I knew everything and it was all over between us, and not to contact me again, which was perhaps the coward's way out.

I should have done it long, long ago.

Then I relayed everything to Jason and Orla at the pub in order to have my wounds washed clean with sympathy, although by then they were already pretty well rinsed with whisky.

Somehow I seemed to have lost my usual healthy appetite for food.

I think it was Kyra getting pregnant by Max that did it: the final curtain on a long-running and sorry bedroom farce.

After that I might have slid into the deep, dark pit of depression, but fortunately inspiration for a new novel dropped on me from a great height on my way home from the pub. As soon as I got back I started a new book of a Frankenstein persuasion, about a doctor heroine who is mining a Max-like character for spare parts.

The working title is *A Good Heart Is Hard To Find*.

Chapter 19: A Plague On It

. . . a rancid tale of torture and terror. Strong stuff. Buy it!
Exposé Magazine:
'On The Shelf', with Lisa-Mona Bevore

Next time I bumped into Rosetta – and Eddie, that goes without saying now – I told her that if Jason asked if there was room at the inn, she was to say no.

'Too late,' she replied, looking surprised. 'I did say we were full – which we are, until we get more bathrooms to go round, but he begged me to at least find him a bed for Saturday night because he had to get away. He didn't say what from.'

'Nothing, unless his son Tom's home for Easter. He's just being protective and interfering.'

Rosetta looked vaguely puzzled, but I was not about to explain the ups and downs (or the ins and outs) of my relations with her brother.

'Oh? Well, in the end I *did* say he could have the little box bedroom at the back, although it isn't very comfortable and it's miles from a bathroom.'

'Oh blast,' I said. 'Does Dante know? Only I haven't seen him about,' I added mendaciously, because although he has been avoiding the pub I did see him when I was out walking one night, and he turned and strode off without a word.

'I haven't mentioned it, because he's really left all the B&B stuff to me . . . and Eddie,' she added, smiling adoringly at him. 'Eddie's been great, doing things in the house and garden.'

'Someone's dumped an old car in the lily pond,' Eddie said cheerfully. 'The ducks stand on it.'

'That's nice,' I said, since he seemed to think this was a good idea.

'Have you and Dante fallen out?' Rosetta asked timidly. 'Only I thought he quite liked you, but if I mention your name now he sort of grinds his teeth and leaves the room.'

'We never fell *in*, in the first place, Rosetta. I don't suppose you know what he wants me to do over Easter, for my slave duties? Perhaps it's just to help you with the guests?' I asked hopefully.

'He said if you were going to haunt him you might as well make yourself useful and do it up at the Hall,' Eddie offered, with that disconcerting knack he sometimes has of repeating an overheard sentence as if it was in a language he didn't speak.

'Dante does seem to think you're going to be the resident ghost over Easter,' Rosetta agreed doubtfully. 'But I thought you didn't want to do that?'

'He knows very well I don't want to, but since it would clearly provide him with pleasure to see me suffer, I'll haunt with a smile on my face and a song on my lips instead,' I said tartly.

'You!' Eddie said, laughing delightedly.

'Yes, mournful old me!' I agreed.

Seeing the conversation was going nowhere fast I hastily excused myself and went home.

Clearly Dante didn't stride away gnashing his teeth at the mention of my name *next* time Rosetta brought it up, because I found a note shoved through my door the following day that said, in a familiar jagged black script:

Cass,
Glad to find my slave so biddable. Don't bother bringing a costume for the haunting – I'll provide one – and you don't need one for Betsy's appearance.
I've now read the whole of your interesting manuscript, and I don't think you ought to be allowed to breed.
Got the dog yet?
Dante.

I'll show the bastard biddable! And does he seriously think I'm going to streak down the Long Gallery at midnight? Dream on, Dante Chase.

196

Re. the rest of the letter, which was obviously meant to provoke, I stoically managed to stop myself going out and ravishing Jason just to show him I didn't care what he thought, but then realised that part of me would much rather seduce Dante himself again to show him, but I am not sure *what* I would be showing him. Or why.

How is it that I understand the motivation of the characters in my books, yet do not have any inkling of my own? Why does the thought of Easter weekend make me feel aghast, panic-stricken, excited and stomach-churningly nervous all at the same time?

Am I now so far round the bend even Laphroaig won't get me back?

I told Orla about Jason booking into the Hall for the Saturday night while I was helping her retrieve the money people had thrown down the Haunted Well.

She stared at me, her hands full of slimily dripping coins. 'But I thought Rosetta was full up? And I've got plans for Jason over the weekend!' she protested.

'I'm sorry, but it's not my fault. *I* didn't want him to do it.'

'Oh well,' she said, cheering up, 'it might be a good thing after all now I think about it. My Barbarella costume's come, and one of Rosetta's guests got my number and booked me to go up and deliver a birthday telegram early Saturday evening to her husband. She chose Marilyn Monroe, but I'll have a sudden attack of confusion and wear the new outfit.'

'Orla, you can't do that!'

'Yes I can, and if this get-up doesn't knock Jason's eye out I'll give up and we can *both* buy dogs.'

'What will you sing?'

'Just "Happy Birthday", I think. She's ordered a cake shaped like a ghost from Clara – she phoned Rosetta and asked her for ideas, that's how she found us. Rosetta's put a large sitting room aside for the visitors, and they mean to have a little cake and wine celebration in there, everyone welcome.'

'I wouldn't miss it for the world, invited or not,' I said, helping her to replace the grating over the mouth of the well, and the sign inviting people to toss their money down it for good luck. (Good luck for Orla, that is.) 'After all, there has to be some perk to compensate me for being Dante's slave for a whole weekend.'

'I think being his slave *is* a perk,' Orla said. 'Are you mad?'

'No, but something seems to have made *him* mad with *me* and now he's read the whole of my manuscript he's even angrier. I'm afraid he's going to spend the whole weekend punishing me for implying he has an immortal vampire ancestor.'

'I bet you can hardly wait!' she said unfeelingly.

When I got home Mrs Bridges gave me a bouquet of red roses that had been delivered in my absence, with the message 'Forgive me! Love You Forever, Max.'

When hell freezes over, I will.

The entire tape on my answerphone was also taken up with one long loving message. Max not only wasn't taking no for an answer, but was afraid I'd been influenced by hearing some of the lying stories that were going around about him and Kyra. Kyra was a sad, unbalanced woman, and actually he and Rosemary were going to fire her for dishonesty . . . And so on and so on.

When he's being persuasive and charming Max uses his warm honey voice, the one that trapped me like an insect in amber nectar for far too long.

For a moment or two I might have felt a touch of the old enchantment, but the bit at the end where he said he'd now shaved his beard off especially for me, like my knight had just gone out and personally slain me a dragon, made me laugh out loud.

Although I was dreading a weekend that might bring two-fold retribution on my head (divine in the form of Pa, and infernal in the case of Dante), yet I managed to completely forget it for large stretches of time as I became more and more involved with the world inside my new book.

The heroine, Dr Amulet Bone, firmly believes that genetically modified androids are the way to go, and if you can't find the perfect man you might as well construct him.

Somehow, I don't think her two-timing ex-fiancé is going to be in full agreement with that one.

Thus it was that I'd so lost track of time that when Orla phoned me up one day and hissed conspiratorially: 'Cass? Your family's arrived!' I was quite taken by surprise.

'I thought they weren't coming until Friday?'

'It is Friday: *Good* Friday.'

'Oh bugger, that's all I need,' I said ungraciously. 'The Black Death has hit Westery and we might as well close the boundaries until it festers itself out.'

'I don't think that's a nice way to talk about your family!' she said reprovingly. 'Francis is right here – he wants a word with you. Your dad's good-looking, isn't he? In a demented prophet sort of way, I mean.'

'My father is a pustulating bubo on the face of the world, Orla, so spare me the murkier dredgings of your subconscious and put Francis on.'

'Hi Sis,' Francis said. 'Got your note. Looks like we've come all this way for nothing, doesn't it? Is Sweet Baby Jane really in London? Pa says he doesn't believe it.'

'Why on earth not?'

'He says you've brainwashed her into your evil ways, and are hiding her away so she can see her lover, or some such, and he must snatch away the burning brand from the flames, and – oh, you know, the usual stuff?'

'Well yes, but she really isn't here, Francis, and she isn't with a lover, she's simply in London minding Phily while George is away. I've only just found out about the shoplifting. Sorry, the *kleptomania*.'

'We don't mention that to Ma and Pa,' he warned. 'It sets Pa off, even though she can't help it, apparently. Orla says your fella's a widower now, but you aren't going to marry him anyway, he's blotted his copybook?'

'No, I'm going to stay single. And get a dog,' I added for good measure.

'Well, just as long as there are no strange males hanging around your cottage when the parents visit.'

'Visit? What do you mean, *visit*?' I exclaimed, aghast.

'To search for Jane. They're determined not to go home until they see her.'

'Francis, all they have to do is phone Phily in London! I said in my letter.'

'They tried right after they read it, and Phily said Jane was otherwise engaged and started giggling like a lunatic, so they didn't believe her. I think Pa makes her nervous.'

'That woman's a half-wit, and that may be rating her intelligence too high. Jane and Gerald were probably just making it up –

199

he's gone down there for the big reconciliation "forgive me for I know not what you did" scene.'

'Oh? I'll *tell* them,' he said doubtfully, 'but they probably won't believe me, either. Here they come . . . I'll be round later if I can head them off tonight.'

'Tell them I'm out, Francis, and then try and meet me in the King's Arms in the village around seven.'

'I'll try,' he said, and put the phone down.

I was packed and out of that house at the speed of light, even allowing for a quick call to Rosetta to ask if it was all right if I went up to the Hall early. I mean, I was far from wanting to appear keen, but any port in a storm.

It's not that I'm frightened of Pa, either: I'm petrified.

I couldn't do anything about Jane's car still parked outside since I didn't have the keys, but I loaded mine up with everything I thought I might need (including the whisky) and drove by a circuitous route up to the Hall, thus avoiding the middle of the village and any possible parental confrontation.

Chapter 20: Single Cell

A thoroughly purging read!

Charlie Rhymer:
Skint Old Northern Woman Magazine

As I crunched up the freshly weeded drive and came to a halt, Dante sauntered out, looking ravishing in those leather trousers, or an identical pair, obviously his favoured working garb.

Talk about forbidden fruit.

'Couldn't wait, eh?' he said, and I gave him a cold look.

'My parents are staying at Orla's with my brother Francis, because they think I've got Jane hidden away somewhere, but actually she's in London with my sister-in-law, Phily. So I'm only here because I need a bolt hole until they leave.'

'You can have your bolt hole, but don't think just because you've arrived early that I'm going to let you go early,' he said, and gave me that particularly sharp-edged smile before helping me remove my belongings from the car.

I mistrusted that smile: it was the kind that should have the Jaws theme tune playing in the background. De-dum . . . de-dum . . .

'I've got you a sort of white ghost outfit,' he said, dumping my bag on the doorstep. Just as well I'd padded the whisky with my cobweb. 'More suitable than the vampire stuff, though that greenish make-up you've got should look good. I'll tell you what I want you to do later.'

'As long as it doesn't involve running naked along corridors, I am resigned to my fate.'

'Are you?' He raised one straight dark brow. 'I might hold you to that.'

'And I'm quite happy to give Rosetta a hand with her first houseful of guests, too, if that's what you want,' I added, dampeningly. 'Have any of them arrived yet?'

'No, but I think one of them is about to,' he said, looking over his shoulder at the scrunch of wheels on gravel. Then he went still, and something in the quality of his silence made me turn and look too.

A large woman was levering herself out of a taxi, gauzy scarves and improbably scarlet tresses flying in all directions.

'What the hell—?' Dante exclaimed loudly.

She straightened, and leaving the taxi driver to remove her suitcase, strode up to the foot of the steps. She had a roman nose, black eyes, and the face of a middle-aged Bacchae. When she pointed a simian arm at Dante and boomed: 'I am retribution! Cower before me, murderer and unbeliever!' the effect was quite awesome.

'Unbeliever!' she repeated on a rising shriek.

. . . holding his severed head aloft, the black silken hair dabbled in the still-spouting lifeblood, she—

Somehow I found I was standing protectively in front of Dante, with my arms outstretched like a mother hen with one chick. 'Who are you? What do you want?' I demanded.

His hands came down hard on my shoulders and gripped them, and there was a sort of grim amusement in the voice with which he said: 'It's all right, Cass: this is – or was – my mother-in-law, Mrs Dufferin.'

'Duval! *Madame* Duval!' interjected the woman.

Behind her a small man had also emerged from the taxi, which drove away leaving him standing among a pile of luggage.

'I'm not interested in what name you're going under: what I don't understand is why you are here on my property?'

Rosetta came out, looking harried: 'Did I hear voices? Oh! Why didn't you call me to say some of our visitors have arrived, Dante, and—'

She broke off and stared, wide-eyed. 'Mrs Dufferin! What on earth are *you* doing here?'

'Duval, Rosetta,' she snapped. 'Madame Duval! And I'm booked in for the weekend.'

'But . . . well yes, I do have a booking for a Monsieur and Madame Duval, but I didn't realise it was you! And why on earth you want to keep hounding my poor brother like this, I don't know!' she added more fiercely. She turned and said, helplessly: 'Sorry, Dante: I didn't realise.'

'It's not your fault. I should have looked over the visitor list instead of leaving it all to you. Duval is the name she's been working under recently.'

'Working under?' I said, realising that Dante's hands were still gripping my shoulders somewhat painfully.

'As a medium – seances, readings, that sort of hocus-pocus. But I'm not having any of that in my home. In fact, I'm not even having you under my roof, whatever you want to call yourself, so you can just turn around and go back where you came from.'

Monsieur Duval trotted up the steps carrying two bags like a very small packhorse.

'Where do you want these, luv?' he said to his wife, in accents more Liverpudlian than French.

'Inside,' she snapped.

'No,' Dante said flatly. 'I won't have you in my house, I've just said. Rosetta will ring for a taxi.'

'I'm booked for three nights, and three nights I will stay,' she declared vehemently. 'If you deny me entrance, I will merely camp here on the terrace. I will not be denied! There must be one last chance to call back the spirit of my poor child . . . my one reason for living, my little . . . my little . . . Emma!'

Under our horrified gaze she began to turn an interesting if deathly shade of mauve and put one hand to her huge and palpitating bosom.

Dante thrust me aside and grabbed her as she began to crumple. She tried weakly to fend him off: 'Leave me – don't you dare to lay hands on me! Killer! Murderer!'

Her husband dropped the bags and, wresting a small bottle from one pocket, unscrewed the lid and waved it under her nose.

'Not that – the pill, for underneath her tongue!' Dante snapped, and the little man, looking panic-stricken, opened her capacious handbag, rummaged about and came up with a small bottle.

Dante grabbed it, glanced at the label, then shook out a tiny pill and shoved into Madame's mouth like someone worming a particularly recalcitrant cat.

It was ruthlessly efficient, and it worked. After only a few minutes she had straightened and her colour was normal enough for Rosetta to lead her inside, with one apologetic look at Dante, who stared after them looking particularly dark and inscrutable, like Mr Rochester with a bad attitude (and a bad hair day.)

I sincerely hope there isn't a madwoman in his attic, for although Pa confidently expects me to burn, I hope to delay the experience for as long as possible.

'Sorry about that, lad,' Mr Duval said apologetically. 'We've only been married a couple of months – a whirlwind romance it was – so I'm not too nippy when poor Louie gets these funny turns. You must be Dante Chase?'

'Yes, and without wishing to appear rude, I would like you and your wife out of my house as soon as she's sufficiently recovered.'

'Yes, but it takes it out of her, this sort of thing, poor luv,' he said. 'You can't send her off like that or maybe *her* death will be on your head too . . . though the way she explains about poor Emma, it doesn't seem to me you could help the poor girl dying!'

'No, but the aneurysm might not have killed her if she hadn't been pregnant, and she was only pregnant because she thought it would bring us back together – and I don't know why I'm standing on my own doorstep discussing my personal history with a complete stranger!'

'Almost your dad-in-law,' he said, with a natural cheeriness that was bound to become very, very irritating exceedingly quickly.

Rosetta came back out looking worried. 'She's gone upstairs with Eddie – she said he had a lovely aura.'

'They all say that,' I commented.

'Dante, she'll have to stay now: I can't put her out. Perhaps she'll be too unwell to do or say anything particularly awful?'

'I doubt it, these attacks have never stopped her before. Rosetta, this is her new husband.'

'Reg Bangs.'

'Does he?' I said without thinking.

Dante gave me an evil look. 'You'll have to excuse the hired help.'

'Ha! ha!' laughed Reg. 'I get that one all the time! But my Louie, she likes to be called Madame Duval for professional reasons. I was Rupert Swayle myself when I was on the stage, but you can call me Reg. Now don't you worry,' he said to Dante and Rosetta, 'I'll keep Louie in line.'

'I don't see what she hopes to gain by coming here and hounding me like this,' Dante said. 'I let her hold her damn seances after Emma died because I'd promised to do it and I wasn't going back on my word, but I'm certainly not having any of that here.'

'I'll tell her.'

'Tell her I'll put her out, heart attack or no heart attack, if she tries!' he said harshly.

Eddie appeared, looking slightly puzzled. 'Louie wants her stuff,' he said. 'This it?' He effortlessly hoisted up two large suitcases and went back in, followed by Reg carrying an assortment of smaller bags.

'Don't look now, but here comes what looks like the Ghost Grabbers,' I said as another taxi drove up and disgorged two men of that incalculable age between greying and dust, and a slender white-haired woman wearing a gold-encrusted wedding sari in a shrieking shade of pink.

'Spectrology Group, and I'm beginning to seriously doubt that this B&B thing was a good idea,' Dante said. 'Rosetta, if you need me for anything – desperately – I'll be in the west wing! I'll see *you* later,' he added to me, before retreating.

'Yes, headmaster!' I called after him, though I'm not sure he heard. *Demon* headmaster would have been more appropriate.

'Oh dear,' Rosetta sighed, looking after his retreating back.

So did I, but not in a sisterly manner: it was well worth looking at in those trousers.

'I hope . . . well, maybe this ghost-hunting theme wasn't such a good idea after all? Why do all our guests look such total cranks? And I wouldn't have had Mrs – Madame – Duval here if I'd known, because she's been haunting poor Dante and it really wasn't his fault at all,' she said earnestly. 'I mean, Emma had an affair with another man when he was away on an assignment, and she only went back when he dumped her! The reconciliation and the baby were entirely her idea.'

'Oh? Her mother doesn't seem to see it quite like that, does she? Though I suppose it's understandable,' I added thinking about it. 'Poor woman!'

'Poor Emma, too,' Rosetta said, 'because she was brought up on planchettes and the supernatural and then she went and fell in love with Dante, who didn't believe at all. There was this huge power struggle between Dante and her mother when they got married which he won, but then Emma fell under the sway of this man her mother introduced her too, another medium, and—'

Dante stuck his head out of the front door again and bellowed: 'Cass!'

'Coming, master!' I called sarcastically. 'Can you manage all right, Rosetta? Eddie will have to carry their luggage up in relays, I've never seen so much for one weekend!'

'Yes, you go if Dante needs you. Eddie will be down in a minute: he's so strong and calm and wonderful, isn't he?' she said dreamily

'Is he?' I said doubtfully, wondering if she was on the pot, as it were, too. 'I mean, yes he *is*, isn't he? Brace yourself, here come the Spectral Spectators!' and hurried off after Dante towards the lonely west wing carrying my own unimpressive luggage.

He showed me to a monastic little newly whitewashed room, muttered something about work and made to leave. When I imperatively called him back he turned reluctantly.

'A table.'

'What?'

'I need a table to work on. In the night. I've started a new book.' I said in short, easy to understand sentences.

He gave me an evil look, but did come back hefting a small papier mâché desk a few minutes later, which although a trifle ornate seemed sturdy enough.

I thanked him.

'The only thanks I want is for you to leave my property and putative ancestors out of any of your future mental dribblings,' he said offensively, and went off, slamming the door to his study behind him.

I went straight after him and flung it open again so that it crashed satisfyingly against the panelling: 'I *strongly* object to the use of the word "dribblings". My thought processes are definitely more in the nature of a free-flowing river carrying all before it,' I told him with emphasis before turning on my heel and marching back to my cell.

Behind me Dante muttered something which was fortunately inaudible, but it was a full five minutes before he closed his study door again: quietly. I was listening.

Charles would probably say that this weekend was in the nature of a penance for past misdeeds, and I should suffer in silence. But there might be some benefits, too, for at least over this weekend I will have lots of time to think about *A Good Heart* while I'm haunting and soaking up the ambience. Who knows, maybe I will actually see Betsy, or some of the other colourful characters reputed to infest the place?

After all the excitement I could have *killed* a pizza, but did not think I was about to get one if it was left to Dante, who seems to have forgotten the joy of food. But shortly I would sneak down to the King's Arms to meet Francis and could eat something there.

I hung a couple of things up, set out my pallid palette of stage make-up for later, put my notes and things on the desk, then went to offer my services to Rosetta for a while.

She was in the kitchen, distractedly rattling pots and pans.

'This is all a big mistake,' she moaned, wild-eyed. 'It's all very well managing a small hotel, but then I didn't have to do everything myself, including unexpectedly cooking dinner for five guests!'

'But I thought you weren't providing meals? Send them down to the pub like Orla does with hers.'

She ran a nervous hand through her curly brown locks. 'I thought that's what they'd do, but Reg – Mr Bangs – says his wife is too prostrate to leave her room tonight.'

'Well, that's a blessing anyway!'

'Yes, but he asked if it was possible for them to have a light meal served in their room! Soup or something. I couldn't very well refuse, could I?'

'I suppose not: but you don't have to cook for the other three as well!'

'I wouldn't, only that weird woman in the sari – she's the sister of the small fat man and married to the tall, thin one – overheard and said she felt quite faint from the long journey and she'd like to do the same. Then the other two said in that case they only needed a snack too, because they wanted to walk down and visit the graveyard and the haunted well later in the evening when the atmosphere would be right. Right for what?'

'Goodness knows. Where's Eddie?'

'He's gone down to Emlyn's in his van for cans of soup and garlic bread, and more fruit to make a big fresh fruit salad.'

'If I'd known he was going I'd have asked him to get me a pizza – I'm starving! Anyway, tell me what I can do.'

'Could you lay the table for the two men in the breakfast room? They're quite nice actually – Mr Bream and Mr Shakespeare.'

'Shakespeare?'

'Yes, but Frank, not William. Then I need to lay those two big trays ready for taking upstairs.'

'I can do that, too. I only hope you're going to charge them through the nose for this kind of service.'

'I certainly am!' she said, a martial light appearing in her eyes. Then we heard Eddie's footsteps outside and she leapt to open the kitchen door. He staggered in laden with cardboard boxes of supplies.

There was a banana in the top pocket of his bib and brace overalls which became somewhat bruised if not flambéed by the enthusiasm of their reunion.

I removed the cartons and began to set about heating bread and soup.

'What would I do without you, Eddie?' Rosetta said. 'Let me just get through this weekend and never again! But Dante's going to be so disappointed with me when we leave next week!'

I stopped slicing bread and stared at her, baffled: 'What do you mean, leave?'

'I'm going off with Eddie.'

'How can you go off when you've got a B&B to run? And do you mean in his van?'

'Of course! Though actually I wondered if Dante would let us use the lodge as our base, especially in winter, so we could come back from time to time? He'll be angry at first, but I know he just wants me to be happy. And I will be, with Eddie.'

I thought she might be being a bit sanguine about that. Another thing came to me, too: 'Eddie, Ma and Pa are staying in the village at Orla's. Francis brought them because they want to see Jane. That's why I'm here already, I'm hiding.'

Eddie smiled cheerfully: but then, like all the boys, he has grown out of being afraid of Pa. And Jane, of course, never had cause to be.

'You won't tell them I'm here if you see them, will you, Eddie? They're looking for Jane – they think I've concealed her somewhere. I'm going down to the King's Arms shortly to see Francis and find out what's happening.'

'I'd come too, Cass, but I can't leave Rosetta. She needs me . . . bad vibes.' He shook his dreadlocks sadly so all the little

208

beads clicked. 'I'll be glad to get her out of here after this week-end. But it's good news about you and Dante, because Rosie won't be so worried about him if you're here.'

'What about me and Dante?' I demanded. 'There *is* no me and Dante! What do you mean?'

Eddie gazed placidly at me. 'Isn't that what the auction was about? The best man won?'

'No, you pot-smoking addle-brained hippie, the richest, most pig-headed man won! And whatever he thought he was winning, he wasted his money.'

Eddie just grinned, impervious to my insults, which anyway he has heard before.

'I think he just wanted to buy time with you so he could get to know you,' Rosetta suggested timidly. 'I knew he was interested in you, only he's been through hell, what with being a hostage and seeing his friend killed, and then finding he'd lost Emma and the baby too. It's made him—'

'Bitter, twisted and suspicious?' I finished for her. 'And I think you're wrong – he now knows me as well as he'll ever want to.'

'He was a bit narked that you gave him a vampire ancestor in the book,' Eddie said.

I stared at him. 'What? Did he tell you that?'

'Yes, he said: "She's put my ancestor in her sodding book as a corrupt, bloodsucking monster!" '

'A very attractive monster,' I said without thinking, and Eddie grinned.

I resisted the urge to throw something at him, since I'd have hit Rosetta too. They were still partially entwined to the point where it was hard to see where one stopped and the other began.

'If Pa sets eyes on you and Rosetta like that, you'll be married before you can say Eternal Damnation!' I snapped

Eddie shrugged. 'It doesn't matter, does it, Rosie?'

'Not to me, but it might be easier for the baby.'

'Which baby?' I said, losing the thread of the plot.

'Eddie's baby,' Rosetta said proudly.

'What? *Already*? Does Dante know?'

'No – I've only just started it. I'll tell him later, before we leave.'

'But you can't have a baby in a van!' I protested weakly.

'I could, but maybe Dante will let us have the lodge when we need it. And by then, maybe you two will—'

'No we won't. Forget it,' I interrupted hastily. Then I had a sudden warming thought: 'I'll be an auntie!'

My eye fell on the kitchen clock: 'Look at the time!' Quickly I swirled cream on to two bowls of soup, took the bread out of the oven and arranged the trays.

'Put Eddie down, Rosetta, and take one of these. I have to go out and meet Francis.'

Chapter 21: The Ghost Of Her Former Self

Publication date of Cass Leigh's next novel, Shock To The Spirits, *has been brought forward to April 20th. If it's anything like her previous works, it will certainly live up to its title . . .*

Book News

I walked down to the pub, but it was still early and there was no sign of Francis, just Jason eating steak and onions.

By then, having missed lunch, I was sort of past being hungry so just ordered a sandwich and picked at Jason's chips until it arrived.

'Where have you been? I tried to phone you earlier,' he said, curving his arm protectively around his plate and moving it out of my reach. 'I can only stay at the Hall tomorrow, but I thought I could drive you up there tonight anyway, and just make it clear to Dante that you're not doing anything that isn't on your list!'

'No need, thanks, Jason – I'm already up. I mean, I took my things there earlier, because of Ma and Pa arriving. Didn't Orla tell you? They don't believe that I'm not concealing Jane in my cottage, so I thought I'd go and hide at the Hall until they give up and go. I'm expecting my brother Francis here around seven to discuss strategy.'

'You're already there? Then I hope you've made it plain to—' Jason had begun, single-mindedly, when suddenly his brown eyes went wide and his jaw dropped open – very Neanderthal.

When I turned round all was made clear. In fact, most of Orla was made clear even to the most casual glance, because her slinky

Barbarella costume was as moulded to her curvy figure as if it had been painted on. (Which I wouldn't put past her if the fancy took her.)

The whole room went quiet, and even Charles, on looking absently up from his papers, seemed a trifle startled. Then one or two regulars leaned over the bar wolfwhistling, which seemed to break the spell.

Orla, beaming, came and sat down with us. 'I can see this is going to be a popular outfit,' she said happily. 'Who said the age of curves was dead?'

'Not me!' Jason said, seemingly unable to take his eyes from the grand canyon of her cleavage, temptingly revealed by the partly-open zipper down the front of what could only be described as a clingy, leather-look, gold catsuit. I don't remember Barbarella in one of those: but hell, a woman's entitled to a little artistic licence.

'Do you like it?' Orla asked softly, leaning towards Jason. With the zipper that far down I couldn't see how she'd worked the gravity-defying trick. I'd have to ask her later.

'Like it . . . ?' he murmured absently, then pulled himself together and said severely:

'I don't think you ought to wear that get-up in public – it's way too revealing!'

'What do you mean?' she asked with hurt innocence. 'I'm Barbarella – it's my new singing telegram personal.'

'Are you booked to do one tonight?' I asked. 'Or just trying it out?'

'Just a trial run. What do you think?'

'Truly amazing. If you do any stag nights, though, I'd take Jason with you for protection.'

'She's not doing stag nights, or any other nights, dressed like that!' he said firmly, like a Victorian papa.

'Sez who?' Orla demanded.

'How about a short gold cape?' I suggested. 'For between the car and the venue and back again, at least?'

'Why? Does my bum look big in this?' she demanded suspiciously.

'Big and curvy, like Jennifer Lopez, and it doesn't seem to have done her any harm.'

'Even with a cape . . . ' began Jason stubbornly.

'You're so dog in the manger!' Orla exclaimed provocatively. 'You're not interested in me yourself, but you don't want other men looking at me!'

'Who said I'm not interested in you?' Jason said, staring at her as if he was seeing her for the first time. I don't think he'd so much as glanced my way since she'd arrived.

It was all looking very promising: they were starting to bicker already.

My brother Francis walked in, glanced around, caught sight of Orla, and stood looking poleaxed, so I seized my chance to leave them to it.

'Would you both excuse me? There's Francis now, so I'll just get him in a quiet corner for a little talk. Jason, shall I tell Rosetta you won't be coming tomorrow after all?'

'What?' he looked up, brow furrowed.

'I said, shall I cancel your booking for tomorrow at the Hall?'

'Funnily enough, I'm making my first Barbarella appearance there tomorrow,' Orla said brightly. 'One of the guest's birthdays. A Mr Bream.'

'Definitely not Marilyn Monroe then?' I said.

She shrugged. 'My dress is at the cleaner's – but I don't suppose he'll complain.'

'I don't expect *he* will but his wife might,' I objected.

'Don't you dare!' Jason said. 'If you show up tomorrow night dressed like that I'll—'

At that interesting point I had to leap in Francis's path and head him off before he honed in on Orla and spoiled everything. He was single-mindedly transfixed: her bosom clearly held the same lure for him as mountain peaks.

Taking him firmly by the arm, I steered him to a seat some way away with his back towards her, then asked him the state of play.

'State of play?' he said vaguely, then gave himself a sort of mental shake. 'Oh yes, the parents. Pa's been round to the cottage and seen Jane's car there, so he's even more convinced that you're hiding her. But I'd told him you were away, and he could see for himself that there were no lights on, and the telephone was ringing and ringing with no one answering it.'

'Max,' I said resignedly. 'I might have known he wouldn't take no for an answer.'

'Oh? Have you broken up with him? Trust you to do it just when you could finally get married and placate the parents!'

'Even if I had married Max, it would never have made things right again,' I told him.

'Maybe not. Well, anyway, then this old bat next door opened her window and started screaming at us, and singing snatches of "Men Of Harlech", and Pa told her she was possessed by the devil and she must be a great sinner.'

'Oh dear! Mrs Bridges *will* keep watching *Zulu*, and it always upsets her. Perhaps I ought to steal it next time I'm in her house? Or Eddie, if he goes round there to do something for her?'

'Is Eddie here? In Westery?'

'Yes, didn't you know? His van's up at the hall because he's helping Rosetta – she's the sister of Dante Chase, the new owner of Kedge Hall – to run her Ghostly House party. Sort of a themed country house weekend.'

Francis looked at me like I was mad but *I'm* not the one who swings about on sheer rock faces on a bit of string.

'Maybe I'd better not mention Eddie,' he suggested. 'Ma would want to see him, but I always worry that Pa will have a stroke. It's touch and go with his outbursts lately, sober or not.'

'No, better keep Eddie quiet if you can.'

'Jamie isn't still here somewhere too, is he? Only Ma and Pa were expecting him home, and he never turned up. He just sent a postcard that didn't make sense.'

'No, he was here, but he lost his bottle and bolted. So, what's Pa's next move, Francis?'

'Well, he asked me where you were, but luckily I didn't know. But then he asked Orla. Great outfit, by the way!' he added enthusiastically.

'Stick to the point,' I told him severely.

'Right. So Orla told him you were Dante Chase's slave for the weekend. That went down a treat.'

'I'll have to thank Orla for that one. What was she thinking of?'

'Well, you know Pa – can charm the birds from the trees when he's sober and puts his mind to it, even if he's damning them all to hell-fire for wanton tweeting ten minutes later.'

'True. I suppose I'll have to forgive her.'

'So now Ma and Pa think you're having some kind of dirty weekend with bondage and stuff, but at least it should put them off following you up there to demand Jane's whereabouts. I tried phoning Phily's house again to speak to Jane, but there was no answer.'

'Probably out having fun. *I* remember fun – I think,' I said bitterly.

'Orla explained to me about the slave auction. She said you were going to frighten the guests, that's all.'

'Perhaps you should let Pa come up, he'd frighten them even more,' I suggested.

'I'm hoping that I'll manage to get hold of Jane on the phone tomorrow and then they will have to admit she isn't here and we can all go home. After all, I've been away for days and I've got a business to run.'

'And mountains to climb,' I agreed. 'I'll give you a ring at Orla's tomorrow and see if you've succeeded.'

'Right.' He downed the rest of his pint and got up. 'I'd better go before they miss me.'

I fished in my bag and handed him an Extra Strong Mint. 'Here – suck this on the way back, or you'll be excommunicated for devil-brew drinking.'

Orla and Jason seemed to be having a promising quarrel, so I just slipped out and walked slowly back. I was tempted to return to my cottage for a while, since Pa'd already visited it so it should be safe; but then thought it would be just like him to sneak back later and try and catch me out.

On the way up the drive the two male Spectral Investigators, Mr Shakespeare and the Birthday Bream passed me, going the opposite way, probably heading for the graveyard and other haunts.

They didn't see me, since I stepped into the bushes when I heard them coming. If I was going to appear as a ghost later, I thought it better that they didn't see me by moonlight now in case it gave them suspicious ideas.

I wonder what Mr Bream will think of his singing telegram? And what will Mrs Bream think of the change of character? Marilyn Monroe is one thing, and Barbarella is quite another. Especially Orla's version of it.

I went round to the kitchen, which was empty and quiet apart from the dishwasher chugging away under the counter, and Dante sitting morosely at the kitchen table with a glass of red wine and a copy of *Britain's Most Haunted Houses*.

He frowned at the sight of me and snapped: 'Where have you been?'

'My bondage doesn't start until midnight,' I pointed out. 'But if you really want to know, I've been down to the pub for something to eat and to talk to my brother Francis.'

'Oh . . . sorry,' he muttered. 'Have a glass of wine?' He pushed the bottle towards me and I noticed that his greeny-blue eyes glittered a bit.

I held the bottle up to the light, and there wasn't a lot in it. 'Have you drunk all this?'

'Yes. I needed something to take the taste of guilt out of my mouth.' He got up and opened another bottle and handed it to me as if he expected me to drink it straight down like a wino.

'You've nothing to be guilty about,' I said, opening and shutting cupboard doors until I found a glass, because I'm not one to leave a man to drink alone – though you'd think I'd have learned my lesson by now with *this* one.

'I have at least one outstanding guilty verdict against me, according to my delightful former mother-in-law. She's demanding we hold a seance here – one last one – and if I co-operate and Emma doesn't contact her she will give up and leave me alone.'

'So what did you say?'

'That I wouldn't do it. I've already done everything she asked me, even though I knew it was all dangerous nonsense. But Reg – who is an inoffensive little man, too good for her – is afraid she'll work herself up into a full-blown heart attack if I don't agree. And I suspect she'll try and hold one secretly anyway, even if I refuse.'

'I share your feelings about seances and that sort of thing, though probably for different reasons. But maybe it would be worth it just to get her off your back once and for all?' I suggested. 'Hopefully, no harm will come of it, but if it does, we'll get the vicar to come in with bell, book, and candle and sort it out.'

'I said I'd sleep on it, in the end,' he said, running his fingers distractedly through his dark hair. That was probably as close to being combed it had come to for some time, and it all instantly sprang back into a wild mane anyway.

Getting up he poured us both more wine. It was good stuff.

'Have you been in the cellar again?' I asked, but unfortunately my innocent remark brought a reminiscent glint to his eyes, and also seemed to remind him that he had a grievance or two against me.

'I'm afraid so,' he said gravely. 'And neither of us will be doing much sleeping tonight. Or tomorrow night.'

'Oh?' I stared at him, my glass halfway to my lips. 'We won't?'

'No, we'll be a-haunting. I've told the Breams and Mr Shakespeare about Betsy's midnight runner and the haunted rose garden and they're all agog'

'I didn't agree to do Betsy!'

'But I thought you were going to do anything I wanted?' he said. 'Though I'll let you off nude: I've put some floaty white ghost clothes on your bed that should look pretty effective. You can run down the corridor looking as if you're silently screaming and terrified.'

If he carried on looking at me like that I might be *loudly* screaming and terrified.

'I only start my slavery at midnight,' I pointed out.

'But you could stretch a point and get changed and in position for midnight? Then you can do it again tomorrow, but I'll let you off on Sunday,' he offered.

'Gee, thanks.'

'I half-expected Jason to insist on coming here tonight as well as tomorrow to protect you from my wicked wiles. Are you losing your charms?'

'I don't think I've got any to lose, and Jason's busy tonight. If he does turn up at all tomorrow I don't think he will make much of a fuss, because Orla's managed to distract him with her new singing telegram outfit. You'll see it tomorrow.'

He'll see most of *Orla* tomorrow, too.

'Will I?'

'Yes, because it's Mr Bream's birthday, and his wife has hired Orla to come here, and Rosetta says we're all invited for cake and stuff at four tomorrow in the big sitting room. But Mrs Bream thinks she's getting Marilyn Monroe.'

'And in fact she's getting—?'

'Wait and see,' I said darkly. 'Where are Rosetta and Eddie?'

'They said something about an early night because of cooking all those breakfasts tomorrow, and left me to it.'

'Yes . . . ' I said slowly, looking at Dante's dark and shadowed face. 'I think Rosetta's finding the weekend a bit more exhausting than she thought. But then, she didn't bank on your ex-mother-in-law coming along, and everyone wanting meals on trays and birthday teas, and all the rest of it.'

Dante rose to his feet and said abruptly: 'Come on.

'Where?'

'Back to the lonely west wing, I've got something I want to show you. Bring your glass, and I'll take another bottle.'

'I think you've had quite enough,' I said severely. 'And what do you want to show me?'

'Wait and see.'

I went, although not without certain nervous qualms, but he led me straight to his study, where he had now ranged the diaries in date order and typed up the first as Chapter One. There was a title page, too: 'Travelling to Alaska'.

'What do you think? Is it set out right?'

I was quite touched that he'd used my suggested title. Picking up the chapter, I flicked through it, then went back and started to read from the beginning.

... my New York hotel bedroom at first seemed a far remove from the earth-floored dark hut I shared with Paul for so many months of our captivity. Yet in a way it still seemed to cage me from the urban jungle outside with its different dangers ...

When I looked up from the last page of the chapter I realised that I'd sat down with it at some point. Dante was sitting opposite me on one of the old armchairs, quietly and intently watching me.

He raised one black brow. 'So you're back?'

'Sorry – it's gripping stuff. I'm dying to read the whole thing when you've finished it.'

'So you think this way of writing it is going to work, then?'

'Work? It's brilliant!' I said enthusiastically. 'I couldn't put it down, you must have seen that?'

'Well, I couldn't put *Lover, Come Back To Me* down, if it comes to that,' he replied. 'But for entirely different reasons. I kept wondering if any of the characters were based on real ones – especially Vladimir, who this Keturah seems to find so very attractive but scary.'

'Oh, no, I make them all up,' I said hastily. Which I do, I only borrow aspects of people I find interesting and jumble them up with some invented bits to make a new character.

218

'You don't find *me* attractive but scary, by any chance?' he asked with interest. 'Just wondered.'

'No, not at all,' I said firmly. 'I made Vlad's character up entirely. And it's Keturah who felt that, she's such a wimp! Or she started out as a wimp, until she took a turn for the worse and got more interesting.'

'Interesting? I suppose that's one word for it!'

'Well, interesting to me.'

'You know, it's a pretty disturbing book, especially if you happen to have both a house and an ancestor with starring roles in it. The ending, particularly, was *deeply* worrying.'

'Oh, I always have a surprise ending – a twist in the tail.'

'It certainly surprised *me*,' he agreed. 'Especially what you did to Sylvanus. Doesn't your lover find it a bit unsettling, the stuff that's going on in your mind?'

'I haven't got a lover, I told you: I've finished with Max.'

'That's not what he thinks. He told me how you've loved each other for all these years, and that you're going to get married once you are over your upset feelings about Rosemary's letter.'

'He said? When did he say?' I demanded, startled.

'When he phoned me up to warn me to mind my manners while you were here,' he said amiably. 'Said he'd just spoken to you, and you were worried about coming here in case I made a pass at you, and so he wanted to tell me not to lay a finger on you, or else.'

I stared at him: 'Doesn't he ever listen to a word I say? I finally finished with him when Jane's husband told me he'd been having an affair with some physical fitness instructor over there.'

I told him about Kyra and a push too far. 'And I told you even before that that I'd decided it was over. Not that it's any of your business,' I added tartly. 'I'm going to my room.'

I got up and laid the manuscript on the table. 'When do you want me?'

He raised a quizzical eyebrow.

'When do you want me for the *haunting*,' I qualified. 'I didn't actually sign up for anything else.'

Come to think of it, I didn't even sign up for that.

'How about just before midnight, so we can get you into place well beforehand?'

'All right, but how will I get away afterwards without being seen? If I hide in one of the rooms they might catch me.'

'I've discovered a secret stair at the end of the hall, and I'll be waiting for you. Actually, it wasn't that secret since it's in the house documents, but it isn't in the haunted house books, so the Spectrologists won't know about it.'

'It will be a waste of time if they don't watch me – or manage to catch me!'

'I've told them they will only see the ghost from the balcony at the end, because if anyone's in the Long Gallery she doesn't appear. By the time they get down from there you'll be long gone.'

'Like the wine: that's long gone, too,' I said tartly. 'You'd better not drink any more tonight.'

His eyes glittered like chips of ice floe, and he pushed his black hair back off his bony face with both hands, like he wanted to study me in detail.

'If there are going to be any resurrections it might have to be the *brandy* again,' he said. 'And aren't I supposed to be the one giving orders?'

I gave him a look and went to my room, locking the door firmly behind me, but I think that might have been to keep myself in rather than him out, since Dante in his black T-shirt and leather trousers brings the words 'moth' and 'candle-flame' strongly into my mind.

I did not go quite so far as to toss the key out of the window, though, because when I turned around something white and gauzy stirred and whispered within the open wardrobe.

It was a white dress. A white Ghost ghost dress, to be exact . . . expensive and quite beautiful, a long gossamer concoction.

I've never been the Woman in White . . . and absolutely *nothing* could have stopped me wearing that dress tonight.

It was a strange but fortunate coincidence that although only the more frivolous items of my underwear are white, I seemed to have packed them along with the sensible everyday black things . . .

I tried the dress on, and I looked like someone else. I felt like someone else. And if I accidentally stood in front of a light, I'd be nearly fully exposed to everyone else.

That would be pretty authentic for Blind Betsy. Which reminds me, I can't remember what she was running from or to, but she must have known the house well if she was doing a head-long streak down the Long Gallery. Must ask Dante later if he knows.

If he expects me to flit round the garden in this outfit afterwards I'll catch my death even with all that wine inside me.

I wonder if Dr Amulet Bone always wears white?

. . . chained to the bed he saw her coming slowly towards him, a glimmer of white in the darkness. Then he heard the soft susurration of her long skirts against the cold stone floor and began uncontrollably to shiver . . .

As the clock sonorously struck midnight somewhere down in the dark depths of the house, I ran barefoot down the carpeted hall, my gauzy draperies streaming behind me.

My eyes had adjusted to the faint moonlight coming from the tall windows down one side, but as I reached the dark, blank panelling at the end where the gallery turned, a dank waft of air touched my face and then something – or someone – snatched me into cold, muffling blackness.

My scream must have been cut off by the closing of the secret panel behind me, and was probably most effective, but as I drew breath for another mighty shriek, a large hand covered my mouth.

'Shh! It's only me – you're safe!' hissed Dante. He must have felt me shaking uncontrollably, because he gave an exclamation and, wrapping his arms around me said apologetically: 'Sorry, Cass – I was so made up with finding this stair and the panelling that I forgot about the cupboard effect. And it isn't a cupboard, because there's a way out.'

I rested my head against his broad chest : déjà vu again.

'If you ever do anything like that to me again, I'll kill you, Dante Chase,' I promised, waiting for my heart to stop pounding away.

'It must have looked pretty authentic to our spectrologists, though – they were up on the balcony when you ran from under it, bang on the stroke of midnight. Come on,' he added, switching on a small torch and pointing it down some shallow, twisting steps. My Chinese shoes sat sedately side by side on the top one. 'It's the rose garden now.'

I noticed that he was wearing his ruffled shirt and breeches again.

'You're going to do some haunting too?'

'*We're* going to do some haunting, as the doomed lovers who walk the rose garden.'

221

'We are? I don't remember hearing about those.'

'Probably not, since I took a leaf out of your book and made it up. However, it's a sad and tragic tale. Come on.'

We emerged on the kitchen floor through what looked like a china cupboard, and leaving the house by a side door, sneaked around to the rose garden.

Dante took my hand in a lover-like fashion, but when I shivered he put his arm around me instead, which was much warmer and equally authentic. As we strolled through the formal pathways I wondered how many of the visitors had read Dante's thoughtfully printed hand-out and were even now observing us through the windows.

It can't have been very exciting.

When I said so, Dante suddenly suggested he add some reality to an unconvincing performance and kissed me.

It would not have been in character to struggle, but when I could speak again my mouth said: 'Call that a convincing performance?' without asking my brain's permission first. I knew drinking in Dante's company was a bad idea.

He was already breathing a trifle heavily for a ghost, but this put him on his mettle, and things might then have got a trifle out of hand had not the scrunch of gravel alerted us to the fact that one or more of the visitors were creeping up on us.

Hand in hand we fled down the rose garden, crept along the far side of the overgrown yew hedge and into the side door of the west wing, which Dante locked behind us before we collapsed in a breathless heap.

Chapter 22: Family Party

After reading Cass Leigh's last novel, Grave Concerns, *I swore I'd never read another. Why, then, did I buy her latest one,* Nocturnally Yours, *then spend the week after reading it too afraid to put the lights out at night?*

The Fiction Review

'You can let go of my hand now, there's no one here to see us,' I said firmly, for once we were back in the brightly lit west wing sanity had returned.

At least, I *think* it was sanity. Certainly I'd suddenly recalled that Dante was probably still a bit piqued with me, as men can be for no particular reason that a sensible woman can see, and that seducing me might be his way of punishing me.

Not exactly my idea of a fate worse than death, but still, I'd been seduced once before and look where that got me. I've no intention of making a mess of my life again.

No ties, and a nice dog, that's what I need, not another quick fling with something darkly Byronic.

Dante released me, looking at me in the sad, hungry way that made me think of big dark jungle cats sizing up dinner, and suggested we have a drink in his room. But I've been there, done that, and we all know what happened last time . . . or we would if we'd been sober enough to remember it all. Anyway, duty called.

'No thanks, I'm going to go back to my room to do some work,' I said with resolution. 'If you don't need me any more tonight, that is?'

'Not in your slave capacity,' he agreed. 'But I thought we could get to know each other a bit better?'

'And I thought you'd already discovered everything there was to know about my subconscious from my books, and didn't find it very attractive?'

'Haven't I made it clear that I find the *rest* of you attractive? Maybe your psyche will grow on me, and mine on you. I never meant to frighten you,' he added unexpectedly.

'Oh, I'm not scared of you any more,' I assured him. But actually, even now there are moments . . . Or then again, perhaps it's me I'm so scared of? 'I mean, I never was really: you just looked so big and sort of grim-looking the first time we met, and then there was all that guilt.'

'I meant frightening you when I grabbed you and dragged you into the secret chamber tonight, actually.'

'Oh, that. It was just a bit too cupboard-like, but I was all right when I knew it was a passage and stairs, and you were in there, and not . . . not something nightmarish.'

'You're such a weird mixture of impervious chronicler of the undead, and frightened child in the dark,' he said softly. 'But tonight, just to confuse me even more, you look more angel than vampire in that dress.'

'Angels are golden-haired,' I said coldly, edging away.

'I don't see why.'

' "Light good, dark bad" is a basic tenet of life.'

'Not mine. Whatever I've done, or not done – whatever I'm accused of – I don't really think I'm a bad man. I hope I'm not a bad man, even though I can't have been any great shakes as a husband,' he added moodily, 'or Emma wouldn't have had an affair with someone else.'

I think she must have been madder than her mother, but that's just a personal opinion. How did she dare? And why on earth would she want to?

'I don't see why anything that happened is your fault,' I said. 'You're not responsible for your friend's death, and if you hadn't been taken hostage you would have been home with Emma when she was taken ill, so that isn't your fault either.'

'I don't know,' he said bleakly. 'It's a chain reaction, one thing leading to another all along the line, like I'm the kiss of death to anyone close to me.'

'Well, Rosetta's absolutely flourishing, and you're fond of her,' I pointed out. 'And the person who was there when Emma was ill

224

and *didn't* take her to hospital is her mother, so she's projecting her own guilt on to you; but of course, if mediums really can contact the spirits of the dead, which is something I'm not entirely convinced of, the presence of someone like yourself who is extremely antagonistic to the whole idea would probably throw a spanner in the works, don't you think? So Madame Duval *might* have a point there.'

'So – what? I ought to brainwash myself into believing in the afterlife and let her hold her seance? Because I'll tell you something else: I took Emma back, but I didn't love her any more after finding out she'd been unfaithful. I think I'd known we were wrong for each other soon after we married, when she started trying to get me to change my job.'

I sighed. 'Like my love affair with Max: I knew that was a mistake right from the start too, once I found he was married. I did resist him, you know. I even got a job and moved here without telling him, only he found me again and persuaded me into our affair.'

'But he was the married one, you must have been very young, and you did try and make the break, so where is your blame?'

'Well, it's all water under the bridge now, isn't it?' I said. 'For both of us. I really have finished with Max for ever, even if he's refusing to accept it. The final straw was that this Kyra got pregnant when I desperately wanted children and he wouldn't hear of it. And now it's probably too late,' I said sadly.

'Why should it be?'

'I'm forty-four, probably past it.'

'You're wearing very well,' he said, with that twitch of the mouth. 'And I don't think I'd give up yet if that's what you really want. Only not with Jason: why not try me again?'

'I didn't try you in the first place!' I said hotly. 'I mean, I wasn't trying to – I wasn't even *thinking* about getting pregnant!'

'So you wanted me for myself alone? I'm flattered.' It was a full-fledged smile, this time, unnervingly.

'Well, don't be, because it was mostly the brandy . . . and a sort of affinity, I think,' I admitted reluctantly. 'Don't you think we're alike in some ways?'

'Dark and guilty?'

'Something like that. And both with personal demons to slay.'

'Yes, you through your books – and maybe now me through

mine. And I suppose I must let our Mrs Bangs – as she apparently now is! – make her distasteful final attempt tomorrow, and close the door on that one for ever,' he said slowly.

'And I may have no choice about facing my father again, if he follows me up here. Which he will do if Francis doesn't manage to head him off.' I shivered.

'He's not that scary, is he?' Dante asked mildly. 'You stood up to my mother-inlaw in my defence, after all.'

I just looked at him pityingly. 'She's not even in the same league!'

'Then if he comes, I'll be there to defend you,' he promised, which was strangely reassuring.

We'd reached the door of his study by now (so clearly I was mistaken about his earlier intentions) and he paused, a hand on the latch and raised an eyebrow: 'A nightcap?'

'No, thanks, this is the time of night when I generally work,' I explained, backing away.

'Is it? Well, it's the time of night I generally *don't*,' he said. 'I'll leave you to it then, but my door is two down from yours if you should want me in the night . . . for anything. Breakfast in the kitchen tomorrow? You don't want me to wake you up?'

'No, thank you. I like to wake naturally, mid-morning, and since I did your haunting bit in the night you can't expect me to be on duty at the crack of dawn. But I'll help Rosetta with her guests if she needs me when I get up. Am I haunting tomorrow night?'

'Yes, same old haunts,' he agreed. 'I'll be working in here during the day, but feel free to disturb me. More than you do already, I mean.'

It was an effort to get the old legs to turn round and march me out of there, but it had to be done. There seemed to be too many unresolved issues hanging like a dark miasma in the air.

Actually even my room seemed to be imbued with a dark and powerful force, but whatever it was, it was *very* conducive to writing, and once I was working I forgot everything.

The house was quiet when I emerged late the following morning. I peeped in the open door of Dante's study, but he was hammering away at the keys of his laptop, so absorbed he didn't notice me.

I could probably have sheared off all that floppy raven hair without him knowing I was doing it, but I resisted the temptation and stole away.

. . . Dr Bone sized him up: he was so very nearly perfect. Just a few, slight adjustments, an enhancement of the gifts Nature had bestowed upon him, and he would be truly her own creation . . .

I'll have to watch that Dr Bone, because far from starting out as a wimp like Keturah she seems to be a bossy-boots who always thinks she knows best – hence her desire to improve on nature.

And I don't mind what she does to the Max figure, but she isn't getting her knife into anyone remotely resembling Dante: he's been through enough.

The only sign of life in the main part of the house was Rosetta, sitting at the kitchen table with a cup of coffee, looking limp and wan. The dishwasher was chock-full of greasy breakfast dishes and the room smelled so strongly of bacon that every breath loaded my system with cholesterol.

That was probably what sent Eddie away, because he finds the smell of any animal cooking repugnant.

'Are you all right?' I asked, concerned, and she looked up and gave me a weak smile.

'Oh yes, just exhausted! Not just by all the cooking and clearing, but by the most spectacular scene. After breakfast Madame – Madame Duval, as we have to call her – spotted Dante in here, and threw a major wobbler. She says she saw Emma last night in the Long Gallery, and it was a clear sign that she was coming for Dante's soul if he didn't let her mother contact her, and stuff like that.'

'I'm sorry I missed it,' I said sincerely, scouting around for bread and peanut butter, but settling for marmalade. 'Was everyone there?'

'Oh yes, they all managed to get down for a full cooked English breakfast!' Rosetta said bitterly. 'Poor Eddie had to go out – he went quite pale when I put the sausages and bacon on. He's gardening, I think. Otherwise she had a full audience, and she even staged a heart attack, only her colour stayed perfectly normal so I knew it wasn't real.'

'What did Dante say?'

'He said she could save the histrionics, because he'd already decided to let her hold a seance early this evening, on the understanding that she left the house tomorrow and never contacted him again, no matter what happened at the seance. I was surprised, because he's so against that sort of thing!'

'We were talking about it last night a bit,' I said. 'And he feels it would sort of end the chapter if he let her do this one last time.

227

And if anything nasty happens I'll get Charles – the vicar – to sort it out, don't worry.'

'I don't really believe in that medium stuff, do you?' she asked. 'But I do wish I'd never had this idea in the first place! What could I have been thinking of, when I knew how Dante felt about that sort of thing? Although at least by coming here I met Eddie!' she added on a brighter note. 'So *some* good has come of it all.'

'Yes,' I agreed, 'and I think you will be very happy together. You haven't told Dante what you intend doing yet?'

'No, we thought – after the guests have gone, you know? How was the haunting? Leo Bream and Frank Shakespeare are setting a camera up tonight in the hope of catching Betsy on film, and Mrs Bream is going to operate a tape recorder, because they said there was a terrible faint scream just as the figure vanished.'

'I'll have to remember that,' I said.

'And they saw the figures of two lovers in the rose garden too,' she added. 'But not near enough to be clear. Was that you and Dante?'

'Yes,' I admitted.

Rosetta brightened. 'I knew he really liked you! When I'm gone you and—'

'Rosetta, your brother is years younger than me, and he doesn't like me that much!'

'He's thirty-eight, old enough to know what he wants,' she said. 'And he's so different since he met you: you're good for him. I was afraid for him when he got home from Colombia, he was so desperately unhappy and seemed to blame himself for everything. *I* blame a lot of it on Madame Duval.'

'Mrs Bangs!'

We both grinned.

'Reg is a nice little man,' she said. 'He helped me clear the tables after breakfast.'

'I'm sorry I wasn't here earlier to help, but I worked for a few hours after the haunting, then slept in.'

'Yes, Dante said, and that it was clear any lifestyle adjustments were all going to be on his side.'

I looked at her: 'You mean, while I'm staying here?'

She shrugged. 'No idea.'

'Well, what can I do to help you now? And where is everyone? It's as quiet as the grave.'

228

Unfortunate turn of phrase! And they're none of them very quiet in any of my books.

'They've all walked into the village together to explore, and then have lunch at the pub, thank goodness. Clara Williams is bringing the birthday cake later, that Mrs Bream ordered for her husband's surprise party – tea, cake and fizz in the sitting room at five. I've told Dante he's got to be there, as Lord of the Manor. Will you come, too?'

'I wouldn't miss it for the world: Orla's turning up to do a singing telegram.'

'Yes, Mrs Bream asked if anyone did them locally, and I told her about Orla. Oh, and your Jason phoned up and said he'd be here about four, he's closing his shop up early today. He's nice, isn't he?'

'Yes he is, but he's not *my* Jason – or not any more, I hope!' I said, and she looked puzzled. However, she often looks puzzled, which is probably what makes her a perfect match for Eddie, who understands nothing he can't smoke or fix with his hands and does not care in the least. 'It was always Orla he really fancied, I just side-tracked him with my kinky vampire gear.'

So I helped Rosetta for a while, and then she went off laden with a basket of vegetarian goodies for Eddie's lunch, like Little Denim Riding Hood, and I thought I'd go and have a look at the rose garden in daylight to work up an appetite before I raided her supplies for lunch.

The rose garden, a formal affair of gravelled paths and trees like so many green pompoms on sticks, happened to be overlooked by Dante's study window.

Unfortunately it was also overlooked by one of the wider loops of the drive up which Pa, with a reluctant entourage of Ma and Francis, was proceeding in search of one of his two twin ewe lambs.

He halted abruptly when he spotted me, then veered off into the shrubbery, which swayed wildly as at the approach of some large wild beast.

I cravenly contemplated bolting – but where to? He clearly wouldn't be leaving until he'd satisfied himself that Jane wasn't here. Might as well get it done with.

So I stood my ground, staring at him as he grew closer, noting the grey in his fair hair and the increased stockiness of his build.

His impressive head, a demented John the Baptist set on a body not quite magnificent enough, was ruddy with rage, the eyes blazing a mad light blue.

Despite the full daylight and there being no cupboards anywhere in the near vicinity, my knees began to shake and I was filled with a sensation of intense panic.

'Perverter of the Innocent! Spawn of Satan, sent to lead the Pure Lamb to eternal damnation!' Pa ranted, the volume increasing as he strode closer.

Francis and Ma made no attempt to hinder or remonstrate with him, of course – it was always pointless, even when he was sober. Ma looked smaller. Frailer. Her curly hair was quite silver now.

She didn't look at me directly, but hovered nearby, hands folded and eyes meekly downbent, even when I said beseechingly: 'Ma!'

Pa came to a halt in front of me and pointed an accusing finger. Bolts of lightening didn't shoot out of it, but I flinched anyway.

'You have stolen her away with your foul wiles! What have you done with your sister Jane?' he demanded.

Whatever *did* happen to Baby Jane?

'Hello, Pa,' I said, reasonably steadily. 'I haven't done anything with Jane – she's in London staying with George and Phily. How are you? And Ma?' I added politely, as though we were acquaintances rather than twenty-years-estranged family members.

Francis, looking resigned, cast his eyes up to heaven. 'I did tell you, Pa! She's gone to London to keep Phily company, and Gerald is there now, too. You can speak to her on the phone later.'

'You're all in a conspiracy to hide her from me!' he declared, rounding on him. 'Has she fooled you too, this fiend disguised as your sister?' Froth was beginning to fly and he advanced on me, fingers twitching and face working.

Shocked by the unbalanced rage I took an involuntary step backwards, for clearly Pa had tipped right over the edge. Sober or drunk, he'd never been quite this ranting and unreasonable before, even over the phone.

'I knew the moment I set eyes on the infant – Seed of Satan, planted in *your* womb, Sarah!' He swivelled and pointed at my unfortunate mother, who cowered. 'To remind you of your evil desires all your days!'

'No, no, Samuel, I didn't – I couldn't!' she whimpered. 'A throw-back! My grandmother Rosie was—'

'Silence!' he roared.

In the ensuing hush I heard the gravel scrunch under approaching feet, and then Dante's arm was around me. I half-turned and clung to him like a wet extra from *Lorna Doone*, my knees crumpling.

Pa stared at him. 'Who is this man? He is too young to be your paramour – unless, evil child, this is *another*? Is this the fornicator who has paid for your services, as I am told? Can no—'

'You must be Cass's father, Mr Leigh? I've heard all about you – and all of it true, it seems,' Dante interrupted, in a voice incisive enough to cut steel. 'I am afraid you are trespassing on my property, and unless you want me to forcibly eject you from it you will have to behave in a reasonable manner.' He glanced at Francis and added in a quieter voice: 'Doesn't he have any medication to calm him down when he's like this?'

I don't remember *anyone* speaking to Pa like that. I gazed at Dante in wonderment, and so did Francis. I *think* it was wonderment.

He half-smiled down at me and added: 'And I would like to say that I am not a fornicator, and that my intentions towards her are perfectly honourable.'

Well, there's a disappointment, I thought.

Pa rallied and said in slightly modified tones of outrage: 'So she has fooled you, too? Unhappy man! But I will waste no more time: tell me where my innocent child, my Jane, is hidden, and I will take her and go from this vile place.'

'Jane?' Dante raised one eyebrow. 'Cass's twin sister? I met her some time ago when she called in here on her way to London. To stay with her sister-in-law, I think she said?'

'Is this the truth?'

'I keep trying to tell you, Pa – I got Phily on the phone this morning and she said that Jane was there,' Francis interrupted and got a glare for his pains.

'It's true, Pa,' I said. 'She's in London.'

Pa looked from one to the other of us. 'If it is not true, then judgment will fall on all your heads!' he roared. 'But I weary – I must go home to my flock and wait for my Jane to come home! I must leave the house of the Whore of Babylon—'

'Do you mean Orla?' I blurted, startled.

'She who dresses as a strumpet for the temptation of men.'

231

'That's Orla.'

'Do you joke about such evils?' he demanded, coming a step closer. I must have flinched, for Dante's arm tightened. Pa looked at him and said: 'I see she has fooled you, but I will tell you what she is!'

'Your daughter? The one you cruelly abused and traumatised when she was a child?'

'It is no crime to try and take the devil from the child. It was retribution – in the cradle she was the very image of the man her mother lusted after.'

'No, no, Samuel!' whimpered Ma.

'Yes! Did I not come back from my preaching tour to find you lusting after him? Did I not find the photographs in your drawer, the records hidden in the attic?'

'No, no!'

'Yes, and the devil sent this child made in his dark image to pervert my own innocent babe, my Jane. Devil's Spawn!'

'Rubbish,' Dante said crisply. 'If you weren't clearly demented I'd knock you down for what you did to Cass. And you!' he turned to Ma. 'How could you let your child be shut in the dark for hours, punished for something she didn't even understand?'

'She couldn't help it, Dante!' I whispered. 'She couldn't stand against him – look at her!'

'The woman and man are as one,' Pa declared. 'I did what was necessary, what was right. But I do not stand here arguing with you if my daughter is not here.'

'One daughter is,' Dante said quietly.

'No child of mine. She will burn – and you with her. It is clear to me now,' he added heavily, 'that you are her match in iniquity. Evil! Evil! I must guard the pure flame! I must—'

'Go before I kick you out?' Dante said pleasantly, but there was that in his voice that caused Pa to shut his mouth on his final words, turn on his heel and stride regally off.

Francis gave me a comical look and plunged after him, but Ma was halted in her tracks by Dante's voice: 'Mrs Leigh!'

She paused, half-turned like some timid creature unused to daylight. Her eyes flickered to me and away.

Dante pulled me towards her. 'Don't you want to look at your daughter after all these years? To wish her well, with me?'

'She is not mine – the devil's,' whispered Ma.

232

'You know very well that isn't so,' Dante said more gently. 'Your husband is out of earshot, so tell me the truth about this man he said you were lusting after. Who *is* the dark sinner he sees when he looks at Cass?'

She stared at him, then at me: 'Perhaps she is the devil's way of tormenting me for my sins? For I *did* lust after him for a time, it is true: he was like a fire in my soul.'

I stared at her. 'Did you have an affair with another man, then Ma?'

Ma took a slow step back, her eyes fixed on Dante's face. 'No: but in my lustful heart I was guilty. He was dark like you,' she added, looking at Dante. 'The King.'

Now I knew she was as mad as Pa. Can insanity be catching?

'Elvis,' Dante said. 'Of course! You had a crush on Elvis!'

'*Elvis*? You mean I was punished because my mother had a crush on Elvis Presley?' I exclaimed indignantly. 'That was all it was about? And I don't look anything like him!' I added.

I could see Dante's lip twitching in that way that meant he was finding it all highly amusing, but I seemed to have had an acute sense of humour failure.

'No – she was *my* punishment every day, reminding me!' Ma cried.

Something in my head blazed like a great light and I exclaimed: 'In my dream – Elvis was the awful thing in the cupboard I wanted to escape from and never could! I remember touching you, Ma, when I was too small to understand what I was reading in your mind, and you were looking at me and thinking of this great, dark, sneering monster in a glistening white suit: and you hated both of us!'

'Not hated,' whispered Ma.

'Sarah!' bellowed my father. 'Sarah!'

Ma took two more steps backwards, still not looking at me, though my arms were stretched out towards her like she might suddenly touch me with the love she had never ever shown to me, only to Jane.

Then she turned and ran jerkily after Pa and Francis.

'All those nightmares,' I said disgustedly. 'And after all, it was only Elvis in the cupboard!'

'Let's hope he has now left the building,' Dante said with a straight face.

233

Chapter 23: The Pendulum and the Pit

*Cass Leigh's new novel is a bursting boil on the face of publishing
. . .*

*(Extract from a letter to the editor,
by Outraged of Upper Slaughter)*

My legs (together with my brain) ceased to function with dramatic suddenness, though I don't know whether it was the shock or the anti-climax that did it. Or maybe it was the fearsome image of the monster, freshly released from the cupboard, in his tight, white, rhinestone-studded suit?

As I crumpled, Dante swept me into his arms and carried me back towards the west wing, and over his shoulder I saw Max, a surreal figure in silky Armani suiting, step through an archway into the rose garden and stop dead, staring.

His appearance was even more incongruous than Pa's, but just as unwanted. I put my arms around Dante's neck and turned my face into his shoulder.

I did glance back once, but Max had gone.

Had he really been there? And if so, had his beard really vanished, and been replaced by its own ghost in white skin? Neither question seemed very important any more.

I was not quite so out of it that I didn't notice and appreciate how effortlessly Dante carted my not – inconsiderable weight about . . . And I now have no idea *what* film I'm starring in, except that it seems to be somewhere between *Gone With The*

Wind and a remake of *Jaws*, where the shark turns out to be the good guy.

Far from being afraid of him any more I now didn't want to ever let go. He was safe, strong, solid, sensible, and even my father had backed down from a confrontation with him. (He was also tall, dark, brooding, haunted and intense – but hey, who isn't?)

I decided to elect him Champion of my Sanity, and once I was curled up cosily with him on the old sofa in his study, hovering somewhere between hysterical tears and laughter, it was tempting to elect him something else, too.

He held me close, murmuring comforting words and stroking my hair, and then after a while I gave him a watery smile and he kissed me . . . and I kissed him back, and one thing led to another.

Only unfortunately it didn't lead all that far, since he said I was deeply shocked and upset and he wasn't going to take advantage of me, and *I* was definitely too exhausted to take advantage of him . . . this time. It was nice of him, though, and I certainly wasn't about to disillusion him by saying I'd appreciate a little less consideration and a bit more action.

Eventually he remembered the birthday party and seance and duty called, so I went to my room to wash and tidy up. Then we went down to the visitors' sitting room for Ghost Cake together: for after all, why shouldn't the Lord and Master of the Manor take his hired help around with him if he wanted to?

The room had been decked out in ghost-shaped Halloween balloons, and Clara's cake occupied a small table in a central position. While her knitted sweaters are all extremely zany she is not the most artistic of cake designers, so the cake was just round and blue with a cut-out icing ghost in a conventional white sheet on top, and 'Happy Birthday, Leo' picked out in yellow around it. There were a few token candles.

Eddie and Rosetta were setting out glasses, teacups and little plates of sandwiches and stuff and looked pleased to see us, although Eddie always looks pleased to see everyone, so that's nothing new. His hair was tied up in a flowered silk square, like a sunny-natured pirate.

The others were all grouped in an incongruous tableau around a table at the end of a room: Madame Duval, vast in midnight blue velvet and Egyptian beads, with Reg in anxious attendance; Jason and Mrs Bream bending over what seemed to be a map, watched with keen interest by her husband and brother.

'What's going on?' Dante asked suspiciously. 'Oh, you've all met Cass, haven't you?' he added, without bothering to add who or what I was, which was probably just as well since even *I* was finding my position pretty hard to define.

'Jason just got here,' Rosetta explained nervously. 'Mr and Mrs Bream visited his shop earlier and got talking, Dante, and it turns out that Mrs Bream can find missing people using a map and items of their belongings and a crystal. Jason's wife disappeared, you know . . . and I thought you wouldn't mind if they tried?'

'I can hardly complain, since I'm going to let Madame hold her seance later,' he said bitterly. 'It sounds perfectly harmless by comparison!'

Dante and I watched as the crystal pendulum hung still over a detailed map of the area around Westery. I suppose they were making sure she wasn't nearby first before going for the large-scale stuff.

Then suddenly the crystal began to move. Mrs Bream muttered a bit, her eyes half-shut, and a slither of cerise nylon sari unfolded down her arm. Then she opened her blue-lidded eyes and laid a pointed fingernail on a spot on the map. 'There!'

We all crowded up but Dante, being taller than the others, was the first to spot the significance: 'That's on my land,' he said. He leaned closer. 'Somewhere in the overgrown flower gardens beyond the pond?'

'There's a new rockery,' Eddie said unexpectedly. 'In the old gardens. Someone made a rockery.'

We all looked at him.

'Jack Craig? Must have been, no one else would have bothered,' I said. 'But why? Surely he—'

'He must have liked rockeries,' Eddie said simply.

'Or he made it to hide something!' Jason said, leaping slightly wildly to his feet. 'My wife had been having an affair with him just before she vanished but I came here that night looking for her, and he swore he hadn't see her!'

Dante laid a restraining hand on his arm. 'Don't jump to conclusions, Jason. There's probably nothing in it. Anyway, the light's gone, there's nothing you can do until morning.'

'A torch.' Jason exclaimed, looking wildly round as though one might materialise.

'Absolutely not. It's all ridiculous nonsense, but if you really want to go out and dig the garden up at dawn tomorrow, feel free.'

Mrs Bream was still twiddling her pendulum. 'There's definitely *something* there,' she murmured with slightly less confidence. 'I'm not sure . . . perhaps it isn't the one you're searching for? But if there's a connection . . . Shall I try again?'

'No thanks,' Dante said crisply. 'And isn't that the doorbell?'

Rosetta hurried out. Jason ran his hands distractedly through his brown hair and said aggrievedly: 'It's all very well for you, Dante, but I think you ought to let her have another shot at it. I'm not going to sleep a wink tonight until—'

He stopped dead and gaped at the apparition in the doorway, his eyes going glazed, as did all the men present except Dante, who merely looked amused. (Though you'd have to know him to realise it.)

Had it been possible, I'd have said Orla's costume was tighter than before. Certainly the zip was a perilous inch or two lower, and the name Barbarella, embroidered across the chest, was stretched nearly flat.

'Where is the Birthday Boy?' she asked seductively, fluttering her gilded eyelashes. But before Leo Bream could do more than gulp nervously and Mrs Bream utter an outraged hiss, Jason had sprung to his feet, tossed an embroidered Chinese shawl over Orla like someone extinguishing a particularly noisy cage-bird, seized her by the arms, and hustled her out.

You know, I think he had that planned.

'Happy birthday, Mr Bream,' I said kindly.

'Leo,' he murmured weakly, gazing after them as after a vanished dream.

'Shall we cut the cake?' asked Rosetta brightly into the ensuing silence. 'Mr Bream – Leo – I'm lighting the candles, if you'd like to blow them out?'

He had barely enough breath but he managed it in the end, and then we all had a slice of cake that had been exhaled all over, and toasted him in something cheap, thin and sparkling. (A bit like his wife's sari.)

Jason and Orla didn't return, and I wondered if they'd retired to Jason's room or if he'd insisted on taking her home. Whichever, I hoped she was managing to take his mind off tomorrow's excavations.

After the normality of the tea party, if such it could be called with Dante looking as if he was about to be involved in something noxious (which he was), Madame said we might as well rearrange the room and have what she called her 'little gathering' right away.

'But shouldn't it be later – after dinner?' I said, surprised.

'It's late enough, and the light's gone,' she said in her deep voice. 'Besides, I never partake of food or drink before I call upon the spirits.'

It was true she'd eaten and drunk nothing, but then neither had Mrs Bream, who seemed to be exhausted after her pendulum swinging (and possibly the shock of Orla's appearance).

Dante shrugged: 'As well now as later. The sooner we get this nonsense over the better.'

Madame Duval bridled. 'I hope you are going into this with a positive attitude, unlike previous occasions when you have maliciously prevented my poor child from contacting me. *This* time I had hoped—'

'I'll do my best,' Dante promised. 'I said so, didn't I? One last time, and that's it.'

'We will support you, dear,' Mrs Bream said. 'And we three are not unbelievers, but open to all new paranormal experiences.'

'And I'll stay, and Eddie,' Rosetta declared firmly. 'I want it finished with, too.'

'And me,' I said.

Dante looked at me. 'No.'

'I want to, Dante. I want to be here for you,' I said stubbornly.

'It could be dangerous. You've had enough upsets for one day.'

'Let her sit with us,' Madame said. 'It is clear to me she has some connection with you, and so might provoke my poor aban-doned child to speak. To speak!' she exclaimed on a slightly more rising note that had poor Reg scrabbling for the smelling salts.

But her colour remained steady, and she bossily directed the repositioning of the chairs around two of the tables, pushed together, and the extinguishing of all but one dim wall light and the flickering log fire.

We all sat around the table holding hands, with Dante next to Madame and me on his left. Reg sat on his wife's right, saying cheerfully: 'What larks!'

Even through the gloom I could see Eddie's white teeth as he smiled at me across the table with happy unconcern. Mrs Bream took my left hand in her cold, bird-boned claw.

'Open your minds,' whispered Madame Duval thrillingly. 'Close your eyes, and let the Others make contact with us . . . Are you there? We hear you!'

There was a silence, during which I for one was not thinking about lost wives, but about Dante, and about how we seemed to be strong for each other when we couldn't be strong for ourselves, and of how I felt slightly affronted by the ghastly secret in my nightmare cupboard merely being Elvis.

I mean, how scary is *he*? Even Jane made a more satisfiying monster.

'There is a dark presence here, trying to bar our way . . . one who seeks to stop us making contact with the Other Side,' Madame hissed rather pointedly, and I heard Dante give an exasperated sigh.

'But we are stronger – we will open the door to our loved ones!' Mrs Bream declared. 'I feel them close to us, waiting.'

After that it was all very peaceful for several minutes except for the crackling of the logs, until Mrs Bream's hand jerked in mine and she gave a sudden snoring snort.

I jumped, and was just about to nudge her awake when she said in a deep voice totally unlike her normal mincingly precise one: 'I am here. Who summons me?'

Leo Bream leaned forward and whispered: 'She's in a trance! That is her control, Two Bison, an Indian chief.'

'Two Bison?' I queried, feeling the hysterical laughter bubbling again, but then there was an intake of breath from Madame's direction, probably indignation due to being upstaged in the medium stakes.

But if so she managed to control it, saying clearly: 'Welcome, Two Bison! Can you give us news of our loved ones, now passed to the other side?'

'Some are here awaiting,' said the deep voice. 'Whom do you seek?'

'My daughter. Emma, my daughter — is she there?'

There was a pause.

'Mother . . . ' whispered a thread of a voice that seemed to issue not so much from Mrs Bream but from thin air.

'Emma? My Emma – at last you have come to me!'

239

'Mother,' sighed the voice. 'Leave him be.'

There was a gasp: 'Who – what do you mean? I—'

'Leave him. The baby . . . not his. Leave him, leave Dante . . . alone.'

There was a muffled exclamation from Dante, and I pressed his hand in the darkness.

'Emma . . .' sobbed Madame Duval. 'Emma . . .!'

'Emma has gone,' Two Bison said levelly. 'Soon I too must go, but first Paul is here. Paul wishes me to say: Dan, my friend. Always my friend. Not your fault.'

Dante's fingers clenched painfully over mine.

'If you're still there, Two Bison,' I found myself saying to an entity that might, or might not, be real, 'can I just ask you if Tanya is there? Can Tanya speak to us?'

There was the ghost of a laugh. 'She is not here, but she is closer than you think,' he said, and then there was nothing except the sound of harsh breathing and Madame Duval's sobbing.

As you can imagine, that was pretty well the end of that, although Madame got even more hysterical and told Dante that she'd known it wasn't his baby all along, but it was all still his fault.

Then she sort of collapsed, and had to be escorted by Reg to her room.

Eddie, who seemed to have sailed through the experience with his mind on other things, went to help him, then came back and started rearranging the room.

Dante hadn't said anything at all to Madame Duval, or indeed anyone else, just sat there looking somehow drained. I simply didn't know what to think about the whole experience, except that Mrs Bream looked pretty well flaked out, and that seemed genuine enough.

'She's always like this afterwards,' Leo explained, tenderly helping her to her feet. 'And we didn't expect the spirits to come through her tonight, but through Madame Duval, or she'd never have tried the pendulum for Jason first. She's exhausted, and had better go to bed.'

'Oh God, more trays!' Rosetta muttered.

Mrs Bream protested weakly at being removed: 'No, no, Leo! The haunting tonight . . . we must stay up to record and film. The manifestations are the strongest we have come across!'

'I think the spirits have been disturbed enough for one night,' Dante said, raising his head to show eyes like glacier melt-water. 'I doubt that anything more will happen after this commotion, so I should call it a day and try again tomorrow.'

'I suppose he's right,' Mr. Shakespeare said reluctantly. 'Things have been stirred up, and it might be better to leave it for now.'

'Much better,' I agreed thankfully, smiling at him. 'How sensible of you, Mr Shakespeare.'

'Call me Frank,' he said. 'I don't think any of us need to be on formal terms after that experience.'

'You won't leave me alone tonight, Leo, will you?' pleaded Mrs Bream.

'Of course not, Nancy.'

'Perhaps I'll just spend the rest of the evening writing my notes up on last night's manifestations,' Frank conceded. 'It's all been pretty tiring, so if we are to make an attempt to record the spirits tomorrow, an early night for us all would be in order. Perhaps I might take some of these leftover sandwiches up with me?' he added plaintively.

'Of course: let me get you a fresh plate,' Rosetta said. 'And I'll bring a tray up for Mrs Bream and Madame Duval shortly,' she added wearily.

Slowly they dispersed, and Rosetta and Eddie went into the kitchen.

Left among the incongruous birthday debris Dante heaved a sigh, got to his feet, and said abruptly: 'I'm going back to the west wing.'

'I'll come with you,' I said. 'I don't know about you but *I* don't feel like being alone tonight.'

'Are you afraid?' he asked, looking at me searchingly. 'But all our ghosts seem to have been laid to rest today, haven't they, Cass? Though how or why Emma . . . ' He shook his head. 'I still don't believe it was her . . . But then, how would Mrs Bream know about the baby? Or that Paul always called me Dan?'

'Telepathy?' I suggested. 'Madame Duval knew about Emma's baby, and I knew from reading your diaries that Paul called you Dan, and I suppose other people might have had a sneaky look at them. But who knows? And the truth is out now, for both of us, and I'm not really afraid any more, I just feel terribly empty and insecure and sort of adrift.' (And a bit puzzled, too, actually: why

241

on earth didn't Rosemary put her four penn'orth in, while the opportunity was there?)

'We've both undergone a sort of catharsis today,' he agreed, 'I think that's it. Come on.' He held out his hand and I took it.

The west wing was starting to feel like home.

We spent the night together, but neither took advantage of the other, we just held each other close, and it was good.

At some time in the night I got up, switched on the little desk light Dante had found for me, and wrote furiously for a couple of hours.

He half-opened his eyes when I got out of bed, but closed them again and slept on until I climbed back in again and snuggled up for warmth some time just before dawn.

I do love a heavy sleeper.

Dante'd gone when I woke up next morning, rather earlier than usual, although that was probably due to the sound of loud voices under my window.

Looking out I saw him talking to Jason and Orla (she was dressed in Jason's jeans and shirt with the sleeves and legs rolled up), who carried various digging implements and last night's map.

After a few minutes conferring they all set out in the direction of the lake, and I began rather languorously to wash and dress, still feeling strangely detached and, truth to tell, a smidgeon anti-climaxed.

By the time I finally got down to the excavation they had been joined by Leo and Frank and were down below the rockery into loose earth, digging carefully.

Then there was the clink of metal on something hard, and they all stopped and stared down into the hole.

'There's something there,' Jason said unnecessarily.

Chapter 24: Buried Treasures

Shock To the Spirits, *yet another macabre offering from horror writer Cass Leigh, certainly lives up to its title. I am never going to see the word 'goulash' (or should that be* ghoul*ash?) on a menu again without wanting to throw up* ...

Surprise! Magazine

There was silence except for the sound of soil being shifted, then a rather incongruous crockery-rattling noise.

'Careful,' warned Jason, muffled. 'It seems to be some kind of china bird, loosely wrapped in sacking. And there's another . . .'

'*A collection of porcelain cockatoos?*' I quoted.

Dante looked up. 'I suppose it must be. Let us hope he didn't bury the Tunbridge Ware boxes down here too, or the damp will have ruined them.'

'What? Why cockatoos?' demanded the others, baffled, and I explained about Jack Craig and the missing valuables.

The excavation revealed a lot of birds, none of them Tanya, and a couple of nice bits of Chinese pottery.

'So it's just a cache Jack Craig's hidden away meaning to recover later?' Jason asked. He was still pale, but sweating from his exertions.

Orla, brushing earth from bright cockatoos, said indignantly: 'He might have packed them up a bit better! Some of these look valuable.'

'Oh well, that's good news then, isn't it?' asked Leo. 'I mean, Nancy wasn't quite sure she'd found what Jason was looking for, but she did find *something*.'

Dante was exploring the bottom of the hole to see if they'd

missed anything. 'The soil's loose at the bottom – I think there's something else here,' he said, brushing more earth away, 'Something that feels like . . .'

He stood up suddenly, staring down, and we all crowded up and stared too.

A hand as white as marble, the fingers curled upwards, seemed to be pushing its way up from the dark soil like yet another resurrection.

. . . pushing through the dark soil, the white fingers clawed for . . .

No, as you were, I've already done that in *Lover, Come Back To Me*.

Jason said hoarsely: 'Oh God, it's not—?'

'It's Diana, I think,' Dante said coolly, and bending down irreverently tapped the naked white arm with the end of his trowel.

'Diana?' echoed Jason.

'Second niche on left in the rose garden wall?' I asked. 'The missing statue, possibly Roman, or an Italian copy?'

'That's the one,' he agreed, excavating further. 'But that seems to be it – the ground's like a rock below her. Well, I suppose I'd better let the police know . . . *and* the insurance company.'

He eyed the collection of cockatoos with disfavour, but actually I thought they were quite jolly.

Jason was sitting on the ground looking white and a bit sickly. 'For a minute there, Cass, I thought it was Tanya,' he said faintly.

'Really, Jason!' I said impatiently. 'That statue is half life-size and Tanya was a strapping woman, how could it possibly be her?'

'But you must admit that arm looked a bit grisly, pointing out like that,' Orla agreed, sitting down next to Jason and putting a comforting arm around him. 'And after all, we *were* looking for Tanya, weren't we?'

'Yes, but not in the form of a calcified midget,' I pointed out a trifle tartly. 'Still, I suppose it was unexpected. We all seem to be having shock therapy this weekend, don't we? Let's hope that's it.'

'Except for pleasant shocks, like good manifestations tonight when we've got the cameras and recorder set up,' Frank said.

We trooped back to the house with our booty just in time to see the departure of one problem: Madame Duval was seated in a taxi on the drive, while Reg was taking his leave of Rosetta and Eddie. As we came up he extended a hand to Dante, too.

'Goodbye, lad,' he said genially. 'Sorry for the kerfuffle, but all's well that end's well, eh?'

Dante seemed a bit lost for words, but took the offered hand. Reg started down the steps and as he drew level with me I put a hand on his arm and whispered on impulse: 'Mr Bangs – Reg – just what exactly *did* you do when you were on the stage?'

He twinkled and said: 'You're a sharp one! I think you've guessed, though.'

'Ventriloquism?' I suggested.

'Reg!' shrilled his wife from the open taxi window, and he winked conspiratorially, gave me a friendly buffet on the arm, and strolled off to the taxi, whistling.

'Off with a Bang,' I said, waving after them and feeling suddenly much cheerier. Presumably Ma and Pa had also left yesterday, and were on their way home – and if they hadn't they would by now be leaving in high dudgeon over the disappearance of their hostess.

'Oh Jason,' Rosetta said, 'there was a phone call from your son – Tom, is it? He said could you go home urgently, something's come up.'

Jason sighed. 'He's probably had a rave and wrecked the house. I was going to call in on my way to open the shop for the afternoon.'

'I hope he hasn't done anything dreadful,' Orla said apprehensively.

He smiled at her. 'I don't think I care any more. But I'll just get my things from my room, and then I can drop you at home on the way.'

'I'll come round to the shop later . . . or you could come round to my house when you've closed?' she suggested, and they exchanged one of those very private smiles.

Looks like our nightly Singles Club is about to be reduced to Single Club of one: *me*.

I went back to my room and caught up on my sleep while Dante dealt with the police and the insurance company, and then later we went for a walk together, not saying very much, and I for one strangely weary but content.

While we were out Jason had left a message asking us to go down to the pub tonight.

What on earth had Tom done?

*

We found Jason and Orla already there and, despite the night being young, pretty well oiled.

'Are you celebrating?' I asked. 'What? Tom's left home for ever or something?'

'Tanya's turned up!' Jason announced.

'Well, not so much turned up as made contact: she's written through a solicitor, asking for a divorce!' Orla explained. 'Tom, being that kind of boy, opened Jason's letters and read it.'

'But where's she been? Did she say?'

'Spain. Now she wants to get married again and she says she just wants a quickie divorce, and no maintenance or anything. Suits me,' Jason said, 'but Tom's a bit upset, because she didn't mention him at all, not even to ask how he was.'

'Poor boy,' I said charitably.

'Yes,' Orla agreed. 'Of course, now he insists that he wants to go out there and see his mother, so Jason is giving him the money.'

'Serves her right.'

'I've never met this repellent-sounding youth, but I'm beginning to feel sorry for him,' Dante commented.

'He's not that bad,' Jason said automatically. 'In fact, he's taken this better than I expected: he seemed to have had some silly idea that I'd killed her, because he overheard our argument and her telling me I wasn't his father. He was afraid if it was true I'd throw him out, but I've said I'll never do that – he's my son, whatever happens.'

'He doesn't deserve you!' Orla said warmly

'He deserves better than he's got,' Jason said. 'And I hope he can make some sort of peace with Tanya, though she can never make up for deserting him like that.'

'Have another drink?' suggested Orla happily. 'After all, there's more to celebrate than not.'

'Not for us, I'm afraid we'll have to get back,' Dante said. 'We've got a heavy night's haunting ahead of us before the Spectrologists depart, hopefully with a lot of hazy shots of Cass. Luckily the moon is far from full tonight, it'll make it easier.'

'One last haunt,' I agreed.

'And then no more Ghastly Weekends,' Orla added. 'You can have your home back to yourself, which must be a relief.'

'No more weekends like that, certainly,' Dante said firmly.

'No more at all, unless you run it yourself,' Orla pointed out. 'Once Rosetta's gone off with Eddie, I mean.'

246

Dante paused in the act of putting his jacket on and gazed at her. 'Once Rosetta's gone where with Eddie?'

I was pulling faces at Orla behind his back when he glanced round and caught me.

'What do you know that I don't?' he demanded.

I sighed resignedly. 'It's not for me to tell you, but now Orla's let it out I suppose I'd better: Rosetta was waiting until after the weekend to tell you that she's going to live with Eddie.'

'Live with Eddie?' he echoed blankly. 'So, how would you describe what she's doing *now*?'

'In his van, travelling about with him, I mean. I think one weekend of the B&B trade has been enough for her. Anyway, they're in love!'

'You mean I set all this up for nothing?' he demanded.

'I wouldn't say that, Dante! A lot of good has come out of the weekend.'

'It certainly has!' agreed Orla enthusiastically, and Jason grinned and put his arm around her.

'It's *not* good that my only sister intends travelling about the country with a shiftless, pot-smoking layabout in an old van!' snapped Dante furiously.

'He's not shiftless,' I said coldly, 'he's very useful. And he's good-tempered, so he will always be kind to her. I'm sure they'll be very happy.'

I didn't mention the baby. Time enough for that when he'd cooled off a little.

His lips were back into that knife-crease origami fold again and he maintained a deep silence all the way back to the Hall, but he did have a firm grip on my hand, though whether to stop me making a bolt back to my cottage or not was a moot point.

He stopped just before we got there, turned my face up to his, muttered: 'Oh, to hell with it!' and kissed me.

After that, I wouldn't say Rosetta and Eddie had his blessing, just that he temporarily lost interest in their future plans.

I gave a faint scream and then ran silently down the dimly lit, carpeted hall, my eyes and mouth stretched wide in terror, gossamer white draperies flying behind me . . .

Only this time I was running towards the fearsome thing in the dark cupboard, not away from it.

'Got you!' Dante whispered, snatching me into the blackness and the panel slid silently shut behind me.

He certainly had. The Superglue of love welded our lips together, while faint and faraway scratchings and squeakings from the frustrated Spectrologists told of their fruitless search for poor blind Betsy's secret.

'Past midnight – and you're free,' Dante said at last, though he showed little signs of suiting his actions to the words.

'Free?' I echoed, thinking I was never going to be free again.

'You're no longer my unwilling slave.'

'I never was.'

'No, it was pretty much the other way round from the minute I saw you. Damn!' he added, as the thumpings and mutterings grew closer: 'They'll find the opening to the panel in a minute if they carry on like that! Come on, we'd better go.'

We exited into the garden, then sneaked back into Dante's tower and carried on where we left off.

After a bit Dante said: 'Marry me?'

I pulled away and looked at him. He looked back, tall, dark and gloomy.

'Marry you? I was thinking more of applying for the post of madwoman in the attic,' I blurted.

His straight brows drew together in a frown, then his face cleared: 'Mr Rochester? You'd like to maim me a bit and set my house on fire?'

'Not really: though I always felt more akin with the wife than with Jane, I consider burning the house down to be taking revenge a little far,' I assured him. 'But I can't marry you.'

'Why not?' he asked simply.

'I'm way too old – *much* older than you.'

'Physically maybe a few years, but mentally you're still adolescent.'

'Thanks.'

'Is that your sole objection?'

'No – I mean, when it comes down to it, I'm not sure I could live with someone all the time. I'm not domesticated, and I'm used to being alone a lot, and there're my strange nocturnal writing and night-hike habits.'

'This house is big enough for both of us to be alone whenever we need to be. You can even be my madwoman in the attic if you really want to – as long as you agree to marry me first. And I can live with your habits, though I might accompany you on the hikes.'

I stared at him. 'I think we're too alike.'

'We're two sides of the same coin and need to be together, Cass,' he said.

'Think about it, Dante,' I tried to hold him off a bit. 'You'd want children, and I'm probably way past it.'

'I don't think I'd want to risk it anyway. I'd rather have you.'

It came to me that he was right: that although I still felt that great yearning for a child, what I desperately wanted and now couldn't imagine ever losing, was Dante himself.

'Be my Dark Lady?' he said enticingly.

'I don't think Shakespeare got much further than adoring her from afar in his sonnets, did he?'

'Then I've outdone the Bard already.'

'You are a very unusual man,' I said staring at him.

'Because I read poetry? And is that a point in my favour, or against me?'

'For, definitely for,' I said.

'Good, I don't think you'd really be happy cooped up in my attic.'

Reader, I married him: but only after he added the clinching lure of a late honeymoon tour finishing up in Mexico to coincide with that popular festival, The Day Of The Dead.

That did it: I knew he was the man for me.

Not that I'd had any doubts once I'd accepted that we are the same kind of animal under the skin, and so understand each other's demons. I helped him to finish his manuscript before we left for the trip, and it began to be serialised in the newspaper while we were away, the proceeds going to Paul's widow and family.

Meanwhile my book is nearing completion, Mexico proving to be a rich source of inspiration both to me and to Dante, who has written a series of brilliant articles about the culture and political state of the country which seems to be turning into another book. I've thought up a great title for it: '*Death: Enemy or Friend? Four Months in Mexico.*

From being convinced that I could never live with someone

permanently, I now find I cannot bear to be apart from him for very long: the fear that there is something bad out there waiting to spring will never, I suppose entirely go away.

And pictures of Elvis still make me shudder.

While we were away Pa went past the point of no return and was committed, and since then Ma seems to have taken on a new lease of life in the Highlands with Francis and Robbie.

It's autumn now, but as things die, new life is flourishing forth.

Eddie and Rosetta are in the lodge, awaiting their baby's arrival.

Francis and Robbie, too, are expecting the surprise advent of a little Annapurna or Kathmandu, we are not sure yet which . . .

And as for me, far from being obsessed with motherhood I entirely forgot about it until it suddenly dawned on me that either I've started an early menopause or a late baby. But I'm not mentioning either possibility to Dante until we are back home in Kedge Hall.

We will take what comes, because whatever happens we will always have each other.

Oh, and a lot of *wonderful* Mexican Day of the Dead souvenirs.

Epilogue: Famous Last Words

Dante, who loved well because he hated,
Hated wickedness that hinders loving.

Elizabeth Barrett Browning.

Back home in the late autumn, when dead leaves lay like forgotten memories on the bed of the duck pond, and dead wives lay dormant awaiting the Eternal Spring, I realised how much I had learned in only a few short months:

I've learned that in the cycle of life sometimes you have to go back to go forwards. That some are born evil, but some have evil thrust upon them; that understanding is the path to forgiveness; and that it's never too late to get laid, but a younger lover probably increases your chance of pregnancy.

And finally, and most importantly, as Dr Amulet Bone discovered in my latest novel: a good heart is hard to find.

noel Schraufnagel

Columbos GA, os
(SA)